THE WORST OF ALL POSSIBLE ORBITS

Keene sat before the communications screen and looked at the lean, hawkish features of Idorf, captain of the Kronian ship. "Captain," he asked, "what's going on? Do you know any more than I do? . . . What is this all about?"

"Nobody's told you yet, eh?"

Keene showed his palms. "I've been trying to find out all day. It's almost like you said. The whole of Washington's acting as if a war is about to break out."

Idorf regarded him fixedly for a few seconds; then, he seemed to make up his mind and nodded. His expression was grim. "Yesterday evening, I passed some news down to Gallian that had just come in from Saturn. Our observatories there have been able to make measurements that won't be possible here for a few more days until Athena moves further out from the glare of the Sun."

Captain Idorf paused for a moment, then continued. "It seems we can forget further speculating about whether the electrical environment can be altered, Dr. Keene. Athena has come out from perihelion on a changed orbit. It isn't going to cross fifteen million miles ahead of Earth as was previously thought. *It's coming straight at us!*"

By James P. Hogan

Inherit the Stars
The Genesis Machine
The Gentle Giants of Ganymede
The Two Faces of Tomorrow
Thrice Upon a Time
Giants' Star
Voyage From Yesteryear
Code of the Lifemaker
The Proteus Operation
Endgame Enigma
The Mirror Maze
The Infinity Gambit
Entoverse
The Multiplex Man
Realtime Interrupt
Minds, Machines & Evolution
The Immortality Option
Paths to Otherwhere
Bug Park
Star Child
Rockets, Redheads & Revolution
Cradle of Saturn

CRADLE OF SATURN

JAMES P. HOGAN

CRADLE OF SATURN

This is a work of fiction. All the characters and events portrayed in this book are fictional, and any resemblance to real people or incidents is purely coincidental.

A Baen Books Original

Baen Publishing Enterprises
P.O. Box 1403
Riverdale, NY 10471

ISBN: 0-671-57866-9

Cover art by Dru Blair

First paperback printing, May 2000

Library of Congress Catalog Number 99-19563

Distributed by Simon & Schuster
1230 Avenue of the Americas
New York, NY 10020

Production by Windhaven Press, Auburn, NH
Printed in the United States of America

Dedication

To the work of Immanuel Velikovsky
and the untiring efforts of Charles Ginenthal.

Acknowledgments

The help and advice of the following people is gratefully appreciated:

Doug Beason, USAF; Jim Dorris; Steve Fairchild; Andrew Fraknoi, Astronomical Society of the Pacific; Charles Ginenthal; Jackie Hogan; Les Johnson, NASA, Marshall Spaceflight Center, Huntsville, AL; Frank Luxem; Melinda Murdock; Jeffrey Slostad; Brent Warner, NASA, Goddard Spaceflight Center, Greenbelt, MD; Betsy Wilcox, USAF

PROLOGUE

Times had always been plentiful. Since the beginning of the age when their ancestors first walked in the world, the People had lived in harmony with the spirits and the elements. Their language had no words for *war* or *want, famine* or *drought*. The forests were vast, the plains fertile. Fair winds brought rain from warm oceans. All of life flourished in abundance.

No memory had been handed down of where the People came from.

Some taught that they were born of Neveya, who ruled the skies during the times of lesser light when the smaller but brighter Sun was absent, and at the end of mortal life they would return to her across the Golden Sea in which the world floated. They learned to farm the lands and tame animals; to study the ways of wood, and stone, and metals; to admire and create music, likenesses, and things of beauty. Their sages pondered over the mysteries of mind and the senses, life and motion, of number and the nature of things.

1

Communities grew under social imperatives and marketplaces for ideas, and became centers of government and commerce.

Iryon stood near the mouth of a broad river, between arms of green hills rising to distant mountains. It was not the largest of cities, but its buildings had been shaped and ornamented with a care that made the whole as much an expression of art as the carved gates and gilded window traceries, or the marble reliefs surrounding the central square. At the summit of one of the five hills on which Iryon was built stood the Astral Temple, where priests of Neveya charted the cycles of the heavens.

Each day began with the world looking out across the immensity of the celestial Ocean that extended away to Neveya's orb, dividing it equally like the plane of a blade halving a water-fruit so that only the upper hemisphere of Neveya was visible. Then the Ocean would rise, tilting and narrowing as it did so until it became an edge crossing past the world to reveal briefly all of Neveya's countenance; from there, now above, it broadened again to expand its underside, at the same time obscuring Neveya's upper part to reach its half-day low, after which it would fall and cross back again. This cycle repeated 5,623 times in the year that the stars took to turn through their constellations.

The proportions of light and dark making up the days changed according to whether the Sun was visible as well as Neveya, and in what situation—which varied with the seasons. The "blue hours" came when the Sun shone from the far side of Neveya, transforming its normally orange glow into a black shadow cast across the Golden Ocean. At certain times in the course of the year, as the Ocean crossed past the world during the blue hours, the Sun would vanish behind Neveya completely, turning day abruptly into darkest night. These were the times when the other worlds that moved about Neveya revealed themselves in their full glories of form and color. They were known as the days of "Dark Crossings." Multitudes would come from afar to Iryon to attend the rites and ceremonies that took place on these occasions.

The pyramid was built such that, from the Eye Stone at the center of the semicircle of astronomers and priests where the Speaker of Neveya stood, the orb was seen as if supported on its apex like a cloud grazing a mountain. Since Neveya never changed her position in the sky, the disk remained balanced in that manner always, varying only from yellow jewel through shrinking face to waning crescent as the Sun rode its distant course about both her and the world, and the celestial Ocean rose and dipped through its daily cycle. As the moment of the Dark Crossing approached, she glowered at the world with full face, black and featureless, fading into the glare as the Sun touched her shoulder.

The crowds assembled on the slopes were hushed as the Speaker intoned the Verses of Passage. Around the temple and across the city below, torches had been lit in readiness for the Darkness. At the top of the pyramid, Neveya reappeared suddenly out of the glare as a black arc sliding across the Sun, her shadow lying now like a black ray cut out of the Ocean, moment by moment advancing closer. When it fell across the world, connecting it to Neveya like a bridge spanning the Ocean, then, it was taught, the souls whose time had come to return would depart on their journey.

A murmuring of awe and wonder, more a wind than a sound, stirred through the crowd as the sky darkened. The astronomers readied their instruments and recording tablets, while the Speaker turned, opening his robed arms wide to greet the spectacle. For an instant Neveya's outline flared into a thin curve of light as if the extinguishing Sun were trying to claw its way back around the edge. . . .

And then all the light went from the sky, and the stars appeared. Above and to one side of Neveya, the pink globe of Jenas became visible, while beyond it Sephelgo's white-veined features shone as crescents of crystal. Lower was Aniar, graying and mottled, swimming to the side of Neveya, transfixed by the spear of the celestial sea seen edgewise, with the white speck of Delem farther out still along the same line. As the astronomers peered and recited their measures, scribes marked the stone that would later be cut for incorporation into the records.

The picture showed a disk pierced by a shallowly sloping line, standing on an arrowhead. Smaller circles showed the other visible worlds and their dispositions, with major stars represented by their symbols. A table incised beneath the design gave precise directions and elevations.

PART ONE

JUPITER—
Creator of Worlds

1

Almost twenty years before, as a nineteen-year-old engineering student at college, Landen Keene had astounded drivers on the interstate near the campus by overtaking them with ease in a 1959 Nash Rambler body fixed to a reinforced chassis on racing suspension, mounting an L88 Corvette engine. He had also more than impressed the two state troopers who handed him a ticket, but they were unable to cite his handiwork on a single safety violation. One of them had even indicated interest if Keene ever found himself of a mind to sell. "Keep at it, kid," he had told Keene. "One day you'll make a damned good engineer—supposin' you live long enough, of course, that is."

These days, it seemed, things worked the other way around. Outdated engineering camouflaged in futuristic-looking shells was hyped as a wonder of the age, the best that taxpayers' money could buy. Keene sat in the cramped crew compartment of the NIFTV—pronounced "Nifteev," standing for Nuclear Indigenously Fueled Test Vehicle—wedged comfortably into

7

the seat at the Engineer's station by the mild quarter-g of sustained thrust cutting the craft across freefall orbits, and stared at the image on the main screen. It showed the elongated body, flaring into a delta tail-wing with tip-fins, of the spaceplane riding twenty-five miles ahead off the port lower bow, closing slowly as the NIFTV overhauled it. Officially, it was designated an "Advanced Propulsion Unit." Its white lines were illuminated in direct light from the Sun showing above the silhouette of Earth, revealing the insignia of both the U.S. Air Force Space Command and United Nations Global Defense Force. (Exactly what the entire globe was to be defended from had never been spelled out.) The NIFTV, by contrast, with its framework of struts and ties holding together an assemblage of test engine and auxiliary motors, external tanks, and crew module, was ungainly and ugly. The APU looked sleek on the covers of glossy promotional government bro-chures and was pleasing to bureaucrats. The NIFTV was a creature of engineers—a space workhorse, born of pragmatism and utility.

Ricardo's voice came over the circuit from the Ccom station—Communications and Computing. "We've got a beam from them now. I'm windowing onto the main screen, copying you, Warren."

"Gotcha." Warren Fassner, research project leader at Amspace Corporation's Propulsion Division and coordinator of the current mission, acknowledged from the control room at Space Dock, at that moment orbit-ing twelve thousand miles away above the far side of Earth. *"It looks like you guys are on stage. Make it a good one. We're getting the hookups."* To avoid giving somebody officious somewhere an opportunity to inter-fere, Keene had persuaded the public relations people at Amspace to hold until the last moment before slip-ping word of the mission to the networks. Since it was something new and sounded exciting, the networks were interested.

A helmeted head and shoulders showing a gray flight suit with Space Command insignia appeared in a one-eighth window at the top right of the screen. *"This is Commander Voaks from USAFSC APU to approaching craft U-ASC-16R. You are entering a restricted zone posted as reserved for official Space Command operations. Identify yourself and announce your intentions."*

Joe answered from the Pilot station, squeezed centrally behind the other two, which were angled inward to face the bulkhead carrying the screens. "Captain Elms from U-ASC-16R acknowledging APU. We are a private research vehicle owned and operated by the Amspace Corporation."

"We are about to commence a high-acceleration test. For your own safety, my orders are to warn you off-limits."

"We're paralleling you outside the posted limit. Just taking a ringside seat. Don't mind us. Let's get on with the show."

Ricardo cut in again: "We've got another incoming—military priority band prefix."

"This is General Burgess, Space Command Ground Control Center, and I demand to speak to—"

Joe shook his head in the background behind Keene's console. "We're gonna be too busy here for this. I'm throwing this one to you, Warren."

"Sure, switch him through. We'll handle it," Fassner said from the Space Dock. It had been expected. Ricardo clicked entries in a table on one of his auxiliary screens, and the irate general was consigned off to a string of comsat links around the planet.

"APU to Amspace 16R. You have been warned in accordance with regulatory requirements. Be advised that your continued proximity to this operation will not be taken as indicative of a desirably cooperative attitude. Negative consequences may result. This is APU, out." The window vanished.

"Negative consequences, guys," Keene repeated. "That's it—it's all over for us. They'll find some bug in our parking lot that needs to be protected now. Close down the head office."

"Where do they get those guys?" Ricardo asked as he scanned his displays and made adjustments. "I mean, do they have to be programmed to talk like that? . . ." His voice trailed off, and he leaned forward. "Okay, this is it. We're registering their exhaust plume on thermal: preboost profile." As Ricardo spoke, the APU's image sprouted a tail of white heat, growing rapidly to extend several times the length of the vessel.

"Full burn," Joe's voice confirmed. "We're looking at about, aw . . . two gee initial. Downrange radar is tracking." The Air Force spaceplane was accelerating away, commencing its test. While Joe continued reading off time checks and numbers, Keene rechecked his own panel to make sure all the NIFTV's systems were ready, then turned his eyes again to the image shrinking and foreshortening on the main screen. *Advanced propulsion*, he thought to himself scornfully. Pure hydrogen and whatever they called the latest oxidizer, it was still chemicals. NASA, circa 1960s, repackaged in an Air Force suit, its adequacy a giveaway of what it was intended for: a high-altitude police cruiser to patrol the envisaged one-world state. NIFTV had the potential to bring the Solar System into Earth's backyard, but the powers that Earth's destiny depended on weren't interested. If the day ever arrived when their one-world order looked like becoming a reality, that, Keene vowed, would be when he'd leave it all and go out to join the Kronians. But with enterprises like Amspace still able to find backers, there was hope yet.

Fassner, having evidently passed the general on to someone else, reappeared on the beam from Space Dock. *"Okay, that's looking good now. Let's go after 'em."*

"On standby at Fire-Ready," Keene confirmed.

"Go, engine. Take it up to eighty," Joe ordered.

Keene initiated the start-up and felt himself being squashed back in his seat as he increased reactant flow to bring the NIFTV quickly up to eighty percent power. Lead gloves encased his hands. He felt his cheeks and lips weighed back over his facial bones, baring his teeth. Smaller screens on the bulkhead in front of him showed deformed parodies of the faces of Ricardo and Joe.

"Lateral thrusters on. Pulsing to commence roll now," Joe grated, his mouth barely moving.

"APU ahead low, declination twenty-seven degrees and increasing," Ricardo reported. "We're twelve-point-two miles off the axis and holding. Course projection is clear."

It was a stunt to get the world's attention. The news channels had publicized that the Defense Department would be testing a new propulsion system designed for low-orbit maneuvering and announced it as a breakthrough. While the space-plane was now in its maximum acceleration phase, the NIFTV was not only overtaking it but tracing a spiral twenty-plus miles in diameter about its course—literally running rings around it. A comm beam latched on again to deliver another tirade. Ricardo looked questioningly at Joe; Joe made a tossing-away motion with his head; Ricardo grinned and switched the call over the detour link to Control.

"*Yeaaah!*" Keene whooped, smacking the armrests of his seat. "Was that a bird? Was it a plane? No, it was us, guys. Hey, look at that thing. It's like a dead duck in the water out there."

"Eat our dust, General," Ricardo sang.

The APU went into a slow curve. Joe altered thrust parameters and stayed with it easily. He ran an eye over the monitors and gave a satisfied nod. "Okay," he said to the others. "Take her up to full burn. Now let's show them what we can really do."

As the NIFTV accelerated along its continuing spiral course, a white haze of more distant light appeared along the top edge of the screen, moving slowly down to blot out the starfield background. It grew until it became part of a vast band extending off the screen on both sides, losing the APU spaceplane in its brilliance as it became a background to it.

2

The planetoid had come out of Jupiter. It was christened Athena.

For more than half a century, there had been astronomers dissenting from the mainstream view of planetary origins, trying to make themselves heard. The generally accepted nebular theory, in which the Sun, its planets, and their satellites all condensed together from a contracting cloud of primordial gas and dust, they maintained, was not tenable. The observed distribution of angular momentum did not fit the model, and tidal disruption by Jupiter would have prevented the accretion of compact objects inside its orbit. Some proposed an alternative mechanism for the formation of the inner planets based upon analysis of the fluid dynamics of Jupiter's core. According to this theory, the giant planet's rapid rotation and rate of material acquisition would result in periodic instabilities leading to eventual fission and the ejection of surplus mass. The bulk of the shed matter would most likely be thrown out of the Solar System, but lesser drops torn off in the process could go into solar-capture orbits.

In the main, the reaction of the scientific orthodoxy was to dismiss the suggestion as too much at odds with established notions and find arguments to show why it couldn't happen. Then, after the onset of sudden irregularities in Jupiter's rotation followed by several weeks of progressive deformation in shape beneath the gas envelope, it did.

Rivaling the Earth itself in size, white-hot from the energy that had attended its birth, and blazing a fiery tail tens of millions of miles long, Athena had been plunging sunward for ten months, all the time gaining in speed and brightness. Spectral analysis showed it to be composed of a mix of core and crustal materials trailing an envelope of ionized Jovian atmospheric gases. Currently crossing the Earth's orbit sixty million miles ahead of the Earth, it was visible to the naked eye across a quarter of the sky before dawn and after sundown. During the next month it would accelerate into a tight turn around the Sun, bringing it to within a quarter of a million miles at perihelion, covering more than a million miles in an hour and practically reversing direction to pass little more than fifteen million miles ahead of the approaching Earth on its way back to the outer Solar System. It was predicted that the spectacle would dim into insignificance any comet ever before seen in history.

3

Space Dock was built in the form of a short, fat dumbbell passing radially through a cylindrical hub. Cramped and dirty, noisy and oily, it normally accommodated between twenty and thirty people. It had been built several years previously as a joint venture by a consortium of private interests, of which Amspace was one of the principals, to provide an orbiting test base for space vehicles and technologies at a time when depending on government to provide facilities had been too fraught with delay and political uncertainties to be reliable.

A stubby-winged surface lifter lay docked at the far end of the hub when Joe attached the NIFTV at one of Space Dock's ports. A minishuttle bearing the Amspace logo was standing a short distance off. It was forty minutes since the NIFTV parted company from the Air Force spaceplane, by which time it had pulled fully a hundred miles ahead despite having traced its circular pattern continuously. The three crew were jubilant as they hauled themselves through the lock into the cluttered surroundings of pipes and machinery to the welcoming shouts and back-slaps of their waiting colleagues. Keene, coming first, waved and grinned in acknowledgment. Behind him came Ricardo, his mouth frozen wide, setting his teeth off white against his Mediterranean-olive skin, with Joe making a double thumbs-up sign as he floated out last. They were making the best of the enthusiasm around them while they had the chance. It was not exactly representative of the reaction they expected from the world in general, which for the most part would no doubt be shocked rather than appreciative. But that, after all, had been the whole idea.

Warren Fassner, in track pants and a red T-shirt, was waiting in the suiting chamber past the lock, where a technician began helping Keene out of his flight garb. Fassner had red hair with a matching, ragged mustache, and a large frame with an ample fleshy covering that gave the impression of sagging slightly when in gravity. Here, it was more evenly distributed, making him appear sprightlier, if maybe a little bloated, compared to normal.

"Great show, Lan!" he greeted. "That should make the high slots this evening. Looks like the baby performed just fine."

"Just as much your show. It's your baby." Keene pushed himself forward to make room as Ricardo and Joe crowded in at the end of the chamber behind. "And how goes it with our friends?" He meant the branches of officialdom connected with the APU test.

Fassner pulled a face, grinning simultaneously. "Mad as hell. Corpus Christi has got lawyers from Washington on the line now."

"Already?"

"Probably being aimed by wrathful agency heads. Marvin says they're trying to come up with some kind of permission or approval that we should have obtained first."

It had been expected, even though nothing had

violated any explicit prohibition. Thanks mainly to the reticence of the Russians, Southeast Asians, and the Chinese, the world had not actually banned the launching of nuclear technology into orbit. It was just that nobody had thought that any organization outside government would contemplate doing it, while everyone on the inside was too vulnerable to pressure groups and public opinion to want to get involved. Now the regulatory agencies would be vying with each other to placate the eco lobbies by showing who had the most teeth.

"Anyhow, you've done your part," Fassner said. "The Corpus Christi office can deal with Washington. That's what it's got a legal department for." He clapped Keene lightly on the shoulder and used a handrail to haul himself past to say a few words to the other two. "Hey, Ric, can't you do something about that grin? You're dazzling my eyes here."

Ricardo's smile only widened further. "Didn't we make a meal out of those turkeys, eh?"

"Joe, you were right on, all the way. So how did the modified RTs handle? Pretty good, I guess."

"Like a dream, Warren, like a dream. . . ."

Keene stowed the last of his gear in an end locker and signed that the technician had retrieved the diagnostic recording chip from his suit. Feeling less restricted now in shirtsleeves and fatigue pants, he exited through a pressure door and transverse shaft outside Number Two Pump Compartment to enter the "Yellow" end of the Hub Main Longitudinal Corridor—the walls in different sections of Space Dock were color coded to help newcomers orientate. More well-wishers, some in workshirts and jeans, others in coveralls, one in a pressure suit, were waiting to add their congratulations as he passed through. He came to "Broadway"—a confusion of shafts and split levels leading away seemingly in all directions, where the hub and the booms

connecting the two ends of the dumbbell intersected—and wove his way through openings and
between guide rails to the "Blue" well. Several more
figures were anchored or floating in various attitudes.

"You guys made the day, Lan," one called out.

"Great stuff, man!"

"Still ain't stopped laughin'. Even if it gets the firm
shut down, it was worth it."

Keene reversed to glide into the transverse shaft
feet-first. He pushed himself off, using one of the
hand hoops along the vertical rail, and felt the wall
to one side nudge against him gently. As he progressed farther, the motion imparted by the rail grew
stronger, causing him to move faster with a distinct,
growing sensation of heading "down." By the time he
reached the three-level wheel forming the Blue end
of the dumbbell, he was using the hoops to retard
himself. He began using his feet to climb down ladder-fashion as he passed through the upper deck, and
stepped off at the mid-deck to find Joyce and Stevie
waiting for him outside Ccoms.

"Damned good show," Stevie offered. He was
thirtyish, British, and sometimes talked like an old
movie. Keene nodded and returned a strained smile.
He knew they all meant well, but this was getting a
bit tiring.

Joyce was the senior comtech. She was one of those
who did their best to look clean and professional, but
her white shirt and sky blue pants, although no doubt
clean that day, were showing grime, and there were
flecks of grit in her black, close-trimmed hair. That
was one of the facts of life that came with the territory. Dirt in zero-g didn't fall obligingly to the floor
and accumulate in out-of-the-way places to be
removed when convenient. Despite all the ducts and
filters and fans, space habitats tended to be smelly,
too.

She smiled, managing to convey the suggestion of

freshness in spite of it all. "Even better than you promised," she complimented.

"Always make your surprises pleasant ones," Keene said, yawning in the close air. "People forget bad predictions that were wrong. But tell them one time that things will be okay and be wrong, and they'll never forgive you."

"Getting philosophical? Is this a new postflight syndrome or something?"

"I don't know. But I could sure use a postflight coffee."

"I'll get one," Stevie said, and moved away along one of the passages.

Joyce nodded to indicate the doorway through to the Ccoms room. "We've got PCN on now, asking to talk to one of the crew. You want to take it?"

"Sure. Who is it?"

"Somebody called John Feld from their Los Angeles office. He's linked through via Corpus Christi."

"Uh-huh." Keene followed Joyce between the communications equipment racks and control panels. "Have we a friendly native?"

"It's difficult to say," Joyce answered as they came to a live screen on one of the consoles. The face showing on it was of a man in his forties with clear blue eyes and straight, yellow hair brushed to the side. He turned to look out full-face as Keene moved within the viewing angle of the console pickup.

"Hello. I'm Landen Keene—NIFTV's flight engineer; also one of the principal design engineers involved with the project."

"John Feld, Pacific Coast Network news."

"Hi."

"You are with the Amspace Corporation, Dr. Keene?"

"In a way. I run a private engineering consultancy that Amspace contracts design work and theoretical studies to."

Feld looked mildly surprised. "And does this relationship result in your going into space often?" he asked.

"Oh, Amspace and Protonix—that's the name of my company—have known each other for a long time. I go wherever the job demands. A desk has more leg room, but this way we get to have more fun."

"As we saw," Feld agreed. "That was a spectacular performance you people gave up there earlier."

"And it was in spite of everything this country has done in the last forty years, not thanks to any of it," Keene replied.

"So what were you demonstrating? Obviously you were doing more than having fun. Is it another version of the message we hear from time to time about private enterprise being able to do things better than government?"

Keene shook his head. "Hell no. What we were telling you has to do with the whole future of humanity, not somebody's political or economic ideology. The world is still burying its head in the sand and refusing to face what Athena is telling us: the universe isn't a safe place. For our own good, we need a commitment on a massive scale to broadening what the Kronians have pioneered and spreading ourselves around more of space. What we showed today is that we can start doing it right now, without needing to negotiate any deals with the Kronians—although if you want my opinion, we should avail ourselves of any help they offer. We already have the technology and the industries. The vehicle that we demonstrated today was a test bed for a Nuclear Indigenously Fueled engine. That means it uses a nuclear thermal reactor to heat an indigenous propellant gas as a reaction mass. 'Indigenous': native to a particular place."

Feld seemed to understand the term but looked puzzled. "Okay. . . . But where are we talking about, exactly, in this instance?"

Keene spread his hands. "That's the whole point: anywhere that you're operating. You see, it works with a whole range of substances that occur naturally just about wherever you might happen to be. Venus is rich in carbon dioxide; the asteroids and ice moons of the gas-giants give unlimited water; others, such as Saturn's Titan and Neptune's Triton have methane; you can also use nitrogen, carbon monoxide, hydrogen, argon. In other words, it opens up the entire Solar System by affording ready refueling sources wherever you go. Today we were using water, and you saw the results. Methane would perform about fifty percent better still."

"So was today's effort to get publicity for a new technology that you've developed? If so, it certainly seems to have been successful."

"New? No way. It was being talked about back in the 1960s. But antinuclear phobia took over, and we've been at a standstill. What we're trying to do is more wake the country up again."

"Ah, but weren't there good reasons?" Feld seemed on more familiar ground, suddenly. "Surely there are hazards associated with taking such devices into orbit that haven't been resolved yet. Isn't it true that if the radioactive material from just one reactor were spread evenly through the atmosphere—"

"It isn't going to get spread evenly around the planet. There's enough gasoline in every city to—" Keene broke off as he saw that Feld was glancing aside, as if taking directions from somewhere off-screen. He looked back.

"Thank you, Dr. Keene. Apparently Captain Elms is standing by up there in the Amspace satellite now, and we would like to hear a few words from him too while we've got the connection. That was very interesting. Let's hope you have a safe trip back down."

"My pleasure," Keene grunted. The screen blanked to a test mode.

Joyce, who had moved away to talk to the duty supervisor on the far side of the room and then come back, stepped forward from where she had been watching. "See, you've scared them off again, Lan. You always have to start getting political."

"Hell, the problem's political," Keene grumbled. "How is it supposed to get solved if we can't mention it?"

Stevie reappeared carrying a plastic mug of black coffee and handed it to him. Keene nodded, sipped to test the heat, then took a longer drink gratefully. "But you're right," he told Joyce. "I should know better by now. It's gotten to be something of a reflex, I guess."

"Falling into patterns of habit is normal with advancing age," she assured him cheerfully.

"Thanks. Just what I needed."

The supervisor called over to them. "They're on hold now, Joyce. Do you want it through there again?"

"Yes, we're done with Pacific," Joyce called back over the consoles. "You've got another call waiting," she told Keene. He drank from his coffee mug again, as if fortifying himself. "Oh, I think you'll like this one," Joyce said. She gazed expectantly at the test pattern on the screen. It changed suddenly to present a face once again, this time a woman's.

Keene blinked in surprise. "It's Sariena!" he exclaimed.

She was in her early thirties, perhaps, with the finely formed features combining just the right amount of firmness with a softening of feminine roundness that fashion modeling agencies and cosmetics advertisers will scour a continent for. Her hair was shoulder-length, richly dark with a hint of wave at the tips, and her skin a clear dusky brown, setting off a pair of light gray, curiously opalescent eyes which at first sight jarred with such a complexion, but produced a strangely fascinating effect as one adjusted to them. Keene could have pictured her as an Arabian princess of fairy tale, or a rajah's daughter. And that was just from electronic images; they had never actually met. For Sariena was not of Earth at all but from Kronia, the collective name for the oasis of human habitation established among the moons of Saturn. The name came from Kronos, the Ancient Greek name for Saturn, who had ruled the heavens during Earth's Golden Age.

"Hello, Lan," she greeted. "And is that Joyce with you there?"

"I'm here," Joyce put in, coming closer.

"Ah yes, it is." Sariena's smile was restrained enough to preserve dignity, wide enough not to appear cold. "I just wanted to let you know that the shuttles are in orbit with us now, and we'll be on our way down to the surface later today, arriving in Washington this evening."

"Sorry if I've been out of touch," Keene said. "I've been a bit busy lately, as you've probably gathered."

Sariena was aboard the Kronian long-range transporter vessel *Osiris*, now parked in Earth orbit after a three-month voyage from the Saturnian system. In that time, the communications turnaround delay had decreased steadily from over two hours when the ship set out. With preparations for the NIFTV demonstration taking up all his time, Keene hadn't talked with the Kronians at all during the past week. Now, suddenly, it was a pleasant change to find himself able to interact with them normally.

"Yes. We all thought that show of yours today was terrific," Sariena said. "The timing was perfect. It'll give us a good opening theme for the talks. Gallian asked me to say thanks, and that he's looking forward to meeting you in person at last too." Gallian was the head of the Kronian mission.

"You should thank the Air Force Space Command

more than us," Keene replied. "They picked today for their test. We just went along with it."

"So do you have any idea yet when we'll be able to meet you?" Sariena asked.

"Well, you're probably going to be tied up with formal receptions and so forth for a while," Keene said. "I try not to get involved in things like that. But I've made time to be in Washington for a few days, starting Monday. We could probably work something in then."

"I'll let Gallian know," Sariena said.

Besides being a consultant to Amspace in Texas, Keene also acted as an advisor on space-related nuclear issues to various government offices, and maintained a Washington office for the purpose. He evaluated official reports and proposals, prepared recommendations, and testified before committees. A lot of congresspeople and other denizens of the Hill also consulted him privately for off-the-record views and background details. Most of them were better informed on issues that concerned them than the required public posturing sometimes allowed them to admit.

He looked at the face that he knew only from screens, outwardly so composed, yet what kind of agitation and uncertainties—fear even—had to be churning inside? In all her adult life, she had never seen an ocean, breathed a planet's air, or walked under an open sky. She had been taken to Kronia as a child in the early days when the original base, named Kropotkin, was constructed on the moon Dione. Now she was returning for the first time as one of the deputation that the Saturn colony had sent to Earth following the Athena event to press the same case that Keene had summarized to Feld.

Keene raised his coffee mug. "And before any of those guys in tuxedos have a chance to get started with their toasts and speeches, let us be the first to say, Welcome to Earth, finally. The main thing you have to remember is that leaving the outside door open is okay. But don't try walking on the blue stuff."

Sariena laughed. "Will you be able to make it to Washington too, Joyce?"

"Sorry. Not for a while, anyhow. I'm stuck up in this grimy can for another three weeks."

"Is that all?"

"Yeah, right, okay—you've got me. I was forgetting. What's three weeks in space to you guys?"

"But their accommodation is probably a bit more roomy," Keene said to Joyce.

"When are you going back down, Lan?" Sariena asked.

"In a couple of hours, probably. The firm's bus is up here waiting already." He gave Joyce a sideways look. "Then it'll be a shower and a swim, clean clothes . . ." He watched the look forming on her face. "And maybe a good steak and some wine out somewhere nice tonight."

"Pig," Joyce muttered hatefully.

The Amspace minishuttle detached from Space Dock a little under three hours later. As the craft fell away, Keene was able to catch a glimpse of the *Osiris* passing above as an elongated bead of light in its higher orbit. Low to one side, partly eclipsed by the curve of Earth's dark side, stretched the awesome spectacle of Athena's braided tail streaming in the solar wind as the supercomet fell toward the Sun.

4

Amspace's headquarters offices were located in Corpus Christi, southeast Texas, on North Water Street, a couple of blocks inland from the marinas on Corpus Christi Bay, at the fashionable, downtown end of Shoreline Boulevard. The company's main manufacturing, engineering, and research center was twenty miles south of the city at Kingsville, with a launch facility thirty miles farther south at a place called San Saucillo, on the plain of sandy flats and sage brush between Laredo and the Gulf. It was Oil Country, and much of the company's founding impetus had derived from the tradition of independence rooted in private capital and sympathetic local politics. All the same, taking an initiative toward developing the longer-term potential of space was a contentious and uncertain issue, and as insurance the corporation was constructing a second launch complex over the border in Mexico, on a highland plateau known as Montemorelos. Besides affording backup capability, Montemorelos would provide a means of continuing operations in the event that San Saucillo was shut down by politics.

It was late morning when the minishuttle carrying Keene and the other two NIFTV crew, along with several others from Space Dock who had been involved in the test mission, landed at the Saucillo site under a sun beating down through a dust haze that tinted the plain blue with distance. A bus carried the arrivals from the pad area to the assembly and administration complex at the far end of the landing field, where there was an interview session with waiting TV reporters. From there, a company helicopter flew them to the main plant at Kingsville for a post-mission debriefing over a burgers-and-fries lunch with senior technical staff in the office of the Technical Vice President, Harry Halloran. A lot of numbers and preliminary flight data were bandied about, and the NIFTV's performance analyzed. The consensus was that the demonstration had comfortably exceeded expectations.

By rights, that ought to have been good news. But such were the circumstances of the times that negative reactions could be expected as a virtual certainty too. And, indeed, by afternoon the protest had already started, ranging from diplomatic notes being delivered in Washington to poster-waving in the street outside Amspace's Corpus Christi offices. All the news channels were airing comments or polling views, and the company's switchboard and electronic mail servers were overloading. So if it was true that there really is no such thing as bad publicity, and since the whole object had been to get attention, then there could be no serious grounds for complaint.

As it turned out, many of the incoming messages were supportive. The British government expressed the hope that the demonstration might mark the beginning of a turnaround in world opinion that was long overdue. A Russian corporation revealed that it was working along similar lines to the NIFTV and would be flying a test engine of its own within six months.

By three o'clock, Amspace had received twenty-six inquiries from hopeful would-be pilots. The meeting ended with the hope that the coming weekend might afford a forced cooling-off period. After that, the case the Kronians had come to argue for Earth expanding its space effort would endorse Amspace's position strongly. So all in all, events seemed to have worked themselves in quite a timely fashion.

While people were still collecting papers together and shutting down laptops, Wallace Lomack, the company's Chief Design Engineer, came over to where Keene was sitting with Joe Elms and Ricardo. "It was the Rambler all over again, Lan," he said jovially. "Right?"

Keene looked up, momentarily nonplussed. "Hi, Wally. What?"

"A long time ago, you told us that story about the Nash Rambler that you souped up and wiped out everything on the highway with back when you were a student. The stunt today was the same thing all over again, right? That was what gave you the idea."

Finally, the penny dropped. "Oh, you still remember that story, eh?" Keene said.

"I never heard that one," Joe murmured, tidying up his notes.

"Lan's history of dreaming up crazy schemes and getting everyone to go along with them goes all the way back," Wally replied. Then, to Keene, "I bet you never thought it would come to anything like this, though, eh?"

"You're right. I never thought it would. . . ." Keene shrugged. "So what are you up to over the weekend, Wally? Anything wild and exciting?"

Lomack left his tie loosened and slipped on his jacket, not bothering trying to fasten it over his ample midriff. "Oh, bit of boating, bit of fishing—something to amuse the grandkids, you know. How about you, Lan?"

"We're the mission crew. We don't have no weekend," Ricardo put in, next to Keene.

"They've given you the whole of tomorrow morning to rest up," Keene pointed out.

"Oh, yeah. How could I forget that?"

"Then Les has got a press conference organized in town that we have to be at," Keene replied to Wally. He was referring to Les Urkin, head of Amspace's public relations. "Then I arranged to be in Washington next week. Things are no doubt about to start flapping there."

"When are you flying up there?" Wally inquired.

"Probably Sunday night."

Joe raised his eyebrows and made an *O* in the air with a thumb and forefinger. "Aha! And planning to meet the delectable Saturnian, I'll bet. Can't say I blame you, though, Lan."

"Sure, if the schedules work out," Keene agreed. "Why not? We've been talking to them long enough."

"Is a romance between the planets about to happen?" Ricardo asked, grinning.

Keene shook his head. "Not me. I've been there already. Burned, bitten, and shy. You know how it is."

Wally thought about that, then made a face. "Well, the first two, I might buy. Anyhow, have fun, young feller."

"You too, Wally," Keene said. "And don't let those grandkids tip over your boat. You're needed back here for the profile evaluations next week."

Lomack moved away, while Keene finished stuffing his papers into a document case. As a matter of fact, he had forgotten all about his student escapade with the Nash Rambler. What had given him the idea for showing off the NIFTV when the Air Force was testing its APU was something he'd read about Charles Parsons, the English inventor of the steam turbine, who had used the celebration of the Queen's Jubilee in 1897 to arouse the interest of the British Admiralty.

On that occasion, the Royal Navy had assembled 173 warships to be reviewed by the Royal Yacht and a grand flotilla of craft containing the Lords of the Admiralty, various colonial premiers, the Diplomatic Corps, and members from both Houses of Parliament; but Parsons stole the show by roaring around the fleet in his 2,000 horsepower turbine-driven yacht *Turbinia* at thirty-four knots, which was faster than anything the Navy could send in chase. In fact, it was the fastest boat in the world at the time. Such was the spirit of the age, that the British Admiralty had responded by promptly ordering two turbine-powered ships. As he zipped up the document case and rose from his chair, Keene wondered if they could expect a similar display of magnanimity and perspicacity from the Defense Department.

After leaving Amspace, Keene stopped by his own company to show his face and check on how things had gone during his absence. Protonix occupied a five-room suite in an office park on the south side of Corpus Christi, near the interchange between the Crosstown Expressway and South Padre Island Drive. Besides himself as president, it had four other staff, all female. Vicki was Keene's associate and second-in-command; Celia acted as her assistant; Judith had a math Ph.D. and looked after the computers, while Karen was the receptionist, secretary, and general errand-runner. The engineers at Amspace referred to the firm enviously as Keene's Harem. In fact, as a point of professionalism and out of the sheer practical consideration of getting things done in an environment that was complicated enough already, Keene kept business strictly separate from anything personal. As with marriage, he had suffered the consequences of those kinds of involvements in earlier years. Sometimes he thought that the first half of his adult life had served partly as a rehearsal for the second, in which he was finally managing to get a few things right.

He was greeted with laughter and applause, a bottle of Bushmills Black Bush Irish whiskey, and an old astronaut-style cap from the souvenir shop at the Johnson Space Center in Houston. The girls had watched the demo that morning and said it was terrific. Karen thought that Keene looked great on TV—that unshaven, mildly haggard look was exactly what movie producers were hunting for. He ought to apply for a part, she told him. Keene assured her that there had been nothing mild about it.

Although Protonix hadn't been named in any of the coverage, the political and media insiders who knew Keene were already clamoring to get ahold of him, and Shirley, who ran the office that he used in Washington, had called with a tentative list of meetings scheduled for Monday. But the *big* news was that Naomi had presented Celia with five kittens: two tabby, one black, one gray, and one "kind of stripey something," Celia said. . . . Oh, and yes, apart from that, Judith had left early to attend the computer show in Dallas tomorrow; there were problems with machining some of the parts for the reactor Westinghouse was fabricating in San Diego, that Vicki needed to talk to him about next week; the guy in Japan who had done the thermal studies had downloaded the reports that Keene was interested in; and the parking lot would be closed next Friday and over the weekend for resurfacing. When a few more minor items were disposed of, Vicki followed Keene into his office with a list of things to check for Monday, leaving Karen and Celia clearing desks, organizing purses, and exchanging plans for the weekend.

Vicki had light brown, almost orange hair that contracted itself into wiry curls no matter how she tried to comb or wave it, and a freckled, angular face accentuated by a pointy nose, sharp chin, and straight mouth. Her body was petite and lean-limbed, shaped by that chemistry that can eat anything all day and metabolize energy without an ounce of gain. She lived for her work, and she was good. Originally a radiation physicist at Harvard, she had met Keene when he moved there to become a theoretician from conducting plasma physics research at General Atomic in San Diego. She had grown disillusioned with the academic scientific community at about the same rate as he, and rejoined him back in the real world soon after he quit, moved south to Texas, and set up the business that later became Protonix. She had a fourteen-year-old son called Robin, whom she had raised from toddlerhood by herself, and Keene had become something of a father figure as well as a business colleague.

"So . . ." Vicki stared across the office from one of the two visitor chairs below a wall of framed pictures of launch vehicles and satellites, including a spectacular shot of the Kronian *Osiris*.

"So," Keene echoed. They were both flopped loosely, unwinding, happy to forget the week's routine events for the time being.

"You get to go again. I told you, the others can take care of the office. Why do I get this impression that male animals are fickle?" One of their standing jokes was that Keene would get Vicki up on a mission too one day. It had long been a dream of hers to go into space.

Keene put on a mock pained look. "If I didn't know you better, I might think you didn't believe me."

"How can you say that? You know I have undying trust."

"And I have an image of mystique to keep up. You know how the guru thing works: always promise nirvana tomorrow."

Vicki turned her eyes resignedly toward the ceiling and changed the subject. "Did I hear you say they're actually giving you tomorrow morning off to rest up?"

"The galley slaves have to get some air sometime," Keene replied. "Les has got a press conference fixed for the afternoon."

"You want to stop by for a late breakfast at the house on your way in? Robin has been asking after you. I think he wants to show you some of the latest that he's been getting into."

Keene rubbed his chin. "Sure, why not? . . . So how is Robin?"

"Just fine."

"What's he been getting into this time?"

"Dinosaurs. Apparently they couldn't have existed."

"Oh, really? A mass hallucination, then. . . . So how come?"

"It gets involved. Why not ask him tomorrow?"

"Okay."

Vicki searched her mind for anything else. "Did you talk to Sariena? I was at Kingsville when they redirected the call from the *Osiris*. That was just after your spot with John Feld ended."

"Yes, I got it," Keene replied. "She just wanted to let us know that Gallian was happy with the way things went; also, that they'd be on their way down to the surface pretty soon."

"They're down," Vicki said. "It was on the news this afternoon—while you were at the debriefing. Big reception dinner at the White House tonight. Everybody who thinks they're somebody is going to have to be there." She tossed a hand out in a motion indicating both of them. "So how come we didn't get invitations?"

"We left the rarified academic heights, don't you remember? People would probably worry that we might show up in coveralls, carrying wrenches." Keene rubbed his chin. "We could stop for a quick one while it's still happy hour at the Bandana," he offered. "Not exactly black tie, but do you think it would do instead?"

Vicki smiled and gave a snort. "The company might be an improvement, though—I'll say that." She stretched, held the position for a few seconds, then relaxed. "So never mind the pageantry over the weekend. How will things go when they get down to the real talking? Any guesses? . . . I know we've got a lot of the world's attention, but is it really going to take any notice? I mean, okay, Athena's there. But most people are treating it like a spectator sport, not something that actually connects to their lives. Are the Kronians going to be able to change that?"

"They must think they stand a chance, otherwise they'd hardly have come this far." Keene showed his palms briefly. "All they have to do is get the powers that shape science in this world to see the obvious."

"Wow," Vicki said dryly. "Now I really feel better."

Kronia's scientists had reached the conclusion that the conventional picture of a stable and orderly Solar System repeating its motions like clockwork since the time of its formation, was—simply put—wrong. Cataclysmic encounters between planetary and other bodies had, they maintained, occurred through into recent historic times, and there was no reason to suppose that such events would not continue. The Kronian leaders accepted this view and for years had been exhorting Earth to put a greater investment of effort and resources into spreading a significant human presence across the Solar System. For as long as the human race remained concentrated in one place, they insisted, it was vulnerable, literally, to extinction. In fact, they claimed it had almost happened in the not very distant past.

But Earth's institutions remained wedded to their dogma of gradualism, which maintained that only the processes observed today had operated in the past, and, apart from temporary local fluctuations, had done so at the same rates. Extrapolating backward the currently measured rates of such processes as sedimentation and erosion had yielded the immense ages assigned to geological formations, which had come to be regarded as unquestionable.

In the main, Earth's policymakers had rejected the Kronian urgings in preference for the orthodox view. With the military no longer able to press as compelling a case as in the days of superpower rivalry, and other lobbies jostling for a share of largesse at the federal trough, expansion of the space sciences and industries had not been a high government priority. For the private sector, ventures much beyond the Moon were too massively demanding in outlay and too risky to interest the major institutional investors, who looked to areas of secure returns such as launch systems for satellites and limited scientific payloads—which conventional technologies served adequately. Comfort and security had become the world's foremost concerns. Only fringe outfits like Amspace, and a few visionaries who were prepared to back them, had continued pushing for a general commitment to broadening what the Kronians had pioneered, and were calling for the enterprise that advanced, long-range, spacegoing capability would open up: *colonization*. Hence, organizations like Amspace had found themselves natural allies of the Kronians, communicating and cooperating for the same end: the Kronians to impart a cultural imperative; the Keenes of the world—and the Joyces, spending weeks on end in a cramped, orbiting boiler room; the Wallys, hoping to create a better world for their grandchildren—pursuing lifelong dreams.

Then Athena happened—and surely, they had all believed, that would change everything. But astoundingly, it had changed things hardly at all. Of course, the early months had seen a media orgy of sensational

pictures of the planetoid and a deformed Jupiter
gradually regaining its shape; hurried explanations by
scientists; and endless lurid articles and documentaries
that the public eventually grew weary of. Sales of
amateur telescopes, astronomy books, and videos
soared; related college classes reported record enroll-
ments; catastrophism saw a dramatic revival. And yes,
the scientific community conceded, with some hem-
ming and hawing and smoothing of ruffled plumage,
that their theories needed revising—and then clam-
ored for more funding to support the new research
that needed to be done. But the kind of research they
had in mind involved bigger and more lavishly
equipped departments, computers that even the
particle physicists would envy, more chairmanships
and committees, and appointments to oversee
unmanned missions to various parts of the Solar System. The mainline contractors got in their bids where
they saw opportunity, but practically without excep-
tion the equipment and techniques envisaged were
all safe, proven, and more of the same. Nothing they
talked about anticipated any meaningful move toward
getting *people* in significant numbers *out there* anytime soon. Finally, in desperation, the Kronians dispatched a political-scientific delegation to present their
case firsthand in an attempt to shake Earth out of
its complacency.

There was a tap on the door, and Celia stuck her
face in. "We're off now," she said to Keene and Vicki.
"Have a good weekend."

"'Bye," Karen's voice called from the outer office
beyond.

"Take care with those cowboys out there," Keene
called back. One of the ongoing news topics of the
office was Karen's latest boyfriend. He nodded a
goodnight to Celia. She disappeared, closing the door.
Keene looked back at Vicki. "We'll just have to wait
and see what the next few weeks bring," he told her.

As he saw things, it was the last chance. If this didn't bring about a change in Earth's outlook and policies, nothing would. Then he and Vicki might well end up applying for jobs at the Bandana instead of just stopping by for happy-hour drinks.

5

Thirty years earlier, the world had scoffed and said it was impossible when two extraordinary personalities got together and announced an intention to establish a human settlement among the moons of Saturn. After the parade of mediocrity that had marked the closing decades of the twentieth century, it seemed that leader figures with the charisma to inspire followings had conceded the stage to rock stars and sports idols. Then, one day, a disenchanted California trial attorney with the unremarkable name of Thomas Mondel gave up a promising career to denounce the world's economic system with the contention that humans were made—created, evolved, or "just there"; whatever one chose to believe—for better things. There was something wrong with a society that spent millions trying to make computers and robots imitate humans while at the same time raising humans to behave like robots. California had seen more than a smattering of fads and cults before, of course. But this was different in several ways that mattered. Mondel was not another beard with sandals and beads, reaching out to lost sheep and adolescents of all ages desperate to find escape from the hopeless corners of life that they had painted themselves into. He was professional, articulate, wise to the ways of the world, and he knew how to get attention. His appeal was to the slowly atrophying cost accountant stuck in traffic twice a day, two-hundred-fifty days every year, with the IRS waiting to mop up whatever of his year's income survived Christmas; to the marketing wage slave sitting out a four-hour layover at O'Hare, looking forward to a microwaved TV meal in a solitary apartment and wondering what happened to the glamorous, high-powered executive that she'd created out of movie images in the years she was at college; to the frustrated who had worked to be scientists or teachers or ministers or healers, but found themselves turned into full-time form-fillers and fundraisers instead. In short, to all those people to whom it didn't make sense to have to labor year-in, year-out in dismally unfulfilling ways in order to be allowed a modest share of the produce in a world whose biggest preoccupation seemed to be with moving overproduced merchandise that nobody really needed. And it was amazing how many people like that there turned out to be.

It was hardly the first time that somebody had denounced money value as the sole measure of worth of all things. In the past, Mondel claimed, some such indicator to keep track of who owed what to whom had always been necessitated by scarcity. But knowledge and the limitless capacity that it equated to in today's world made that no longer true. In terms of ability, humanity's material problems were solved. What hadn't been solved was finding the right incentive to induce people to realize that ability. Trying to mesh twenty-first-century technology with nineteenth-century notions of economics produced the constant clashing of gears that the world had been hearing. When the wants of those with the means to pay determined the demand that was supplied, and not what the rest of the people needed, eventually the ones with the needs would resort to force to satisfy them, which was why war, unrest, and rebellion refused to go away.

"Mondelism" caught the mood of the times and spread, attracting followers from all stations in life committed to creating a mutual support network based on principles of obligation and trust, service and duty, instead of buying and selling. But it also attracted a lot of free riders too, as the skeptics had said it would, giving rise to hostility within and ridicule without, and in general the movement wasn't a success. But neither was Mondel a quitter. The problems didn't reflect on the soundness of the idea, he insisted, but resulted from its having to be sown in fields already choked by weeds. The followers continued to believe, and sustained by a core of tireless disciples and some quite influential backers, tottered on through intermittent triumphs and crises for several years. And then Tom Mondel met a geneticist-entrepreneur by the name of Clement Waltz.

Waltz had started a biological engineering company called Genenco that hit on a method for detecting and correcting a number of common genetic birth defects. Health-care systems worldwide rushed to license the process, since the cost of screening was significantly lower than that of the treatment programs avoided later. The result was that Waltz became a multibillionaire before he was thirty, upon which he grew bored with it all and cast around for something more meaningful to occupy himself with than continuing to make money, which he had come to despise. Some scientific and business colleagues introduced him to Mondel, and Waltz was immediately captivated. Mondel, by this time, had reached the conclusion that what his system needed was a clean start in an untainted environment removed from Earth. Accepting the irony that in a money-dominated world, money was necessary to gain freedom from the contamination of money, Waltz assembled sufficient assets from his own resources and sympathetic backers to solicit the Guatemalan government's cooperation in constructing an assembly and launch center at a place called Tapapeque. He imported scientists from Japan, manufacturing know-how from China, disgruntled rocketry experts from NASA and the former Soviet military, and announced that he was going to establish a Mondelist colony elsewhere. The world chortled and jeered—until test shots from Tapapeque circled the Earth, and three months later a four-man lander touched down fifty miles from the UN experimental base at Tycho in a single-stage jump from an Earth-orbiting platform. Here was an illustration of what dedication and human creativity untrammeled by power-lust and greed could achieve, Mondel and Waltz told the astonished world. In the isolated Central American microcommunity, Mondelism worked. They then announced that the promised extraterrestrial colony would be founded not on Mars, as most commentators had assumed, and where a tiny international scientific reconnaissance group lived a hardy life with visitations twice a year; not among the Asteroids, which would be bypassed and exploited later; not even above Jupiter, whose high-radiation environment posed uncertainties; but all the way out at the remoteness of Saturn. This time the world didn't jeer, although there was no disguising that its credulity was strained. . . . And, by God, they made it!

Thereafter, despite the distance and the infrequency of return voyages by the first ship, and—later—more departures by others, the colony grew at a surprising rate. The stories that came back of science free to function as an instrument of pure inquiry, unconstrained by establishment dogmas or the political agendas of funding agencies, attracted a particular kind of mind—not just physicists and engineers but builders, inventors, philosophers, explorers: the curious, the restless, the innovators of every kind. They were drawn by the accounts they heard of a society-in-miniature that seemed to function without budgets or accounting, where value was reflected in what an individual contributed to the common enterprise. Some gave the closest description they could find for the social order there as "monastic." The measure of worth— "wealth"—was knowledge and competence. It couldn't be stolen, hoarded, taxed, or counterfeited. If left to lie unused it effectively didn't exist.

Invariably, there were those who couldn't fit in and came back. And the vast majority on Earth, even if they ever thought about such matters and could relate to them, were unable to comprehend how anyone would choose living amid ice deserts and breathing machine-dispensed air to taking in a movie after a day's shopping at the mall, lying on the beach, or harvesting corn in Iowa in October. But just a few here and a couple there from places scattered the world over proved sufficient to fill the transports lifting out from orbit and establish further bases on Tethys, Rhea, Titan, and Iapetus in a time period that confounded all the experts. Nevertheless, it was still widely regarded as a crazy venture destined eventually to peter out or come to an abrupt end. Earth's commercial and political institutions made no rush to follow, since for them there was nothing to be gained. It was only in the surreal system of economics that Mondelism had created, where a huge infusion from altruistic benefactors had put up the stake money and some of the best talent that Earth had produced was prepared literally to work for nothing, that any significant investment in operations over such a distance could be contemplated.

There had been times when Keene too had thought about going in one of those ships—not during the early days, for he had been too young, but later, when he would have had something to offer out there. The period following the breakdown of his marriage had been one such time. Others were when he despaired that no Earth-based initiative would ever follow to build on the unique combination of circumstances that had founded Kronia—at least not while he was still a young man. But he had stayed, knowing those moods would pass—and they always had.

It would have felt too much like giving up. Big changes were never easy, and always they depended on the rare kind of people who seemed capable of believing in anything except the impossible. And besides, he liked to watch sunsets too—and to scuffle through autumn leaves, eat out at a good waterside restaurant, and lie on beaches. Why should he have to leave all that to people he disagreed with when he could fight them for it? And right now, the prospects for finally getting official recognition that expansion outward was imperative to the security of Earth's culture looked better than ever. He wasn't prepared to become an exile just yet.

The colony's original intent had been to maintain a cooperative relationship with Earth based on some kind of exchange of Kronian technological innovations in return for products and materials that Earth could supply more conveniently. But when Kronia went on to realize in twenty years advanced propulsion systems that Earth had put on hold, attitudes on Earth became more wary, causing the Kronians to withdraw and manage their own affairs. Mondel and Waltz both died together in a craft that broke up on reentry over Titan eight years previously, making them instant martyrs of the movement. But by that time Kronia was established and virtually self-sufficient. The Tapapeque complex was handed over to the Guatemalan government, who maintained shuttle operations to ferry up departing emigrants when a Kronian ship was in orbit, and at other times leased surplus capacity to various national and private interests, providing a welcome supplement to the country's income.

Did Keene really believe that a bunch of mavericks and misfits that most of the world dismissed as deranged or incomprehensible could reroute human destiny? "Sure," he told innumerable reporters and interviewers who called him throughout the rest of the evening. "Just the same as we can run rings around the Air Force."

6

Southeast of Corpus Christi, a bridge connected across an inlet to a peninsula called Flour Bluff, at the end of which lay the Naval Air Station. Beyond the peninsula, a causeway continued to Padre Island, one of the chain of sandy offshore islands fringing the Gulf shore from west Florida to Mexico. That was where Vicki lived, in an aging but well-kept and homey single-family house that she had acquired when she moved from the northeast to join Keene after he set up Protonix. Robin's father, a Navy man, had been killed some years before in a political bombing incident in the Middle East. Keene's slipping into the role of family friend and father substitute filled a vacant space in both their lives, as well as making a big difference for Robin.

He arrived shortly before ten, after a twenty-minute drive from his townhouse on Ocean Drive, facing the Bay on the southern side of the city, clad in a sport shirt with slacks that he could throw a jacket over for the press conference later. Vicki greeted him in a weekend casual top and shorts. Robin joined them, and they sat down to breakfast in the glass-enclosed summer room that had been added as an extension of the kitchen. Keene had always thought Robin a great kid with a natural ability to get along with anybody, who deserved to have known a natural father. He was fair like his mother, although his hair was more yellow, and his skin, unlike hers, kept a year-round tan. His features seemed to alternate between deep frowns when he was intent on something, to wide-eyed vistas of distant blankness when he was off into the realms of . . . wherever he went. Keene sometimes wished he had kept a notebook to list the questions Robin had come up with in the time they had known each other. For a while, someone at Robin's school had formed the opinion that he had an attention-deficiency problem, but Vicki thought it was more the result of a communications failing somewhere; any kind of communications channel has two ends. It hadn't been Keene's place to interfere, but in his own mind he had agreed with her. He knew from his own experience that Robin was capable of fearsome and sustained concentration on things that interested him.

Besides her job with Protonix, Vicki had a sideline creating advertising graphics at home. When she wasn't breadwinning or single-parenting, she managed to find time for a mix of interests that never ceased to amaze Keene, ranging from biology and medieval history to pen-and-ink drawing and decorating, in between which she desk-published the newsletter for a local church group, made sure that Robin fed and looked after his menagerie, and amassed books on seemingly every subject imaginable. She believed nothing on TV or in newspapers that was of interest, and had no interest in the things she did believe. When she seriously wanted to know something, she dug and pestered until she found sources that were reliable, or she went to someone who knew. She had first entered Keene's world of awareness through tracking him down when they were both at Harvard, to answer questions she had about the electromagnetic properties of space after finding the theories of dark matter to account for anomalous motions of galaxies unconvincing.

"The hounds are baying," she told Keene, referring to reactions that had been building up to Amspace's stunt the day before. "But we knew that would happen. Have you caught much of it?"

Keene shook his head. "I've been screening those out. That's what Amspace has a PR department for. No doubt I'll get my share this afternoon. Who's saying what?"

"The EA secretary was bilious," Vicki said—the name of the former EPA had been shortened, after some thought the original form sounded too alarmist. "He called it criminally irresponsible and wants a formal ban on space nukes to be declared internationally."

"He's got an image to keep up for the faithful," Keene replied. "It'll never happen. The Defense people need to keep an option open to match the Chinese if they have to, and the Chinese will never buy it."

Robin attended to his eggs and bacon, his mind roaming in whatever realms it turned to when grown-ups got into politics. Keene watched Vicki refilling the coffee cups and then let his gaze wander over the kitchen, searching for a change of subject. Sam, the household dog, lay in the doorway watching him with one eye open, still unable, quite, to figure out whether or not Keene belonged. Labrador and collie contributions were discernible, with various other ingredients stirred into the mix. Vicki had originally christened him "Samurai," but he just didn't have the image. The parakeets squawked noisily in their cage from the kitchen beyond.

There were a few more pictures and drawings

adorning the wall. A model of a tyrannosaurus had appeared on top of the refrigerator. "Oh, what's this?" Keene murmured. He remembered what Vicki had said at the office the previous evening. "Is Robin going through his dinosaur phase? I guess he's at just about the right age." Robin returned immediately from wherever, registering interest.

Vicki nodded with a sigh. "His room is practically papered with prints that he's downloaded. It's like one of those science-fiction-movie theme parks. I think he must have checked out every book on them in the local library."

"I hope that won't mean more additions to the private zoo, CR," Keene said, looking at Robin. Keene had dubbed him Christopher Robin, after the character from the British children's books.

Robin appeared to mull over the possibility, then shook his head. "Too much cleaning up after. And they'd probably bother the neighbors."

"What's this I hear about them not being real?" Keene asked. "Has everyone been imagining things all these years?"

"Oh, did Mom tell you about that?"

"Right."

"Theoretically they ought to be impossible," Robin agreed. "They couldn't exist." Keene waited, then showed an open palm invitingly. Robin went on, "Well, you're an engineer, Lan. It follows from the basic scaling laws. The weight of an animal or anything increases as the cube of its size, right?"

Keene nodded. "Okay."

Robin shrugged. "But strength depends on the cross-section of muscles, which only increases as the square. So as animals get bigger, their strength-to-weight ratio decreases. All this stuff you read about insects carrying x times their own body weight around isn't really any big deal. At their size you'd be able to walk around holding a piano over your head with one hand."

Keene glanced at Vicki with raised eyebrows. "Robin's been doing his homework." Keene was familiar with the principle but had never had reason to dwell on its implications regarding dinosaurs.

"That's Robin," Vicki said.

Keene looked back at Robin. "Go on," he said.

"As you get bigger, it works the other way. Do you know who the strongest humans in the world are?"

"Hmm. . . . Oh, how about an Olympic power lifter?" Keene guessed.

"Right on. Now, take one, say, doing dead-lift or a squat. The most you'd be talking about would be what—around thirteen hundred pounds including body weight?"

Keene shrugged. "If you say so. It sounds as if you've checked it out."

"Oh, he has," Vicki threw in.

"Now scale him up to brontosaurus size, and his maximum lifting capability works out at under fifty thousand pounds," Robin said. "But the brontosaurus weighed in at seventy thousand; the supersaur even more than that, and the ultrasaur at—would you believe this—three hundred sixty thousand pounds!"

"My God." Keene sat back in his chair, staring hard as the implication finally hit him. "Are you sure they were as heavy as that?"

Robin nodded. "I got those estimates from a guy called Young, who's Curator of Vertebrate Paleontology at the museum in Toronto. And I checked it with somebody else at the Smithsonian, too." It sounded as if Robin had been picking up tips from Vicki. His expression remained serious. "But the point is, the strongest man in the world wouldn't have been able to stand under his own weight, let alone move—and that's when you're talking about practically being made of muscle. These other things were all digestive system. So how did they do it? See what I mean—they couldn't exist."

Keene looked across at Vicki quizzically. It was a challenge for any engineer. Vicki tossed out her free hand and shook her head. "Maybe they had better muscles," Keene offered as a starter, looking back at Robin.

Robin was clearly prepared for it. "No, that doesn't work. The maximum force that a muscle can produce is set by the size of the thick and thin filaments and the number of cross-bridges between them," he replied. "It turns out they're about the same for a mouse as for an elephant—and it holds true across all the vertebrates. That means the only gain you get from larger size is what comes from the bigger cross section."

"There's no increase in efficiency," Keene checked.

Robin shook his head. "In fact, it goes the other way. Gets worse."

"Okay. . . ." Keene searched for another way to play devil's advocate. "They were aquatic. I saw a picture in a book once that showed them snorkeling around in lakes and swamps."

"Nobody believes that anymore," Robin countered. "They don't show any aquatic adaptations. Their teeth were worn down from eating hard land vegetation, not soggy watery stuff. They left tracks and footprints. That doesn't happen under water."

"Did he find all this out by himself?" Keene asked, turning back to Vicki.

"I helped him with some of it," she told him—which Keene had guessed. "But it does seem to be a real mystery—a big one. You just don't hear about it." She made a vague gesture. "On top of the things Robin's mentioned, you've also got the problem with the circulatory system of the sauropods—those were the ones that were all neck and tail. How did they get the blood up to their brains? A giraffe's head might be twenty feet up, and it needs pressure that would rupture the vascular system of any other animal. Giraffes do it by having thick arterial walls and a tight skin that works like a pressure suit. But a sauropod's brain was at fifty or sixty feet. The pressure would have needed to be three or four times that of a giraffe. The people who've studied it just can't see it as credible."

"Hmm. Maybe they didn't hold their necks upright, then," Keene tried. "What if they walked around with them horizontal? . . . No." He shook his head, not even believing it himself. What would have been the point of having them? And in any case, even without knowing the exact numbers, his instinct told him that the stress generated at the base would be more than any biological tissue could take.

Robin concluded, "And then you've got things like the pterosaurs that somehow flew with body weights of three hundred fifty pounds, and predatory birds of up to two hundred. The most you get today is about twenty-five, with the Siberian Berkut hunting eagle. Breeders have been trying to improve on that for centuries, but that's as far as you can go and still get a viable flier."

Keene looked at Vicki. "Any bigger, and you end up with a klutz," she said. "The big gliding birds like albatrosses aren't good flyers. They often need repeat attempts to take off, and they can be real clowns on landing."

Robin nodded. "That's why they're called gooney birds."

Vicki sat back and finished her coffee while Keene thought about what she and Robin had said. There didn't seem any further line to pursue. "And the people in the business know these things?" he said finally. Of course they did. It was more for something to say.

"Well, we sure didn't make them up," Vicki replied. "I guess they put it out of their minds and get on with cleaning up the bones and fitting them together or whatever. So what's new?"

It was Athena all over again—the reason Keene had quit physics to return to engineering. Most workers just got on with the day-to-day job that brought in the grants and kept the paychecks coming, without worrying too much about what it all meant. It was safer to write papers and textbooks about things that everyone agreed they knew than go dragging up awkward questions whose answers might contradict what people in other departments were saying *they* knew. Before long the whole edifice would be threatened, and the result would be trouble from all directions.

"There must have been something vastly different about the whole reality that existed then," Vicki said distantly. "I don't mean just with the dinosaurs, but about everything: the plants, the insects, the marine life. Walk around the museums and look at the reconstructions. It was all on a different scale of engineering. You can't relate it to the world we know today. Something universal has altered since then. And the only thing that makes sense is gravity. Earth's gravity must have been a lot less back in those times than it is now."

Keene looked at her, coming back from his own line of thought. His brow creased. "How?"

"I don't know. But if it wasn't, dinosaurs couldn't have existed. Yet they did. So what other explanation is there?"

Robin massaged the hair at the front of his head in the way he did when he had some way-out suggestion to offer. "I can think of one. Maybe it wasn't Earth's gravity that was different," he said.

"Huh?" Keene frowned. "What else's, then? I mean, where else are we talking about?"

"You know how what wiped the dinosaurs out was supposed to be an asteroid or something. . . ."

"Uh-huh."

"Well, suppose they weren't on Earth at all before

it hit, the way everyone assumes. Suppose they came here with it."

"Came with what? You mean with the asteroid?"

"Yes—or whatever it was." Robin made an appealing gesture. "If Earth's gravity was too big for them to have existed, then they must have existed on something else. That's logic, right? Well, suppose the something else was whatever Earth got hit by. It doesn't have to be an asteroid like we think of them—you know, just a chunk of rock. It could have been, maybe, like something that had an atmosphere they could live in."

"Wouldn't it need to have been pretty huge, though, to have an atmosphere?" Keene queried.

"Not necessarily, if it was cold with dense gases. Titan has an atmosphere. . . . And in any case, the whole thing didn't have to hit the Earth. Maybe it got close enough to break up, and only part of it did."

Keene's first impulse was to scoff, but he checked himself. Wasn't that just the kind of automatic reaction that he was having so much trouble with from the regular scientific establishment? He could see reasons for not buying the suggestion, but simply the fact that it conflicted with prior beliefs wasn't good enough to be one of them. Robin was trying. Keene paused long enough not to be dismissive.

"What about the impact?" he asked. "These things explode when they enter the atmosphere, like that big one over Siberia, oh . . . whenever it was. Or imagine what must have happened when that hole in Arizona was dug. You're talking about bones being preserved intact enough to be put together again. Eggs. . . . And we've even got footprints. Would they really be likely to survive something like that?"

"That was what I wondered when Robin put it to me," Vicki commented.

"Maybe, if they were encased inside chunks of rock that were large enough—say that came down across a whole area like a blanket," Robin persisted. "The air might act as a cushion."

"So you're saying they might not actually have *lived* here at all," Keene said, finally getting the point.

"Exactly. They lived on . . . whatever." Robin looked from him back to Vicki as if to say, *well, you asked for suggestions*.

Keene sat back and snorted wonderingly. Ingenious, he had to grant. But being ingenious didn't automatically mean being right. There was still that other small factor known as "evidence" to be considered.

"I don't know, but I'll tell you what I'll do," he said. "I'll put it to a couple of the planetary scientists that I know. We'll see what they say." Robin deserved that much.

"Really?" Robin looked pleased. "Hey, that would be great!"

"Sure. Why not?"

After breakfast they watched a replay of the Kronian landing and motorcade into Washington from the day before. Seeing the Kronians alongside native Terrans for the first time brought home something that Keene had never really registered before: they were *tall*. Sariena was a natural for the cameras to single out for close-ups, and she came over well when taking her turn to respond to the welcoming address by the President. Keene noted that the Kronians remained seated, and all of them wore sunglasses outside.

Keene and Robin spent an hour experimenting with a new electronic paint board that Robin had just added to his computer. Playing father figure was good for Keene's self-image in enabling him to claim the capacity to be socially responsible if he chose. All in all, it was a relaxed, easygoing morning—the perfect way to recharge after the past week and prepare for the equally demanding one ahead. And then, just as

Keene was getting ready to leave to go back over to the city for the press conference, Leo Cavan called from Washington, rerouted from Keene's private number, with some news he said he'd rather not go into just now, but which had to do with the Kronians. Was Keene still planning on coming up to D.C. first thing the coming week? Keene confirmed that he was—probably flying up tomorrow night. Fine, Cavan said. Could he make it earlier in the day so that they could meet for dinner? Sure, Keene agreed. It sounded important. Cavan said yes, he thought it was. And Cavan wasn't the kind of person who did things without good reason.

7

The press conference was held in the boardroom of Amspace's headquarters building in downtown Corpus Christi. Ricardo Juarez and Joe Elms, the NIFTV's other two crew members, were present with Keene. Wally Lomack joined them at the table facing the cameras as the official corporate spokesperson. Les Urkin, who headed public relations, and Harry Halloran, the technical VP, were present also in off-screen capacities. The assembly they faced was a fairly even mix of print and electronic news journalists, some hostile, some supportive, most simply following to see where the story led. With the tensions of the previous day's test now over and preliminary evaluations of its results exceeding expectations, the Amspace team was in high spirits.

As had been expected, the initial questions involved the political furore being kicked up over the unannounced testing of a nuclear propulsion system in space by a U.S.-based company. Liberal and environmental groups were committed to protest on principle, and much of media opinion was sympathetic. Joe

Elms and Ricardo ducked that issue on the grounds that their line was flight operations, happy to leave Keene the brunt of responding—which made sense, since it was a case he was used to presenting. For a while, he reiterated the line he had begun with John Feld the day before: the risks that had been propagandized for decades were exaggerated and trivial compared to others that the world accepted routinely; energy *density*, not just the amount, was what mattered if you wanted to do better things more efficiently; the densities involved with state-transitions of the atomic nucleus were of the scale necessary to get out into space in a meaningful way, whereas those associated with the so-called "alternatives" were not. None of this was particularly new. But Keene's main hope while they had the world's attention was to emphasize again that a commitment to such propulsion methods would be essential for the expansion across the Solar System that the Kronians were calling for, which was crucial to the security of the human race. The opportunity came when one of the network reporters asked for a response to allegations that Amspace was using the Kronian cause to promote its own commercial interests. Not being on the company's staff, Keene couldn't comment. Wally Lomack took it with a show of shortness.

"Obviously, it would be hypocritical to deny that we'd hope to benefit. But I'm getting tired of these people who seem to think that we're incapable of looking beyond the bottom line of the current quarter's balance sheet. If a serious space development program becomes our official policy, every contractor will be looking for a share of the action, and sure, we'd expect to take our place in line with everyone else who has something to offer. But the issue that should concern all of us is the safety and future of humanity. Look at the western sky tonight just after sundown if you've forgotten what I'm talking about.

It's happened before, and now we've just come too close for comfort to seeing it happen again. Saying that you and I won't be around next time isn't an answer."

"The *Kronians* say it happened before," somebody at the back of the room called out. "But they're the ones on a limb out there who need Earth to bail them out. Is it just a coincidence that the line of business you're in happens to be what they're telling us we have to do?"

Ricardo shook his head violently, looking along the table for support. "They're not out on any limb. Hell, man, they've got drive systems that could run rings around what *we* put up."

"But Kronia is economically nonviable," somebody else threw out. "Admit it, their system's shot. They have to get Earth's support somehow or go under."

"That's just a line that the politicians take," Joe Elms retorted, sitting next to Keene on his other side from Lomack. "They don't want to think about what it might do to their budgets."

"Me neither. Would *you* want to pay the taxes?"

"It doesn't have to be a tax-funded thing," Joe answered. "Taken as a whole, this planet has enormous resources. We spend more on cosmetics, alcohol, entertainment, and pet food than—"

"Corporate interests again," another voice chimed in. "That's the whole point that some people are questioning."

Keene didn't want this to degenerate into an airing of suspicions they had all heard before. There were vaster issues to be focusing on. "Look," he said, raising both his hands. "Can we just put all this aside in our minds for a minute? These things are trivial compared to what we should be talking about. What we should be talking about concerns all of us. . . ." He gave the mood a second or two to shift. "It isn't just the Kronians who are saying that Earth has undergone major cataclysms in its past from encounters with other astronomical objects. Scars and upheavals written all over the surface of this planet and its moon say it. Abundant records of violent mass extinctions say it. Evidence of sudden climatic changes and polar shifts say it. And records preserved from cultures all over the world say that it has happened within recorded human history. Traditionally, they've been dismissed as myths and legends, but they show too much corroboration to be coincidental. The facts have been there for centuries, but for the most part we've remained collectively blind to what they've been telling us. Athena is telling us that we can't risk that kind of blindness any longer."

"Exactly," Lomack pronounced, nodding vigorously.

A dark-haired man who was sitting near the front raised a hand, then pitched in. "Phil Onslow, *Houston Chronicle*. Do we take it, then, that you endorse this idea that the Kronians have been pushing about Venus being a new planet?"

For a moment, Keene was surprised. He had assumed it was obvious. "Well . . . sure. It's intimately connected with what we're trying to say, and what yesterday's demonstration was all about. Three and a half thousand years ago, the human race came close to being wiped out."

"And if we buy that, you're asking us to spend trillions of dollars," Onslow persisted. "But isn't it true that scientists have been refuting that claim for years?"

"Yeah, right," Ricardo scoffed. "The same scientists who said that comets couldn't be ejected by Jupiter, let alone a planet-size body. Then look what happened ten months ago. And they're *still* saying it!"

"Not quite. They're saying there's no proof that it happened before," someone pointed out.

"Then they're still in as much a state of denial as they have been for years. That's all you can say," Keene answered.

What the Kronians had been trying to get accepted since before Athena's appearance was that around the middle of the second millennium B.C., Earth experienced a close encounter with a giant comet. Its axis was shifted and its orbit changed, causing seas to empty and flow over continents, the crust to buckle into mountains, and opening rifts that spilled lavas as much as a mile deep across vast areas of the surface. Climates changed abruptly, bringing ice down upon grasslands and turning forests into desert; civilizations collapsed; animals perished in millions; entire species were exterminated. These, the Kronians maintained, were the events glimpsed by the Hebrew scriptures in their descriptions of the "plagues" inflicted on Egypt, along with the events recorded subsequently.

The "blood" that turned the lands and the rivers red, followed by rains of ash and burning rock and fire, were consistent with the proposition of Earth moving into the comet's tail to be assailed by iron-bearing dust, then torrents of gravel and meteorites, and finally infusions of hydrocarbon gases that would ignite in an oxygen-laden atmosphere. Then came the enveloping darkness as the smoke and dust from a burning world blanketed out the sun. The same succession of events was described not only in writings from across the entire Middle East, but in legends handed down by the peoples of Iceland, Greenland, and India; from the islands of Polynesia to the steppes of Siberia; and places as far apart as Japan and Mexico, China and Peru. The accounts of shrieking hurricanes scouring the Earth and tides piling into mountains read the same in the Persian *Avesta*, the Indian *Vedas*, and the Mayan *Troano* as in *Exodus*, and were similarly narrated by the Maori, the Indonesian, the Laplander, and the Choctaw. And finally, the titanic electrical discharges between the comet's head and parts of its deformed, writhing tail became clashes of celestial deities depicted virtually identically whether as the

Biblical Lord battling Rahab, Zeus and Typhon of the Greeks, Isis and Seth of the Egyptians, the Babylonian Marduk and Tiamat, or the Hindu Shiva or Vishnu putting down the serpent.

"I don't think you're being fair," Onslow objected. "A lot of scientists now agree that something extraordinary occurred around that time. A close flyby by a large comet is proposed in a number of models. But Venus is much bigger than any comet."

"Any comet seen in recent times, anyway," Joe said.

"It's a lot like Athena could look three and a half thousand years from now if it lost its tail," Lomack suggested.

The mood of the room pivoted on an edge. The three just back from space were heroes for the day, and the journalists' professional instincts were not to put them down. Onslow was still frowning but seemed disinclined to press his negative sentiments further. On the other hand, they had been heavily influenced by the official line heard over the years. Keene sensed a chance to bring them closer and perhaps win one or two of them around if the case could be put persuasively. He studied his clasped hands for a moment and looked up.

"You're all media people. How do you refer to that thing out there in the sky that's not the same as anything we've seen before? One of the most frequent descriptions I've seen over the past few months is 'giant comet.' Well, people in ancient times were no different, except they thought of celestial objects as gods. In the languages of race after race and culture after culture, the names of the gods they associated with these events turn out to be not only interchangeable with or identical to their word for 'comet,' but also the name that they applied to Venus." Keene looked around. The room was noticeably stiller, eyes fixed on him.

"I hadn't realized that," a new voice said. "This is

interesting." Onslow busied himself noting something in his pad and didn't comment.

Keene answered, "It is, isn't it. And I'll tell you something more that's interesting. Old astronomic tables from places as far apart as Egypt, Sumeria, India, China, Mexico—and the accuracy of some of those tables wasn't equaled until the nineteenth century—all show *four* visible planets, not five. And in each case, the missing planet is Venus." He waited a few seconds for that to sink in. Here and there, heads were turning to glance at each other. He concluded, "They all added Venus at about the same time. They all showed it appearing as a comet. And they all described it losing its tail to evolve into a planet. So come on, guys. How much more do you want?"

Afterward, they all agreed that it had gone well. In the chat session that followed over refreshments, most of the questions conveyed genuine curiosity and interest to learn more. Keene felt more than satisfied with the way things had gone, and Harry Halloran was looking pleased. As the session was breaking up, Les Urkin returned from taking a call outside and drew Keene to one side.

"You're still going up to D.C. tomorrow night, Lan, is that right?"

"I switched to an earlier flight," Keene replied. "I'm meeting someone for dinner."

"Good. The Kronians are having an informal reception at their suite in the Engleton on Monday evening. Gallian heard you'd be in town, and he wants you to know you're invited. Want me to confirm? Or I can give you their number."

"Sure, I'll be there," Keene said. "Let me call them, Les. I get a kick out of talking to them without any turnaround delay now. So now we get to meet them finally, eh?"

Things were looking better and better.

8

The next day, Sunday, Keene arrived at Washington's Reagan National Airport around mid-afternoon, and caught a cab to a Sheraton hotel that he often used when in the area, overlooking the Potomac outside the city on the far side of Georgetown. After checking in, he called Cavan to confirm that everything was on schedule. That gave him a couple of hours to shower, change, and catch up on some of his back-logged work via the room terminal before Cavan was due to arrive.

Leo Cavan worked as an "investigator" in what was effectively an internal affairs department of a bureaucratic monstrosity called the Scientific and Industrial Coordination Agency, or SICA, charged with planning and overseeing the implementation of a national scientific research policy. Keene had gotten to know him when Keene was at General Atomic. Cavan had started out in the Air Force hoping for a life of travel and excitement, and ended up instead preparing quality control reports and cost analyses in an accounting office. When he put in for a transfer to Space

Command to get a chance to go into orbit before he was too old, he was drafted to Washington to review regulations and procedures instead. He had never fit the role well in Keene's experience, being too technically knowledgeable to project the ineptness normally expected from officialdom, and too ready to overlook transgressions of no consequence when his judgment so directed. The result was that the two of them had gotten along splendidly and remained friends after Keene's exasperation with the politics of government-directed science returned him to the world of engineering to develop nuclear drives for Amspace.

Cavan had taken to him, Keene suspected, somewhat in the manner of a father figure seeking to live through a surrogate son the life he would have wished himself. He led a strange kind of double existence. Outwardly a diligent creature of the system, he apparently found a pernicious satisfaction in subverting that same system by leaking inside knowledge that might help its opponents and compensate its victims. It seemed to be his private way of getting even with the forces that throughout his own life had deceived and then entrapped him. He also had one of the oddest senses of humor that Keene had ever encountered.

The restaurant was at the rear of the hotel, looking out over lawns sloping down to the tree-shaded riverbank. Keene had found a window table and was sipping a Bushmills while watching a flotilla of ducks on inshore maneuvers, when Cavan appeared through the entrance from the lobby. He spotted Keene and came over. Keene stood to shake hands, and they sat down. A waiter came to the table to inquire if Cavan would like a drink, and Cavan settled for a glass of the house Chablis. "I assume you wouldn't risk your reputation by fobbing us off with a bad one," he told the waiter. "Or have the accountants taken over writing the wine lists these days, like everything else?"

Cavan couldn't have been far away from retirement. Everything about him suggested having been fashioned for economy, as if over the years the idealizations of his profession had infused themselves and ultimately found physical expression in his being in the way that was supposed to be true of owners and dogs. He had thinning hair and a sparse frame, on which his plain, gray suit hung loosely, a thin nose and sharp chin formed from budgeted materials, and a bony, birdlike face that achieved its covering with a minimal outlay of skin. Even his tie was knotted with a tightness and precision that seemed to abhor extravagance of any kind. But the pale steely eyes gave the game away, alive and alert, all the time scanning for new mischief to wreak upon the world. Of his private life Keene knew practically nothing. He lived somewhere in the city with a Polish girlfriend called Alicia whom he described as crazy without ever having said why, although sounding as if they had been together for years.

Cavan had followed Friday's event, of course, and added his own congratulations. He pressed for details that hadn't appeared in the news coverage, enjoying immensely Keene's descriptions of the spaceplane's robotlike commander and the splutterings of the Air Force brass, and expressing approval that the media reactions were not all hostile. The wine arrived and was pronounced acceptable. For the dinner order, Keene had worked up enough appetite after traveling to try the prime rib and a half carafe of Sauvignon to go with it. Cavan settled for Dover sole. "And I see they've been keeping you busy since," Cavan resumed when the waiter had left. "I saw that clip that Feld did with you while you were still up on the satellite, and then the press coverage of all of you together yesterday. You came over well there, Landen. That should give a lot of people something to think about."

"I got the feeling that for once we were getting through," Keene said. "You can say the same thing to reporters for months, spell out all the facts, and nothing will prise them away from the official line they've been given. But this time we got them listening." Cavan nodded, but without seeming as gratified as Keene would have expected. Keene could only conclude that what Cavan had wanted to talk about offset the good news.

"And are you still finding time in all this for the ladyfriend?" Cavan inquired, evidently choosing not to go into it just at that moment. His eyes were twinkling.

"You mean Vicki?"

"Of course."

Keene sighed. "Leo, you know very well we're just business partners. And sure, over the years we've become good friends as well. Why do you keep trying to make something more out of it?"

"Well, it's none of my business, I suppose, but a fellow at your stage of life could do worse than consider stabilizing things a little." Cavan sipped his wine. "She has the young son, and does ad work, yes?" Probably through habit, Cavan always sought confirmations and cross-references of information, Keene had noticed. In another life Keene could picture him as a tax auditor.

Keene nodded. "But I've got too much going on right now. In any case, I need my own space."

Cavan indicated the upward direction with a motion of his head. "You mean there isn't enough for you out there?" He studied Keene for a few seconds, swirling his glass. "Are you sure you're not keeping your options open until you see how the land lies with that other lady you've had hovering on the fringes of your life for a while?" Keene frowned at him, perplexed. "The one who'd be a natural for the lead in a Queen-of-Sheba movie," Cavan hinted.

Keene stared. "My God! Are you talking about Sariena?"

"I am, of course. Why act surprised?"

"What on earth makes you think that?"

"Excitement. Something different. The allure of the alien and unknown." Cavan's talonlike hands broke apart a bread roll and commenced buttering one of the pieces. "A perfectly understandable reaction, Landen— especially for somebody of your adventurous disposition. I mean, you've been in communication since before the *Osiris* left Saturn." He paused, glanced up as if to be sure Keene was listening, and then went on, making his voice casual. "I could see your point, after all. She really is stunning. Everyone I talked to thought so when we were with the Kronians last night."

"What?" It hit Keene only then that this was Cavan's strange way of leading around to the subject he had wanted to discuss. And it had worked. Keene couldn't deny that his first reaction was a twinge of resentment. "You've met her already?"

The meals arrived then, and Keene was able to let his surprise abate while plates and dishes were positioned, covers removed, and the glasses refilled. Having had his fun, Cavan became more serious. "I was at another dinner on Friday: the official White House reception for the Kronians—to be introduced to my 'marks,' for want of a better word." He eyed Keene suggestively for a moment, as if inviting a response. Keene waited. Cavan explained, "The department has come up with a new angle on what an investigator does. Now, it appears, I'm supposed to cultivate the confidence of our guests of state, the purpose being to spy on them. It's getting to be a tacky world that we live in, isn't it, Landen?"

Unable to make anything of this so far, Keene merely motioned for him to continue.

"I'm one of several persons who have been assigned positions as official host representatives—tour guides, if you will—who will have constant contact with the Kronians. Our brief is to get close to them in order to get as much advance information as we can to help our own negotiators shoot them down." Keene's hand stopped with his fork halfway to his mouth. Cavan nodded somberly. "It's a nonstarter, Landen. A policy ruling has already been made that Earth isn't buying the Kronian line. Our side's only interest is to discredit the whole business and get it out of the public limelight as quickly as possible." For the moment, Keene was too stunned to do more than stare. He looked down at his plate and found that suddenly he didn't feel so hungry anymore. Cavan added after a few seconds, "Sorry if I've spoiled your dinner. The tab's on me, if that helps."

There was a silence. Finally, Keene said, "What's going on, Leo? Are they all blind or something?"

"It's not so much a case of being blind as of not wanting to see," Cavan replied over his soup. "You know the way things work in this business. The academic establishment sees the Kronians as invaders of its turf and a huge potential threat to traditional funding—which has been thinned down in recent years in any case. Government science sold out long ago to become an instrument for justifying government policy, and nobody on the Hill wants to talk about the expense. For the private sector the investment would be colossal, and the return on it just isn't there. That's why the space program was shifted to a lower gear in the first place."

Keene shook his head disbelievingly. "One day, none of that's going to matter. This is something we can't afford *not* to do. I mean, we're not talking about selling laundry detergent here, Leo. Maybe we have to learn something from the Kronians. The know-how and the ability is there, and it's something that *needs* to be done. So you forget all the shopkeeper economics, and you just *do* it."

"Logical enough, and eminently sensible," Cavan agreed. "But the powers who run things here can't think like that."

It didn't need to be spelled out further. Keene stared at his glass and sighed. "So what's the line going to be? The one we've been hearing for a while: The whole Kronian venture was ill-conceived from the start; imagining that a society could function viably at that kind of distance was ridiculous all along . . . ?"

Cavan was already nodding. "And now they're waking up to reality and finding themselves overextended," he completed. "This story about supercomets and the end of the world is a concoction dreamed up to exploit the Athena event and milk support from Earth's governments. That's our line. And naturally the establishment's scientific big guns will have their act coordinated to back it. We wouldn't want to let down the people who ladle out the honors and write the checks, after all, now, would we?" Cavan spooned the last of his soup into his mouth—thin and straight, sparing on the lips—and watched, seemingly until Keene was just recovering sufficiently to tackle his food again. Then he added, "One of the big guns they'll be wheeling up is a certain professor of astronomy and faculty head at Yale, recently nominated for the presidency of the International Astronomical Union. I wouldn't imagine he needs any introduction."

"You don't mean Voler?"

"I do, of course."

Keene's fork dropped slowly back to his plate. For Herbert Voler was the paragon of perfection that his own former wife, Fey, had fled to and later married when Keene confounded her social ambitions by abandoning the prospect of scholastic accolades to return to the grubby world of engineering.

"I'm not quite sure how that might be relevant at this stage," Cavan confessed. "But conceivably the situation could take a turn whereby the social connection offers possibilities unavailable in the purely formal context. In any case, it was an option that would apply to nobody else, so my first thought was to approach you."

Keene made an inviting motion with his free hand. "Approach me for what, Leo? You still haven't told me what this is all about."

"Let me first give you an idea of how they intend playing it," Cavan suggested. "Then it will be clearer. The softening-up program to condition the public has already been going on for a while. Did you see your friend Voler on TV yesterday?"

"No, I have been kind of busy, as you pointed out. What was this?"

"He gave a talk at Columbia, ridiculing the claims about all those ancient records. . . . But it was planned months ago to coincide with the Kronians' arrival." Cavan produced a compad from his jacket pocket. "Let's watch him." He activated the unit, fiddled with commands to retrieve a stored playback from the net, then turned it the right way around for Keene to see and passed it across. Keene's features remained neutral as he gazed at the familiar figure.

Voler was fortyish, maybe—on the young side for the titles and credentials that he was able to brandish. He had a full head of black hair styled collar-length like a media celebrity, and a tanned complexion which with his pugnacious jaw emphasized a strong set of white teeth that his mobile features put to good effect, constantly splitting into broad smiles and grimaces. To Keene, he had always come across as a little too smooth and slick for a figurehead of academic excellence—but then, perhaps such qualities helped the political image equally necessary to attaining the rarified heights. Keene could have seen him as a pushy prosecution counsel, maybe, or a hustler on Wall Street. Behind him on the screen was a chart carrying names of planets and ancient deities, presumably referred to earlier. Keene turned the volume up just enough to avoid being an annoyance to nearby tables.

"... four ways in which the same legend could come to be found among widely separated cultures. One, Common Observation: all of the cultures witnessed a common event and interpreted it in a similar way. Two, Diffusion: the legend originated in one place but traveled to others with the wanderings of humankind. Three, Commonality of Psychology: Humans everywhere are so alike that their brains create similar legends reflecting common hopes and fears. And Four, Coincidence." Voler paused, grasping the podium, and surveyed his audience. "I think everyone would agree with me that we can reasonably discard the last. And we simply don't know enough to propose number three, Common Psychology, with any confidence—although in my view it seems unlikely." Due court having been paid to reasonableness and modesty, the focus narrowed to the brass tacks. Voler's confident smile broadened, stopping just short of open derisiveness. "The Kronians, of course, are saying that we are therefore forced to accept the Common Observation hypothesis, as if it were the only alternative. But in this they are surely dismissing far too casually—one hopes in their impetuousness—the second possibility, namely that as various peoples dispersed across the globe, they took their myths and legends with them, just as they did their languages, their religions, and their technical skills. . . ."

"You can see what the game plan is," Cavan broke in from across the table. "The Kronians will be projected into roles of sincere but misguided children. After a few days of recuperation from the voyage, they'll be taken on a whistle-stop tour of some selected spots around Earth. None of them can remember much of Earth, and some were never here at all. So we'll see pictures of them gaping at the Grand Canyon and the Amazon, or gawking like tourists in London and Paris, with chaperones like myself pointing out this and explaining that. Earth will have been magnanimous; Earth will have been accommodating. But you see what it will do for their image. They arrive here naive, and we have to acquaint them with reality. The same image will carry over to what the world will perceive as the science, and their case won't have a prayer."

By now, Voler was expounding on details of various human migrations. Keene had heard enough and snapped the unit off. "And what about the evidence written all over the surface of this planet?" he demanded. "None of that counts?" He meant the anomalies in the geological, fossil, and climatic records—all independent of anything that any humans of long ago had to say. There were such things as marks of sudden sea level changes, in some cases measuring hundreds of feet, found the world over; agricultural terraces close to sea level when they were cultivated, now disappearing under the snow line eighteen thousand feet up in the Andes; the remains of millions of animals and trees, torn to pieces and broken, found piled in caves and rock fissures from Europe to China and across the Arctic, in some places forming practically the entirety of islands off northern Siberia; huge herds of mammoths, buffalo, horse, camel, hippopotamus, and other beasts wiped out abruptly a thousand miles or more from any vegetation growing today that could support them. And all in the middle of that same mysterious millennium that the writings of old had chronicled. Was all that to be ignored?

"They'll stay away from all that if they can," Cavan said. "The Kronians make some good points, and many scientists outside the political-academic orthodoxy are siding with them. Nobody argues much anymore that terrestrial catastrophes have happened. Where they'll try and draw the line is with *planetary* catastrophes—that Venus could have been an earlier Athena. If that's allowed, then the whole foundation of the economic power structure as we know it would have to change, which in effect is what the Kronians are saying. But of course that would be unacceptable. So the line will be to discredit the Kronian arguments by any means until Athena has disappeared out of the Solar System and been forgotten—apart from as an anomaly that will generate Ph.D. theses for years—and then we'll all be able to get back to the safe, comfortable lives that we know."

Finally, Cavan took back the compad. He went on, "The reason I wanted to talk to you before you meet them tomorrow, Landen, is that the Kronians need to be made aware of this. But I can hardly bring it up in my position. You, on the other hand, are not saddled with having to wear an official hat. And being in touch with the Kronians already . . ." He left the obvious unsaid.

"Sure, I'll handle it," Keene agreed. There really wasn't anything to have to think about. He picked up his knife but sat toying with it.

"I was sure you would," Cavan said. He paused and refilled Keene's glass. "Oh, do stop staring and try some dinner, Landen. You've come all the way from Texas for it, and it looks so delicious."

9

For a desk and a base to work from in the Washington area, Keene rented space at an agency called Information and Office Services. Shirley, who ran the facility and acted for him when he was away, had arranged several Monday appointments from the calls that had begun coming in on Friday. The first was not until 10:00, and Keene spent the first part of the morning returning other calls that Shirley had listed. One was to a David Salio, who described himself as a planetary scientist at the Aerospace Sciences Institute in Houston, which Keene had visited on occasion. The Kronians had been getting attention in the Web news groups and independent media of many like Salio who were not among the circle of academic and government scientists fearful of money being diverted into the space corporations. Salio had favored the young-planet theory of Venus for some time and possesed a sizable collection of facts and data supporting it from modern-day space and scientific researches, independent of what ancient writings said. Athena was a clear warning that action had to be taken along the lines that the Kronians were calling for, and he wanted to know what he could do to help. Keene was immediately interested to hear more and suggested stopping by on his way back to Corpus Christi, which would be via Houston in any case. He would let Salio know when he had a firm return date.

Next was somebody called Barney from one of the Washington-based news services, who had tracked Keene down through his connection with Amspace. "What, you're in Washington now!" he exclaimed when Keene called. "Hey, never mind taping an interview over the phone. We'll send a couple of guys over to the hotel. It works for a better atmosphere. How would four o'clock suit? It'll still be going out by this evening. Don't worry, we do it all the time. No problem."

Keene checked with his schedule and agreed. A couple of other concerns were happy to tape from the hotel, and a science magazine with a local office arranged to send a feature writer over that evening, after the TV taping. Keene spent some time confirming and fixing more appointments for the next two days that he would be in town, then left for his first meeting that day, which was with one of the senators for Texas in an office in the Senate Building.

In a TV interview over the weekend, the senator had told the reporter of the need to bring companies like Amspace to heel and enforce a greater compliance with "social responsibility." He explained to Keene that he had to talk that way in order to preserve an acceptable public image. "But I want the people at Amspace to know that they can count on me to be realistic too." Which could be taken as a warning or a wink and a nod, but either way translated into: "Keep the contributions coming and pray." Keene tried to broach issues that went beyond appeasing activist groups while at the same time keeping the corporations sweet, but made little impression. The senator lived in his own world.

Lunch was with a documentary producer called Charles McLaren, whom Keene had known amiably for about two years. McLaren wondered if Friday's event might resurrect the general nuclear-antinuclear controversy for a while and was thinking of putting together a fast tie-in for the public-affairs channels and newsnets. Would Keene be willing to act as a consultant again on short-call if they went ahead? Sure, Keene agreed. McLaren put accuracy before sensationalism and was meticulous in trying to get his facts right; Keene knew he could be sure of getting fair representation. But it was with weary assent. The discussion was pitched at helping a good technician do a job relating to a topic that was expected to be transient. There was no suggestion of a documentary to tell the world that it had come close to seeing the end of its civilization.

By early afternoon, he was in the cocktail lounge of a hotel off Pennsylvania Avenue to meet one of the technical aides to President Hayer. He wanted Keene to convey unofficially back to the management of Amspace, and through them to other allied interests, that as a sop to domestic outcries and world opinion it might be necessary to pass a bill banning the launching of nuclear devices from U.S. territory by private corporations. But the message was to keep up the development effort because provision could be engineered for a repeal in circumstances deemed vital to national security—but not until after the presidential election next year. In fact, the defense agencies were stressing the Chinese threat and could probably be induced to channel in some discreet funding to compensate for the shorter-term inconveniences. The aide paused to assess Keene's reaction, then asked, lowering his voice to impart a note of confidentiality, "Out of curiosity, what would be the chances of matching the kind of propulsion the Kronians have, say within five years—given a suitable financial incentive? The Air Force already has an eye on extending its activities to trans-lunar distances. I can tell you that they for one are particularly interested."

"Give me the top ten names in contained plasma dynamics, superconducting cryogenics, spontaneous vortex computational theory, and nuclear transition phases, get rid of all the political obstructionism, and you can have it in three," was Keene's answer.

The aide looked intrigued. "Really? And you know who these people are?"

"Sure I do. It's my field."

"Just suppose, for argument's sake, that we decided to try and get them to come over to work for us here, in the States. What do you think it would take? Is it something you might be able to help us organize?" The aide paused as if pondering a point of some delicacy. "I'm sure we could see fit to being . . . extremely generous."

"I'm not sure it's something that we have options on anymore," Keene replied. "They all moved to Saturn."

Keene grabbed a half hour to stop by at the agency and check on things with Shirley, then returned to the Sheraton to freshen up and change before the Kronian reception at seven. By that time he had consolidated his thoughts sufficiently to call Marvin Curtiss, Amspace's president and CEO, to update him on the situation that Cavan had described the evening before, and Keene's further impressions after his day in Washington. It was all pretty much in line with what Curtiss had been finding out independently.

"It doesn't look as if we're going to be able to count on much support from the main contractors," he told Keene from the hotel room's terminal screen.

"They're taking the line that it isn't the business of corporations to decide what's scientifically true or not. That's what we've got universities and national laboratories for." He didn't have to add that it also meant they could look forward to a continuation of low-risk contracts that referees from those same universities and laboratories would feel comfortable with and approve, and which wouldn't frighten investors.

"I don't know, Marvin," Keene sighed, tired after a long day. "How do you deal with it?"

"Just keep saying what we've always said: that we believe the claims the Kronians are making deserve serious consideration, and everyone should forget their vested interests and try to be open-minded to what appear to be the facts." That was what Keene had expected. If Curtiss weren't a fighter, he would hardly have been running an operation like Amspace to begin with. Curtiss went on, "One thing we might try is getting Les working on organizing more voice and visibility for the scientists out there who have been taking a more independent stand—like this character Salio that you talked to. We need people like him."

"I've arranged to meet him on my way back," Keene said.

"Good. Find out what his story is and who else he talks to. Maybe we don't have to let the establishment have a monopoly on the media."

"What about the political side?" Keene asked. "How much do you trust this talk about a defense loophole and Air Force money coming through the back door if that bill goes through?" That news hadn't come as a total surprise to Curtiss, who had apparently heard something similar from another source.

"If it happens, then fine, but I've always believed in insurance," Curtiss answered. "I've been talking to the people here about bringing forward the schedule for getting Montemorelos operational." He meant the backup launch and landing facility being constructed

in the highlands not far south of the border—outside
U.S. jurisdiction. "Not marginally, but making it our
top priority."

"That makes sense," Keene agreed. "But it might
only tide us over for a while. The Mexicans are still
vulnerable to pressure from our side."

Curtiss nodded. "I know. Beyond that, we're
reviewing the options we've negotiated on possible
sites farther from home."

"I think there's some for lease at the original
Tapapeque complex in Guatemala," Keene said.

"There is?"

"So I heard around a month or two ago."

"We'll look into it." There was a blur in the foreground on the screen as Curtiss checked his watch.
"I'm due for another appointment, Lan. It should be
interesting meeting the Kronians tonight. Call me
tomorrow and let me know how it went."

"I will," Keene said. "Take care, Marvin."

Keene still had some time before the TV reporters were due. Out of curiosity, he scanned the news
searcher for items relating to the Kronians and
selected one of the current leaders, which turned out
to be an NBC panel hookup to debate whether
ancient sources constituted a valid basis for formu-
lating scientific beliefs.

"Absolutely not!" was the opinion of a speaker, cap-
tioned as Dr. William Ledden, an astronomer at the
University of California. "Repeatable observations and
measurements determine what is properly termed science. What writers of old manuscripts say happened,
or think happened, or think ought to have happened
simply has no place . . ." He waved a hand agitatedly, as if too exasperated to be capable of further
coherent thought.

A gray-haired woman, president of an archaeologi-
cal society in Vancouver, agreed. "It has taken centuries to establish reliable methods and standards for

disentangling fact from fancy. I agree with Dr. Ledden. This kind of thing will probably sell some Sunday supplements, and we're going to be hearing a lot about it in the news, but it has no place in science."

"So you're saying we should be good hosts and neighbors, but not get carried away by this," the moderator checked sagely.

"Exactly."

That line seemed to be the consensus of the others. The converse view—rather timidly put, Keene thought—came from a historian and author somewhere in England. "I hesitate to cast the dissenting vote here, but is it unthinkable that peoples of ancient times might have described events that they actually witnessed, and maybe have something important to tell us?"

"It's scandalous that we should even be discussing this!" Ledden fumed. "Why are people who call themselves scientists concerning themselves with Biblical quotations? Are we going to be talking about walking on water and dead bodies coming back to life next? The Kronian phenomenon grew from a quasi-religious cult. This whole business is an attempt to give credibility to scriptures by means of concocted pseudoscience. Very possibly there's fundamentalist money behind it. They've got to be supporting themselves out there somehow."

Keene grew more perplexed as he listened. The Kronians had never made any appeal to scriptural beliefs. They used Biblical references purely as accounts of historical events, and then only where corroborated by other sources. The Englishman tried to make that point but was ineffective.

Barney's TV crew showed up on time, but the interview, conducted on the grassy riverbank at the back of the hotel, was aimed too much at trying to provoke Keene into admissions of the dangers of nuclear devices in space. The journalist who arrived afterward had a more balanced approach, but they got deeper into technicalities than Keene had anticipated and ran out of time, arranging to continue over breakfast the next morning. Finally, Keene boarded the cab that had arrived to take him to the Engleton.

"So how was your day?" the cabbie asked over his shoulder as they pulled out from under the lobby canopy.

"Never a dull moment," Keene told him with feeling. "How about you?"

"Aw, not so bad. You know how it is. Just a couple of years more of this to bring a bit more money in, and then it's retirement. Just me and the wife now. We figure we'll move to Colorado. Got some grandkids there. Mountains, scenery. Nice place to take it easy."

"Sounds great," Keene said from the back seat. Sometimes he had to remind himself that most people—probably the vast majority on the planet—didn't think too much about Athena, or care—one way or the other.

10

The Kronian mission, along with the security and administrative staff attending them, were on the top two floors of the Engleton, which had restricted access from the general part of the hotel and was one of the regular accommodations for official visitors to the city. In all, there were twelve delegates and eight crew members, the numbers having been kept low to leave capacity for the *Osiris* to carry emigrants back on the return trip. Some of the crew, however, had been left to maintain a skeleton presence on the ship and would get their chance to come down to the surface later.

On arriving, Keene went straight up to the eighth floor as he had been directed and checked with the security people in room 809. A personable young man in a dark suit verified that he was expected and escorted him to one of the larger suites on the floor above, where two more security men in suits admitted them through the doors. From the hubbub of voices, the party was evidently already in progress. Keene recognized the white-haired figure of Gallian, the leader of the Kronian delegation, seated a short distance inside, talking to an Oriental couple who looked as if they had also just arrived—apparently he was greeting everyone personally. Gallian spotted Keene and waved him over, introducing the couple as a Japanese space-technology administrator and his wife. He apologized for the unusual way of receiving guests. "It's the gravity, of course—and then two days of functions and presentations on top of it. Your people are working us hard already. But anyway, why am I making excuses? At my age one doesn't need any excuses." Keene grinned, told Gallian that he didn't know how many times this had been said already but " . . . welcome to Earth," and shook hands heartily. The Japanese couple exchanged pleasantries and were then ushered on to meet others in the room by another Kronian, who Gallian said was Thorel, from the *Osiris's* regular crew, and who must have stood at around seven feet.

Gallian turned back to regard Keene. He had a crusty, puckish-nosed face with eyes that were clear and mischievous. From their few long-delay message exchanges, Keene had formed an impression of bustling energy and a person who could never be content doing one thing at a time. Already, everything he saw was starting to confirm it. "Well, Lan, hello," Gallian said. "So here we are. You see, we made it. And so did you. Les Urkin obviously got the message through. I'm glad."

"I heard they're taking you off on a tour," Keene said.

"Yes, New York City to start with, then Niagara Falls . . ." Gallian waved a hand. "I'm not sure where after that."

"When will this start?"

"Well, it was supposed to be first thing tomorrow . . ."

"So soon? You're kidding."

" . . . but that may have to be postponed."

"Oh?"

"Allergic reactions," Gallian said.

"Yes, of course. I'd forgotten about that." It was a known risk for Kronian-born making a first-time visit to Earth. Keene shrugged sympathetically. "There's nothing anyone can do?"

"Not much, apparently. Immigrants like me don't have a problem. We prepared the first-timers with the recommended drugs, but several of them are affected all the same. Two are in bed, knocked off their feet. We'll know in the morning what the situation is."

There was a tap on the doors; one of the security men opened them, and two men and a woman were shown in. Gallian extended an arm. "Anyway, I must press on with my hostly duties. Go on in and meet the others. Sariena's around somewhere. We're informal tonight. There's a buffet in the suite. All of us agree, by the way, that whatever its other problems, Earth food is exquisite. And I'm finding that I'm particularly partial to wines. Vineyards are a luxury that we haven't graced Kronia with yet. Our synthetic efforts really don't compare. I'll definitely try to get that changed when we return." Gallian caught the attention of another Kronian, brown skinned and distinguishable by her tall build and casual, brightly colored trouser suit—distinctly not customary Washington dinner wear. "Polli, this is Landen Keene, an old friend of ours. Look after him and introduce him around, would you?" He looked back at Keene as the three arrivals approached. "I'll seek you out and pin you down with more serious questions to spoil the party with later, I promise."

The buffet was set up in the center of the suite, dispensed by hotel staff—a salad bar selection, cold cuts and cheeses, several hot dishes, dessert trolley, and a beverage bar. There were between one and two dozen people so far, Keene estimated, although the far end of the suite had an L-bend so there could have been more out of sight. Sariena was with a group on the far side by the windows, perched on an arm of a couch. And on the far side of the bar, to Keene's mild surprise—although it shouldn't have been, given the kind of job he had described—talking with two men, was Leo Cavan.

Polli was also an *Osiris* crew member, she told Keene as he selected a plate of cold assortments and took a glass of wine from the bar. Four of the ship's eight-person complement had come down with the delegation. The four who had stayed aboard included the captain, whose name was Idorf. Polli was astonished and delighted to learn that Keene was one of the three who had been in the news the previous Friday, and called Thorel over as he passed near after depositing some used plates on a side table. "You know who we have here, Thorel? Landen is one of the Terrans that we saw, who raced with the spaceplane the day we arrived."

Thorel was perhaps thirtyish, curly-headed, sallow-faced yet hefty, with an open and amiable manner. His field area was engineering too, and for several minutes he and Keene talked technicalities about the NIFTV and its performance. "So how is it you have all this trouble trying to convince your governments of things that should be obvious?" he asked in conclusion. "It seems such a waste of energies. And here you need all the energy you can get, just for standing up."

Keene had noticed that nearly all the Kronians around the room were sitting. "Is that how you're finding it?" he asked Polli.

"Also, it is bewildering," she told him. "Already I have seen more human beings than in all the rest of my life put together. And I still get attacks of . . . What is it when you fear going outside?"

"Agoraphobia?"

"Yes, that is right. We trained for the gravity, but it doesn't really prepare you for it. But the brilliance of the daylight is the most astounding. Nothing on screens can come close. But then, at night you have hardly any stars."

Thorel went to collect some more arrivals from Gallian, and Polli took Keene around to meet more of the guests. Besides other Americans, he was introduced to more Japanese, two Russians, and one each German, Chinese, Brazilian, and Australian. Sariena saw him from across the room and acknowledged with a wave. While still tall by Earth standards, she was smaller than average for the Kronian group. Keene remembered her as saying that she had gone to Saturn as a child, with most of her rapid-growth and developmental years completed. The younger ones, born to the environments of Saturn's moons or the low-*g* orbiting habitats, were uniformly one to two feet taller.

The word went around that one of the space crew from "that thing last Friday" was present, "The one who was on the news this evening—didn't you see it? That's him over there," and Keene found himself much in demand.

"Do you really think it has a future—foreseeably, in the practical sense?" one of the Americans asked dubiously. He was a director of Chase Manhattan, it turned out. "Where's the payoff? What can you bring from out there that we don't have already, and cheaper?"

"It iss interesting zat your ship can connect viss der UN shuttle zat brings you down," Keene overheard the German saying to one of the Kronians, who had a blotchy face and was sneezing intermittently. "Do you build to der same mechanical mating specifications zat you exchange maybe, ja?"

Everything inside Keene wanted to lean in and murmur, *Ve haff vayss of making it dock*. But he behaved himself, bit his tongue, and refrained.

Gallian appeared again and sought him out, accompanied by a man called Druche from an office of the Defense Department that dealt with space matters, whom Keene had met before on one or two occasions. "This is the man you should have building spaceships for you," Gallian told him. "Landen understands how long-range systems have to work. Lan, you would appreciate a real spaceship. Before we go back to Saturn, we must show you the *Osiris*."

Keene blinked at him, surprised. "Are you serious?"

"I don't play jokes on my friends. We'll sort out something for you, don't worry. Make sure you talk to me later about it," Gallian told him.

Gallian and Druche moved on, and Keene was promptly buttonholed by three more Japanese who seemed to be together. "Who are the other companies partnering Amspace?" the one who appeared to be the senior asked when they had been talking for a few minutes. "We could be interested in discussing further funding. How can we get in touch with the correct people?"

Keene mentioned Marvin Curtiss and offered to arrange an introduction. The Japanese seemed pleased. As Keene detached himself, Cavan drifted by, nursing a glass. "Just doing my job, you see," he murmured. " 'Pump them when they don't suspect it,' is what I was told. A tacky world we live in, Landen. Tacky world." And then he was gone again.

Before anyone else could pounce on him, Keene made his way over to Sariena. They had managed to exchange barely a few words so far. She was sitting on the arm of one of the couches, still managing to do justice to the unpretentious but stylish dress that she was wearing—black and sleeveless, with a high, oriental-style neck and just the right touch of trim—but closer he could see that weariness was beginning to show. A slim woman in a light green dress, with graying hair tied high, was standing talking to her.

Keene remembered her being introduced earlier as with the Smithsonian but couldn't recall her name. Sariena smiled as he approached.

"Lan, do join us. Have you two met yet?"

"Oh, we all know who he is," the woman said.

Keene smiled uneasily for a moment. "Smithsonian," he managed.

"Catherine Zetl," the woman said, getting him off the hook. "I'm the historian."

"Oh, right."

"Ancient—the history, not me. Well, I hope not too much, anyway."

"Catherine has been telling me some fascinating things," Sariena said. "She's just back from Arabia— involved with the Joktanian discoveries there."

Keene searched his memory. There had been a stir in the news a couple of years back, and occasional mentions since in the scientific literature. "Some civilization they found from way back, isn't it? Caused some surprises for the specialists." Which about exhausted his knowledge of the subject.

"That's putting it mildly," Zetl said. "It's turned all our ideas upside down. The Sumerians and Babylonians were supposed to have been the earliest to settle and build, but these people date from much earlier. Yet some of their architecture and workmanship appears more sophisticated. And there's no obvious relationship to the cultures that came later. It's as if they represent some lost age that flourished long before it should have been possible. For some reason it ended abruptly, and then what we've always thought was the beginning of civilization was a second start that came much later."

"Isn't it fascinating, Lan?" Sariena said again.

"So do we know what ended it?" Keene asked, getting more interested. "Was it your Kronian supercomet again?"

"Oh, I'm impressed by the Kronians' arguments, but

I refuse to be dragged into any of that tonight," Zetl said, holding up a hand. "In any case, it couldn't have been the comet, Venus, or whatever. This race existed long before the Egyptian Middle Kingdom and the Exodus. And I use the word 'race' deliberately. They were large—comparable to the Kronians around here."

"The name Joktanian comes from Noah's grandson," Sariena informed Keene. "I didn't know that."

"That's who the ancient Arabic legends say the first people of the southwest peninsula were descended from," Zetl said, nodding. "Their word is Qahtan." She glanced away. "Oh, there's somebody about to leave that I must catch. Excuse me." She laid a hand briefly on Sariena's arm. "Sariena, we do have to talk more about all this. Do call me when they give you a moment—if they ever do."

"I certainly will."

Zetl excused herself again and hurried away.

Sariena looked at Keene, sighed, and rotated her face slowly to stretch her neck. "Oh my. Is this what it's like to be what you call a celebrity? You do it all the time? Where do you get the stamina? What's the secret?"

"Not really," Keene said. "Most of the time I deal with reactors and engines. This is just temporary, since Friday. Attention spans on this world tend to be short." He looked at the glass that Sariena was holding. "Want me to get you another? Save your feet."

"Oh, please. Any kind of fruit juice with a touch of vodka. . . ." She handed him the glass. "Do I look unladylike up here on the arm like a bird on a perch? If I sit down in this couch I can't get up again. It digests you."

"I don't think you could look unladylike in a boiler suit," Keene replied. "Something more to eat?"

"Thanks, but I've had enough."

He went over to the bar and got a refill, along with a straight Scotch for himself. He wasn't driving tonight.

Might as well make the most of it, he figured. "Anything else for you, sir?" the cocktail waiter tending the bar asked. He peered at Keene more closely. "Say, aren't you one of those three guys who—"

"You've got it," Keene murmured, covering his mouth and slipping a ten into the glass set aside for tips. "But don't spread it around."

He went back, handed Sariena her drink, and looked at her while he sipped his own. There had been so many things he'd listed in his mind that he wanted to ask her when they finally met. He wanted to know about her world and what it was like to live out there; how it felt to be without a planet that automatically self-renewed and replenished everything necessary for life; to be totally dependent for survival itself, every moment, on machines. He wanted to know how a moneyless system could function and still sustain—evidently—all the complexities of a technological society. What motivated people to provide for each other in place of the penalties and rewards that just about every authority on Earth insisted were indispensable? . . . So many things. And now here they were, and suddenly none of it felt appropriate.

"Well, you've certainly created some attention," Sariena said. "Let's hope it's a good omen for the talks."

"We can but try," Keene said.

"So what brought you to Washington so soon? Was the President so impressed that he wants you to put together a real space program for them at last?"

"I wish." Keene sipped his Scotch and saw that Cavan was watching them inconspicuously from across the room. "As a matter of fact, somebody wanted me to talk to you while I was here. Not the President, but it was to do with your mission." Sariena waited, curious. Keene looked around. The suite was in the penthouse, with an exterior balcony all the way around. "Let's go outside," he suggested. "Gallian says you need to get used to the air."

Sariena rose and moved toward one of the sliding glass panels that had been opened. Keene picked up a chair and followed her along the balcony to a corner, away from the others who were outside talking. Keene placed the chair by the wall and leaned an elbow on the rail while Sariena sat down. He began: "The person that I mentioned is on the inside here. And I've seen something myself today of what reactions are going to be." He shook his head. "Earth isn't going to buy this line about Venus being an earlier Athena. Yes, Athena happened and the standard theories were wrong. Nobody can deny that. But they're going to fight any suggestion that the two have anything in common. As far as they're concerned Venus is a planet and moves like a planet. Athena is a one-time anomaly that will be a spectacle for a year until it leaves the Solar System. . . ." Keene paused, thinking for a second that Sariena wasn't listening. She was sitting back against the window glass, staring up at the sky with a faraway, almost rapturous expression.

"I love stars," she said.

Keene looked away and turned his head upward. "Polli told me we don't have any," he replied. It was a clear night, not bad by Washington standards. The angle of the walls faced roughly north, making just a wisp of Athena's tail visible behind the building to their left. It only occurred to Keene then that until the last couple of days, Sariena's only recollections of seeing a sky had probably been from inside some kind of enclosure or a helmet.

"Paltry," she agreed. "But you know that, Lan. You've been out there too. . . . But what you've never seen is Saturn from one of its moons. This sky has nothing to compare with it. Pictures don't come close—any more than they can show sunshine.

It's like . . ." She turned her face up again. "All the rainbows you've ever seen stirred together into a glowing ball ten times as big as the Moon. And you're looking at it across the rings seen edge-on. It seems to be floating in a golden ocean that extends away into the sky. If you're on one of the moons that has a tilted orbit, the ocean seems to be rising and falling." Sariena looked back at him. "Did you know that there are many legends from the distant past—before the beginnings of our literate age, like those people that Catherine was talking about—that make Saturn the greatest god in the sky and describe it as rising out of an ocean? Isn't that strange? It's almost as if they'd seen it too." Keene frowned at the city lights, searching for a way of turning the subject back to more immediate matters. "Can you pick out Saturn in the sky?" Sariena asked him.

"Er, no. . . . I guess not. It isn't really one of my things."

"Not many people can—nor any of the other planets. And isn't that strange too? They're such insignificant pinpoints that most people can't even find them. And yet in just about every system of religion and myth from times gone by, they filled people with awe and terror and were associated with gods fighting titanic battles in the sky—mightier even than the Sun and Moon. Why would that be?" Sariena went on before Keene could respond, "Because the planets moved in different orbits then, that brought them much closer."

She hadn't strayed off the subject, he realized. It was just a roundabout way of addressing the issue he had raised.

She went on, "They *saw* Venus being ejected by Jupiter. To the Greeks it was Pallas Athene springing from the brow of Zeus. The Hindus have Vishnu being born of Shiva. The Egyptians, Horus. All names for the same planets, associated with events in the sky that are described the same way everywhere, over and over. Now tell me that Athena isn't the same thing happening again."

"You don't have to convince me," Keene said. "I'm already on your side, remember? But the scientists who'll determine what our governments decide aren't interested in old myths and legends. They're going to want to see facts and evidence and numbers before they'll budge, and none of them wants to budge because they're happy with the ideas they've got and things the way they are."

Sariena looked at Keene dubiously. "Is that really all that matters here?" she asked. "Comfortable livings and safe jobs? Prestige and promotions? Don't things like where we're all heading in the longer term, and wanting to know the truth count?"

"Maybe they did once—I don't know; you hear these things. But people have always thought things were better in the past. Today, the creed is 'Make what you can now and grab as much as you can get.' There might not be a tomorrow."

"One day, that could turn out to be a gruesome self-fulfilling prophesy," Sariena observed. "I don't understand how a system can function that seems to be based on nothing but antagonism."

Keene smiled humorlessly. "Most people here can't understand how your system can, that isn't."

"We couldn't afford anything else out there," Sariena said. "Everyone's survival is at stake. We have to work together. And look what it's achieving." She paused, waiting, but Keene had nothing to add just then. After a short silence, she said, "Of course we have more than just ancient myths and records. They're just the beginning. We have as much fact and evidence as anyone could reasonably need. Otherwise we wouldn't be here."

"I know about the mass-extinctions and geological

upheavals," Keene agreed. "But there are plenty of other theories going around as to what could have caused all that. How do you positively connect it all with Venus?"

"Venus is a young planet," Sariena answered. "It hasn't been there for billions of years. The evidence has been piling up for decades. A lot of scientists on Earth that we know of are aware of it."

"I'll be meeting one of them on my way back," Keene said. "But even if you're right, that doesn't mean it nearly sideswiped Earth. That's the biggest single problem you're going to have to deal with: how an orbit that could take it from Jupiter to an Earth-encounter could circularize to what we see today. All of conventional theory says it couldn't happen. That's why people here are saying that Athena is something different. No mechanism known to science could reduce its eccentricity to almost zero in under four thousand years. That's what they're going to tell you. How are you planning on answering it?"

Sariena studied him for a moment. "Do you know about the electromagnetic changes that have been occurring all over the Solar System since Athena was ejected?" she asked curiously.

Keene looked at her uncertainly. "Electromagnetic changes to what?"

"The space environment itself. Its properties are being altered."

Keene was still frowning, but with a new interest. "No . . ." He told her. "I don't think I do. Suppose you tell me."

"I don't think it's something that most scientists here are informed about," Sariena answered. "Earth hasn't been putting enough deep-space probes out to get the picture. We have. We must be getting a better perspective."

"What's been happening?" Keene asked.

Sariena motioned upward with an arm to indicate

the night sky. "This white-hot mass, hurtling in from
Jupiter for the last ten months, pouring out a tail of
highly ionized particles that extends for millions of
miles, orders of magnitude denser than that of any
comet ever known . . . It's turning space in the inner
Solar System into an electrically active medium—at
least, temporarily. Now move an incandescent body
in a plasma state through that medium at high
velocity. . . ." She left the suggestion unfinished.

The expression on Keene's face told her there was
no need to say any more. A charged body moving
through an electrically active medium would be subject to forces that in those conditions could conceivably rival or even exceed gravity. Forces that conventional
astronomic theory, based on the assumption of a pre-
Athena, electrically quiescent Solar System, had never
taken into account.

Sariena nodded, seeing that Keene had made the
connection. "Our scientists in Kronia have been
running some calculations. The preliminary results
came in to the *Osiris* just before we came down to
the surface. They're being rechecked before we
present anything here officially. But perhaps you could
arrange for them to be duplicated independently here
on Earth as well—the more confirmation we get, the
better. We'll give you the codes to access the files
of original data from our probes. I think you'll find
the results interesting."

11

Next morning, the over-breakfast continuation of the interview with the science journalist went well, and Keene was happy that the treatment would be accurate. Afterward, he went back up to his room and called Marvin Curtiss as promised. Although Texas was an hour behind Eastern Time, he found Curtiss already in his office. Apparently, Halloran, Lomack, and most of the other engineering and project managers were at work already over in the Kingsville plant too, working out figures for a proposal that Harry Halloran had come up with for getting the Montemorelos site operational sooner, as Curtiss had wanted.

Instead of the conventional above-ground pads as used at San Saucillo, where final testing and any last-minute servicing had to be conducted out in the elements, the Montemorelos facility used an experimental design of silo in which all preparations and launch would be effected in one blastproofed location. Equipment installation was virtually complete, and the next phase called for a live test of the launch systems. A live test meant actually launching something. For something to be launched, it would first have to be there. The existing plan called for a regular (chemical powered) vehicle to be moved in sections by road from Kingsville and assembled in one of the silos. However, a separate surface-to-orbit trial was also due to be conducted in the near future from Saucillo, involving a minishuttle fitted with a modified hybrid engine using solid propellant and a liquid oxidizer. Halloran had proposed combining the two programs by landing the minishuttle at Montemorelos after its orbital trials, where it would then be available for the launch test without anything needing to be shipped by road. The planning committee would be meeting that morning to consider it.

Keene agreed the suggestion made sense, but it was an internal Amspace affair and not something that concerned him directly. He went on to summarize his impressions after meeting the Kronians. The most important thing to come out of it was Sariena's disclosure of the changes the Kronian scientists had detected in the solar environment and the need to verify their calculations of what it implied. "I was hoping Jerry could set it up somewhere on one of the big computers you've got access to," Keene concluded. Jerry Allender was the head of research at Amspace. "If he needs some help from a specialist in celestial mechanics, I could probably put him in touch with a couple of people I know."

"How soon do we need this?" Curtiss asked, not looking enthralled. "We're going to be swamped here with this Montemorelos business as things are."

"I think it's absolutely crucial to have the results confirmed or otherwise by the time the Kronians get back from their tour," Keene pressed. "That means we ought to get moving now. I could get Vicki to take care of liaising with the Kronians and getting the files and material together. Judith could even help with running it and tackling a specialist—she's pretty hot.

All Jerry would need to do would be to set things up."

"What results did the Kronians get?" Curtiss asked. "Do we know?"

"No, they've just offered to let us have their raw data. That's the way it should be done. Sariena just said she thought we'd find them interesting."

Curtiss drew a long breath, then nodded. "Okay, we'll see what we can do," he promised. "Talk to Harry. I'll tell him to expect to hear from you. Now I have to rush. We've obviously got one of those days ahead of us, and I've a commitment in the city tonight."

"What's on?" Keene asked. "Business dinner? Press Club? Some kind of civic function?"

"My stepdaughter Anna is playing the cello. It's her first appearance in public, and it would be more than my life's worth not to be there." Curtiss looked pleased that Keene had asked. He seemed quite proud. Keene liked it when tycoons showed a human touch. It meant there was hope for the race yet.

He called Vicki immediately afterward and caught her at the house just as she was about to leave for the office. "Something came up at the Kronian party last night that could be important," he told her. "Can you pull Judith off that Japanese project and ask her to take a look at it—maybe give her a hand. I want you to access the Kronian research files and find some data they've been collecting on changes in the electromagnetic properties of the space environment during the past ten months. You can get it from the databank in the *Osiris*—no need for all the delays in dealing with Saturn. I'll send details and access codes to you at the office."

"Changes?" Vicki repeated, looking surprised.

"Yes. It seems that all that stuff that Athena's spewing out has been altering the inner-system free-space permeability and permittivity—for a while, anyway, until the solar wind blows it away. But in the meantime we're in a more electrically active neighborhood. I want to compute the forces that would act on a hot, massively charged body and how they would affect its orbital characteristics."

"You want *us* to do this . . . ?"

"No, no—not all on your own, there, anyway. I've just talked to Marvin. He's going to have Jerry Allender set it up in his department over there. But they're all in a panic this morning over something else that's going on. I just want us to do the go-betweening with the Kronians for them. You might need to involve a specialist too. I can think of a couple of names you could try. I'll send them with the other stuff."

Vicki stared at him for a few seconds, thinking rapidly. "Are we talking about Venus?" she asked at last.

"Could be," Keene answered noncommittally.

"Are you saying that our scientists here don't know about this already?"

Keene shrugged. "All too busy writing begging letters to Congress or getting themselves into the Washington black-tie cocktail-party circuit."

The significance was slowly sinking in. Vicki shook her head, looking disbelieving. "Lan . . . do you realize that what you're talking about could upset half of astronomy all the way back to Newton? I mean, you just call on the phone when I'm leaving for work and mention it as casually as if it were a bookshelf you want ordered. . . ."

"Yes, I know, but I haven't got time to go into raptures over the philosophy of it right now. There's probably a cab waiting for me downstairs already."

Just then, a blurred voice called something in the background behind Vicki. She looked away. "I said on the table in the kitchen," she directed to somewhere off-screen.

"Robin getting ready for school?" Keene said.

Vicki turned back again. "You guessed. How do you do it, Lan?"

"And how is he? Anything new with the dinosaurs?"

"It's led into mammoths. But don't ask me right now; I'll mail you a note if you're interested."

"Sure, I'm interested."

"You want to say hi to him?"

"Sure."

"Robin, it's Landen on the line. Like to say hello for a second?"

A few seconds went by, and then Robin moved into the view alongside the image of Vicki. "Hi, Lan. How's Washington? Did you get to meet the Kronians?"

"Sure did. I'll tell you all about them next time I stop by."

"Is that it?" Vicki asked Robin, gesturing at a blue folder that he was holding.

"Yes. I was sure it was upstairs."

"What's in it?" Keene inquired.

"Oh, a project we're doing at school, in the science class. We have to write an essay on the Joktanians and the kinds of things that have been turning up in the places they're digging at."

"That's the old civilization from around Arabia and Ethiopia that was only discovered in the last few years," Vicki supplied for Keene's benefit. "So give the school system some credit—they're keeping up to date."

"Ah yes," Keene was able to reply airily. "Named after Noah's grandson. Legend says the earliest peoples of southern Arabia were descended from him. The Arab word is Qahtan."

Vicki stared hard and blinked. "I didn't think you'd know that."

Keene managed to keep a straight face and replied nonchalantly, while inside enjoying every moment of it. "Why not? I thought everyone did."

She shook her head. "Lan, you never cease to amaze me."

"Just call it talented. Got to go. Check your mail when you get in. I'll probably stay in town tomorrow too. See you Thursday."

The final thing Keene did before leaving the hotel to begin his schedule for that day was call David Salio. Salio was surprised to hear back from him so soon, but pleased. Yes, it turned out that he was flexible that week and could be available. Keene arranged to see him on Thursday and changed his flight arrangements to stop off in Houston on his way back to Corpus Christi. Things seemed to be moving along.

12

The Aerospace Sciences Institute was both a research
and educational establishment, set up jointly by a consortium of contractors and allied interests. It was
funded privately and made no appeals to the public
purse, the goal being to ensure an adequate supply
of competent specialists in the fields essential to the
industry, without complications arising from any yield-
ing of standards to political agendas. NASA layoffs
and the ensuing contraction of the Johnson Center
had provided much of the initial recruitment and been
one of the reasons for choosing Houston as the
location.

Keene was no stranger there, although he had not
dealt previously with the Planetary Studies section,
which was where David Salio worked. The principal
interests of the founder corporations were commercial and defense-related, leading them to focus essentially on launch and Earth-orbit activities, with some
involvement in lunar pilot schemes and the scientific
endeavor on Mars, the latter of which was a small-
scale operation in any case. But putting some effort

into theoretical studies of longer-term possibilities bolstered the image of exploration and adventure that
excited the public, gratified stockholders, and worked
wonders for recruiting ads. And besides, despite their
stereotype to the contrary, many of the executives
responsible for policy were genuinely curious.

The Institute was run in a spirit that conformed
to the open-door tradition of regular universities, more
sensitive and secretive work being conducted elsewhere. Accordingly, a little over ten minutes ahead
of the appointed time, Keene sauntered in from where
the airport cab had dropped him in front of the Glenn
Building, verified from the lobby directory that Salio's
office was on the fifth floor, and went on up without need of signature, badge, or security check. The
elevator delivered him to a carpeted area with plants,
padded leather seating arranged around a glass-topped
table, and a wall of picture windows looking out over
one of the Houston freeway interchanges. A sign
directed him past a vending area into a corridor of
similar-looking numbered doors and occasional bulletin boards, where eventually he arrived at 521, with
a nameplate alongside indicating it to be the office
of DAVID R. SALIO. Keene tapped, waited for a
moment, and then eased the door open. A voice from
inside called out, "Dr. Keene? Yes, do come on in.
I won't be a second."

The office was the familiar combination of over-
flowing desk, computer work station, raggedly packed
bookshelves, and wall board that seemed to charac-
terize the natural habitat of *Homo sapiens technicus*
the world over. Salio was at the computer, clicking
through a series of data-contour images on the screen,
pausing to flag a point here and there or add a
comment to the caption. "Must get this off to somebody at JPL right away. It won't take a minute. Could
you use a coffee or soda or something?"

"I'm fine, thanks. I had plane-food on the way."

Keene judged Salio to be in his mid-twenties to maybe thirty. He had straight black hair, a shadowy chin, and heavy-rimmed glasses, giving him a studentish look that seemed mildly incongruous in combination with the plaid shirt, blue jeans, and pointy cowboy boots. There was an intense, birdlike nervousness about the way he peered at the screen, pecking at icons and hammering quick staccatos on the keys. The desk to one side bore a framed family print showing an attractive woman and two young, happy-looking children. On the wall behind was a poster showing climbing routes up the face of El Capitan in Yosemite, and beside it a cork board with departmental notes, postcards from various places, and a cartoon collection.

Finally, a mail screen appeared and Salio sent the package off to its destination with a flourish. Then he stood and extended a hand. "Sorry about that. One of those things that couldn't wait. Let's see . . . we need to make some room for you." He lifted a pile of books and papers from a chair by the wall and cleared some space for them on top of a file cabinet. Keene sat down, and Salio moved around to pull up his own chair on the far side of the desk. He looked across and pushed his hair up from his eyes. "Well, I admit I was flattered when you got back to me so quickly. I never expected to see you here in person. We don't exactly get a lot of celebrities stopping by in this office."

"Oh, I wouldn't attach too much significance to that," Keene said. "You know how it is. They'll all have found someone else by the end of the week."

"What's your title with Amspace, if you don't mind my asking?"

"I'm not exactly with Amspace. I run a technical consultancy on nuclear dynamics that's been working with them for a number of years: Protonix—also based in Corpus Christi."

"Ah . . ."

"That's what I really do. The stunt and commercial last Friday were coincidental."

"It's stirring up a lot of hostility out there," Salio said. "But you knew that had to happen."

"If you hope to do anything, you have to be visible," Keene answered. "As I said when we talked, Amspace, myself, and various other interests that we're associated with are trying to help promote the Kronian case because we believe it's too important an issue to let politics and scientific dogmatism get in the way of the truth—which is what's happening. You said you'd like to help. We're interested enough that I'm here."

"This is all very gratifying, Dr. Keene. It's something I've been battling over for years."

" 'Landen' is fine. So can we talk about the kind of work that you and the other scientists that you said you're in touch with have been doing? Particularly about Venus being a young planet. You said a lot of evidence points to it."

"I can't say whether or not it had anything to do with Moses," Salio cautioned. "Things like that aren't written in thermal signatures or atmospheric compositions. But what I can show you is that practically everything we know about Venus is consistent with the notion of a young, recently very hot body." Salio tilted his chair back and clasped his hands behind his head. "The first thing every schoolkid knows is that what the first American and Russian probes found back in the nineteen sixties came as a big surprise— at least it did to the orthodox theory. The expectation had been that since Venus was about Earth's size and had clouds, it would be pretty similar—maybe a little warmer through being nearer to the Sun. What they found was virtually a volcanic cauldron: surface temperature seven-hundred-fifty degrees K and more—enough to melt lead—and an atmosphere of acids and hydrocarbon gases at ninety times the pressure of Earth's. Not the kind of place to put on your list of vacation spots."

"Supposedly a runaway greenhouse effect," Keene supplied. It was what all the texts said, and not something he had ever had much reason to doubt or look into.

Salio pulled a face. "Yes, 'supposedly'—a good choice of word, Mr. . . . Landen. That theory was contrived as an attempt to square the facts with the established assumption of an ancient planet. But it really doesn't stand up. The main weakness is quite simple: a real greenhouse has a roof that stops the hot air inside from convecting upward and being replaced by cooler air circulating down from above. A planet doesn't have such a lid, and so there's nothing to stop the hot surface gases from mixing with the freezing upper layers. A greenhouse process might raise the temperature some, but maintaining a difference of over seven hundred degrees just isn't credible. You'd reach thermal equilibrium through convection and radiation back into space long before it got anywhere near that. The only way such a difference could be maintained is if the heat source is the planet itself, not the Sun."

"A young, recently very hot body," Keene repeated.

"Exactly. And enough heat doesn't get down to the surface in any case. In fact, hardly any does. For a start, most of the sunlight is reflected off the cloud tops thirty miles up—which is why Venus is so bright. And what does penetrate diminishes rapidly with depth in an atmosphere that thick, so that any solar heating you do get occurs at the top. Thermally it's more like shallow seas on Earth, where sunlight is absorbed primarily in the upper three hundred feet. Venus's surface pressure is about equivalent to that three thousand feet down in the ocean. Even at the equator, the temperature at that depth is only about eight degrees above freezing. You see, the greenhouse effect can't simply be magnified without limit. Increasing the insulation also reduces the amount of sunshine that's transmitted. Taking things beyond a certain point becomes self-defeating: The loss in transmission is no longer compensated for by the extra insulation, and the temperature begins to drop. None of the heat from the bottom of the ocean can escape into space, but it isn't boiling hot."

Keene thought it through but couldn't fault it. He nodded for Salio to continue.

"This all fits with other things that have been known since the earliest U.S. and Russian space shots," Salio said. "The planet isn't in thermal equilibrium as the greenhouse explanation would require. It radiates twenty percent more energy out than falls on it from the Sun. Its dark side isn't cooler, even though night lasts fifty-eight days. In fact, it's slightly warmer. We're talking about a planet with a lot of residual heat."

"Has a cooling-curve model been worked out that's consistent with this kind of temperature from an internal source?" Keene queried.

"Oh yes—and it's quite interesting. If you start out with the assumption of an incandescent state three and a half thousand years ago, which is what the Kronians are saying, the calculated temperature today works out at seven-fifty degrees K—precisely what's observed."

"Why not radioactivity in the rocks?" Keene queried. "It warms us up here. Why not there too?"

"Generating ten thousand times more heat than Earth does?" Salio shook his head. "No way."

Keene frowned as he thought back over what had been said. "And this has been known for years? . . . So why do we keep hearing the same story?"

Salio shrugged. "Once people are trained in a particular theory, they become emotionally wedded to it. They can be literally incapable of seeing anything that contradicts it, and will invent the most amazing rationalizations. That's why you have to wait for a generation to die off before you can move on."

"But how can that be?" Keene invited. "Science is objective, impartial, and self-correcting. All the textbooks say so."

Salio returned a thin, humorless smile. It was clear that they spoke the same language. Keene sensed the way to real communication opening between them. It occurred to him what a lonely professional life Salio must lead. Salio went on, "And then you have the anomalies in atmospheric composition. For example, as most people know there's the sulfuric acid in the upper clouds—probably formed out of sulfur trioxide from the hydrocarbon gases binding with what little water ever existed. But sulfuric acid in the cloud tops ought to have a short life due to decomposition by solar UV. If Venus were over four billion years old, there shouldn't be any sulfuric acid left. But there is.

"The middle atmosphere is rich in carbon dioxide. That should have been dissociated in a few thousand years into carbon monoxide and oxygen, which don't recombine again easily and ought to be abundant. They're not.

"And where are Venus's oceans? In billions of years it ought to have outgassed enormous volumes of water. The conventional explanation is that it was dissociated into oxygen, which combined with the rocks, and hydrogen, which escaped. But a lot of us can't buy that. For one thing, the depth of surface you'd need to 'garden' to absorb the amount of oxygen indicated just isn't credible. And for another, if dissociation produced oxygen, the oxygen should recombine into upper-atmosphere ozone the way it does on Earth, shutting out that UV band and terminating the process. How can you postulate one mechanism and ignore the other?"

Keene could tell there was more. "Go on," he said, staring wonderingly.

Salio tossed out a hand idly, as if inviting Keene to take his pick. "Ratios of argon isotopes. Argon-40 is a decay product of potassium-40 and should increase over time—to a level comparable with Earth's, you'd think, if Venus were as old as the Earth. But in fact it's around fifteen times less. On the other hand, argon-36 is primordial and should have decayed to a level like Earth's. It turns out to be hundreds of times more. Both figures are about what you would expect in a young planet's original atmosphere. . . . And if you want, we could talk about the lack of erosion that you'd expect from dense, corrosive winds, and the absence of a regolith; the flatness of the surface; and the enormous lava flows with huge numbers of collapsed volcanic formations. The books say Olympus Mons on Mars is the biggest known volcano. I think they're wrong. Venus is. The whole planet's a cooling volcano."

Keene had already accepted Salio as the kind of person who took his work seriously and would get his facts right. He sat back and massaged his brow. After a few seconds he looked back up. "I assume you can point me to sources for all this?" he said.

"Oh, sure," Salio replied. "And I'll include some on the Moon as well. Obviously, if something came close enough to the Earth to cause polar shifts and all kinds of devastation, the Moon should show signs of it as well."

"And it does?"

"Yes—all the signs of something passing close by and subjecting it to intense tidal stress and heating on one side. The formation of the maria lava sheets is consistent with melting by tidal forces. If they were extrusions of molten material from billions of years ago, they ought to be covered by a deep layer of regolith. It's practically nonexistent."

Keene nodded slowly. He remembered reading

somewhere that some of the scientists who planned the original Apollo missions had been worried that the landers might sink in the dust.

"The maria extend across one side in a huge great-circle swathe, which is what you'd expect from a passing encounter," Salio went on. "And moonquakes are concentrated along two matching belts, six to eight hundred kilometers down. If the Moon has been dead for billions of years, there shouldn't *be* any moonquakes. What it says is that something deformed the structure recently, and it's still recovering. That would account for the bulge on the maria side too, which has been a puzzle for centuries. If it were primeval, it should have sunk under gravity long ago." Salio spread his hands in a gesture of finality. "You've got volcanic activity that shouldn't be there today. And the maria lavas have a coherent magnetism that means they cooled in the presence of a field far too strong to have been either terrestrial or solar. So where did it come from? . . . Do you want me to go on?"

"It's okay, David. I'm getting the picture. I can check the rest out myself from your references." Keene stood up and flexed his arms, as if it would help him digest all this information better. There was a chart on one of the walls showing a depiction of the Milky Way Galaxy. Somebody had added an arrow with the caption: *You are here . . . or maybe somewhere near here—Werner Heisenberg*. Salio sorted some of the papers on his desk, allowing Keene time to think.

At length, Keene turned. "So why hasn't *your* thinking been channeled along the standard lines that we keep hearing?" he asked. "You seem pretty free to follow where your inclination leads. How come the difference?"

Salio's intense look softened for the first time into something approaching a grin. "Well, it's really what you might call a hobby interest, so nobody around here cares that much. We're not part of the establishment. The concerns that run this institute are interested in technology as opposed to what you and I think of as science. Ruffling academic feathers isn't something we have to worry about." Salio licked his lips and indicated the door. "Are you sure you wouldn't like a drink of some kind? I'm going for one. But then I've been doing all the talking."

"Okay, maybe a cup of coffee," Keene conceded.

"Splendid." Salio rose from his chair. "We can go to the visitors' area by the elevators where you came in, or if you don't mind muck and squalor, there's our own cubbyhole which is closer—but the coffee's better."

"I'll take that. Probably feel more at home anyhow," Keene said. He looked at the poster of El Capitan while Salio was coming around the desk. "Is that something you do—climb?"

"I used to. These days, though, other things tend to take up more of life . . ." Salio looked back at the photo on his desk. "Or maybe I'm just getting older."

"Nice family," Keene complimented as he waited for Salio to lead the way out the door. "What's your wife's name?"

"Jean. She's Canadian—also an emergency-room nurse at one of the hospitals here. I've been offered a sabbatical at a university in England, which will mean moving there for two years. She's very excited about it—well, I suppose we both are. It will be her first time in Europe."

"Sounds terrific."

They followed the corridor and came to a double door. Salio stopped, opened one side, and ushered Keene through into laboratory surroundings. "Now I'll show you what I really do," he said.

The centerpiece of the room was a complex assembly of machined parts housing an array of electronic units, wiring forms, lenses, and mechanisms. The whole stood about the size of a kitchen table and was supported in a wheeled cradle. Two technicians in lab coats, one male, one female, were working over it. A youth who looked like a student was sitting at a console by the far wall.

"Looks like satellite instrumentation," Keene remarked.

"Exactly right. This is a package that we're putting together to go into low orbit over Saturn," Salio said. "There will be some descent probes too."

"Is it part of some deal to do with the Kronians?" Keene asked. A number of concerns on Earth had worked out cooperative ventures with the colony where they could be of mutual service.

Salio nodded. "They'll transport the modules there for us and deploy them. Don't ask me what the reciprocal arrangement is. I'm only interested in the scientific side."

A discussion of technical details followed. Keene commented that walking in off the street to find himself looking at a sophisticated piece of equipment like this seemed, somehow . . . "casual."

"Oh, this is just a prototype that we're testing design ideas on," Salio told him. "The one that'll actually be going is being assembled in California. And you're right. There, it's clean rooms, gowns, filtered air—the works."

Salio led the way through to a workshop area at the rear, where a bench below the windows ran the length of one wall. There were racks for tools and materials, and shelves bearing an assortment of containers, boxes, and pieces of unidentifiable gadgetry. Several tubular steel chairs standing loosely around a scratched plastic-topped table, and a small refrigerator supporting a coffee maker denoted the lunch area. Salio filled a mug for Keene, waved a hand at the milk and sugar containers for him to help himself, and got himself a can of lemon soda from below.

"So, do I take it you're with the Kronians about

Venus being an earlier Athena?" Keene asked, getting back to the subject as they sat down.

"Well, it fits with the heat, the hydrocarbon gases—all the other things we talked about," Salio replied. "Also, its whole atmosphere is in a state of super-rotation in an east-west direction at about a hundred times the speed of the surface, which is consistent with the idea of a dense tail wrapping itself around the planet and still dissipating angular momentum." He peeled open his drink. "And then you've got the comets. The shower of new comets that accompanied the ejection of Athena is forcing a revision of the idea that comets come from outside the Solar System—which, personally, I never had much time for anyway. I mean how else are you going to get material compressed to the density of rock out in space?

"But it goes further. The whole question of how the Solar System was formed might have to be rethought. There's work going back to the last century that no one has ever refuted, saying that neither of the traditional tidal or accretion models can be right. Because of its disrupting effects, none of the inner planets could have formed inside the orbit of Jupiter. If so, then where did they come from? An obvious thought is that if Venus and Athena originated by fission from Jupiter, then maybe the others did too, which makes Jupiter not just a comet factory but a planet factory too. And that's exactly where the Kronian line of thinking is taking us." Salio took a drink at last and paused again to think for a moment. "The biggest problem is to account for the circularization of orbits. Conventional theory doesn't do it, and that's where the Church of Astronomy is going to be digging its heels in."

Keene sat back and looked at him, amazed. They had converged totally. "Would you believe I was talking to the Kronians about just that very thing last Monday night?" he said.

"You've actually met them?"

"That was one of the reasons why I was in Washington."

Salio looked impressed "And do they have any ideas?" he asked.

"Yes," Keene answered. "I think they might." He paused, waiting for a reaction. Salio waved for him to continue. "Well, go on. Now I'm the one doing the listening."

"What would you say to the suggestion that the orbits aren't always determined purely gravitationally?" Keene replied. "Suppose an event like Athena could alter the electrical environment to create a temporary regime in which charge-induced forces became significant. Mightn't that make a difference?"

Salio didn't answer at once but stared at him long and fixedly. "Is there some reason to suppose that's true?" he asked finally.

"I think the Kronians might have some good reasons, yes," Keene replied. He went on to summarize what Sariena had said about the Kronian findings and the arrangements being made in Corpus Christi to compute the implications. Naturally, Salio was intrigued. Keene promised to keep him posted on the outcome.

Back in Salio's office, Keen finally got around to asking the question that had been his prime reason for coming to see Salio. "If Amspace were to arrange media coverage and so forth, would you be willing to go public with the kinds of things you've been telling me this morning?"

"I'd be happy to," was Salio's reply. "Wasn't that why I got in touch with you in the first place?"

"It wouldn't create problems with the people you work for here?" Keene checked.

"No. As I said before, as far as they're concerned it's just a hobby. As long as it doesn't affect their budgets, contracts, or completion dates, no one here is going to worry too much."

Salio offered lunch, but Keene's flight departure time didn't allow for it. He called for a cab to take Keene to the airport, and, to stretch his legs and get some air, said he'd accompany Keene down to the front entrance.

"So what's your version of why so many astronomers don't want to think about it?" Keene asked as they stood waiting. He was curious to see how Salio's view compared with Cavan's. "I mean, you and I don't have a problem. If you tell the ordinary guy in the street that we nearly got wiped out by Venus once, he says 'Say, that's interesting. Tell me more.' Why the difference?"

Salio stared into the distance. Having to ponder the psychology of such things seemed to be something he was not used to. "Maybe if your whole world is built on certainty and prestige, the thought of losing it is something you can't face," he offered finally. "Ordinary people accept uncertainty and insecurity every day."

"Maybe," Keene said. It was a thought, anyway.

Salio went on, "And in any case, it's not true of all astronomers. There's a lot of politics that I try not to get mixed up in. The astronomers I know out on the West Coast would like to see all this debated more openly. But the International Astronomical Union, headquartered at the Harvard-Smithsonian center in Cambridge, sets the official line. That's where the lines and Web links from around the world come in to report observations, coordinate announcements, and so on. Its ties are to Washington investment capital and the defense establishment, both of whose horizons are conservative and Earth-centered."

Keene nodded slowly. Cavan had mentioned Voler's recently being nominated for presidency of the IAU. "So what happens on the West Coast?" he asked.

"There's a kind of parallel information clearinghouse at JPL in Pasadena," Salio said. "The IAU is primarily NSF-supported. JPL is operated for NASA by Cal Tech, which, being a private institution, gives it more autonomy. Certainly, a lot of scientists there would love to start launching stuff all over the Solar System again the way the Kronians want us to, but the catch is being tied to government money."

"Who'd be the person to talk to out there?" Keene inquired curiously.

"The best I can think of would be a guy called Charlie Hu at JPL. He runs their communications center and big number-crunching operations. I wouldn't be surprised if he talks to the Kronians on a direct line the same as you do, but doesn't publicize it much. Anyhow, sure, I can put you in touch with him."

There was only one more thing. As the cab appeared in the gateway to the parking lot, Keene remembered Robin's theory of dinosaurs arriving with impacting bodies and asked Salio what he thought. At the time Robin mentioned it, Keene had thought it outlandish; now it seemed rather tame.

"Well, it's different," Salio said—with an effort to be tactful, Keene thought. "Is it your idea?"

"No. The son of a friend of mine. He's fourteen."

Salio looked surprised and at the same time impressed. "Well, as I say, it's different—but I can see a few problems. Let me think about it. Can you give me his e-mail code? It would probably make him feel good if he got a response from the Institute directly, don't you think?"

The TV had been left on in the passenger compartment of the cab. Keene was about to turn it off, but paused when he realized that the item that had just come on featured a senator from New York giving his views on the Kronians.

"They're overextended with no credit in the bank. If you ask me, this whole line they're pushing is a ploy to sucker us here on Earth into bailing them out of a foolhardy venture that should never have been attempted in the first place. Well, I'm sorry but my answer is, we have problems of our own to take care of. No, sir, I will not be voting my support."

13

Judith was spending a year at Protonix to gain commercial experience before going back to university to continue her postdoctoral work. She confounded all the jokes and stereotypes by being blond, pretty, busty, and leggy, and modeled for girly magazines when she wasn't computing reactor thermal dynamics or charge distributions in ionized gas flows. Her fiancé was from a family that owned a chain of Texas automobile dealerships, but he had passed on his share of the fortune to study and compose music. Keene had never found life to be short on incongruities.

"We need to modify some orbital mechanics programs that Jerry's people downloaded," she told Keene when he stuck his head in her office to ask about progress on his return to Corpus Christi. "I talked to Neuzender at Princeton and he said he'll help out, but can't until something he's working on is done. He asked me to say hi, by the way."

"Okay."

"I'd say, maybe a week or two."

"Um." Keene pulled a face. "I was hoping we'd

have it before the Kronians get down to serious business. Is that the best we can do?"

"I'll keep pushing. Maybe we can shave it down a bit."

"Whatever you can do. How was the computer thing in Dallas on Saturday?"

"Not bad. I found the perfect replacement for this machine. It's just what we need: image-tank driver, voice directable, and with math-pro conditioning."

"Sounds great, but I'm up to my ears saving the world right now."

"Vicki has the brochures, specs, and prices."

"Okay, I'll take a look. How's everything else?"

"Celia's moving along with the Karisaki thing. We should get the draft done by tomorrow."

"Great stuff. Catch you later."

Back in his own office, he reviewed his messages. A note from Karen confirmed a meeting the next morning with Curtiss and other senior Amspace management to update them after his talk with Salio. Wally had called to say that Harry Halloran's proposal was now officially accepted, and the tentative date set for the hybrid shuttle trial out of San Saucillo, followed by a landing at Montemorelos, was in two weeks. Pretty quick. Keene nodded in silent approval. Then a header lower down caught his eye, saying that a recording from Gallian had been filed around midday. Keene activated it, and a moment later the familiar white-haired features were addressing him from the screen.

"Hello, Landen Keene. You're probably busy, so I'll just leave this for when you get back and not chase you around on your personal number. We're leaving Washington for the tour, finally, and looking forward to it—surely the whole planet can't be as hectic as this city. But I just wanted to let you know that I haven't forgotten my promise on Monday to arrange for you to see the *Osiris*. In fact, I have talked to

Captain Idorf and asked him to get in touch with you. It is his ship, after all, and he should be the one issuing invitations." Gallian looked away for a moment. "Well, they're hounding me again. Got to go. Be our guest, as we are yours. Sariena sends regards. More when we've a moment. Bye."

And, indeed, the message from Idorf up in the *Osiris*, inviting Keene to visit the ship, was four items farther down. Idorf regretted that he would have to leave it to Keene to get himself up there, however. Any others that Keene might wish to bring too would also be welcome, since right now there was plenty of space aboard. Keene killed the screen, leaned back, and thought it over. No doubt there would be official vessels shuttling up and down between the ship and the surface for one reason or another that he could probably get a place on, but if his experience was anything to go by it would be a tedious and officious business. The Amspace trial that Wally had said was scheduled to take place in two weeks offered an obvious alternative possibility. Keene warmed to the idea as he mulled over it. If they could kill two birds with one stone, then why not three? He wasn't listed to go on the trial as things stood, since it involved simply a conventional type of engine that didn't involved him, but that could be changed. They were using a mini-shuttle; there would be plenty of spare room. . . .

He sat forward to the screen again and called Wally Lomack at Kingsville.

"Lan, say, what's up? How'd it all go in Washington?"

"Pretty good, Wally. There's been more since, too. I'll be over at Kingsville tomorrow after I talk to Marvin and his people in town in the morning, so I'll fill you in then. Right now, I wanted to talk about the hybrid and Montemorelos mission."

"It's going ahead—targeted for two weeks from now. I sent you a note."

"I know. I've seen it. I don't suppose you were planning on flying yourself, right?"

Lomack looked surprised. "Why, no. It's just a regular trial. Why would I want to go? I've done enough of all that in my time. That's what we have crew for."

"But you're CDE. You could change the flight roster if you had a good reason."

"Lan, quit playing games. What's this about?"

"How would you like to see the inside of the Kronians' ship?"

"The *Osiris*?"

"Right. I've got us an invitation. The fee is that you provide the transport up there."

It took Lomack several seconds to satisfy himself that Keene was serious. He shook his head in amazement. "Hell, you were only with them one evening. What did you do, offer them some free consulting?"

Keene grinned. "As if they needed any. . . . Oh, come on, you know me, Wally. Smooth operator when the occasion calls. So what do you think? Can do?"

Lomack thought, inclined his head, and pursed his lips. "It's a tempting thought, all right. . . ."

"We can offer other places too," Keene said. "Any number up to what a minishuttle can carry. That should help make it more popular."

"That's true enough." Lomack chewed his lip for a moment longer, and then nodded. "Okay, I'll see what I can do. No promises, mind, but I'll put it to Harry. Good enough?"

"Good enough. Take care, Wally."

"You too."

Keene cleared down and sat staring at the blank screen, savoring for a few moments the rare feeling of everything in life going right for a change. Murphy's Law also operated on itself, which meant that it didn't always work . . . which meant that it did work. He'd never quite been able to figure out the logic. He got up and sauntered into Vicki's office, where she was busy over pages of program code that she had been working on with Judith. "How's life on the lower decks?" he inquired, scanning casually over the sheets.

"It's going to be tight, but with Neuzender's input from Princeton I think we'll make it."

"Good." Keene let it hang for a second. "Maybe we've a cause for celebration, then. Never say that the firm doesn't appreciate the galley slaves."

Vicki glanced up. "What does that mean, Lan? Another happy hour at the Bandana?"

"Well, it would give you a chance to tell me about Robin's mammoths, which you were going to send and never did," Keene said.

"That's right, I never got around to it. Well, we have had this little thing to work on while you've been seeing the sights around Washington, you know."

Keene grinned and studied her curiously for a few seconds. "Suppose I said I can fix that trip into space for you that you've been waiting for? Would that beat a beer at the Bandana?"

Vicki stopped and looked at him as if she couldn't have heard him right. Her eyes interrogated him silently. They had worked together long enough that Keene had the feeling she could bypass sensory intermediaries and verify directly what was going through his mind. "You're serious, aren't you," she pronounced finally.

Keene made a gesture that was at the same time both nonchalant and expansive. "Even better. How about seeing the *Osiris* as well?" This time Vicki did come close to looking as if she thought this might be a sick joke after all.

Keene nodded, his face splitting into a wide grin. "It's real. So do you feel like celebrating? . . . Oh, and one more thing to add to your list. I want us to order a mixed crate of the best Californian wines to take up as a present to Gallian for organizing it. Did you know he's partial to wines? They don't make any of the real stuff on Kronia yet."

14

Accelerating ever faster, Athena crossed Mercury's orbit and vanished into the glare of the Sun. After attaining a million miles per hour at perihelion on the far side, it would reemerge and become visible again in just over two weeks. While Judith continued working with Jerry Allender and the Princeton advisers on the computations that it was hoped would throw new light on Venus's early behavior, Halloran put Lomack's proposition to Marvin Curtiss, and approval came down for extending the San Saucillo–Montemorelos operation to include a rendezvous with the *Osiris* in the way Keene had suggested. Keene's and Vicki's places were confirmed, and after some debate within the company, a draw between members of senior management and technical staff was announced for the remaining seats.

With that side of things going so smoothly, there had to be some negative news too. The opposition groups who had been stirred up by the NIFTV demonstration were still seething, and the forthcoming trial offered a timely opportunity to register their protest.

That the vessel involved this time was not nuclear didn't matter. The target for attack was the company name.

A couple of days before liftoff was due, Cavan called Keene at home in his townhouse on Ocean Drive. It was mid-evening. Keene had just been sharing a couple of beers by the pool out back with a neighbor from across the street.

"Hello, Landen. I'm returned at last to the land of the comparatively sane. Are you in the middle of anything? I have something that I'd like to show you."

"No, I was taking it easy for once. So, welcome back. How were Hawaii and Japan? Did the Kronians survive it all intact?"

Cavan had been one of those accompanying the Kronian party. The strategy he had outlined for manipulating the public's image of the Kronians had begun to reveal itself. Instead of the independent, free-thinking scientists that Keene had seen personally, they were typically shown as naive, trusting tourists.

"Most of them are bearing up well, a few feeling the strain," Cavan replied. "They'll be going back up to their ship in relays to take a break from the gravity before the negotiations start."

"Sounds like a good idea," Keene agreed. "How's Gallian? He has to be the oldest."

Cavan snorted. "He's got more energy in him than a football team. That's one that you don't have to worry about."

"Now why doesn't that surprise me?" Keene made an empty-handed gesture. "Anyway, what have you got?"

"I've been picking through what's been going on. The name of your friend David Salio at the Aerospace Sciences Institute has been turning up a lot in the department here. The media seem to be showing an interest in him all of a sudden. It's upsetting a lot of people."

"The Amspace PR people have been busy," Keene said. "I put them on to that guy Charlie Hu on the West Coast that Salio mentioned, too, and he's proved a big asset. *Science* magazine might be running a friendly article, and *New Frontiers* is interested in putting together a documentary. It's really moving along."

"Did you know that Coast-to-Coast wants to get Salio on the *Russ Litherland Show*?" Cavan asked.

"We've got this launch coming up. I haven't been following all the details."

"He received a call recently to confirm that he was interested in participating. But the call didn't come from anyone at Coast-to-Coast. It was from a woman called Maria Hutchill, who had gotten wind of their intention. Does that name mean anything to you, Landen?"

Keene felt unease and let it show. "Leo, this makes me nervous. I thought SICA's business was supposed to be national science policy. But it seems we can't mail a letter without you knowing about it. It makes me feel really glad that you're on my side. . . . At least, I hope you are."

"I told you, Landen, we're all spies now. It's a tacky world. Science has been taken over by the mentalities that run everything else. The only way to feel secure is to know everyone else's secrets and think they don't know yours."

"I get by okay just managing my own business," Keene said.

"But you're not neurotic. You had the sense to get out."

"If you say so. Anyhow who's this Maria . . ."

"Hutchill. She's effectively Herbert Voler's second in command at Yale." Keene's eyebrows lifted at the mention again of his former wife's present husband.

Now he was all attention. Cavan went on, "Voler has emerged as the coordinator of the campaign to discredit the Kronians. The verdict is political and has already been decided, but the case for the jury needs to be made to look scientific."

Keene stared hard at the image on the screen. "Did you guess that this would happen, Leo? Was that why you came to me?"

"It seemed fairly certain early on that Voler would be involved, yes," Cavan admitted. "The job dovetails well with his own personal agenda."

Keene nodded without needing to be told what Cavan meant. Voler's credentials and professional ambitions had made him the ideal for Fey to turn to when Keene committed the great betrayal of turning his back on the prospects of social eminence and distinction in academia. Keene had suspected a certain bedazzlement on Fey's part in that direction before he announced his decision, but he hadn't made an issue of it since his guess had been that she wouldn't be around for too much longer after that in any case. Voler's sights at that time had been set on becoming Director of Observational Astronomy at NASA, which meant running all their ground-based, orbiting, and lunar observatories. The position was coveted by several notable figures in the academic world, and success in the current task of defeating the Kronian mission would significantly improve his chances.

"Have you been keeping track of him over the years since your paths crossed?" Cavan inquired.

"Oh, come on, Leo," Keene snorted. "Why should I have? You know I got out of all that. I've got better things to do than play the jealous, stalking ex. In any case, I wasn't jealous."

"His pet scheme that he's been trying to get Congressional action on is for a new federal overseeing agency to coordinate all major research in government, the academic centers, and major industrial labs," Cavan said. "With himself chairing the supervisory board, of course."

"Of course," Keene agreed sarcastically. "We really need another one."

"Ah, yes. But the line he's pushing is that science has been getting sloppy, letting in New Age and Mother-Earth mystics, and what's needed is an office with clout that can clean up the faith and reinstate proper discipline. He's got the ear of a lot of people with problems they can blame on deteriorating scientific standards. So you can see what an opportunity this Kronian situation is for him to show everyone he's the man for the job. And it would be particularly valuable to him at the present time, in view of his bid to become NASA's astronomy supremo. He has the support of the academics, but there are other rivals that many of the scientists within NASA itself would prefer—in JPL, for example."

Keene nodded. "I heard something about that from Salio. So where does this call to him from Maria . . . Hutchill come into it?" he asked again.

"She's a disciple in the cause," Cavan replied. "If Herbert makes it big-time, she flies high too. I just happen to have a recording of the call. . . ." Keene shook his head but said nothing.

The screen split vertically to show Salio on one side, and a woman speaking in front of a background of bookshelves and part of a window on the other. Showing just his mop of black hair and heavy-rimmed spectacles, with no jeans or cowboy boots to offset the image, Salio looked even more the student than when Keene had met him. Hutchill was probably in her thirties, a little on the plump side with rounded features, and short, unpretentiously cut hair. Her eyes had a sharp look, however, and her voice was firmer than her appearance would have suggested. Keene sensed a potential antagonism being consciously kept under restraint.

"Dr. Salio?"

"Yes."

"I hope I'm not calling at a bad time. Do you have a few minutes?"

"Not if it's insurance, siding, or you want to lend me money."

Hutchill forced a smile. "No, I'm not selling anything. My name is Dr. Hutchill, from the Department of Astronomy at Yale. It's in connection with the plan to put you on the show with Coast-to-Coast."

Salio looked more interested. "Well, it's not exactly firm yet."

"Yes, I understand that. What I'm concerned with is getting an idea of the probable content to assess its suitability."

"Oh . . . okay. What would you like to know?"

"Note how she's giving the impression of being connected with the show as if she's some kind of official advisor," Cavan put in from his side of the screen.

"Yes, I did pick that up," Keene replied.

The conversation opened with a trading of views on theories of the formation and stability of the Solar System. Salio was candid in the way he had been with Keene, maintaining a humorous note and declining to be unduly deferential. Eventually, they closed over the matter of comets originating from Jupiter. Hutchill's manner became more penetrating. The issue, basically, was whether the shower of new comets that had been born with Athena provided adequate evidence that the previously existing short-period comets—the ones with aphelia showing a statistical clustering at the distance of Jupiter's orbit—had originated in a similar episode involving Venus. Salio's answer was, sure they did. You didn't need the other mechanisms that been speculated about over the years and could throw them away. Hutchill was determined to see them as exceptions.

"There simply aren't grounds for making such a sweeping generalization on the basis of an event that has been observed only once," she insisted. "You're ignoring the transfer of long-period comets to short-period trajectories by perturbation, which is still the dominant process on any significant time scale."

Salio grinned, evidently having expected it. "That's what the textbooks say," he agreed. "But when has it been observed even once? I can point you to a string of papers going back to before 1900 which show that such a mechanism isn't viable. It's a myth that has been exposed now for well over a hundred years."

Displeasure showed through Hutchill's demeanor for the first time. "I think I'd advise caution before dismissing something that's so widely accepted," she said.

"But if acceptance were the thing to go by, then a popular but wrong theory could never be changed," Salio pointed out. "Let's try plausibility instead. All the estimates that I've seen agree that the probability of Jupiter deflecting incoming comets from vast distances on parabolic orbits to an elliptical one is about one in a hundred thousand. So that's the ratio of short-period to long-period that you ought to get. In fact what you have is close to sixteen percent. The number of long-periods is far too small. How many comets are there in the Jupiter family—about seventy? And the typical lifetime would be what . . . four thousand years?"

"Hmm. . . . Maybe."

"Let's take that figure, then, and suppose that Jupiter has to replenish them by capturing long-period arrivals at the rate of one in a hundred thousand. To give seventy in four thousand years would require seven million long-period arrivals, which works out at seventeen-hundred-fifty a year, or five every day. Allowing for the transit time in and out of the Solar System would give us about nine thousand present

in the sky by my calculations, of which let's say half
would be brighter than average. A pretty spectacular sky." He shrugged and waved a hand, seemingly
enjoying himself. "So where are they? And then
you've got the problem that all of the short-periods
orbit the Sun in the same direction as the planets,
as they should if they came from Jupiter. But by
capture, some should be retrograde—in theory half
of them. You see, the numbers just don't work out."

"Sufficient long-term comets can be produced by
periodic disturbances of the Oort Cloud, as I'm sure
you're aware," Hutchill said.

Cavan interjected, "It's the same as what I'm supposed to be doing with the Kronians. She's leading
him on to sound out his arguments. The idea is to
have one of their own people on the show as well,
ready to take him on in a debate."

"She looks like she might be getting more of a
debate than she expected," Keene commented. "This
guy's good."

On the screen, Salio's grin had broadened. "What
Oort Cloud?" he challenged. "It's never been actually
observed, has it? And it's supposed to extend maybe
halfway to Centauri. Comets from interstellar distances would arrive on wide hyperbolic orbits. The
short-period comets that they're supposed to turn
into don't exhibit the distribution of orbits and
inclinations you'd expect from an all-sky parent
population."

"I wasn't referring to short-period," Hutchill said
shortly. "They are postulated as coming from the
Kuiper Belt, near the planetary plane."

"Postulated," Salio echoed. "You've still got the
problem of velocity mismatch, which tells against
capture. Whatever way you look at it, the number of
short-periods is still far too high."

"Dark matter in the galactic disk would put more
of them onto an injection trajectory," Hutchill said.

Salio's face registered delight. "So now we have an unobserved Oort Cloud and a postulated Kuiper Belt that's influenced by invisible dark matter. And even if all of them existed, they wouldn't produce the distribution and prograde consistency that we see. Yet what the Kronians are proposing fits all the facts without any inventions. All you have to do is throw out some ideas you've grown up with. So isn't it time we changed the textbooks?"

The rest of the exchange went into more details that didn't change the essentials. Hutchill ended by thanking Salio for his time and hanging up visibly disturbed.

"Interesting," Keene pronounced when Cavan had expanded back to fill the screen. "It's going to be quite a show. Are they just going to let it go, do you think? She obviously wasn't happy. What can they do?"

"All I'm going to say at this point is, don't underestimate anything," Cavan replied. "And that was really why I called. Your man is bright and knows his stuff, Landen, but he's too trusting. Maybe it's just his way of telling the world that he has nothing to hide, but it's giving the opposition a lot of free information. The Kronians make the same mistake consistently."

"You want me to talk to him?" Keene asked.

"Precisely. I can't intervene—you know my situation. But someone should wise him up a little on the ways of the world. In particular, caution him on who he talks to and how much he says to people he doesn't know. If he's going to take on the big guys in front of a couple of hundred million people, he needs to learn something about the rules."

But then Keene became embroiled in last-minute details connected with the impending space shot, and somehow he never did get around to calling Salio before the day arrived for the launch.

15

The coverage that the San Saucillo launch received, and the distances over which throngs came to join in the protest, suggested coordination on a national scale. By early morning, the site was already besieged by crowds disgorged from cars, trucks, and campers that had been arriving all night. Tents and sunshades had been set up, several bands were in action, and the atmosphere would have approached that of a rock festival were it not for the angry undertones and the cordon of state and county police and vehicles maintaining a perimeter. Amspace security reported that the approach by road was problematical, and the sheriff was calling on the company to act with minimum provocation. Accordingly, Keene and Vicki were directed to the Kingsville plant to join the rest of the flight complement who were not already at the launch site, and lifted out by helicopter.

Keene looked down somber-faced as the administration and assembly buildings of the San Saucillo site came into view ahead. The launch area itself was situated two miles farther west, at the far end of the landing field with its two vehicle transporter tracks running along one side. Although some problems had been reported with groups trying to breach the security fence marking the two-mile safety zone south, west, and north of the pad area, the crowds were mainly concentrated around the east end of the complex and its approach road. As the helicopter descended, a ripple of hand-waving and gesturing followed it among the upturned faces below. In some places, signs that were being displayed were turned to point upward, although it was impossible to make out what they said. The pilot commenced a pattern of evasive weaving.

"What's happening?" Vicki asked tensely from her seat next to Keene.

"Just a routine precaution. It isn't always like this, you know. You just picked a bad day for your first space hop."

"The story of my life. It never fails."

They landed among an assortment of helicopters and small aircraft on the concrete apron in front of the control building at the end of the landing field. A raucous cadence of several thousand voices chanting in unison reached them from the far side of the main gate and the perimeter fence as they boarded the bus waiting to take them to the assembly and flight preparation area. There was a little under three hours to go before the scheduled launch time.

In one of the admin buildings they met the others who would be going. There were twelve in all: the regular test crew of three, expanded to include Wally Lomack and another engineer from the design team named Tim; Keene and Vicki; and the five winners of the Amspace lottery. They were: Milton Clowes, the financial vice president; Alice Myers from one of the secretarial offices, already uncontrollably jittery—she said the only reason she was doing it was to keep face with her three teenage children; Les Urkin's assistant, Jenny Grewe—much to the chagrin of Les, who had missed by one number; Phil Forely from marketing; and a new hire to the Navigation Systems Group, Sid Vance, who was barely out of college and had been with the firm less than a month. All of the five, like Vicki, would be making their first trip into space.

After changing from regular clothes into flight suits and taking time for a snack, they met with representatives from the mission management team for a final briefing and update. Weather conditions were good at the downrange emergency abort sites in Florida and Algeria, and a "Go" was expected. Demonstrators on the north side of the pads had attempted to compromise the launch by crossing the boundary river in boats, but were being contained by police landed from choppers. The group went back out to the bus and left the main complex to be driven along the edge of the airfield, beside the tracks that carried the heavy vehicle-transporter platforms to the pad area.

For the most part they were quiet as the spires of silver and white ahead loomed closer and taller. By the time they arrived and climbed out from the bus, service trucks and other vehicles were beginning to pick up and withdraw. Ground crew conducted them to the access elevator and across the entry bridge when they emerged a hundred feet above the ground. Minutes later, they were securing themselves into harnesses to settle down for what Keene knew from previous experiences could be the Long Wait—although the latest update was that they were still on schedule. The ground crew who had come aboard to make final checks left the cabin, and the lock was closed. TV shots from outside showed the last vehicles filling up and departing.

In the forward stations, the captain and flight engineer exchanged prelaunch jargon and offhand remarks with ground control. Farther back and below, in the passenger section of the cabin, the first-timers cracked nervous inanities to show they weren't nervous. Beside Keene, Vicki looked around the cramped surroundings of bulkheads, control panels, equipment racks, and cabling. A whirr of machinery sounded through the structure, followed by the clunk of a hatch closing somewhere. "We need your seven-dee markoff," a voice said from a speaker up front.

"Roger," the captain replied. "We have, ah, seven-oh-ten, nineteen-zero-four, and . . . four-six showing on two and five-one on ten."

"Okay, gotcha."

"And how's it going with the Oilers and the Bears? Any news?"

"Let's see . . . last we had was Oilers ahead by six points."

"Yeah, right-on!"

"*Guys!*" Vicki breathed.

Keene grinned. "Life's great once you weaken."

"I think some of it must be rubbing off. I mean, what am I doing here, Lan? You let them strap you to the top of a ten-story bomb that nobody who knows what's going on will stay within two miles of. . . . Is that the kind of behavior that would normally qualify as sane?"

"*Women!*" Keene threw back. He made an appealing gesture to Wally, strapped in farther across, who had heard and was smiling. "For years she gives me a hard time about wanting to come on a mission. Now I'm getting one for bringing her. What does a guy do?"

The captain's voice came over the internal address speaker. "Attention, folks. We've had a slight hold because of the trouble on the north perimeter, but things seem to be under control there now. We're looking at a little over fifteen minutes. The skies are pretty clear across most of North Africa and Asia. We should get some good views."

Places halfway around the world, Keene reflected as he lay back in the harness, waiting. He had expected he might get used to the thought, but he never had. It hadn't been so long ago when people had spent years of their lives traveling distances like that; now they were talking as nonchalantly as if it were a bus ride. In a way it would be little more than just that. The boost into orbit would be measured in minutes; then there would follow nine circuits around Earth for testing the hybrid engine and putting the shuttle through its paces; a day's visit to the *Osiris*; and then back down in time for dinner tomorrow. The Kronians were already talking about going anywhere in the Solar System in ninety days.

Vicki seemed to be thinking along similar lines. "You know, we've worked together all this time," she said to Keene. "I think I'm only starting to realize how frustrating it must be to believe in something as much as you do and have so much of the world not understanding it. Especially when they all stand to gain in the long run."

"Hm. . . . Yes, I think Christ and Giordano Bruno probably knew the feeling," Keene said.

"When I was at Harvard, we had the same kind of thing. It was practically impossible to convince people that low radiation levels are not only harmless but essential for health. We used to call it Vitamin R."

"Should I look for it in the health food store?" Clowes asked from the far side behind Wally.

Anxieties rose as the countdown entered its final phase, and the cabin fell silent. The crew recited their final check dialogue with control. And then the voice from the speaker up front was sounding off the final seconds.

Liftoff came with an all-enveloping roar and sudden force squashing the occupants back in the seat moldings. Vicki's hand groped over the armrest instinctively to find Keene's, and squeezed. A screen in front showed the craft sliding up past the gantry amid clouds of red and white smoke, while another gave a more distant view of it emerging on top of a column of light, with demonstrators on their feet, waving and gesticulating in the foreground. The force intensified, stretching flesh back over face bones. Ground fell away and was replaced by ocean. And already—Keene never ceased to be amazed at how rapidly the perspective changed—the outline of the Gulf was taking shape, glimpsed in parts below an immense whirl of banded cloud. Up front, the exchange between dispassionate voices and ground control continued. The boosters detached and fell away to deploy extendable wings for remote-piloting down to a recovery field in Cuba, while the orbiter engine continued driving the main vessel faster and higher. Florida and the Caribbean passed by below, followed by the huge, unfolding, speckled expanse of the Atlantic. . . .

Suddenly, the sound inside the cabin cut and was replaced by stillness and quiet. It was if they had been transported from the world of humans and machines to some different, ethereal realm. The shuttle was no longer a creature of violence fighting its way free from gravity, but floated serenely now—content, seemingly; at ease in the element it was meant for. The pressure that had pinned everyone immobile was no more. Gradually, the hum of unseen machinery and the subdued hiss of air being drawn into the extraction filters impressed themselves as the only sound breaking the silence. Then the captain's voice came again over the internal circuit:

"That's it, folks. Welcome to orbit."

The faces in the passenger compartment looked about them wonderingly. Milton Clowes let his arms hang weightless in the air in front of him. "Well, I'll be darned," he told the others. "Look at that."

Alice finally let go of her armrests, which she had gripped, white-faced throughout the launch. "I don't believe we're still here," was all she could manage.

"How many times is this for you, Wally?" Tim, the engineer who was with Lomack, asked.

"I don't know. I've lost count. I thought I'd retired from any more of this kind of nonsense."

The captain spoke again: "Yes, I know the first thing you're all dying to try is the zero-g. Anyone who feels inclined to experiment now, go right ahead. Take it easy, though. It works better than you think. People who turn into missiles inside here don't make themselves too popular." It was just a reminder. They had been through it all in the preflight briefings.

The passengers exchanged glances. None of them really wanted to be the first to risk being a spectacle. Finally, Vicki felt for the buckle securing her harness, then hesitated and gave Keene a questioning look. He nodded encouragingly. "Nobody here's gonna laugh," he told her.

She released the catch and eased herself cautiously out of the harness to float above the gee-couch, turning slowly. A touch on the cabin wall stopped her and sent her turning the other way; a push on the wall made her drift toward Wally. Clowes gave her some handclaps by way of applause, and a couple of the others followed.

"This is fantastic!" Vicki told them as she started to get the feel of it. "It's like being a whale with a whole ocean to frolic in. I want to leap and dive."

"Doesn't it make all that business back at the complex seem kind of unimportant now?" Jenny Grewe mused distantly. Vicki drifted down the center of the cabin, turning in a slow cartwheel.

"Hey, that looks cool," Phil Forely said. "I have to try it too."

One of the flight crew had unhitched and was moving back. "Okay, but let me give you a few tips first," he told them. "Just a couple of you at a time, guys. You'll all get a turn, don't worry."

Keene had seen it enough times to leave them to it for a while. He turned his eyes back toward the screen in front and watched the image of the deserts of northeast Africa and the Middle East passing by below. So much had been written about the proliferation of life on Earth. But the planet's real potential for life had never been really grasped because in recent times there had been nothing to give a measure of it. Earth was still only recovering from its devastation.

He remembered how, years ago, when he first started making regular airline flights eastward from the West Coast, it had amazed him that after leaving the oases of human habitation around San Diego, Los Angeles, or the San Francisco Bay Area, there would be nothing for a thousand miles to the Mississippi valley—just parched mountains, deserts, and canyons; everywhere, the dryness. It was only later, when he began grasping the true scale of the planet by seeing it from orbit, that he realized that had been just a small part of the picture. The vastness of the wildernesses extending from Mauritania on the Atlantic side of Africa to Afghanistan, then onward through Mongolia, and in the southern hemisphere, those of southwestern Africa and virtually all of Australia, staggered the imagination.

It hadn't always been that way. There had been times when the Sahara was green, Arabia and Iran fertile; what were now the deserts of northwest India and Afghanistan had supported flourishing civilizations. The Sphinx was older than the great pyramids and showed water damage and erosion that couldn't be accounted for by the conditions that had existed through recorded history.

What it all pointed to was that Earth's climatic bands had been different then, with narrower tropics and broader temperate zones that had brought rain where there are now deserts and caused grasslands and forests to extend into what is today the Arctic. Such conditions were consistent with the Earth's axis being more perpendicular to its orbital plane around the Sun. Something, then, had caused it to shift and increased the planet's tilt, creating the northern and southern desert belts and extending the polar regions.

The flight crew got busy commencing the engine trials that had been the original purpose of the mission. Wally and Tim spent much of the time forward, following events, and Keene got involved in the technical proceeding, too. Vicki made the best of the opportunity to get to know more Amspace people. She seemed to get along especially well with Jenny, Les Urkin's assistant in public relations, Alice, and Phil from Marketing. Sid, the new hire straight out of college, was still too mesmerized by the torrent of events that had overtaken him to be capable of much coherent thought.

"Are things always like this here?" he asked when the group was struggling to master their first peel-wrappered, squeeze-bottle lunch. "I mean, after the way things were at Berkeley, I expected life in the commercial world to be kind of dull. They haven't found me a permanent desk yet, and I'm in orbit already."

Later, he got to talking with Vicki, and then her and Keene, about the Kronian theories and Keene's work with Amspace. Sid was enthusiastic about space development, which was why he had sought a position with Amspace in the first place, but he'd had no inkling of the deeper implications of what was at stake. It all came as a revelation, which he devoured avidly. A solid recruit to the cause, Keene decided.

However, as hours passed by and the novelty wore thinner, weariness akin to that of a long airline flight

set in. While at the forward end of the compartment the voice exchanges with ground control at San
Saucillo and other stations monitoring the flight
continued against a background of electronic beeps
and bursts of static, conversation in the rear section lapsed. Some of the passengers dozed or tried
to read. About halfway through the mission the
Osiris made contact to get confirmation that the
Amspace vessel would be on schedule; also, there
was a message for Keene from Sariena letting him
know that she would be one of the Kronians up
resting from terrestrial gravity while his party was
visiting. Soon after, he found himself with Vicki and
Sid, watching yet another turn of the globe sliding
by on the cabin screen.

"Did I tell you that Robin got an e-mail from
Salio?" Vicki asked. "My eternally curious fourteen-
year-old son," she added for Sid's benefit. They had
told Sid about Salio briefly when talking about the
Kronians' planetary theories.

"I don't think so. He said he would," Keene said.

"Robin was thrilled to bits. Salio knocked a few
holes in his dinosaur theory, but it was nice of him
to find the time to respond." She explained to Sid,
"Robin came up with this idea that the dinosaurs were
on the body that impacted Earth, since he doesn't
think they could have existed in Earth's gravity."

Sid pulled a face. "A bit farfetched, isn't it?"

"Give him a break. He's fourteen."

"David Salio's an okay guy," Keene said. "He's going
to be dynamite on the shows . . . which reminds me,
I was supposed to call him." He thought for a
moment about calling Salio right there, from orbit,
but then decided that the topic wasn't appropriate for
an audience. "You never did tell me this business
about Robin and the mammoths, either," he told Vicki
instead.

"Oh, that's right. I never did, did I?"

"He's not saying that they came from someplace else too, surely?" Sid said.

Vicki shook her head. "Oh no. It's just that in following his inquisitiveness, he stumbled on a lot of controversy that's been going on for years—that even I didn't know about—about when they died out."

Keene made an inviting gesture. "Well, we're listening. I always thought it was supposed to have had something to do with over-hunting."

"Somewhere around ten or eleven thousand years ago, wasn't it?" Sid said.

"That's the conventional line," Vicki agreed. "That date was thought to have been soon after the arrival of people. But now it seems pretty certain that humans were in the Americas much earlier. So they and the mammoths had coexisted for a long time. That theory doesn't really hold up."

"I never thought it made much sense, anyway," Keene said. "Elephants are notoriously dangerous and difficult to bring down even by hunters equipped with iron and horses. But they were never hunted to extinction. Yet a sparse population armed with stone-tipped spears was supposed to have done it? All those millions of mammoths, mastodons, giant deer, you name it . . . piled up in thousands in some places? They'd have needed nuclear weapons."

Vicki looked at him dubiously. "So why are you asking me about them? It sounds like you pretty much know the problem already."

"It was something I came across when I got interested in evidence for catastrophes," Keene said. "I was curious to hear Robin's take on it. What else did he come up with?"

"Do you know about varves?"

"No. What are varves?"

"Layers of sediment that are deposited in lakes and so on, which change color from summer to winter and can be counted like tree rings. They contain pollen grains, which tell you what vegetation grew in the area over the years. And in the Arctic during the Ice Age, which is when standard thinking says the mammoths and all those other animals were supposed to have been around, there simply wasn't anything growing there that they could have lived on. It was all just frozen desert."

Keene nodded, at the same time looking puzzled. "Well . . . okay. What else would anyone expect to find in the Arctic in an Ice Age? Am I missing something?"

"I sometimes wonder if I am," Vicki said. "Do they really make people professors for coming up with ideas that it could have been different?"

Sid looked from one of them to the other. "So what it sounds like you're saying is, when the mammoths and all those other animals did live there, it couldn't have been an Ice Age."

Vicki nodded. "Exactly.

"So when was that? Do we know?"

"It has to have been during a much warmer period that came later," Vicki said. "They couldn't have been buried eleven thousand years ago under Arctic conditions. The soil below a few feet down is permanently frozen. So how could all those bodies and bones and trunks of trees have been buried under it? A few might have been caught by things like slides and collapsing crevasses, maybe, but nothing on the scale that's found. And even if they did, nonfossilized bones and body tissue would never have survived degradation through thousands of years when the warming occurred. So they must have been wiped out and quick-frozen much more recently, in some event that marked the end of that warm period."

Keene and Sid looked as if each was waiting for the other to fault it. It seemed that neither of them readily could. "What about carbon-14 dating?" Sid asked finally. "I thought that supports the Ice-Age extinction theory."

"The data that have been published over the years do," Vicki conceded. "But now it's beginning to look as if maybe the indicated dates were too high."

"How's that?" Keene asked.

"The Arctic has huge natural carbon reservoirs—permafrost soil, peat deposits, methane hydrate in the oceans—that would release lots of carbon dioxide into the atmosphere if a mild warming occurred for any reason. We're talking about billions of tons a year. . . . And that 'old' carbon would be breathed and ingested and find its way into plant and animal tissues, making all the dates too high if today's levels with a cooler climate are assumed as the reference."

"How do you know the climate's cooler today?" Keene challenged.

"We don't have big herds of large animals inhabiting the Arctic today."

Keene stared at her. There it was again. If the conventionally accepted dates were high by a significant factor, then once again they were led to the conclusion of tremendous and destructive happenings worldwide around that same mysterious time, several thousand years ago.

Sid drifted away across the cabin to listen to Clowes telling Alice and Jenny some anecdotes from Amspace's history. Keene and Vicki remained buckled into the restraint harnesses in one of the corners, watching the screen. They talked about the time when she had left Harvard after he and Fey split up, and the support they'd found in each other that had led her to follow him south when he set up the consulting deal that had grown into Protonix. They talked about Karen's succession of cowboy boyfriends, Judith's odd mix of talents and even odder-seeming engagement, about David Salio and his case for Venus, and Celia's cat. Keene was glad to have a chance for once to ramble on with Vicki about whatever took their fancy, free from the pressures that never seemed to let up when they were in or anywhere near the firm. The loyalty that she had always shown to everything he did and the things he believed in had played a big part in enabling him to keep going through the rough parts, but he had never found a way of expressing adequately how much it had meant. Hence, it was gratifying that he had been able to keep his word to get her up on one of the missions one day, even if whenever he mentioned it he had made it sound like a joke. Flippancy came naturally as part of his armor for dealing with the world, and sometimes, he feared, brought the risk of having things like promises not taken seriously. It was nice, even if over so small a thing, to be able to feel that it wasn't so.

16

The UN shuttle that had brought the Kronians up from the surface was in the process of detaching from the *Osiris* when the Amspace vessel arrived, climbing from a lower orbit. The captain waited several miles off in a matching orbit while the maneuver was completed.

As well as being larger than the types of craft that Keene was used to, the *Osiris* had a unique variable geometry design that combined linear and rotational accelerations to provide a normal internal gravity simulation whether the vessel was in freefall or under drive. Its basic form was of a wheel attached to one end of an axle. The axle formed the main body of the vessel and was shaped like an old-fashioned potato masher, with a handle projecting from one end of a thicker cylinder. The "handle" consisted of the reactant tanks and propulsion system, while forward of it, the "masher" section contained other heavy equipment, cargo bays, and the docking port. Four booms projecting radially from the masher carried the accommodation modules at their ends and were interconnected by a circular communication tube to complete the wheel. The booms pivoted freely to trail back like the spokes of an umbrella when the craft was under acceleration, the angle automatically finding a value such that, whatever the combined motion, the resultant of the forces generated by rotation and forward thrust was always perpendicular to the decks. Telescopic sections in the connecting ring compensated for changes in the wheel's circumference when the trailing angle of the booms altered. The engineers among those studying the details on the screen aboard the minishuttle were impressed. "It makes you wonder if those guys out there are still taking applications," Tim commented to Keene.

Eventually, the UN craft cleared the vicinity and fired a retro burn to begin falling back toward Earth, and the Amspace minishuttle was cleared to approach. Its lock connected with a coupling extended from the *Osiris*'s front-end docking port, and minutes later the occupants were hauling themselves along guide rails into the Kronian ship.

Two Kronians who introduced themselves as Baur and Semad were waiting for them. The first item on the agenda would be an introductory tour of the hub and propulsion section while they were in the central body of the ship, they informed the visitors; after that, they would ascend one of the boom elevators to meet Captain Idorf and the other Kronians in the Command Module, which was the only module being occupied while the *Osiris* was parked in Earth orbit. Refreshments would be available there, in the crew messroom.

In many ways the maze of galleries, shafts, and machinery compartments was reminiscent of Space Dock. But in the unity of expression that he saw in its design—perhaps fitting for a vessel that could cross the Solar System as opposed to a service platform constructed in Earth orbit—Keene sensed a work of inspiration that had found form, rather than a collection of compromises of the kind he had seen too often, hammered out by committees working in semi-isolation to imposed deadlines. It was the difference between a chateau and a shantyville, a patchwork of trailer lots and a landscaped park. If this was an example of what a tiny colony of misfits and dissidents could do, given simply the freedom to become what they were capable of, then what, he asked himself, might the potentials of all the peoples of Earth be capable of achieving?

He and Wally had been curious about two housings on the outside of the wide end of the axle that they had noticed as the shuttle closed in. They were perhaps the size of an average automobile, located diametrically opposite each other at the rear end of the wider hub section, overlooking the projecting spindle forming the tail. They didn't seem to be communications mountings or external tanks, and seemed unrelated to the propulsion system. The locations seemed unlikely places to put machinery associated with the spoke elevators, and they seemed too small to accommodate independent vehicles of some kind, say for external maintenance.

Keene had more or less forgotten about them and was lagging behind the others to study the layout of an instrumentation bay that they were passing through, when a low voice sounded from a short distance behind him. *"Hey, Lan."* Keene turned and looked back. Wally had drifted off the route and gone through a steel door to one side that he had apparently tried and found open. Now he had come back to the opening and was beckoning. "What do you make of this?"

Keene aimed himself in a slow bound through the microgravity and peered inside. Most of the chamber was taken up by what looked like some kind of hoist mechanism connecting from an enclosed structure below, visible through a stairwell beneath ducting and floor plates. There was more machinery above, crammed into the base of something extending upward. Keene looked back the way they had come, reconstructing in his mind the route they had taken and estimating distances. Unless he was mistaken, they had to be right under one of the strange housings.

Wally indicated the walls of the structure they could see part of below. "Look at the thickness of those sections there and all over there . . . and those panels under the walkway. We're in a hub location here—built for permanent virtual zero-g, right?" He looked at Keene oddly. "This isn't for structural strength, Lan. It's containment. But what's it doing here?"

Keene was a nuclear engineer too, and recognized radiation shielding when he saw it. As Wally had said, the layout didn't add up. They were in the wrong part of the ship for it to have any connection with the propulsion reactors or fuel and waste storage. He looked around, trying to make sense of it. There were signs reading LAUNCH COOLANT, EMERGENCY FLOOD VALVE, and AUTO EJECT. A panel at what appeared to be a local control station carried the legends: *Door Sequence, Inner/Outer, Destruct Override, Acquisition/Director.* Before he had a chance to voice any thought, however, Baur came hurrying back, obviously looking for them.

"That door should be secured. . . . You shouldn't be in there." His voice was short. He seemed agitated.

"Oh . . . sorry." Wally came out, smiling. "I wasn't sure which way you'd gone."

Baur closed and fastened the door, entering a code into its electronic lock. "There's nothing to see in there anyway," he said, ushering them to follow the rest of the party. "Just auxiliary power plant."

Not saying anything, Keene and Wally exchanged glances as they moved on. Each read the same in the other's eye. The *Osiris* was armed. And whatever the weaponry was that it was carrying, it had been devised with a lot more in mind than turkey shoots.

❖   ❖   ❖

Idorf, not long back from visiting the surface himself, was waiting on the Control Deck with a female officer called Dayda, the remaining member of the skeleton crew, to welcome the visitors. He was characteristically tall, with a lean build bordering on scrawny, a mop of unruly reddish hair, and one of the few beards, short and ragged, that Keene recalled seeing on a Kronian. His face was hollow-cheeked and hawklike, but was saved from an appearance of gauntness by the unwavering eyes and a ruddy, weathered-looking complexion that was perplexing considering the environment he was from. Keene could have pictured him as the captain of a Louisiana shrimp boat, or maybe an old-time frontier-era itinerant preacher. "I'm not yet recovered from being in a place that counts its people in billions," he told the arrivals as Baur and Semad conducted them through from the spoke elevator. "This kind of number, I think I might be able to handle."

With Idorf and Dayda, still wearing orange flight suits, were Sariena and the two other Kronians who had just transferred from the UN shuttle. One of them was called Vashen—a planetary scientist with the delegation, whom Keene had spoken to briefly at Gallian's reception. The other was Thorel, the crew member that Keene had also met on that occasion. Thorel waved an arm to indicate the surroundings. "So you come to see some quality engineering at last, eh, Dr. Keene?" he joked. "Here we can move. Not like those doll-house spaceships you make us squeeze into." Keene couldn't argue with that. Designed for people of Kronian proportions, the *Osiris* was spacious compared to Terran-built craft.

There was a round of introductions for those who had not already met, and then Idorf showed the way to the messroom where the food and drink had been laid out. A lot of it looked familiar, presumably shipped up. It seemed that Earth food was a hit with the Kronians. Rather than make speeches and have his guests paraded around like tourists, Idorf left them to mingle and wander off to be shown other parts of the ship as suited their interests. Wally and Tim stayed with the Amspace crew to learn more from Idorf and Dayda about the *Osiris's* control and communications systems. The other five Amspace people, with Baur, Semad, and Thorel, drifted off in smaller groups, which left Keene and Vicki with Sariena. The two women knew each other from video exchanges while the *Osiris* was in transit, and for a while they swapped small talk while getting better acquainted. Keene thought that Sariena looked surprisingly fresh for having just been through the rigmarole of launch and the flight up. He said so, wondering if it was due to her being out of surface gravity or escaping from the demands of the official schedule. "Just being back in familiar surroundings after so much strangeness," she told him. "The *Osiris* got to feel like a second home during the voyage out. It probably seems like metal boxes full of pipes to you, but we lived here for almost three months."

"Was Earth really so much stranger than you expected?" Vicki asked curiously.

"I'm still awed by the sheer numbers of people wherever you go," Sariena replied. "We all are. Nothing in Kronia prepares you for that. You see the pictures, yes, but there's a . . . a *mood* created by so many being present all together in the same place, that you *feel* only from being there. . . . And the ocean! Hour after hour of it. I never imagined so much water existed in the universe. The waves at the beach in Hawaii were terrifying."

"Was the gravity very tiring?" Keene asked her.

"Well, I won't pretend it isn't nice to be back up in the ship. But I've had an easier time than some of us. I think that having been born on Earth must make a difference."

"Do you find you've remembered much?" Vicki asked.

"Not as much as I thought I had. A lot of what I thought I remembered must have been imagination." Sariena moved a few paces away and turned, flexing her arms and stretching her head back as if exhilarated by not being weighed down anymore. "I also have feelings that the talks with your governments will go well. The people we've met had a lot of questions. The preliminary tour was a good idea, even if a bit exhausting."

Keene frowned as he listened. No doubt the people asking the questions had been informants placed close to the Kronians in the way Cavan had described. The Kronians didn't seem to be picking up on the negative rumblings sounding in the media, or else they were being shielded from them. He couldn't see them dealing adeptly with Earth-style politics. It wasn't that they were incapable, so much as never having needed to learn how. Their politics back home—or whatever word better described the managing of Kronian social affairs—presumably worked differently.

"How are those orbital calculations going?" Sariena asked.

"What's the latest from Judith?" Keene asked Vicki.

"There were a few delays, but the last I heard was that we could be seeing some of the results anytime," she replied.

Sariena looked around. "We don't have to stay here among things that you see every day. Come on. Let me show you more of the Command Module . . . and something spectacular."

They left the messroom to reenter the Control Deck and walked along one side, past a row of empty crew stations. Sariena described the functions briefly, giving Keene and Vicki an idea of the *Osiris*'s operating procedures. At the far end was a cross-passage with metal stairwells leading to levels above and below. Beyond, they descended some steps into a recess containing low tables with padded seats set around and against the wall, where the low lighting contrasted abruptly with the brightness they had just left. It seemed to be a kind of viewing gallery, perhaps a rest area, with one wall of glass looking out at the slowly wheeling stars. The window was on the module's forward side, with no other part of the *Osiris*'s structure in sight.

"I don't know how much you got to see from the shuttle," Sariena said. "But this has only become visible in the last few hours. Wait . . ." The sky turned for about a quarter of a minute. Then, the shadows inside the gallery sharpened as the Sun came into view low on the right. The window material darkened to suppress the glare as the light intensified, revealing the sharp edge of the solar disk. One side of it had what appeared to be a bump, from which a finger of whiteness streamed away fully half the width of the window, pointing almost horizontally left. "Athena, just emerging," Sariena said. "The tail is over thirty million miles long now."

Keene and Vicki stared, spellbound. After the close pass at perihelion the tail would be at its longest. They were seeing it virtually from the side as it pointed away from the Sun. In the following month its tip would sweep past Earth like a searchlight as Athena swung into its return path, growing even more spectacular as it crossed Earth's orbit fifteen million miles ahead.

"We saw a shot of it on the screen but it was nothing like this," Vicki murmured, not taking her eyes of the scene. "And you're right. That was a few hours back, and it's grown even in that time."

"How does this compare to when we were looking at the stars in Washington, Lan?" Sariena asked. She studied the sky as the Sun and Athena disappeared from view at the top of the window and the glass lightened again. "I don't think we'll be able to see Saturn this time, though—not from this side of Earth, anyway. You know, it's strange. I still haven't gotten used to seeing it looking so small."

"Tell me something about life there," Vicki said. "I've never quite followed it. You have all those talented people moving out. What is it they're looking for? Do they find it?"

"People have always sought something bigger than themselves," Sariena replied. "Something that will give their lives meaning that makes sense, that will still be there after they're gone. Why else did medieval masons pass their skills down through sons to grandsons who would complete the cathedrals that they began?"

Keene turned his face away from the window. "Is that really true? I don't know. It sounds too idealistic, somehow. . . . I thought ideas like that pretty much went out of style two hundred years ago."

"True, for the most part," Sariena agreed. "And look at the disaster that followed. The civilization that could have enlightened the world degenerated into conflicts of squabbling fanatics. Humanity should have become a vigorous, spacegoing culture by now, expanding across the Solar System and gathering itself for the move out to the stars. Instead, it has turned back within itself. We represent what could have been, and we're considered misfits. But there are some from Earth who will never succumb to whatever the disease is. And so they come to us."

"Maybe you're in too much of a hurry," Keene suggested. "Earth is tired. It's played its part. Maybe the culture you're talking about will have to grow from Kronia. But that won't be for a while."

"Maybe."

There was a silence. Keene got the feeling that Sariena didn't entirely agree but was not of a mind to press the subject just at the moment.

"So how does it work?" Vicki asked. "You all have

this shared vision, and that somehow provides an alternative reward system to what we have? Is it something like that?"

Sariena's brow creased. "I'm not sure I know how to explain it. I have no experience of your money systems, so it's difficult to find the right terms. I don't expect any overt reward for what I do. I do the things that need to be done."

"But how do you know what's needed?" Keene asked. He was curious himself. "Money's only a common way of measuring obligations. What do you have instead? How do you know who owes what?"

"Owes? . . ." Sariena shook her head. "Owes to whom?"

"To each other, to society in general. . . ." Keene searched for an example. "Look, you told me you're a planetary geologist. That involves a lot of study and ability, knowledge, hard work. Why do you do it?"

"Why? . . . It's, simply . . . I told you. It's what needs to be done."

"But *why*?" Vicki pressed. "What's in it for you? What do *you* get in return?"

Sariena looked at them uncertainly, as if hesitant to state the obvious. "In return, I am alive. I experience life. It was not *I* who designed and built this ship that we are talking in. Others did. Others made the clothes that I wear and produced the food that sustains me. And when we return to Kronia, the same will apply to everything there that keeps me alive: the habitats we live in, the machines that provide our needs. All those things exist because of the work and skills of thousands of people. And you ask me what I get in return?" Sariena shook her head again, this time with an expression of amazement. "You want me to measure *how much* I owe in return? The only answer can be, the best that I am capable of. That is my worth."

Keene had the uncomfortable feeling that it was

something she would have expected a child to understand but was being too polite to say so. But they were too close now to so many things that he too had wondered about for a long time for him to feel offended. "But wouldn't you still have all those things if you didn't put in the effort?" he said. "I mean, what are they going to do—throw you out on the ice?"

"Of course not—no more than they would an invalid or a mental incompetent." Sariena shook her head again. "But why would anyone do that deliberately—deprive themselves of the fulfillment of being needed? That's surely what the essence of being human is all about. Has Earth really forgotten?"

Keene stared at her. The message was finally getting through.

"Kropotkin," Vicki murmured distantly. "The first base that they established on Dione was called Kropotkin, wasn't it?"

"Some Russian, oh . . . way back, wasn't he?" Keene said. He was still digesting what he had heard from Sariena.

"Peter Kropotkin," Sariena confirmed, nodding. "Mondel adopted a lot of his ideas. He was a revolutionary who tried to change the face of revolution by arguing that people need each other. The necessity of mutual aid should be sufficient to guide human affairs. On Earth, he failed. But . . ." She waved a hand resignedly and let the sentence hang. Maybe it had just needed the different environment, the gesture seemed to say.

A system that measured success by giving, not taking; where "wealth" was assessed not by possessions but by what one was able to contribute. Perhaps such a scheme came naturally in an environment where the survival of all depended on the competence of each. Keene tried to visualize what it would feel like to be part of such an order, to be motivated by its values. But he was unable. He didn't have the conditioning.

Inwardly, he was also skeptical. Such utopian-sounding ideas had been tried through the ages—often with some success in the early phases—but always, invariably, as numbers grew, the ideals of the founders became diluted, and the realities of human nature asserted themselves, such experiments had ended in eventual strife and disintegration. Maybe, as Sariena said, in a new environment removed from Earth and its legacies from the past, the social dynamics could evolve differently. Time would tell.

Vicki seemed fascinated. Perhaps being away from Earth for the first time and seeing it in a new perspective against the vastness of everything else was affecting her. "Is it just a social structure?" she asked Sariena. "Or is there some deeper belief system involved too?"

"Why do you ask?"

"Oh . . . it sounds pretty close to what all the great religions tried to teach for thousands of years—originally, I mean; not the political counterfeits that always end up taking over."

"Kronia doesn't have anything like a formal church," Sariena replied. "It's more of an internal, personal thing." She waved an arm at the panorama outside. "But most of our scientists believe that all of that and our being here talking and wondering about it suggests design for a purpose more than the meaningless, impossible accident that your systems teach. It means that our sciences operate within a different intellectual climate. If you insist that 'science' only deals with the mechanical and material by definition, you might turn out to be excluding it from the only questions that really matter."

Sariena's answer surprised Keene and touched a skeptical note. "So is this intelligence behind it all the same God that armies hacked each other to pieces for, and people used to get burned at stakes over?" he asked dryly.

Sariena shook her head—a trifle impatiently. "Of

course not. Those are results of the political counterfeits that Vicki mentioned, when the heirs of a religious tradition sell out to the power structure and give them a means of social control. I doubt if the intelligence I'm talking about has any concern with the day-to-day affairs that we imagine are so important."

Keene fell silent with a nod. It was close to what had been happening with the heirs of the scientific tradition on Earth, too.

"But you think it has a purpose?" Vicki said to Sariena, before Keene could pick up on the political aspect again.

Sariena's expression became distant, highlighted by the glow from the turning pattern of stars outside. "I believe so. It all seems too directed to be otherwise: stars manufacturing elements, fine-tuned to eject them at the end of the production run; planets as assembly stations for complex organisms programmed to evolve toward the expression of consciousness; consciousness, the instrument for accumulating experiences. And if we accept whatever our role happens to be as contributing a stone to the cathedral of eventually bringing the universe to life, then maybe yes, I suppose you could say that Kronians have their religion."

All very fine idealistic stuff; but it caused Keene's misgivings to return. He just couldn't see these people negotiating effectively, Earth-style with hostilely disposed Terrans. The very concept of starting with maximum demands in return for the minimum they thought they could get away with would be alien to them. Instead, they would offer the best they could afford and expect reciprocation. It was by willingness to give, not the power to take, that they valued each other.

"Is Gallian a visionary like that too?" he asked Sariena. "You know, the people that you're going to be dealing with when you go back down there aren't going to be exactly falling over themselves to find reasons for diverting resources out to Saturn. They've got too many other concerns that are closer to home. I'd just like to be sure that Gallian is mindful of things like that."

"You sound as if you might be trying to warn me of something," Sariena said.

"It's just . . . What I'm trying to say is, attitudes here won't be the way you're used to. Hiding one's hand is considered a mark of shrewdness on Earth. You can't take everything you're told at face value."

"We have studied Terran history and ways," Sariena said.

"And that's good," Keene agreed. "But I'm not sure it can be the same as living them."

Sariena gave him a long, thoughtful look, as if she were weighing up something. Then she said, "There is something more, that we haven't made public yet or brought up with your people so far— but nobody has specifically forbidden us from talking about it. We didn't come here expecting to outdo Terrans at Terran political games. Our objective is a scientific one: to gain acceptance for our beliefs on the basis of the evidence, not through debating tricks."

Keene smiled, but with an effort not to appear condescending. "That's a nice sentiment. Maybe you manage to keep science and politics in separate compartments out at Saturn, somehow. But life here is more messy. They have this tendency to get mixed up."

"We're aware of that," Sariena said. "And that was why we chose to bring our case formally to Earth now, when we did. It wasn't just to take advantage of the Athena event—although that was certainly timely. It was to present what we think is our strongest item of proof."

Keene frowned. This was an unexpected turn. "Proof? . . . You mean about Venus being the comet of the Exodus?"

Sariena shook her head. "Much more radical than that. I'm talking about the stability of the entire Solar System, not just a single event in Earth's history. We've believed for a long time that the planets had different configurations in previous ages. Now we're certain of it." She shifted her eyes to look at Vicki, who was waiting just as intently. "Let's go back. I'll show you what I mean."

Keene and Vicki followed Sariena back the way they had come, into the deserted part of the Command Deck. She led the way to one of the consoles and activated it. The layout was unfamiliar, but a standard communications format appeared on one of the screens. "I just want to get Gallian's okay first," Sariena murmured by way of explanation. Moments later, Gallian was looking out at them.

"Sariena!" he exclaimed. "I presume you're back up in the ship by now. No problems, I trust? Have Landen and his friends arrived yet?"

"Yes. He's here with me right now, and so is Vicki."

"Ah, good. You have my unmitigated envy at being up off the surface, if only temporarily. Walking down here still makes me feel as if I am carrying a dead horse. Is that the correct figure of speech? Never mind. I only have a moment and must be brief. What can I do for you?"

"I'd like to show them the Rhea finds," Sariena said. "They're relevant to something we've been talking about. I just wanted to check first that you have no objection."

"The Rhea finds," Gallian repeated. His eyebrows rose. "I didn't want any announcement until we've had the reactions next week."

"This will be strictly unofficial. You know how Lan and his associates have supported us. I don't think we need have any fear that the information will go further."

Were Gallian leading a political deputation on Earth, it would probably have been pointless even to have asked the question in such circumstances. The Kronian, however, thought for no more than a few seconds, then nodded. "Very well. If you think it desirable, Sariena, I bow to your discretion." He remained on the line long enough to greet Keene and Vicki, asked them what they thought of the *Osiris*, and then excused himself and was gone.

Sariena shut down the console and moved toward a doorway leading from the main floor area. "This way," she said over her shoulder. Keene and Vicki exchanged curious looks and followed her again, this time into a small room filled with electronic equipment, screens, and panels, with a worktop extending along one wall. Sariena sat down in the chair at a station in front of a glass enclosure looking somewhat like a small fish tank and began touching buttons and entering commands. A misty glow appeared in the space, which was obviously a holo-viewer. "The articles themselves are in freeze storage in one of the *Osiris*'s other modules," Sariena said as the glow brightened. "We'll be taking them down to the surface with us when we return. For now I can just show you the images. We sent the same images ahead some time ago for evaluation by your experts. As Gallian said, we're hoping for some kind of public announcement next week."

She manipulated a control on an adjacent screen, and a form materialized behind the glass. It looked like a tablet of dark stone with fine white veins, shaped into a semicircle at the top and with a corner missing below. Sariena rotated the image slowly, bringing into view a design etched into the surface. It suggested a disk standing symmetrically on an arrowhead, pierced by a shallowly sloping line. Smaller circles and other shapes appeared to the sides, while below was what looked like the top part of a tabular array of strange symbols.

Keene shot a mystified look at Vicki, frowned, and peered closer over Sariena's shoulder. What they were looking at was clearly a product of an artistic culture. "Did you say Rhea?" he asked her, baffled. Rhea was one of Saturn's moons. Vicki said nothing at once, but stared at the image with an odd expression on her face.

Sariena nodded, keeping her eyes ahead. "A number of items and fragments like this were discovered in the ice fields there. Obviously they are artifacts. We have no idea what the markings mean. There is no life there today, nor even the conditions to permit the emergence of any, let alone an advanced race. So what are these objects doing there?" She turned her head finally to regard the two visitors. "You see what this means. The Solar System *hasn't* been the same for billions of years as your scientists believe. Some things about its past were very different from what we see today. And if that's true, they could become very different again."

17

After eight hours of sleep aboard the *Osiris*, the visitors breakfasted with the Kronians before departing. The descent back to the surface and landing at the new Montemorelos facility went smoothly, and an Amspace plane flew the passengers and crew back to the San Saucillo site in Texas. After the postflight debriefings and changing back into their own clothes, Keene and Vicki were among the group that left by helicopter to return to Kingsville, where they had left Keene's car on the way out. The demonstrators were gone by then, since the mission had terminated elsewhere, and work crews were busy around the site and along the sides of the approach road, clearing up the trash left behind.

"Courtesy of our friends of the environment," Keene quipped to Vicki, who was staring fixedly out as the helicopter rose and headed north. She didn't seem to hear. He moved a hand up and down in front of her face. "Hello. Earth to Vicki. You can come back now. The rest of you is already here." She blinked and smiled faintly. "Where were you—still up in the *Osiris*?" Keene asked.

Vicki didn't answer at once. "In a way. . . . I was thinking about those markings on the things Sariena showed us from Rhea. I know this sounds crazy, Lan, but I'm sure I've seen them before . . . or something close. I just can't put my finger on where."

That *was* crazy. How could she have seen markings from objects only discovered within the last year that hadn't even arrived at Earth yet? "Maybe they got into some transmission from Kronia somehow, that you saw," was the only thing he could think of to suggest.

Vicki shook her head. "No, I'm sure it wasn't anything like that. It was in a book or something. I've been dabbling in so many different things lately: Venus and Mars, dinosaurs and mammoths, Biblical history, ancient legends. . . ."

"Yes, but it couldn't possibly have been—" The phone in Keene's pocket beeped and cut him off. "It's started already," he sighed, taking it out and activating it. "Hello, Landen Keene here."

"Lan, it's Judith. You should be down by now. Are you anywhere near getting away yet?"

"We're on our way to Kingsville in a chopper right now."

"Vicki's there?"

"Of course, sitting right next to me."

"How'd it all go?"

"Just great. But that obviously isn't whatever couldn't wait. What's up?"

"I just heard from Jerry. He's finished the preliminary run and sent me the figures. They're dynamite. I'm on my way over to Kingsville right now to see the complete outputs. So I guess I'll see you there."

"All *right*!" Keene pocketed the phone and clapped Vicki's shoulder. "That was Judith. Jerry's finished the first run. She's leaving the office now and coming up to Kingsville. It sounds as if there might be some interesting news."

After clearing more formalities at Kingsville, Keene and Vicki went straight to Jerry Allender's section. Judith still hadn't arrived from Corpus Christi, but Allender took them into his office and showed them the preliminary results. Essentially, tidal pumping induced through combined electrical and gravitational forces in a hot plastic body of the kind Venus was theorized to have been would drive an initially eccentric orbit toward a minimum-energy state, circularizing it much more rapidly than anything in conventional theory permitted. It didn't prove that Venus had originated that way; but it showed that it was possible.

Keene was jubilant. Added to what he and Vicki had seen aboard the *Osiris*, this was a powerful argument for taking the Kronians seriously. Judith arrived and joined them while Allender was still expounding on the details. Keene, however, had already seen enough. Leaving the others still poring over the printouts and putting more images up on the screens, he went into an empty office and called Les Urkin at the downtown building.

"Hey, Les. First, I just wanted to let you know that we brought Jenny back okay. We're at Kingsville now, in case you haven't heard from her already. It went well. She did real good."

"Yes, she called me about half an hour ago. . . ."

"The other thing, Les: I've just talked to Jerry, who's got the results of those computations. It really puts the whole thing on a solid foundation. Jerry says the buzz is going around among the astronomers already. I think we should try for some good general coverage at the same time to tie in with the start of the Kronian talks. Let's get some exposure for Salio, Charlie Hu at JPL, all the other guys we've been talking to who don't buy the party line, and . . ." Only then did Keene register the solemn expression on Urkin's face, and that he wasn't reacting to Keene's enthusiasm. Keene's expression changed. "What is it, Les?"

On the screen, Urkin shook his head and looked bleak. "It's all changed, Lan. Things have been going on that I don't understand. We've lost Salio. He's not going to be in it anywhere. And I don't think he'll be the only one either. I—"

"*Lost* him? What do you mean, lost him? How can we . . . ?"

"He—" Somebody interrupted Urkin from one side. He looked away and muttered something. More voices sounded indistinctly in the background. "Lan, look, I'm sorry but we're right in the middle of something right now. Why don't you give him a call, and I'll talk to you about it later—say, thirty minutes to an hour. Can we do that?"

"Why, sure, Les. . . . Shall I call you back?"

"Sure. . . . Or we could grab a sandwich. I still haven't had lunch."

"Okay. Want me to come into town?"

"If you wouldn't mind. My treat."

"See you then, Les."

Keene got the number from the directory in his pocket phone and called Salio right there via the office unit he was using. Salio was at once awkward, as if he had been expecting the call and not looking forward to it. There was no point in beating around the bush. "I'm just down from orbit and talked to Les," Keene said. "He tells me there's some kind of trouble."

"There isn't going to be any appearance on Coast-to-Coast, Dr. Keene," Salio said heavily.

"Why not? What's happened? Are you saying you were dropped?"

Salio shook his head. "It was me. I canceled out. . . . I got a letter from the university in England raising questions about my legitimacy to conduct what they termed 'serious scientific investigation,' and hinting not very subtly that the invitation for the two-year sabbatical might be subject to reconsideration." He looked embarrassed. "It's more than just a job. Jean's got her heart set on going there, and it would be so valuable for the children. . . . I know it's important to you, but . . ." Salio shook his head. "I'm sorry, Dr. Keene. I don't think I can help you. I'm sure you won't have too much trouble finding someone else."

Vicki looked up from studying a plot of field intensity contours when Keene came back out into the main computing lab. "This is astounding, Lan. If we'd had probes out there too, our scientists would have known about this too, months ago."

"Uh-huh."

"Oh. And Judith says that Karen is probably going to be leaving us. It seems the current boyfriend is from Dallas and can get a job for her, so she'll be moving there. Just when she was beginning to fit in and get the hang of things, too. It's a pity. She's been doing a good job. I guess we have to start going through the replacement routine again."

"Um. How long have we got?"

"About two months, apparently, so it could be worse. . . ." Vicki saw that Keene was only half listening. "Lan, what is it, Lan?"

"I'll tell you later. Look, can you get a ride back with Judith? I've changed my plans. I have to dash into town to see Les."

"It's not just with Salio," Urkin said tiredly across the table of the booth. They had walked a block from the headquarters building to a coffee and sandwich shop that a lot of the downtown Amspace staff used. "There's a campaign being orchestrated from somewhere to kill our side of the story. And it's not just your neighborhood eco club saving bugs or weeds. Look how high they went to persuade Salio to back off—and were able to get attention."

Keene had a pretty good idea where from. He nodded grimly. "Okay. So what else have we got?"

Urkin tossed up a hand while he stirred his coffee. "Two talk-show appearances mysteriously canceled at the last minute in the last few days. You remember that guy Herrenberg that I told you about—the astronomer from Hawaii that we were putting on last Saturday night?"

"The one Charlie Hu organized. Yes, sure."

"We'd flown him into LA. He was actually waiting in the green room when the interview was scratched."

Keene was incredulous. "You're kidding!"

"Herrenberg was just as much in the dark too. He was just told that there had been a schedule change, and he was paid off. Obviously, somebody got leaned on by somebody somewhere with a lot of weight. I couldn't get anything out of them that made any sense when I called, although the producer's assistant let something slip about one of the science agencies in Washington. . . . Oh yes, and you know the book that we were waiting for to appear this month?"

"Seymour's book?" Keene said. Entitled *Gods, Myth, and Cataclysm,* it was a popular-level treatment supporting the Kronian cause, which had been scheduled months before to hit the stores when the subject was topical.

"Right. Well, now it looks as if it's being put on hold because scientific buyers are threatening to boycott the publisher's textbook division, which is a big line with them. They're also being subjected to a letter and e-mail campaign protesting about the book. . . . And listen to this. I got the name of one of the scientists who sent in the letters—a geologist in Minnesota, called Quine—and I called him out of curiosity to ask what it was, specifically, in the book that he objected to. Want to know what he said, Lan? He admitted he didn't know too much about it. He never got an advance copy, so he'd never actually read it."

"*What?* Then how . . ."

"He said he tried to tell them that, but they said that was all right. They'd write the letter; all he had to do was sign it.

"*'They'*? Who's 'they'?" Keene demanded.

"He wouldn't tell me. He just said they included someone who sits on the review committee of just about everything Quine gets published. You see what he was being told, Lan: his career could be on the line."

Urkin sat back in his seat and toyed indifferently with his salad, while Keene munched silently on a sandwich. Les was normally upbeat and buoyant, managing to keep up an image that went with his PR function, but today all that had gone out of him. He stared morosely through the window by the booth at the early-afternoon mix of people out on the street, and then looked back at Keene. They had been pals socially for a number of years, mutually available for helping out with the fixing of cars and other new-improved-model gadgets, downing a few beers in the Bandana every now and again, and getting in the occasional game of golf. Also, when the pressures built up, Les sometimes used Keene's male preserve across town as a temporary refuge from marital domestic bliss.

"I don't know, Lan," he sighed. "Sometimes you wonder what it's all about. You think you're getting somewhere, actually making a difference to something that matters, and then one day you wake up and look around, and you realize that all you've really been doing is hanging in there while most of what you made ends up in other pockets, and that's about the way it's always gonna be." He took a gulp of coffee and shrugged. "And that's it. That's what it's all about. And you find that some dumb ball game is the high point that you look forward to in your week. It doesn't feel right. Does it to you? Don't you get this feeling inside that we were meant for bigger things, better things? . . . What kinds

of things could we be doing if we weren't wiping ourselves out just trying to make ends meet all the time?"

Starting cathedrals to be completed two generations later, Keene thought to himself. Bringing a
universe to life. He drank from his own mug and
looked around. Three young children at a nearby table
were laughing and giggling, having stopped in for an
afternoon ice cream with their mother. Workers from
a power-company truck parked along the street outside were closing off one of the traffic lanes with
orange cones. "I guess if you leave things even a little
bit better than you found them, it means it was
worthwhile," he said, looking back and trying to inject
something positive. "Philosophers ask the wrong question. They spend years wanting to know if humanity is perfectible. Then, when they finally arrive at
the conclusion that the answer is no—which should
have been obvious in the first place—they get
depressed and commit suicide or something."

"So what should the question be?" Les asked.

"Whether humanity is improvable. And since the
answer will always be yes, there's always something
worthwhile to be doing."

Urkin stared hard as if trying to fault it, apparently couldn't, and settled for a snort. "All right. So
how do we improve this situation we've been talking about?" he asked. "Have you figured out what's
going on? It isn't science."

"Now you want me to play psychologist. That's not
my line, Les. I build nuclear drives for spaceships."

"I'd still like to hear your take, anyhow."

"Well . . ." Keene drew a long breath while he
thought about it. "I guess it's the old story of the
in-club being threatened by a heresy that's getting
attention. You could lose your standing as the
official church and all the gravy that comes with
it, and then your disciples will desert to the other
side. So you fight it with everything you've got."

"Everything?" Urkin objected. "You mean scruples don't matter? I thought there were supposed to be civilized rules of discourse and conduct."

"Oh, those only apply between gentlemen who are in the club," Keene explained. "They don't count if you're on the outside."

"But we've got flagrant censorship going on. Suppression of facts. What happened to all this I heard about impartial weighing of evidence; seeking objective truth?"

Keene waved a hand. "Like with all religions: it was a nice thought in the early days. Then different people move in and take over, and in the end it's the power dynamics that matter. The rest makes good reading for indoctrinating the initiates."

Urkin looked across curiously. "But that's not true with everyone, is it?" he said. "I mean, how about you? You still seem to care about those things."

"Sure. And that's why I run a five-person office that works with a maverick outfit somewhere in the south of Texas instead of handing out the contracts in Washington. But at least that gives me a reason. What's yours?"

Urkin just shook his head in a way that gave up trying to understand it.

Keene knew he was drifting into being flippant again. It was his reflex defense mechanism while he absorbed the impact of what had happened to Salio and the other things he had heard. But underneath it, now, he could feel his anger rising, like the slow building up of wind before a storm. And he wasn't going to accomplish anything to alleviate it here, or with people like Salio, or by talking to the Kronians, or flying stunts around the planet. The only place to take it was where the source of the problem lay.

Could Cavan have really seen this coming all along?

18

Keene arrived at Protonix the next morning with a mood that hung over the office like a temperature inversion. The girls got on with their tasks and stayed out of the way.

He was in the kind of situation that irked him the most: of not being in control of the things that affected him the most profoundly. His professional future was tied to the fortunes of Amspace, which hinged on decisions that would eventually come out of Washington, and he had done all he could do to influence the process that would determine those decisions. And the premonitions he was getting weren't good. To make matters worse, the focus of priorities at Amspace had shifted for the time being from engineering matters that involved him to internal administrative details of getting Montemorelos ready to relaunch the shuttle that had landed there, giving him no ready outlet for his energies.

His approach to life had always been to suspect himself as the first candidate for blame when things went wrong—which put the capacity for learning

173

something and doing whatever needed to be done squarely in his own hands. That was the first prerequisite to being in control of one's life as opposed to a helpless victim of it. The Kronian affair was as far as he was prepared to go in knocking himself out, he decided. If this didn't work out, then to hell with it. He would chuck it all in and go back with them when the *Osiris* departed.

He was still mulling over the thought when Vicki came into his office holding a blue folder and set it down open in front of him. One of the pages showed a contour map of rugged terrain with various locations marked by crosses, squares, and other shapes. The facing sheet had reproductions of what looked like a piece of pottery, a slab that could have been from the base of a statue, and a section of mural relief carving, all with lines of peculiar symbols inscribed, fragmented and obliterated in some parts, others tolerably clear.

"There," she announced, indicating the symbols. Keene stared at them. He knew what she was getting at but acted dumb and looked at her questioningly. "That's where I saw them," she said. "Robin's science project on the Joktanians. I'm sure they're like that script that Sariena showed us on the *Osiris*. I can still picture some of them. The similarities can't be coincidental. They have to be related."

Keene could only point out the obvious. "I'm sure you mean it, Vicki, but I don't have to tell you it's preposterous. How are artifacts from Arabia supposed to have gotten to Saturn? Ancient sea-going cultures making accurate maps of Antarctica before the Ice Age, I can buy. But are they supposed to have built—"

Vicki raised a hand for him to stop. "I know, Lan. I know it's crazy. All I'm telling you is what I saw. I do ad graphics. I've got an eye for things like that."

He made a conciliatory gesture, indicating that he

wasn't going to argue about it. "So, what do you want me to do?" he asked, leaning back from the desk.

"I'm not really asking you to do anything. But I saw the way you looked at me when I mentioned it in the chopper yesterday, and I just wanted you to know that I hadn't been having hallucinations or something."

Keene nodded obligingly. "Okay. . . . So you weren't being daffy-headed after twenty-four hours in orbit. But I never thought that anyway." He waited for her to nod, having made her point, pick up the folder, and leave. She didn't.

"Although . . ." She looked at him as if something had just occurred to her, which Keene didn't believe for a moment.

"What?"

"Well, it's got me curious. You said you met this woman from the Smithsonian when you were in Washington, who's involved in the excavations and so on. . . ."

"Catherine Zetl?"

"Right. Couldn't we get those images sent through for her to have a look at? Surely that would settle it. If I'm wrong, then that's the end of it. But if not . . ." Vicki didn't have to complete it. It would add a whole new dimension of impossibility to something already complex enough.

Keene was not enthusiastic. "I'm not sure it's our place to go showing that material around," he said. "Even Sariena checked with Gallian first, remember. And I don't really know Zetl well enough to go involving her in something like that. We exchanged a few words at a cocktail party. I can see your point, all right, but . . ." He finished with another wave.

Vicki straightened up, looked at him reluctantly for a few seconds, then sighed. "You're right. We're not even involved officially, I guess. It's just . . . Well, it's so darned bewildering!"

"Yes, I know, I know." Keene drummed his fingers on the desk. "Tell you what I'll do. Sariena said those images had been sent ahead, so people here will already be going over them. If there really are similarities to the Joktanian script, surely you can't have been the only one to spot it. Let's wait and see what's said next week when the Kronians bring the artifacts up at the talks. Once their existence has been made public knowledge anyway, I'd feel better about bringing it to Zetl's attention if nothing else is mentioned—because then it would seem very strange. Asking questions would be legitimate. How would that sound?"

"You mean I have to wait a whole week?"

"Think you can stand it? Come on—I fix you a visit to a spaceship from Saturn and all I get is a hard time? What is this?"

"Well, if you put it like that, I suppose—" The call tone from Keene's desk screen interrupted.

"Excuse me," he said, sitting forward to accept. "Hello?"

"Catch you later, Lan." Vicki picked up the folder and left, closing the door.

The caller was Jerry Allender from Kingsville. He was red-faced and shaking his head, and had to wave a hand in the air several times before he could speak. "Lan, do you know what's happened? They're throwing them out . . . just tossing them out as inadmissable! It'll be like they never happened. They won't even be a factor to take into consideration—not even worth a can of beans."

"Jerry, calm down. What are you talking about? Who are throwing what out?"

Allender paused to collect his breath. "I just got word from an astronomer called Tyndam, who's on the scientific committee that'll be meeting with the Kronians next week—chaired by somebody called Voler."

Keene nodded tersely. "And?"

"The orbital calculations that we ran. They aren't accepting them."

"*What?*"

"Voler has ruled that until corroboration can be provided by properly organized studies and review, they're not material to the case. And you know how long that could take for anyone with a mind to stretch things out. But in any case it means that as far as next week is concerned, forget it."

Keene felt himself trembling in outrage. "The Kronians ran them. *We* already corroborated them! There's no reason not to accept them tentatively. Every precedent demands it. Is he trying to say that we and the Kronians are both incompetent? . . . Or worse: that we faked it?"

Allender mouthed awkwardly for a second or two, as if choking on something, and then nodded. "I think so, Lan. That was how it came across to me—and what they're maybe putting around. I think they *are* insinuating just that."

Minutes later, Keene exploded into the reception area, startling Karen, who was sifting through the morning's mail at her terminal. "Yale University, Connecticut," he barked. "I want to talk to Professor Herbert Voler, who runs their astronomy faculty. Either get me through to him or a number that's close to wherever he is. I don't care if he's at his grandmother's funeral. Find him."

Vicki appeared, framed in the doorway of her own office behind him. "Lan, don't you think it might be an idea to let it cool for half an hour before—"

"It's gone far enough. First we get shoddy science. Then the kind of dirty tricks you'd expect in some tin-pot dictatorship somewhere. Now this. *We* are being accused of incompetence or dishonesty . . ." He shook his head, left the sentence unfinished, and stalked back into his own office, slamming the door.

A moment later, he opened it again long enough to throw out, *"By them!"*

He still hadn't begun cooling when Karen announced, "His department says he won't be there for probably two weeks. The woman I talked to isn't at liberty to give out his personal code. She did give me a Washington number, but he won't be accessible through it until tomorrow or the day after. I have got a home number for him in New Haven, though."

Of course, Keene thought to himself. Voler would be getting ready for the circus in Washington. "That'll do," he growled. "Maybe someone there might know where he is. . . . And thanks, Karen." Moments later, he found himself staring at the features of his one-time wife, Fey.

She looked cool, sophisticated, her hair shorter than he had known it, more composed and organized— altered in the same direction as her life, no doubt. She was wearing a powder blue blouse with a sparkling brooch that looked both stylish and expensive, and what looked like a loose, black cardigan. Glimpses of subdued wallpaper and wooden paneling in the background completed the image of polish and refinement—a fitting setting for a senior academician who was going places.

Surprise flickered barely long enough to be visible before being brought under control. The eyes scanned and recorded, extracting in a matter of moments all the information to be had from the screen confronting her. In the way that happens with people who have spent years together, his mood had communicated itself already.

"Well," she said. "The face from a former life. I had a premonition it might only be a matter of time. You've been in the news a lot lately. But I see it hasn't done anything to sweeten your temper. What do you want, Lan?"

Keene drew a long breath in an effort to steady himself. "Hello, Fey. You're right. . . ." As she always was; it infuriated him. "I wish I had some pleasantries to swap, but I'm not in the mood. I need to talk to him. Is he there?"

"By 'him,' I presume you mean my husband. His name's Herbert."

Keene nodded curtly. She was right again. Whatever the grievance, incivility wasn't called for. In any case, it would only be giving away free ammunition. "Yes. Your husband, Professor Voler. If he's there, I need to speak to him . . . please."

"I'm afraid he's not. He's in Washington, preparing for the talks next week with your . . . friends. I'll be joining him tomorrow morning. Didn't they tell you that at his office? You must have tried there first."

"Do you have a number that will get me through to him?" Keene said. "I presume I don't need to spell out that it is extremely important."

Fey eyed him critically for a few seconds. Finally she shook her head. "I don't think so. You're clearly spoiling for a fight over something. I'm not going to be the one to expose him to such disruptive influences with this business next week coming up."

"Dammit, isn't it obvious that the business next week is what I want to talk to him about?" Keene said shortly.

A hint of mockery played on Fey's lips, just for an instant. "I really don't think Herbert would be concerned with engineering details." She made it sound like the chauffeur's job.

Keene felt his blood rush, knew his buttons were being pressed, but was powerless to stop it. "Look, some work that's crucial to those talks has been recently completed here in Texas," he fumed. "I've just heard that the committee has been instructed to disregard it, and that the instruction came from him. This isn't a trivial matter, Fey. It's a travesty of science and deliberate sabotage of affairs vital to the interests of every person in this country. He won't be allowed to get away with it. If he tries, the effects could be very damaging to that precious career of his. Do you understand that?"

"Oh, how pompous. And now I do believe you're making threats. Please tell me you are, because dealing with them is very simple and straightforward. Make my day, as they say."

"Take it any way you want," Keene retorted. "But if you won't let me tell him myself, then convey this to him: That deliberately misrepresenting scientific evidence by someone in his position is bad enough; but we have a truckload of evidence that goes beyond that to organized disinformation and manipulation of the media on a scale that for my money qualifies as criminal conspiracy. I'm talking about things like denial and suppression of dissenting views; intimidation of hostile witnesses; organized censorship. Those things would be criminal if the subject of a court case. Well, how is the public going to judge it when they find out? Because that's what's going to happen if he's not willing to reconsider. I'm talking about full exposure of the whole shit heap. And I'm serious. So you just tell Herbert that."

Fey's expression had frosted over while Keene was speaking. The eyes had turned to steel encased in ice. "I think you've made yourself clear," was her response. "If you have any more to say, I suggest you direct it through your attorney." And with that she cut the connection.

Keene was still simmering late that afternoon when Karen put a call through from Sariena. She was still aboard the *Osiris*, due to come back down in two days' time. Gallian, in Washington, had told her the news about the Terran scientific committee's ruling, and she was distressed. The whole Kronian delegation was in disarray. They had been trying to get some guidance from their scientists back at Saturn, who had worked feverishly to have the probe data available in time, but the two-hour communications delay was making things impossible. So Gallian was trying to organize some defense locally. Neuzender at Princeton had declined to speak at the conference on the grounds that his part had been purely to advise on the mathematics, but Gallian was pushing to have Charlie Hu and a couple of his people from JPL attend. Keene had arranged the corroboration run at Amspace, and Allender had performed it. Would he and Jerry be willing to come to Washington next week and testify on the nature and validity of the work they had done?

"Of course I'll be there," was Keene's immediate response.

He called Allender while Sariena was still connected from the *Osiris*, and Allender's answer was equally unhesitating and affirmative. So at least it seemed they were back in with a chance. But it was going to be a nasty fight.

Leo Cavan confirmed as much when he called Keene at home late that night. He'd heard that Keene had been recruited to help the Kronian cause. "I don't know what else you've been saying, Landen, but you've certainly stirred up a hornet's nest," was the further piece of information he had to proffer. "I've been hearing your name all over the place today, and not with the friendliest of connotations. I have a bit of advice: Tread very carefully, Landen. Check that none of your library books are overdue, make sure not to roll through any stop signs, and don't even look in the direction of a female who's under age. There are departments in the bureaucratic netherworld of this fair capital of ours that specialize in dredging up sleaze, and some of the things they come up with would astound you. You are targeted for anything they can get on you. It doesn't have to have anything to do with the scientific case. If I can find anything specific that they're onto, I'll let you know, but it's hardly the kind of information they leave lying around. In any case, don't underestimate these people, Landen. They can be frighteningly effective."

19

Keene found himself constructing visions of gleaming metal cities and icy landscapes under star-filled skies; of strange habitats orbiting above distant moons; the hugeness of Saturn seen from outside its ring system. He tried to imagine life where science was not dominated by preconceptions, and to grasp the puzzling yet alluring culture with its different concept of value.

All he was trying to do was get Earth's institutions to acknowledge the possibility that they could be wrong about something vitally important to the entire future of the human race. Yet the response was to be ridiculed, shouted down, and now, it seemed, viewed like some kind of political threat to the nation's security. He analyzed his own feelings to ask himself if he was serious about giving Earth up as a lost cause if this attempt failed, and leaving to start anew in Kronia.

He didn't try to deny that his thoughts about a new world and a new life included an element of intrigue for Sariena. Talking to Fey had brought home how

fully he had immersed himself in his work at the
expense of any meaningful personal life since they
split up—not that it had been remarkably great
before. So perhaps new challenge and adventure in
a different direction was just what his life needed.
It surely wouldn't be before time. He thought back
over his conversations with Sariena, looking to see if
there was anything that, with a bit of wishful thinking, he could read as hints or leaders that might have
failed to permeate his pragmatic engineer's filter of
awareness. With someone from a culture that had to
be described as alien, it was difficult to tell. At other
times he grew impatient with himself, asking what
reason she might have for harboring any interest in
him that went beyond the professional. . . . But on
the other hand, why should that have to be a prerequisite to anything? These things had to start somewhere. Sometimes he caught himself half hoping that
the talks would come to nothing and give him a
reason for making the break.

Yet, for all that, another part of him deeper down
was uncomfortable, and the only honest admission was
that he didn't know why. He wanted to rationalize
that it would be quitting and he wasn't a quitter, but
he knew there was more to it. Because it would be
"abandoning" Vicki and Robin, somehow? There was
no reason, really, why that should be. He had never
let a relationship develop with Vicki in a way that
might have implied some kind of commitment, and
certainly she had never indicated that she felt he
owed her any. And yet it was true that he had drifted
into something of a role with them, he supposed,
especially where Robin was concerned, even if as little
more than an emotional anchor and a psychological
prop over the years. But reason and emotion communicate on different wires that don't cross. Had he
anticipated this situation a long time ago and avoided
any involvement with Vicki precisely to give himself

a moral escape hatch now? If so, then had the entire part he'd been acting out for months about caring what Earth did been a charade manufactured to prop up his self-respect, while all along he waited for the time to come when he would follow the course that he had already chosen?

He didn't know. But the effort of thinking about it gradually brought the realization that even if a mental switch were to flip and reveal that going to Kronia was a decision he had already unconsciously taken, suffering defeat here first wasn't necessary as a pretext for a motive. If going there was what he wanted, then that was good enough. In other words, there was no reason why he shouldn't win the battle here first, and still go anyway—and with Earth committed to full cooperation, the prospective future out at Kronia would be immeasurably more promising.

He liked that way of looking at things, he decided. Thereafter, his demeanor brightened considerably. His optimism regarding the forthcoming Washington conference climbed again, and the atmosphere in the offices of Protonix returned to its normal level of productive geniality.

20

The Kronian hearings had been in progress for two days, staged in the conference theater of the American Association for the Advancement of Science's new building on New York Avenue. The active participants fell into three broad categories: the Kronian delegation and Terran scientists from various places and disciplines who supported their position; specialized committees representing the prevalent scientific opinions on Earth in such areas as Solar System astronomy, recent geology, Ice Age chronology, climatology, cultural mythology, and the other subjects under debate; and an assortment of political advisors and delegates concerned with the policies that would come out of it all—potentially international in scope, although it seemed agreed that the lead set by the United States would be generally followed. The move to have two of Hu's scientists from JPL added to the astronomy committee had been contested on the grounds that it would produce internal divisiveness. The committee chairman—Herbert Voler—had concurred and upheld the previously agreed arrangement.

These groups occupied three sections in the front part of the auditorium. The dais facing the room had been furnished with a panel table to accommodate the group concerned with the current topic, and a podium for a principal speaker. Some seats and tables in the center at the front were reserved for the current AAAS president, Irwin Schatz, a physics Nobel Laureate, who was nominally hosting and chairing the event, along with several officials from major scientific agencies and their administrative assistants. The rows across the middle were taken up by journalists, science correspondents, and reporters. The remainder of the hall was by invitation only for anyone with the right connections who had managed to get a pass. Since the event had as much to do with world policymaking and public opinion as with science, there were lots of cameras and microphones around.

Although the work that Keene and Jerry Allender had been involved in was not scheduled for discussion until the third day, they had been present from the beginning. Keene recognized a number of familiar faces from his dealings over the years and was able to catch up on events with some of them in the chat room between formal sessions. Also, he noticed Leo Cavan putting in an intermittent presence, usually in a seat to the side of the hall or standing near one of the doors.

So far, the floor had largely been ceded to the Kronians to recapitulate the work that had led them to their conclusions. Practically all of the material they cited had been available before, but—apart from the more sensational items that the media had been popularizing since Athena appeared— fragmented among specialized journals and for the most part obscure. Gallian had wanted it all consolidated for the record, and there were really no grounds on which that could be denied. They went over the parallels between ancient accounts of terrestrial disruptions and violent celestial events, and the implied connection with cataclysms written into the geological and biological records. They pointed to the evidence for major disturbances to both the Moon and Mars in recent times as showing that the upheavals on Earth had been caused by some external agency, and hence the cherished notion of a stable and orderly Solar System was in error. Finally, they recounted the reasons for supposing that agency to have been an earlier Athena-like object ejected from Jupiter, which had since evolved into the planet Venus.

Reactions had grown more animated and vociferous as the two days went by. The Kronian appeals to ancient records and mythologies had elicited mainly pointed silences as the establishment scientists' way of registering their disapproval. They didn't think that this had any place in a scientific debate of the twenty-first century, but courtesy required that the Kronians be permitted a hearing if that was the way they insisted on playing it. The review of recent geological and biological catastrophes initiated more lively responses, not so much of denial that the evidence existed—for that much was generally accepted—but more of resistance to the suggestion that it testified to something universal and global rather than the unconnected, localized events that the mainstream theories still clung to. There was louder protest at revisions the Kronians wanted made to accepted historical chronology—for example, bringing forward the date for the ending of the last ice age, and doing away with the Greek 1200 to 700 B.C. "Dark Age" conventionally held to have separated the Helladic from the Hellenic periods. This, the Kronians asserted, had never happened but resulted from a misalignment of Greek and Egyptian chronologies stemming from faulty nineteenth-century research. The points of dispute were tabled to be covered during the specialized sessions later.

The real objections and choruses of "No!" "Never!" "Rubbish!" began when Gallian, Sariena, and several of the other Kronian delegates began challenging traditional notions of the origin, age, stability, and recent history of the Solar System. This, of course, was the Terran party line orchestrated by Voler finally emerging. The reality of Athena couldn't be denied, but it was acceptable only as a freak event that would never occur again in the timespan of humankind. To suppose that it could be the latest instance of what in fact was the normal scheme of things, meaning that just about everything that had been believed for centuries would have to be torn up and discarded, was inconceivable. Again, according to the rules, points of dispute and contention were supposed to be deferred until later sessions; but this time the mood of the room had reached the point where frayed tempers and wounded egos wouldn't wait, and matters boiled over. The media had a bonanza, capturing red-faced, spluttering professors hurling pejoratives from the floor, the AAAS president pulping a file folder on the edge of his table as he shouted for order, and Sariena at the podium, quiet and dignified, waiting while one mêlée after another erupted and subsided. In all this, it seemed to Keene that Voler played more a role of egging things along and loudly adding to the controversy rather than acting as any kind of moderating influence. It was in keeping with the significance of the Kronian affair to the career ambitions that Cavan had described. Seldom did anything become a focus of the political-scientific community's attention like the current issue, and Voler was making sure to keep himself at center stage.

Eventually, matters spiraled to the inevitable clash over the origin of Venus. Gallian began summarizing ancient astronomical and mythological accounts again but was interrupted by astronomers protesting

that this material was irrelevant and demanding that
the proceedings be confined to science. Gallian
handed over to Vashen, who presented evidence for
a young planet along the lines Salio had described
to Keene. Despite Schatz's pleas for them to defer
until later, several attendees rose to insist that the
hypothesis was unnecessary since the accepted theory
explained everything adequately. This led to the
Kronians making comparisons with Athena, which was
countered by reassertions that Athena was a totally
different kind of object, moving in a class of orbit
that Venus could never have possessed. Sariena contradicted this, stating that data collected over the past
ten months by Kronian space probes showed a change
in the electrical properties of the space medium
sufficient to invalidate conventional models, and that
calculations based on the revised model showed that
orbits could indeed be circularized in the way postulated, within the requisite time frame. This caused
something of a stir until Tyndam, the deputy chairman of the astronomy committee, no doubt following directions, called for the subject to be ruled
inadmissable. At this point, Gallian jumped to his feet
to protest that nothing pertinent could be excluded
from a scientific debate and challenging the other side
for a justification. Tyndam's reply was that the claim
was unverified—the equivalent of hearsay in a court
of law—and had no standing as scientific evidence
until either confirmed or contradicted by independent studies. The intransigence of this ruling caused
some surprised mutterings. Sariena rose again and
retorted hotly that the results had been verified, and
the people who had conducted the corroborative study
were right here—she indicated where Keene and
Allender were sitting. Gallian demanded to the chair
that they be heard. With curiosity mounting all round,
and feeling himself under mounting moral pressure,
Schatz, clearly with some reluctance, agreed.

Voler's position was most vulnerable here, and he took it upon himself to defend it personally, assuming more the role of a trial lawyer, it seemed, than a delegate at a scientific conference, by coming out from his seat to address the dais from the floor immediately in front of the chairman's table. Keene was at the podium at this point, having just finished describing his part in organizing the computations conducted at Amspace. Allender, Sariena, Gallian, Vashen, and Chelassey, a mathematician with the Kronian group, were at the table to his left, looking out over the hall.

Voler began, "So this wasn't part of any research protocol agreed with the Kronian scientists from the outset. It was decided at a cocktail party after the *Osiris* arrived here. Have I got that right?"

"That's correct," Keene confirmed. He was getting irritated. Maybe that was the idea. It *couldn't* have been agreed any earlier; the first results had only just come in from Saturn. Voler knew that.

"The data files were in the *Osiris*'s computers. You passed on the codes for accessing them so that the calculations could be repeated at Amspace."

"Yes—at least, it was arranged by my business partner and a mathematical physicist employed by our company. Just the original raw data. We had no prior knowledge of what the Kronians' results had been. The solutions computed at Amspace are in full agreement with them. My colleague, Dr. Allender, has complete details of the protocols and procedures." Keene couldn't keep himself from adding, "If you're questioning the competence of Dr. Allender and his staff, their method and setup were worked out in conjunction with Professor Neuzender at Princeton, a specialist in celestial dynamics whose name I have no doubt is familiar to you."

Voler stared for a few seconds and then nodded distantly, his mind seemingly on a different track. "Oh,

I have no doubt as to the abilities of the people involved, and I'm sure that their computations were done validly. I've known Gary Neuzender for years, and if he's given his approval I'll grant the results provisional status." He paused again and turned away briefly before resuming—clearly for effect, and succeeding in getting the room's attention. "But it isn't the quality of the computations that concerns me, Dr. Keene. After all, the outcome of a computation can be no more valid than the data that it's based on; isn't that so? And in this case, you've just told us that all of the alleged data came from one source only, and a source, moreover, that has a significant—to put it mildly—stake in the outcome. Isn't *that* so?"

Exclamations of astonishment greeted the statement. Keene couldn't believe his ears. Voler had as good as directly questioned the Kronians' honesty. He shook his head, momentarily befuddled. "What are you trying to suggest, that the data weren't real . . . ? That they'd been faked or something?" he asked incredulously.

Voler raised both arms in an empty-handed gesture. "I'm simply pointing out that these results which we are being asked to accept depend wholly on data that we have no way of verifying, supplied from a single source at the last moment; and that source hardly qualifies as a disinterested party. One cannot but be struck by how conveniently these results accord with the case that's being argued, yet are incompatible with just about everything hitherto believed. An extraordinary coincidence, wouldn't you agree? Extraordinary claims requiring extraordinary proof. And you're saying it should be accepted purely on assurances."

Farther along the table to the side of the podium, Gallian was on his feet again, his face livid. "What kind of suggestion is this? We came here in good faith, believing this would be a debate of evidence, not an examination of our motives. Are we being called criminals now? Exactly what is Professor Voler insinuating?"

Keene had already seen Fey, sitting with a mixed group of people a couple of rows back from the front. She had a satisfied look, as if this whole thing had a personal dimension to it somehow and was settling some old scores. Keene had recovered sufficiently to think coherently again, perhaps, if not quite coolly. The audacity of the double standard being applied was staggering. After all the things that had been going on presumably with Voler's approval, if not actually under his direct instigation, *he* was now questioning the integrity of the Kronians? Keene couldn't swallow it. He had warned Fey that he was in a position and of a mood to expose what had been going on, and he had asked her to convey the message. Either she had ignored him, or Voler had. Well, Keene told himself, there would never be another opportunity like this.

He raised his head to address the whole floor. "This has gone far enough. If there were sound scientific reasons for questioning the claims that the Kronians are making, then of course this conference would be the place to hear them. But instead, it appears it's being turned into a forum for making accusations that can only be described as scandalous." Cries of "Hear, hear!" came from a few scattered places. Encouraged, Keene gripped the edges of the podium and looked around. "Very well. If that is the way it's to be, then let's have the full picture of things that *have* been happening, not unsupported insinuations or speculations about what might have happened. I would have preferred it if these matters had been referred to a more appropriate quarter." Around the room, heads were shaking; others exchanged mystified looks. "However, since we have been turned in this direction, let's talk about scientists I can name who have been intimidated by threats to their careers from voicing convictions to which years of intensive work have brought them; or about suppression of opposing views from the mass media by direct intervention to cancel already scheduled events at the last moment. Let's talk about actual censorship of publishing conducted through organized boycotts and letter campaigns. . . . And I remind you all again, I'm referring to things that *have taken place*, not exercises in fancy about what might have." Finally, Keene brought his eyes back down to where Voler was still regarding him from the floor, and pointed a finger. "And now the *same person* whose influence I can show as central to all the things I've just listed can stand here and make these kinds of allegations? . . ." Keene raised his hands in a brief appeal.

"I take it we're referring to this wealth of evidence that would prove conclusive if the scientific community and the world at large were permitted to share it without prejudice. Is that it?" Voler fired up at him.

"Thank you. I couldn't have put it better," Keene acknowledged.

Voler seemed unfazed by Keene's remarks but stood with his arms folded confidently. "'Censorship.' 'Suppression,'" he repeated. "Our colleague, Dr. Keene, is quick in his use of strong words. We are accused of intervening in the activities of the media. But since when have the mass media constituted the proper channel for scientific discourse? It seems to me that what we've been seeing is more a case of the other side attempting to shortcut the regular process in order to create a jury of public opinion. When that happens, it's inevitably because the case is incapable of withstanding rigorous scrutiny. Seen in that light, our actions would be more accurately described as moving to prevent the public from being stampeded into graphically and emotionally portrayed beliefs on the basis of suspect claims and half-baked evidence. Well, isn't that what we have scientific institutions for? We've been reminded ceaselessly over recent months of the importance of the decisions that will be made as a result of these hearings. Very well, I'll reiterate it. Let us be mindful of them."

Approving murmurings came from the floor this time. Keene felt the foothold that had seemed so solid starting to slip. Gallian, still standing, was looking confused. Voler couldn't be turning this around. "No!" Keene threw out over the hubbub. "This is not something out of the tabloids. We turned to a public forum precisely *because* the institutions that Professor Voler puts such trust in have refused to see the facts in front of them." He extended an arm sideways. "The Kronians are scientists as competent as any in this room. The evidence they're asking us to look at is as solid and verifiable as anything in your own laboratories."

"Yes, we've just looked at an example of it," Voler remarked derisively.

"*You didn't! You're refusing to look at it!*" Keene shouted.

"Based on data that no one this side of Saturn has seen; allegedly obtained from probes whose very existence we have to accept on faith. You call that verifiable?" Voler taunted.

"What you are insinuating is inexcusable!" Gallian protested again, recovering his voice and rallying with Keene.

"We brought you a lot more than just the data from the probes," Sariena said from beside Gallian. Her face seemed flushed, even with her dark complexion. It was the first time that Keene had seen her registering anger. "Tangible evidence that you can hold in your hand. Was that supposed to be 'alleged'? Did we imagine it? Is that not verifiable enough for you, Professor Voler? Tell us. What else would it take to convince you?"

Voler raised his head sharply and swung to face the hall in a way that said they had just heard something important, so that by the time he turned back toward the dais the room had fallen quiet. There was something triumphant in his manner, as if he had been leading up to this moment all along. Keene sensed that some unexpected turn was about to take place.

"Ah yes, the tangible evidence," Voler repeated. He surveyed the room again, and then walked back to where he had been sitting, while the Kronians exchanged questioning frowns. Voler stooped to lift into view a large cardboard box about two feet along a side and set it down on the table. From it he produced an object wrapped in black cloth, which he uncovered and held aloft to reveal as what appeared to be a broken flake of brown rock, perhaps an inch thick and roughly the size of a dinner plate but with one straight side terminating at a distinct corner. "I assume we're talking about these." The Kronians looked horrified. Gallian started to protest, but Voler waved his other hand. "Oh, don't worry. This is just a plastic replica. The originals are in safekeeping, naturally." He moved back below the dais and turned to face the hall again. Sariena caught Keene's eye but Keene could only shake his head.

"Some of you know about these already," Voler said. "A public announcement was due to be made this week, so I don't think I'll be giving anything away if I bring the essence of it forward a little. Briefly, this is one of a number of objects that, we are told . . ." he paused and turned his head to look up at Keene pointedly for a moment " . . . were discovered in the ice of Saturn's moon, Rhea, around six months ago. They are clearly artifacts from an intelligent culture, and several of them carry samples of a distinct written script and other symbolic markings. . . ." Astonished gasps began breaking out immediately, but Voler raised his voice and concluded, "Holographic images were sent ahead for experts here on Earth to examine, and the actual articles were delivered a matter of days ago. They are offered as proof that the configuration of the Solar System was once very different from what we know today—once again apparently corroborating in a striking fashion the claims that the Kronians have come here to put to us."

This time the flurry of voices took some time to die down. Voler moved back and rested casually against the edge of the dais while he waited. When he had the room's attention again, he half-turned to look up at the podium. "Would you describe your relationship with our Kronian guests as cordial, Dr. Keene?" he inquired. Once again, he seemed to have projected himself into the role of a lawyer conducting a trial.

"Well, yes, I suppose you'd say so," Keene agreed. He had no idea where this was going.

"Friendly, perhaps? You were in communication for many months. You and certain members of their scientific group got to know each other quite well, I understand."

"I guess so. That's natural enough for people who share professional interests. What of it?"

"Ah yes, sharing professional interests. Your interests are tied pretty tightly to whether or not the case that the Kronians are arguing is accepted, isn't it? And the interests of Amspace Corporation, with whom your company does the bulk of its work. If Earth were to initiate a large program of long-range space development in the way we are being urged, then not only would the future of the Kronian colony be assured but the prospects for success and fortune of both yourself and Amspace would be permanently guaranteed. Isn't that so?"

"Kronia's future doesn't need any assurance from Earth," Gallian fumed from behind the table, where he had finally been induced to sit down. "That's a pernicious myth that—"

"Please let Dr. Keene answer the question," Voler requested.

Keene's patience was getting close to its limit. "Yes, it's true," he replied curtly. "So what? Exactly what are you suggesting?"

Voler straightened up and moved forward so that while still addressing Keene, he was facing the auditorium. He raised the piece of imitation tablet aloft again. "Why was the specimen only delivered two days ago? The *Osiris* has been here for almost four weeks. Did somebody somewhere imagine that thorough physical tests wouldn't be possible in that time? If so, they must be getting desperate. Or was it more a case of simple naiveté and inexperience in terrestrial geology?"

By now, Keene was totally flummoxed. "Look, I don't . . . What is this? Will you just tell us what—"

Voler's voice resounded suddenly, cutting him off. "By every test of composition, chemistry, isotope ratios, spectral, neutron activation, and thermoluminescent analysis to which it has been subjected, the original specimen corresponding to this replica that I am holding in my hand is indistinguishable from Lower Cretaceous sandstone laid down here, on our own planet, approximately one hundred and thirty million years ago. Yet we're told it was found eight hundred million miles from Earth on a moon of Saturn. Now, how could that possibly be?"

"I . . . I . . . That's not possible." Keene shook his head.

The Kronians were in consternation. "But we brought them here ourselves," Gallian insisted. "Your analyses can't be as specific as you believe them to be."

Voler nodded and looked pleased. "Yes, I was waiting for that. Of course, the Solar System is just awash with oceans that could have laid down sandstone. Or are our experts supposed to be so inept that they mistake igneous lavas for sandstone? But fortunately, we don't have to rely solely on the word of our geologists. The script that I alluded to has been identified. It turns out to be a version of late Joktanian angular, clearly related to that found in the region of southwest Arabia and the African Horn in recent years, which is yet to be deciphered. In short, there can be no doubt that it came from the same planet that we are standing on, and the people who carved these symbols were of a culture that existed here and not out at Saturn." Voler turned to face the dais again, finally. "And how, Dr. Keene, do you explain *that*?"

Keene couldn't. Snippets of what Vicki had said flew disjointedly through his mind, but he was unable to assemble them into anything coherent. His thought processes had seized up. Farther along at the table, Gallian was looking dazed. "But how could it have?" he asked. "We brought them here ourselves, from Saturn."

"From the same place as the probe data, maybe?" Voler suggested, stopping short of openly jeering but evidently enjoying himself.

"Are you trying to suggest that we faked that too now?" Gallian gasped. By now, the whole floor was listening in disbelief. The reporters at the back were having a field day, some already muttering into phones. At the central table, Schatz was shaking his head despairingly. This was unprecedented.

"I'm simply asking how objects from Earth could turn up on a moon of Saturn," Voler replied. He walked back to the center table and set the tablet down on the wrapping that he had removed. Then he looked up again. "But then, of course, we don't actually have *independent, verifiable* evidence that they ever were at Saturn, do we?" He turned to look back at the Kronians, as if half expecting an outburst.

"The only indisputable fact is that they were brought down from the *Osiris* two days ago by the shuttle that returned a group of Kronians to the surface after spending a rest period up there. Everything else that we are told rests totally on assurances—just as with the data from the probes." Gallian started to rise again, his face crimson beneath his white hair. Vashen and Sariena pulled him back down, but then Voler turned away abruptly, picked up some papers from the table, and moved back to the front of the floor to look once more up at Keene. "And for that one, simple, indisputable fact, I think maybe we do have a simple possible explanation. Do you not think so, Dr. Keene?"

Keene was still trying to collect his wits. He shook his head impatiently. "I wasn't involved in any of this. I don't know what you're talking about."

"Oh, really? Then allow me to refresh your memory of a few things." Voler consulted one of the pieces of paper that he was holding. "The *Osiris* arrived in Earth orbit on Friday, May 6. On the evening of the following Monday, the Kronians held an informal reception at their suite in the Engleton Hotel, which I believe you attended. Is that so?"

"Yes, I did. What about it?"

"You weren't on the officially prepared list of guests, I see," Voler commented.

"I was invited by the Kronians directly," Keene retorted.

"Oh yes, of course. You'd been good friends for a while, hadn't you? . . . And tell me, Dr. Keene, is it true that on that occasion, you were introduced to a certain Catherine Zetl, a paleoanthropologist with the Smithsonian Institution, who has been involved in the Joktanian excavations that have been in progress for some time now?"

"We met, yes," Keene confirmed. What did this have to do with anything?

"And how would you describe Ms. Zetl's attitude toward the Kronians and the case they are arguing?"

"I don't recall that we talked much about it."

"Oh, you didn't. Well, I have it on record that she is extremely supportive of them and critical of what she likes to call 'official stodginess.'"

"Very well, if you say so. Am I being accused of something, or can we get back to what was supposed to be the business of this conference?"

Voler summarized: "So, you have been friends with the Kronians for a long time, in part because your professional interests coincide with their agenda. They arrange for you to attend a social gathering at which you meet another scientist sympathetic to their position, whose work happens to have included studying, cataloguing, and storing the very objects we have been talking about. And now let's move forward almost three weeks to May 24. On that date, isn't it true that you took part in another space mission conducted by Amspace—your long-term business associate who shares the same interests?"

It hit Keene then where Voler was going with this. Sudden dismay jolted him and must have showed. "*No,*" he protested.

"What? Are you saying that you didn't go on the mission launched on May 24?"

"I'm saying that what you're suggesting is ridiculous."

"I haven't suggested anything, Dr. Keene. What was the purpose of the mission?"

"*I tell you this is ridiculous!*" Keene said again, his voice rising.

"Please answer the question."

"What is this circus supposed to be? I came up here to describe our work in repeating the Kronian orbital calculations. Am I supposed to be on trial for something?"

The room had become solemn. "I think you should

answer Professor Voler's questions," Schatz said from behind Voler, voicing the general mood.

Keene drew a long breath to calm himself. "It was to test a design of a hybrid engine," he replied.

"A chemical hybrid," Voler supplied. "This was a test of a conventional propulsion system?"

"Yes."

"But you are a specialist in nuclear propulsion, are you not, Dr. Keene? What was your role in the mission?"

"I wasn't involved in that part of it."

"Oh?" Voler feigned surprise. "There was another part? And what was that?"

"You obviously know damn well."

"Yes I do. And allow me to inform the rest of the people present here what it was." Voler turned to address the hall in general. "At the last moment, the mission was extended to include an additional phase: After completion of the hybrid trials, the Amspace craft made rendezvous and docked with the *Osiris*, where it remained for over twelve hours." Voler peeled off the last of the sheets of paper he was holding and held it high. "I have here a copy of the loading manifest of personal baggage items carried by the Amspace craft on that mission. It lists as an item forwarded for Doctor Landen Keene, one carton of weight fifteen point five kilos, described as containing twelve bottles of assorted wines." Keene looked across at the center table, where Voler had left the box that he had taken the replica from. "Well, let's see," Voler went on, "in my estimation that would be about the size of the box over there. So, a couple of weeks after meeting Zetl, you took a box similar to that one up to the *Osiris*, and lo and behold, two days later the specimens that we are told came from Rhea are shipped down, just in time for this conference. Another amazingly convenient coincidence." Voler wheeled to face Keene fully. Finally, he dropped the playfulness that he had been affecting, and his expression darkened. "Seriously, Dr. Keene, are you really expecting us to . . ."

But the rest was drowned in the rising pandemonium coming from all sides. Keene had no answer to offer anyway. Anything he tried to say would have sounded lame. The Kronians, too, were sitting in silence, stunned. Keene was vaguely aware of figures coming forward into the space below, jabbering, shouting, and gesticulating. Somehow, Cavan's face materialized out of it all. "It isn't true, Leo," Keene said, still feeling this had to be some kind of dream. "You know it didn't happen that way. I can't explain it. Where do we start with something like this?"

"I don't know either," Cavan told him. "But I think that for the time being you need to forget any more arguing with scientists. What you're going to need is a firm of lawyers."

21

Until Voler's allegations were either proved or refuted there could be no continuance under the guise of a scientific debate, and the conference was suspended until further notice. Marvin Curtiss was as bewildered by it all as Keene. It was bad enough that public attention should be so completely diverted from the original issue at this crucial juncture; but even worse was Amspace's being implicated, calling into question the credibility and integrity of all the interests that the company was associated with. "Everything's turned into a political show trial," he groaned over the phone when Keene was finally able to talk to him. "It will take twenty years for this to wear off."

Carlton Murray, the head of Amspace's legal department, left on an afternoon flight from Texas with two of the firm's lawyers. They would meet with Keene that evening, and the following day make arrangements for representation by the company's Washington law firm. An outraged Catherine Zetl issued a public denial and announced her intention to sue, which raised the possibility of acting jointly. After a brief conference in a private room at the AAAS building, Gallian, for once noncommittal and subdued, told Keene to let him know what the lawyers wanted the Kronians to do after Keene met with them that evening. Gallian and the rest of the Kronians then retired to the Engleton for the remainder of the day. Keene told Vicki to expect to be effectively in charge of Protonix for a while, and then stopped by Information and Office Services in D.C. to have Shirley take care of everything there. For the sake of privacy and sanity he changed his hotel to the one that the Amspace lawyers would be checking into and forbade Shirley from revealing to anyone where he had gone. Jerry Allender offered to stick around, but Keene told him the whole business had moved way out of his field and there was little further that he would be able to do. Allender left, accordingly, on the last flight that night connecting to Corpus Christi.

The two lawyers accompanying Murray turned out to be Sally Panchard, an old hand who had been with Amspace for years, and Cliff Yeaks, a relatively new recruit from law school but bright, personable, and enthusiastic. Only when he was able to sit down with them in his room, finally removed from the frenzy that had followed him all day, was Keene able to give any real thought to what it all meant.

And what it meant was shattering. The accusations against himself, damaging as they would probably be to the public perception of the Kronians and which constituted Curtiss's main concern, were not what bothered him. Murray was confident that Voler had carried his theatrics too far, and if the true story were as Keene maintained, systematic investigation of the facts would eventually establish it. That didn't mean that somebody else hadn't taken the artifacts up to the *Osiris*, of course. It was hard to imagine any of the others on the minishuttle being involved, but Curtiss had authorized discreet background checks of all of

them as a precaution. But all kinds of official craft had
been shuttling up and down between the surface and
the *Osiris* since its arrival, so there was plenty of room
for the culprit to be elsewhere.

So did Voler really believe the line he had strung
together about Keene? Or had he simply seized an
opportunity to derail the Kronians when a convenient set of coincidences presented themselves,
knowing that he would be able to admit hastiness
and extract himself later? At this stage, it didn't
really matter. What remained—unless some of the
world's foremost experts were unable to tell terrestrial rocks and the work of an ancient human culture from things that had originated in another realm
entirely—was that regardless of who had taken or
sent them up to the *Osiris*, the artifacts *had* come
from Earth, which could only mean that the story
of their being found on Rhea was a fabrication. And
if that were so, then what reliance could be placed
on the probe data also? That, of course, had been
Voler's real point. The rest, as likely as not, had been
staged to grab some limelight for himself and
embarrass Keene and Amspace at the same time.

In all his dealings with them, it had never crossed
Keene's mind to question the integrity of the Kronians. Was it possible that he could have judged so
wrongly? And if so, what else might he be wrong
about? Maybe the Kronian colony *was* as stretched
to its limit as the politicians and advisors on Earth
had been saying all along, and desperation to the
point of perpetrating a deception such as this was the
result. Whatever their reasons or their situation, the
fantasy Keene had toyed with of going back with them
had exploded. His only desire now, after transferring
all dealings to the lawyers, was to leave things in their
hands from here on, get away from everything for a
while, and then do some serious thinking about what
he wanted to do with the rest of his life. First,

however, it would be necessary for him to introduce the lawyers to the Kronians.

Although he had the direct personal calling codes that the Kronians had been assigned for the duration of their visit, matters were more formal now and he called the general number for the suite. A security man answered, and after verifying Keene's authentication put him through to the floor above. Vashen took the call, and when he saw that it was Keene, passed it over to Sariena. She was sleepy and not very communicative, which was hardly surprising. After checking with Gallian, she confirmed that tomorrow morning would be fine for a meeting with the lawyers. Since everything on their schedule had been canceled, there was little else for the Kronians to do anyway.

The next morning after breakfast, Keene was waiting in the hotel lobby, where he had arranged to meet the lawyers, when three men detoured by him while on their way toward the main doors.

"Aren't you the guy who was all over the news yesterday—the one who took the fake tablets up to the space ship?" one of them said.

Keene was momentarily taken aback. "Excuse me? . . . Oh. No, what they said wasn't true. There's a lot to be uncovered. Don't believe anything you hear at this stage."

"Oh yeah? Well, you tell those kook friends of yours that if they want to go back where they came from and freeze, that's okay. But don't come here expecting us to make it work for them, because it can't work. Especially when they have to lie about it. Okay?"

The three walked away before Keene could respond further. Just a month ago, he'd been a space hero taking on the Air Force. Already, he'd turned into a lackey of alien interests. Celebrity, it seemed, could be a short-lived thing.

✧   ✧   ✧

The mood in the Kronians' suite at the Engleton was very different from what Keene remembered of the last time he was there. Instead of a party atmosphere and optimistic talk of exciting changes to come, the tone was set by somber-suited lawyers with laptops, heavy briefcases, and legal pads. No longer did the Kronians joke about the strange sights and experiences of Earth. Instead, they were listless and reticent, volunteering little beyond what they were asked, giving the impression of going along with something they had no choice in but being already resigned to the futility of it.

Keene didn't have a large part to play after making the introductions, having given his own story the evening before. Murray opened with general preliminaries, explaining Amspace's relationship with the Washington law firm, and since Amspace and the Kronians were implicated together, outlining the advantages of arranging comprehensive representation for all of them. However, that would depend on the outcome of talking with partners of the Washington firm, which he hoped to do later that day or tomorrow. The Kronians had no real questions, and Murray got down to the business of going over the reports and transcripts of the previous days' conference item by item to get the Kronians' version and their verification where quotes were attributed to them. All the time, Sariena kept giving Keene curious looks, while he did his best to avoid her gaze. Gallian's answers to the lawyers' questions became shorter and more strained. He seemed to be containing himself only with difficulty against rising impatience.

Finally, Murray leaned back in his chair, his pen held lengthwise between his fingertips, and contemplated Gallian for several seconds as if weighing how to make a delicate point. Gallian scowled back unhelpfully. "Look, I appreciate that ways of going about things might be different where you're from, and I've tried to allow for that," Murray said. "But I have to say, the answers you've been giving aren't exactly going to serve your best interests. You don't seem to understand how the system here works. We are not your adversaries in this. We're on your side. Our job is to put together a strategy that will get us through with the minimum of damage. But to do that, we need complete cooperation."

Gallian's jaw tightened. "I'm sorry. I thought we were cooperating," he replied.

Sally Panchard put in, "I think what Carlton's trying to say is that whatever else is admitted publicly, *we* need to know where those artifacts came from. But as far as the case itself is concerned, our position will depend on what we think the other side is able to prove. In other words, we give nothing away. Without proof, how can anyone know for sure if the artifacts were ever up in the *Osiris* at all? If they were given to you by someone here on Earth after you landed, who *said* they'd come out of the container that was shipped down, then Lan Keene, you, and everyone in your mission would be exonerated."

"Yes, yes. Those are just the lines I was thinking along," Murray interjected.

Sally went on, "There would still be the images that were beamed from Kronia to account for, but they could have originated here and been turned around. So the whole thing could have been engineered between a group of unknown parties here and in Kronia, and you were all used unwittingly."

Vashen was shaking his head, trying to follow. "But that wouldn't change what Voler was trying to say yesterday. You'd just be making others guilty instead of us."

"That's our job," Cliff Yeaks said. "You and Dr. Keene are our clients. The other guys are not. If Voler can't prove who did it, that's his problem. The thing that matters is, you guys will be off the hook."

Gallian emitted a loud sigh suddenly, got up from his seat, and stamped over to the window to stare out at the Washington rooftops. "*The thing that matters,*'" he repeated. "All this posturing and antagonism, obsessions over who will win and who will lose. When will the people of this world ever learn to stop fighting each other and do things together? Doesn't it occur to anybody that the thing that matters might be *truth*?" He turned back to face the room. "Which side are you people on? All I'm hearing is nonsense about legal contortions and antics that don't interest me that can be dragged out to divert attention from the real issue forever. Is that what you want? I thought this was supposed to be a scientific matter. When are we going to get back to that? The only one among you who speaks that language is Landen, and he has said practically nothing. So why don't we stop talking about what stories we can invent and try concentrating on asking what really did happen?"

Keene answered, since Gallian was still staring at him. "I think that's what Carlton is trying to do. As he said, he needs to know exactly at what point those objects—the actual objects, not some kind of container that they were supposed to be in—came into your hands." Keene paused, then added as the thought struck him, "Come to that, *did* you ever actually see them outside of a container?"

"A good point," Sally said, nodding.

Gallian frowned from one to another of them. "I don't understand. I was quite familiar with them before they were crated. I was involved in some of the studies of them." He waited, inviting some explanation.

"Gallian," Keene said despairingly. "Now you're starting to sound as if they really did come from Saturn. Carlton just told you: he and his people are on your side, yet you're still giving them a hard time. I'm beginning to see his point."

"We're trying to get you out of a mess. This isn't helping." Yeaks groaned.

Total silence hit the room. Gallian stared at the Terrans first in noncomprehension, then with slowly growing incredulity. The rest of the Kronians were exchanging shocked looks or just sitting with dazed expressions. Involuntarily, Keene turned in Sariena's direction with a what-did-I-say? look.

"Oh my God," Sariena whispered. "Even you don't believe it, Lan." She faltered, looking at him in disbelief. "These fairy stories that you're talking about; they're not just for Terran melodramatics. You really imagine that some kind of alternative explanation has to be manufactured somehow."

Keene almost started to laugh. "You're not trying to tell us they're genuine, that they really were found on—"

"*Of course they're genuine!*" Sariena shouted. Keene blinked, feeling as if she had slapped his face. She raised a hand to her brow, started to say something, then rose, shaking her head. "I can't believe . . . Lan, how long have you known us? How long have we communicated, worked together? You know something about our values, our commitment to truth. Could you really imagine we'd be capable of such a thing?" Gallian moved to a chair and sank down onto it.

Keene didn't know how to respond. The two older lawyers saw that they were out of their depth and shut up. Yeaks looked at Sariena and showed his hands. "But how could that be possible? We've heard the evidence from yesterday. Nobody has even hinted of any doubts about it. We can hardly argue that those things didn't come from Earth."

"Oh yes, I'm sure you're right. They came from Earth," Sariena agreed tiredly.

Yeaks glanced at his colleagues as if checking that he hadn't missed something, then looked back at Sariena. "Then how can anyone believe they were found on Rhea? You can't go back out there and keep saying that. Nobody on Earth is going to believe it."

"It's as we said," Gallian declared, speaking to the Kronians. "Getting involved in the complications here will just be a waste of time and achieve nothing. I say we pack up and go back. We'll sort it out ourselves with our own scientists back in Kronia."

"Leave now, just like that?" Vashen said. "What about the emigrants we were due to take back?"

"Get the word out for them to bring their plans forward. Speed things up at Tapapeque. We'll wait for them in orbit," Gallian replied curtly.

Now Keene was confused. "What is there to sort out?" he demanded. "Cliff's point seemed pretty clear to me. You're admitting that the artifacts came from Earth, but at the same time you want to stick to the story that they were found on Rhea. You can't have it both ways, for heaven's sake. It doesn't make any sense. We're here. Saturn is eight hundred million miles away. Are you telling us that the Joktanians are supposed to have had space travel now?"

Sariena came over to sit down across from Keene and looked at him. There was no aggravation in her eyes now but something deeper, sadder—for a moment, it seemed, almost pitying. "Oh, Lan," she sighed. "You've tried so much to think like us, but you're still a Terran underneath, locked into your preconceptions. You really can't turn it around the other way, can you?"

"What do you mean?" Keene said. "Turn what around what other way?"

"We've been discussing it most of the night. Just believe the facts and accept their implication. Don't try to force anything to fit with what you think you

already know. And you end up with only one answer."
Keene looked to the lawyers for help. They shook their
heads helplessly. He looked back at the Kronians.

Vashen raised a hand to enumerate on his fingers.
"Fact one: those objects originated on Earth. Fact
two: they were found on a moon of Saturn. Fact
three: no interplanetary transportation existed at the
time of creation."

"In other words, they couldn't have gone from here
to there," Sariena said.

Silence fell again. "Now turn it around the other
way, as Sariena said," Gallian told him from across
the room.

Keene still couldn't figure what they were driving
at. He looked at Sariena and shook his head.

"Therefore, they must have been created there, not
here," she completed. "They were ejected off Earth
in some kind of impact event, and later fell on Rhea."

It took Keene a further three or four seconds to
grasp the only way in which that could have been so.
Then his eyes widened slowly. "Surely not," was all
he could manage.

Sariena nodded. "Their journey across space wasn't
from here to there, but from there to here. And since
there wasn't the technology to transport them, they
must have come with the Earth itself. *Earth was once
a satellite of Saturn!*"

Was it genuine? Or was it a face-saving ploy to let
the Kronians extricate themselves from the affairs of
Earth and depart? Keene didn't know. His confidence
was not bolstered when Gallian refused to throw the
matter open for debate on the grounds that after
seeing the reaction of Earth's scientists to the Venus
proposal, he wasn't even going to try getting them
to listen to something like this. The Kronians would
go back and pursue the matter themselves, with their
own scientists. They abandoned plans for any further

serious discussion on Earth, and began making departure preparations accordingly.

So, what were they: true visionaries impelled by an ethic that would never be understood on Earth; or failures who had fooled even Keene for a year, pulling out under a contrived pretext when it became clear that their bid to enlist help from Earth had failed? And the *Osiris*: Was it really the exemplar of what freed science could accomplish, as he had believed, or just a one-time showpiece achieved by hurling everything into a single-purpose project? Had the Kronians known all along that their position was precarious, and that they could well end up with enraged authorities on Earth opposing their departure if things went wrong, and was that why the *Osiris* was armed? Keene still didn't know what he believed when, a day later, with nothing more to be accomplished in Washington, he and the three lawyers boarded a plane at Reagan National Airport to head back to Texas.

22

The question nagged at Keene for days, allowing him
to get little else done. Either the Kronians were guilty
as charged and he had made one of the biggest mis-
judgments of his life, or one of the most stupefying
scientific conjectures of all time was being missed
because of politics and petty vanities. If the first, he
was on the wrong side and it was time to redirect
his life toward staking some claims in everything he
had been missing out on. If the latter, then humankind's way ahead lay with the different ethic of the
Kronians, in which case Keene belonged out there
and not here, and if they were already getting ready
to leave he needed to make his mind up soon if he
intended doing something about it.

It all hinged on the proposition that Earth had
once been a moon of Saturn. If that were credible,
then so were the Kronians. So how believable was
it? Keene decided that he needed somebody suitably
knowledgeable to help him untangle the questions
clogging up his head. Most of the astronomers he
knew—especially after the recent happenings in

Washington—wouldn't want to get within a mile of something like this. In the end, he called David Salio. At first, Salio was still embarrassed after what he felt had been a betrayal, but his manner eased when it became clear that Keene was calling about something entirely different. Keene's opening sentences were enough to get him hooked, and they arranged a meeting for that same afternoon. Keene flew up to Houston on the midday flight and spent the afternoon and evening with Salio. Salio couldn't guarantee to Keene that the latest Kronian proposition was not a line they had fabricated to extricate themselves; but neither did he dismiss it as impossible. Certainly, the suggestion that the motions of other planets too, not just Venus, might have been different in times gone by didn't offend him in the way it had other astronomers Keene had talked to.

"There's good reason for supposing that Mars moves differently from the way it used to," he told Keene. "The Kronians think that after Venus's close pass with Earth, it went into an orbit that brought it close again periodically—though never with anything like the devastation of the first encounter, of course. That was why just about every ancient culture watched it so closely, keeping charts to track its every movement and viewing its approaches in trepidation as a portent of destruction. Finally, somewhere around 700 B.C., it came close to Mars in an event once again recorded everywhere as a celestial combat of gods, altering Mars's orbit and afterward settling down to the circularized orbit we see today."

"Cooled down from the plasma state, with the electrical effects dissipated," Keene remarked.

Salio shrugged. "We don't know enough about that yet to say. But if something as recent as that is at least plausible, who's to say what the situation might have been in this more distant era that the Kronians are talking about? Without knowing the truth about those artifacts, I can't tell you that the Kronians didn't make it up. That's for your lawyers to figure out. But it's certainly not grounds for writing them off, either."

Keene caught the last flight back to Corpus Christi, where Vicki met him at the airport—he had lent her his car that day since hers was in the shop. She looked trim and classy in a cool summer dress and greeted him with a hug that felt nice after a long, hectic day. "We could redeem one of the outstanding rain checks at the Bandana," she said as they walked out past Baggage Claim. "Robin's overnighting with a friend, and I can live it up—the life I've always dreamed about."

"You must read minds too," Keene said. "Sure, I could use a beer. Planes and peanuts always make me dry."

"So how did it go with Salio?" she asked as they began crossing the parking lot. "What did he have to say?"

"He was fascinated. Said it was the most exciting thing he'd heard for years. He even came up with some thoughts of his own about it that could answer a number of puzzles that have been going around for a long time. For example, Saturn could have provided a more benign environment for life to have gotten started in than here, close to the Sun. No fierce ultraviolet to break up early, fragile molecules before there was ozone."

"He didn't think it would be too cold out at that distance? That was one of the things that bothered me."

"Not necessarily. If Saturn was a protostar at one time that didn't make it to fusion ignition, it might still have radiated enough to warm its satellites."

"What about when Earth escaped?"

Keene shrugged. "Maybe there's your Ice Age. . . . In any case, with all the other things going on that we've been talking about, Saturn might not have been at the same distance then. I can see why Gallian thinks there's enough new science to keep them busy for fifty years."

Vicki glanced at him silently as they walked. Her expression still held a touch of skepticism. "Could it really have been that recently?" she queried. "Enough for humans to have seen it?"

"Well, it's beginning to look as if things could change a lot quicker than has always been thought. Salio thinks the whole geological and astronomic time frame is screwed up."

"Don't tell me 4,004 B.C. is true after all."

"No. But he's pretty certain that the conventional figures are going to have to be drastically revised downward, all the same."

"So does he buy the idea of a one-time satellite of Saturn?" Vicki asked.

"Until we know for sure one way or the other about the artifacts, he can't say," Keefe replied. "It could be a scam; it could be straight. That's where Murray and the lawyers ought to have been pitching in. Where we go next, I'm not sure."

Vicki handed him the keys. He opened the passenger door for her and saw her in, then walked around and got in the driver's side.

"I'm surprised they didn't stay on in Washington longer," Vicki said as they moved out. "I can see why you and Jerry would be out of it now. But doesn't the legal mess up there need attention?"

"There wouldn't be any point," Keene said. "The Kronians aren't interested. They're going back—either to work on their theory or figure out how else they're going to save their colony. I don't know which. It depends on whether they're genuine or not. The last I heard, Idorf was bringing the *Osiris* up to flight readiness."

"Ouch. I didn't realize it was so soon. It's really that hopeless?"

Keene sighed. "Well, if you and I have trouble buying it, the establishment isn't even going to want to hear. If they really are genuine, then Gallian is probably right in thinking that getting tangled up in legalities would just be a waste of time. He told Murray that no law firm would take Kronians on anyway. After Voler's act, they'd be too worried about the bill being paid in faked money."

Vicki smiled and snorted, but remained serious, staring out into the night in silence for a while. Then she said, "You know, there's a lot more at stake here than I realized before. If the whole thing is a scam, the only thing that makes sense as to why the Kronians should have gone to such lengths is to get a share of the real power structure instead of being just an outpost on the fringes. Because if they'd gotten Earth behind them in this program they came here to sell, that's what it would have meant. It does makes a crazy kind of sense."

Keene shook his head. "It's not crazy at all. That's the jackpot question, Vicki. If it was a scam, and we bought it but the people we thought we were so much smarter than didn't, Kronia is finished. But if it's straight . . ." he sought for a phrase, "then they could be the next leap in the social evolution of the human species."

Vicki fell silent again while she thought about it. "You don't really believe them, though, do you, Lan?" she said finally. "The Kronians. Deep down, you're not convinced."

Keene looked across at her, surprised. "I said I don't know what to believe. What makes you say that?"

Vicki shrugged lightly. "You're here, back in Texas. You didn't stay around to see them off. What does that tell you?"

They pulled into the parking lot in front of the Bandana and parked next to a pickup, where a group of a half dozen to a dozen youths and girls were standing around talking in the flickering glow from the neon signs. The sound of heavy-beat country music from inside greeted them as they climbed out of the car. The air was warm and close after Washington, but with a fresher scent coming in with the breeze off the coastal plain. Keene stretched his arms and looked up at the sky. All that could be seen of Athena now was a pale glow over the western horizon. Even though the time was approaching midnight, a matter of days ago it would have been a bright column climbing halfway up the sky. It meant that the tail was foreshortening as Athena came around from perihelion, swinging around like a lighthouse beam to sweep past Earth before Athena crossed Earth's orbit in just a few weeks time. Between now and then it would become the most spectacular object to fill the sky ever in human history—unless, of course, the Kronians were right about the Venus encounter.

"How ya doin'?" one of the youths inquired genially as Keene walked around the car to join Vicki. He was tall and lean, wearing jeans with a plain shirt and vest, and had a white ten-gallon tipped to the back of his head.

"Doing okay," Keene replied. "How about you guys?"

"Oh, just fine. It's busy in there tonight, I'm tellin' ya."

"We'll risk it."

"Take care, now."

Keene followed Vicki up a few steps up to the entry porch. "I think I'll get a hat and some boots," he said as he stepped ahead to hold the door. "The prettiest girls always seem to hang around with the cowboys."

"Those could be your granddaughters," Vicki told him. The noise intensified suddenly as they went through.

"Even better. . . . Which reminds me, have we heard anything more about what Karen's doing?"

"Yes, she's definitely moving to Dallas. It might be a bit sooner than she thought, though."

"Um." Keene stood looking around. The dance floor was filled, and a mostly male crowd was clustered in the vicinity of the bar. It wasn't going to be easy to get a booth or a table in the front lounge. Keene looked across to the far side. "Maybe we could go through into the restaurant," he said. "They look as if they've got more room in there. I never thought to ask, have you eaten?"

"I did earlier—but I could use something with a drink, sure."

They made their way through the bar and dance area to the restaurant and grabbed a corner table just as another couple were vacating it. A waitress came to clear the dishes and give them menus, announced that she was Julie, and took an order for drinks. Keene decided he wasn't up to a full meal or in the mood for a burger. The steak sandwich sounded good. Or maybe something lighter, like a salad. . . . "I suppose we get the recitation about the specials when she gets back," he said, scanning the Mexican section. "Have you ever noticed? They don't listen. 'I'm Julie, your server. How are you today?' And if you say, 'Suicidal,' it's, 'That's nice. Our specials are . . .' I'll show you when she gets back. . . . But I guess it's not really surprising when they have to say it probably a hundred times a day." There was no response. He looked up and realized that Vicki wasn't listening either, but was staring past him with a strange, fixated look on her face. "Hello?" he said. "Anyone home?"

Vicki answered after several seconds, seemingly from a million miles away. "Dinosaurs. . . ."

"What?" Keene waited, but that was all he got. He turned to see what she was staring at. On the wall behind him was an old movie poster from the nineties or thereabouts advertising something called *Jurassic Park*. It showed a tyrannosaurus, various characters and a truck, and a pack of smaller dinosaurs bounding across a grassy landscape. "What about them?" he asked, turning back.

Vicki remained distant, speaking almost to herself. "They couldn't have existed unless conditions then were very different. Gravity had to have been smaller. The whole scale of the engineering was wrong. . . ." She focused back on Keene slowly. "Lan, how easy is it to figure an estimate of this in your head. Suppose Earth were orbiting a giant primary like Saturn just outside its Roche limit, with one side phase-locked toward it. How far out would that be? And at that distance, how much would the primary's gravity reduce Earth's surface gravity by on that side? Could it be enough to allow things like that to live and move around? And if Earth escaped, the gravity would increase. Could that explain why all of the giant forms died out, and the things that replaced them were smaller?"

Keene looked at the poster again, turned slowly back toward Vicki, but already he wasn't seeing her. In his mind he was picturing a world of gigantic beasts, with enormous plants and trees, and a huge, mysterious globe ever-present in the sky. Gradually, he became aware of a voice saying, " . . . with our own, homemade, Bandana peppercorn sauce. . . . Gee, I don't know why I bother. Nobody listens. Would you like me to give you another couple of minutes?"

"Er, yes . . . please, Julie. Sorry, we were away on something else." Keene picked up his beer, which had arrived unnoticed. "My God," he breathed when Julie had gone.

"They *were* right!" Vicki said in an awed voice. "Earth was out there when those artifacts were made. The Kronians were right. . . . It means they're genuine, Lan. Oh, my God, and look how they've been treated here. Even you didn't believe them in the end, and came back. And they're right. . . . I'd be going back too. Their science might get to the bottom of this. Here, it wouldn't even get a hearing."

Keene pushed himself back from the table, all thoughts of eating suddenly gone. "We have to talk to them about this," he said. "I can't do any figuring or call them with this noise. We need to go back to the office."

"You're going to call them now? It'll be nearly one A.M. in Washington."

"This can't wait. They could be shipping out in the morning for all I know. Come on, we have to leave."

Vicki nodded and rose without protest. Keene took a ten from his billfold and put it on the table. They met a confused Julie coming the other way when they were halfway back across the bar area. "Oh, you're leaving? Was there something wrong?" she asked them.

"No, nothing to do with you. We've taken care of you," Keene told her. "We'll be back another time. Just a rain check."

"It's the story of my life," Vicki murmured to Julie as she followed Keene toward the door.

23

Keene didn't want to wake up the entire Kronian mission at this hour by calling the general number. So, reversing his earlier decision of keeping to a more formal level of dealings, he called the direct personal code that Sariena had given him. She answered sleepily in voice-only mode, obviously having already retired. Her first reaction was surprise. She clearly hadn't been expecting to hear from Keene again—at least, not for a while.

"I'll be honest," Keene told her. He was in his office in the darkened Protonix building. Vicki sat listening in a chair pulled up to one end of the desk, which was littered with scrawled diagrams and calculations. "I left because I didn't know what to believe. I had doubts; I admit it. It's embarrassing to look back at, but it's the way it was. What else can I say?"

"Well . . . I'm glad that you seem to be having second thoughts about us," Sariena said. "And I don't want to sound ungrateful that you called, or disinterested. But couldn't it have waited until morning?"

"That could," Keene agreed. "But there's more that couldn't. I'm with Vicki in the office in Corpus Christi."

"In the *office*! At this time? . . ."

"I think she might have hit on something that clinches your case. It's something she and I have talked about before, but there was never any reason to connect it with Saturn. The whole age of gigantism with the dinosaurs and everything—I don't know if you've ever gone into the scaling implications, but nothing of those sizes could function in the conditions that exist on Earth today. The gravity is too strong. But suppose those conditions didn't always exist. Suppose Earth were a phase-locked satellite, close-in to a giant primary. The primary's attraction would reduce the value on the facing side. Combine that with what you've told us about Rhea. . . . It all fits."

There was a long silence. Finally, Sariena said, "Let me put something on and get to a real phone. Stay on the line. I'll be about a minute."

"Seems like it got her attention," Vicki murmured.

Keene looked across at her. "Boy, isn't Robin going to be pleased."

They waited. Then the screen of the desk unit brightened, and Sariena appeared against a hotel-room background, wearing a dark wraparound robe. She had evidently been doing some hurried thinking. "It appears to make so much sense," she said, then mustered an awkward smile. "It's *I* who ought to be apologizing, Lan. You *can* think like Kronians."

"Thank Vicki," Keene grunted. "Or, maybe we should all thank Robin."

"Who's Robin?"

"Vicki's son. He's fourteen. He's the one who's been telling us that dinosaurs couldn't have existed."

"Are you there, Vicki? Robin sounds like quite a person. Life must be interesting at your house."

"Tell me about it," Vicki called from where she was sitting. "I'm sorry things in Washington went the way they did."

"Well, no doubt we shall survive it. What it tells us is that Kronian and Terran science can't work together. And maybe that was something that needed to be seen and understood plainly. So perhaps, if for no other reason than that, the mission served its purpose. In the long run, it might be for the better in any case. These things that we're still only touching on will lead to a whole rewriting of just about everything we thought we knew. We're probably better off being free to pursue it in our own way."

"You sound as if you could buy this idea of Vicki's, then," Keene said.

"I could in principle," Sariena replied. "It would be nice to see something quantitative that at least fits the picture."

"I did some rough calculations here before we called," Keene said. "To be frank, they don't look too promising. Even with the most extreme assumptions that I can justify, the answers I get aren't anywhere near big enough. . . . But I could be missing something. You're the planetary scientist. I'll leave it with you."

"Well, all we can do is pass all of this new material back to the scientists in Kronia," Sariena said. "They know more about the dynamics of the Saturnian system than anyone. I don't know where it will go from here. We might have to wait years before anything can be answered with confidence."

Even after dealing with Kronians for a year, Keene was astonished at the ease with which Sariena was able to adjust her horizons to accommodate these new possibilities. Already he could sense an entire new program of research about to take shape out at Saturn after the *Osiris* returned. Now that his fears were allayed, all doubts had fled that he should have been going too. But the moment was gone. He had wavered at the crucial juncture, and the effect couldn't be undone. Doubtless, there would be another ship, another time—but not this time. All the same, it was nice to think that until that time, whatever transpired out there now, in a way he would still be part of it.

"Well, I guess that for a while we'll have to leave it with you people," he said. "Do I take it you'll continue staying in touch and keep us posted on developments?"

"But of course." Sariena sounded surprised that he should have thought it necessary to ask.

Keene was relieved. "Do you know when you'll be leaving yet?" he asked.

"No. There's some kind of administrative complication. The arrangements are on hold right now. I'm not sure of the details."

"Maybe if it's going to be a day or two, we could come back up and say so long to all of you properly," Keene offered.

Sariena smiled. "I appreciate the thought, but it isn't really necessary. I'll convey it to Gallian."

"I guess you've got something more to throw at him when you see him in the morning," Keene said. "How's he bearing up under all this?"

"Oh, he's not asleep. He and Vashen are away at some meeting somewhere. They've been gone for several hours."

"*At this time?* What kind of a meeting, for heaven's sake? Who with?"

"I really don't know. Some people came here earlier this evening and talked to him in private, and then he and Vashen left with them. I don't know what it's about. Whatever it was, Gallian was looking very serious."

Mystified, Keene looked across at Vicki as if for suggestions. "Maybe they're billing him for the rooms and just wanted to make sure nobody got away first," she suggested dryly. Sariena didn't quite seem to follow the remark.

"It doesn't look as if you'll be leaving anytime soon, then," Keene said, looking back at the screen showing Sariena. "We thought it might be tomorrow morning. That was why I didn't want to put off calling you."

"Well, I don't think you need worry about that," Sariena answered. "As I said, I really don't know what's going on. But if it's something important, I'll let you know. I'm sure Gallian would want to talk to you again before we leave, anyway."

"Yes, do. I'd like that. Well . . ." Keene made a casting away gesture. "There we are. In case we don't get another chance to say so before you go back, it was an experience meeting you and the others face-to-face finally. Working with you even for this short time has been a revelation. I'm only sorry that your mission here didn't produce a more positive result. But maybe we all realize now that perhaps that could never have been. I get the feeling there's going to be lots going on that we'll be talking about. It's just a pity that it'll be from so far away again."

"And it has been an experience for us," Sariena replied. "This is truly an amazing world. Our whole race is amazing. And it will continue to expand and grow despite these setbacks. That's what we should all remember, and work toward making happen. . . ." She hesitated for a moment. "I'm glad that we didn't part on a note of misunderstanding and bitterness, Lan. Take good care of him, Vicki."

"I just run a business with him." Vicki smiled, got up and moved around the desk so that she was in the viewing angle with Keene. "But I like the things you say, Sariena. And I'm sure you'll be proved right one day. Have a safe voyage."

"Make sure you take care of Robin, then. Perhaps we'll even see him at Saturn one day—at least for a visit. It sounds as if he has the makings of a Kronian already." There was a drawn-out moment of silence. Then Sariena raised a hand. "Good-bye, Lan . . . Vicki, for the time being, anyway. And thanks for all you've done. It won't be in vain. You'll see."

The screen blanked out.

24

Keene slept late and arrived back at Protonix around mid morning. He had already talked to Marvin Curtiss, Les Urkin, Carlton Murray, Harry Halloran, Wally Lomack, Shirley in Washington, and everyone else who had been looking for him during his absence the previous day, so there were relatively few surprises waiting to pounce. Neither, to his mild disconsolation, was there any message from Gallian or Sariena. He waited until noon and then decided to call them, using the general number. The manner of the security man who answered was cool and detached.

"I'm sorry, Dr. Keene, but I can't connect you. You're name isn't on the cleared list."

Keene was flabbergasted. "What? But that's ridiculous. I was one of their guests. . . . I mean, I've *been* there. You put me through yesterday."

"A restricted policy is in force now. I'm not authorized to give you access."

"But, but . . . they're personal friends of mine. This is insane. I demand to speak with Gallian, head of the Kronian delegation there."

"I'm sorry, Dr. Keene, but I have strict orders. I can give you the number of my superior if you wish."

Keene noted the number but sat staring at it for several minutes after he hung up. Deciding he had better things to do than get involved in arguments with layers of officialdom he tried Sariena's personal number, only to get a recording: *We're sorry, but the number you have called, 202-555-3325, is not currently in service. If this appears to be in error, please check with the directory or press 611 for assistance.*

His apprehension rising, he clicked to his own directory and retrieved the off-surface code to connect with the *Osiris*. A jarring tone told him the channel was unavailable. Now certain that something was wrong, he punched in the digits for the long-distance operator.

"I'm sorry, sir, but that service is temporarily discontinued," she advised.

"What do you mean, discontinued? It's the trunk beam up to the Kronian spaceship that's in orbit. I'm a personal acquaintance of the captain."

The robotlike voice repeated, "I'm sorry, sir, but all I can tell you is that the service has been temporarily—"

Keene cut the connection with a snarl, pounded the arm of his chair, and sat staring exasperatedly at the screen for several seconds. Then he rose to his feet, paced over to the door and back, glowered at the screen some more, finally turning for the door and storming through into the corridor just as Vicki was coming out of her own office on the other side. "Oh, not again," she groaned, stepping back a pace to stay out of the way.

Keene strode through into the reception area, where Karen was helping Celia check some figures. "Karen, look up the numbers for Leo Cavan of SICA and track him down, wherever he is, would you? I need to talk to him now, right away, *maintenant, jetzt, ahora, adesso*. If you can't find him, find Herbert Voler."

"Lan, what are you doing now?" Vicki asked despairingly as he turned to head back to his office.

"There's something strange going on," he told her. "I don't like the feel of it. I can't get through to the Kronians or their ship. There are two kinds of people that they won't let you talk to: ones who don't want publicity, and prisoners. The Kronians came eight hundred million miles to try and get publicity. So what does it tell you?"

Karen got through to Cavan ten minutes later on a permanently open personal code that he had given Keene, only to be used in emergencies. He was on his way to a meeting in the SICA offices and had to keep things brief. "I'm not sure what's going on, Lan," he said. "Something's in the wind here, but nobody's talking. I do know it goes all the way to the top. There's an information blackout in force, which obviously includes the Kronians. Even I haven't been able to get access to Gallian this morning. Somebody doesn't want the world talking to them. It was ordered by a security official in the middle of the night. But what seems significant to me is that it's still being applied. It hasn't been rescinded."

"It's more than just an attempt to stop them leaving in such a hurry, then," Keene concluded, which had been his first thought.

"It would be a pretty drastic way of going about it," Cavan agreed.

"Any guesses?"

"I'm afraid not. For once in your life, you have me at a loss, Landen."

Keene drummed his fingers on the desk and hesitated. "The other thing might be to try Idorf," he said, finally. "If it involves their plans or something to do with Saturn, he'd know about it, surely."

"You won't get through. The *Osiris* is restricted to an official channel only," Cavan said.

"I know, I already tried calling. But Amspace can bypass the regular net and get it on a direct beam when it's above the horizon. We've still got the access protocols they gave us to get into their file system. It might be possible to create a message link from there."

There was short silence. Then, "Give it a try, Landen. Keep me posted. And if I learn anything more at this end, I'll do likewise. Must go now. Why does life happen in tidal waves?" Cavan hung up.

Keene went through into Judith's office and found Vicki there. He waited in the doorway for them to finish speaking.

"Oh, is the beast fed?" Vicki checked warily.

"Yes, it's safe. . . . Judy, do something for me when you're through, would you? Lines to the *Osiris* are being blocked. I want to bypass the public system and try getting through direct. Would it be possible to create a connection via a beam from Amspace, using the access codes we've got for the file system?"

Judith thought for a few seconds. "It should be. . . . But with just a skeleton crew up there, it mightn't be set up to get attention at their end."

"Okay, well, get onto Amspace and find out when the ship's due overhead, and give it a try. If it works, I want to talk to Idorf."

"What are you getting us into now, Lan?" Vicki asked suspiciously.

"I'm not getting us into anything. I'm just trying to find out what's going on."

Vicki gave a resigned nod. "That's how it always starts."

Cavan called back around mid afternoon to say that Voler and a number of other leading astronomers had been called to a meeting at the White House, as well

as top officials from the Federal Emergency Management-
ment Agency, the Departments of State and Defense,
NASA, and the principal security agencies. It was
being given a low profile to avoid media attention,
but a lot of encrypted communications traffic was
passing between departments involved in orbital and
lunar operations and space agencies overseas, and all
kinds of routine business was being canceled. There
was a lot of strain and tension in the air. That was
about as much as Cavan knew.

An hour later, Judith called Keene in his office to
say she had Idorf on a link through Amspace. "You
did it!" Keene got up to close the door with a foot
and then resumed his place before the screen. "Good
girl. I knew you'd hack it."

"It wasn't me," Judith told him. "I was still working on it. This is incoming. He's calling you." Moments
later, Keene found himself looking at the lean, hawkish
features with the reddish hair and raggedy beard. Idorf
didn't look in the friendliest of moods; neither did he
have time for social pleasantries.

"Dr. Keene, I'm sorry if this is inappropriate, but
I don't pretend to understand how things work in your
world. I'm contacting you because you are a person
who gets attention and can convey a message to the
proper people; also, I respect you as someone whose
word can be relied upon. I cannot say the same for
many of the others that I've been hearing recently. My
impression is that they are likely to say anything they
think I want to hear if they believe it might get them
what they want. I'm told this is what you call politics."

Play this ree-al easy, Keene told himself. He tried
to look composed. "I appreciate the compliment,
Captain Idorf. How can I help?"

"Are you aware that the departure of our delegation is being obstructed?"

"No, I wasn't. I knew there was a block on communications, and in fact was trying to get through to you

via Amspace to find out more. I'm back in Texas now, away from it all. What's happening?"

"The transportation that was supposed to be made available to bring them back up to the *Osiris* is not forthcoming. I am also informed that the emigrants who have been booking earlier flights to the Tapapeque base in Guatemala have been put on hold." Keene started to inject that he knew something strange was going on in Washington, but Idorf went on, "Today, I announced that if your government was not going to provide a shuttle to bring our delegation up, I would send one of our own surface landers down to get them. I was *warned off* by Terran defenses, Dr. Keene! They advised me that any such unauthorized landing would be treated as a hostile act, and the craft seized. So, are we at war now, eh? Does Earth jump to the only kind of solution it has ever been able to conceive for any problem?"

Keene was aghast. "My God! Look . . . I know something's been—"

"Ah, but that's not the end of it. Two hours ago, I was advised of an intention to send a military boarding party up to this ship and asked to cooperate peacefully 'for our own security and protection,' whatever that is supposed to mean. . . ."

"Jesus Christ! I—"

Idorf's hand appeared in the foreground on the screen, pointing a finger. "Very well, they have made their rules clear. Now this is what I would like you to convey, if you would, to whoever down there should hear it. Years ago, when relations between our two societies were more strained than in recent times, there seemed a real possibility that Earth might send an expedition to take over Kronia forcibly. We devoted considerable effort of the kind that produced vessels such as this one to the development of advanced defense systems, and it has been our policy ever since to build all new ships with a dual-role capability. The

Osiris is armed, Dr. Keene. The weapons that it carries are of extreme potency. We will fire upon any craft, manned or otherwise, that attempts approaching closer than one hundred miles without authorization, whether or not it acknowledges further warnings. I trust you will have gathered by now that I am not of a mood to make jokes. I'm hesitant to put this to the people I've listened to today, because I fear they might attribute the same slipperiness to my words as appears to apply to their own. But as I said, you strike me as someone who will put it in the right way, to the right persons. Have I been clear enough? And if so, will you do as I ask?"

Keene eased himself back in the chair and exhaled a long, silent whistle. "Yes. Perfectly clear, Captain. . . ." He thought furiously about how much it might be wise to divulge. Finally, he decided that the way to respond to candor was with candor. "I already knew that the ship was armed," he said. "When we visited you, a colleague and I strayed off the path we were supposed to be on, and saw inside one of the hub cupolas. The machinery looked like an ejector, and whatever it launches is obviously nuclear. What is it? At a guess—some kind of fission-pumped, multipointing beam device? X-ray laser, maybe?"

Idorf's eyebrows arched. "I respect your frankness, Dr. Keene. And you are remarkably well informed. Each capsule deploys a gigajoule charge and generates multiple, independently targetable beams at a ten-thousandth of an Angstrom. I don't think I have to spell out what that would do to a target at a hundred miles."

Or a thousand, Keene thought to himself. "I am a nuclear engineer," he said. "And I worked in plasma physics research for a while. In fact I've been involved in studies of that kind of system. How much of the specification are you prepared to release?"

Idorf shrugged. "As much as it takes to convince them."

"I think I can do that for you," Keene said dryly. "Okay, let me ask you for some numbers." He paused and looked at the screen quizzically. "But first . . ."

Idorf waited. "Yes?"

"What's going on? Do you know any more than I do? . . . What is this all about?"

"Nobody's told you yet, eh?"

Keene showed his palms. "I've been trying to find out all day. It's almost like you said. The whole of the Washington's acting as if there is a war about to break out."

Idorf regarded him fixedly for a few seconds; then, he seemed to make up his mind and nodded. His expression was grim. "Yesterday evening, I passed some news down to Gallian that had just come in from Saturn. Our observatories there have been able to make measurements that won't be possible here for a few more days until Athena moves farther out from the glare of the Sun. It seems we can forget further speculating about whether the electrical environment can be altered, Dr. Keene. Athena has come out from perihelion on a changed orbit. It isn't going to cross fifteen million miles ahead of Earth as was previously thought. *It's coming straight at us!*"

Keene called Cavan on a secure channel to inform him as he had promised he would. Cavan seemed too stunned to make much by way of reply just for the moment. However, he wouldn't be the person to send Idorf's message through, since doing so would invite questions about his and Keene's previous dealings. Instead, on Cavan's recommendation, Keene contacted a presidential defense advisor called Roy Sloane and passed on Idorf's warning. To back it up, he quoted the figures that Idorf had revealed, adding a few pertinent observations that he and Wally Lomack had made during their visit. He kept strictly to the script that Idorf had indicated, making no mention of Athena. Sloane was familiar with Keene's name, took the warning seriously, and asked Keene to leave it with him. Thirty minutes later, he called back.

"You say that you and your colleague Wallace Lomack actually saw these weapons with your own eyes, Dr. Keene?" he checked.

"Yes, that's right."

"You can describe the construction and layout, detail the main assemblies, give performance estimates?"

"Not of the actual pods, which were in shielded storage. But of the hoist and ejection systems, yes. And some idea of functions from the local backup controls."

"We need both of you here, Dr. Keene. Can you contact Mr. Lomack down there and tell him he needs to get ready to travel tonight? Or would you rather we have one of our people call him?"

"*Tonight?* I don't know if we can get a flight at that notice," Keene said.

"Oh, we'll take care of that. When you're coming to meet the President, it's on Uncle Sam's tab."

Keene called an astonished Wally Lomack and told him the minimum that was necessary at that point. He debated with himself about telling Vicki everything but decided that until he knew more than he did, there was little purpose to be served. So, giving her just the Idorf's-warning part of the story, he entrusted the office into her charge once again and drove home. He just had time to pack his bag once again before a staff car with a lieutenant and a WAVE driver arrived from the Corpus Christi Naval Air Station at the end of Flour Bluff to collect him. From Keene's place they went on to Lomack's house to pick up Wally, and from there to the airfield, where an executive jet with Navy markings was warmed up and waiting. They flew to Andrews Air Force Base, Washington, and were met there by a car from the White House vehicle pool. The radio was running a program about vacation spots in South America for the rest of summer and fall. Athena was due to intercept Earth in less than three weeks.

PART TWO

SATURN—
Nurturer of Life

25

The meeting was clearly destined to run through into the early hours. It was being held in what Keene had been told was the Yellow Room in the South Wing, furnished in Queen Anne period against a background of satin hangings, ochre carpeting, redwood panels, and landscape paintings. Twenty or so people were present, including President Samuel Hayer, David Novek, head of the National Security Council, William Born, Deputy Secretary of Defense, and General Patrick Kilburn of Air Force Space Command. Voler was there also, with his astronomer colleague Tyndam, so far acting as if Keene didn't exist. He spent a lot of time conversing with a man called Vincent Queal, apparently from one of the intelligence agencies. Most notably absent was the Vice President, Donald Beckerson, who was conferring with defense officials at the Pentagon.

A large wall screen uncovered by sliding panels showed several views of the *Osiris* and a chart of its internal layout that the Kronians had released some years previously. On it, the weapon-launch housings were left unidentified and the armory serving them conveniently obscured by other details of the structure. Keene had described his and Lomack's impressions close-up, and outlined the nature of the weapons. After being launched a safe distance from the vessel, each pod would detonate a moderate nuclear charge at the center of an array of heavy-element lasing rods, probably in the order of six feet long, that could be aimed independently at a mix of near and distant targets. In the billionths of a second before the rods and the ellipsoid-walled focusing cavity surrounding them were vaporized, the energy from the bomb would be concentrated into intense beams of X rays aligned along the rod axes, which could be aimed with precision. From the scale of the hoist machinery between the shielded armory where the weapons were stored and the launch housings, Keene guessed that the pods carried a propulsion unit, indicating that they needed to get a long way from the ship before activating. This gave a minimum estimate for their power, which fitted with the numbers that Idorf had supplied. Keene explained from beside a table near the screen, where he had placed his notes.

"A medium hydrogen bomb produces around ten to the power fifteen joules of energy in a millionth of a second, which works out at ten to the twenty-one watts, or a one followed by twenty-one zeros. That's equivalent to the output of a trillion large power plants. That power radiated equally in all directions would be distributed over a sphere, which is divided into four pi units of solid angle called steradians. That gives you a density of around ten to the twenty—twenty zeros—watts per steradian." He paused to let that sink in and invite questions. Solemn silence persisted.

"As a conservative estimate, assuming figures I was using ten years ago, the divergence of a beam generated by this kind of device might be five feet over a distance of a thousand miles, or in other words a millionth of a steradian. That means that anything within the cone defined by that beam will be hit by a bolt of energy a trillion times brighter than a hydrogen bomb. Putting that in practical terms, you could easily destroy an ICBM booster at launch from lunar distance. Or you could take out a harder target, such as a reentry warhead, say, from ten thousand miles." Low whistles and some ominous glances greeted his remarks.

General Kilburn shook his head. "I don't know. . . . You said you were working on this? We could have *had* it years ago. What happened to it all?"

Keene shrugged. "It was talked about. But a lot of people said it was impossible, and they were the ones who were listened to. The same ones who said planes could never fly, satellites were impossible inside a hundred years, and the Moon landing would never happen, I guess."

"So what happened to the other people who were working on it?" Kilburn asked.

"One of the top ones I used to know was Robert Sterman at Los Alamos," Keene said. "He and his family moved out to Kronia. It wouldn't surprise me if he had a hand in what we're talking about now."

Novek from the NSC sat forward on one of the couches to reach for the last of some salmon sandwiches that had been brought in earlier. "So at the hundred-mile limit that Idorf has stipulated . . ."

"Don't even think about it," Lomack said from a chair near where Keene was standing. "Any material absorbing energy at that rate will turn into a piece of the Sun."

Seemingly, Novek had ordered the block on communications with the Kronians as a precaution immediately after he learned of what was still being referred to as the "situation"—which Keene wasn't supposed to know about and Lomack still didn't.

Nobody had criticized the decision, and President Hayer had expressed approval that Novek had done no more than his job. The hold on providing a shuttle to take the Kronians up to the *Osiris* was simply an extension of the same policy until the official line was decided.

More serious was the demand that had been put to Idorf to allow the *Osiris* to be boarded, which Keene obviously knew about since it had been the last straw that prompted Idorf to contact him. The explanation given was that the President had authorized the signal after satellites observed launch preparations at Chinese and European military bases, and intelligence analysts voiced fears that a foreign move to seize the *Osiris* might be imminent. These reports had been exaggerated, and Born had given a contorted account blaming the confusion on a mixup in communications between Defense and State. Keene had no way of knowing whether the story was accurate or just for his and Wally's benefit. He had a feeling of some wriggling and shoe-shuffling going on, and from Hayer's reaction got the impression that the President had suspicions too—but it was hardly Keene's place to comment. Why foreign powers should want to seize the *Osiris* had not been explained.

Hayer's immediate concern was to smooth things with the Kronians before Idorf took it into his head to start broadcasting his grievances to the whole world. "Let's make sure we manage our own public affairs," Hayer said to the room. "That Idorf chose to communicate privately with Dr. Keene tells us he'd still prefer to straighten things out with us than compound the problem, so let's use that chance while it's there. Then we can do something about relaxing these restrictions."

A silence followed. Keene waited for any further technical questions but everyone had evidently gotten the message. Eventually, Voler spoke. "It sounds as if we're talking about just restoring our relationship with the Kronians to the point where we feel we can trust in their discretion, and then sending them on their way."

Hayer nodded. "Yes, that's pretty much the way I meant it, Professor. Their mission here is over, and we're going to have other things to worry about. Did you have something else to propose?"

"I think that the possible seriousness of the situation forces us to be realistic about considering all our options," Voler replied. He looked pointedly in the direction of Keene and Lomack. "However, before continuing, I should point out that there are still people present here who do not possess the necessary clearance for the subject to be discussed. Could I suggest that we remedy that situation before proceeding?"

Hayer eyed Voler pensively for what dragged into several seconds, then shifted his gaze to regard first Keene, then Lomack, with curious looks. Hayer had straight yellow hair parted conventionally, and a somewhat florid face. It was his second term, and while Keene had always regarded him as basically honest in his dealings and well-meaning, he had never been what could be described as a strong leader determined to leave his mark. Although competent and solid enough, he was not a great innovator of change, tending to opt for the easier life that came from preserving the safer, proven ways that the established corporations and institutes thrived on. He kept them happy, while they had kept the campaign funding healthy, and stability and order reigned. It really was no surprise that the Kronian endeavor should have run aground as it had, against such an administration. Keene wasn't sure if the blandness was in Hayer's nature or due simply to the absence of any occasion to rise to. If the latter, then the next couple of weeks should certainly put that right.

"Under normal circumstance you'd be right," Hayer agreed. "But what we're facing is hardly normal. We're going to need more people like these, but we can't use them if they don't know what's going on. In a matter of days, a week at the most, maybe, it's going to be common knowledge anyway."

"I protest," Voler said, tossing his papers down on a table by his chair. "What I have to say is of an extremely sensitive nature."

"I have to agree," Queal chimed in. He was heavy-jowled and stocky, with a shadowy chin and close-cropped black hair. Keene had mentally dubbed him "Bluebeard the Black Belt" when they came in, before he knew anyone's name. "It's a breach of procedure. Unnecessary risk."

"Noted and understood, but I'm pulling rank," Hayer replied. He looked back at Keene and Lomack. "Out of curiosity, have either of you formed any theories concerning what this is all about?' he inquired.

"Something pretty big to keep all you people up at this time of night," Lomack said.

Keene decided he could do a little image polishing without arousing suspicions about Idorf's discretion. Why act dumber than one needs to? "As a matter of fact, yes I have," he replied.

"Namely?" Hayer nodded for him to continue.

Keene glanced around. "Well, we all know what happened at the recent conference at the AAAS. I see that Professor Voler is here. And suddenly the Kronians are being held incommunicado—from what I've heard, because of the risk of them broadcasting something that the public isn't ready for yet. Could it be something they learned from their people at Saturn, which is in a different observational position? My guess is they have been proved right, and what supposedly couldn't have happened with Venus has happened again to Athena: its

trajectory has altered, and maybe we're in trouble."
He looked around the room as if for confirmation
and nodded in a way that said there was no need
for anyone to answer. Keene was glad now that he
hadn't given Lomack the whole story. The shock on
Lomack's face couldn't have been faked. Keene
couldn't resist a lordly look in Voler's direction. Voler
turned his head away ferociously.

"I'm impressed," Hayer said, addressing everybody.
"I said we need people like these two with us. You're
absolutely correct, Dr. Keene. Currently we're waiting for indications to come in of just how much
trouble. Our own observatories have the matter on
top priority, obviously, and we're getting the Kronian
readings transmitted from Saturn. . . . And now,
Professor Voler, you had a point to make."

Voler sat up tersely, still looking ruffled. "Very well.
As I said, in view of the possible seriousness of the
situation, I'll be perfectly blunt. If the first estimates
I've been hearing are close, we could be talking about
major disruption, conceivably comparable to all-out
war. In times of war, one does not settle for half
measures, gentlemen. Until we know more, we cannot exclude the possibility that it may prove necessary to evacuate key personnel from the surface for
a period in order to ensure a smooth reintroduction
of order and social controls after the worst of the
disturbances have abated." Voler raised a hand to
point directly overhead. "In orbit right now over our
heads is the most advanced and dependable means
of affording such capability that we're going to see.
In my opinion, it would be the crassest irresponsi-
bility not to take full advantage—for the nation's
benefit—of the unique opportunity that it represents."

"In plain English, you mean keep the ship here
as a lifeboat in case things get rough," someone said.

"In war, you requisition whatever is needed,"
Tyndam, the other astronomer, replied.

"I second it," Queal informed the room. "Are we supposed to just sit here and let it go back to Saturn when we could end up needing every cubic foot of ship capacity we can get?" He made an appealing gesture that took in everyone. "We're already looking into what we can mobilize from the lunar bases and remote stations. What's the sense in talking about bringing that back while at the same time we're letting go what's already here?"

"So the first overt act of war is to be on our part?" the President queried. "We steal it or impound it by force—supposing we could find a way. That's what you're saying?"

"Not really," one of the defense advisors pointed out. "The *Osiris* only came here with a complement of, what was it—twenty or something?"

"Twelve on the delegation and eight crew," Keene confirmed.

"But it's built to carry a hell of a lot more than that. We'd only be asking them to stay on and help their own kind in an emergency. Is that so unreasonable?"

"And what about the emigrants it was supposed to take back?" Novek asked. "Some of them have already started arriving in Guatemala. More are on the way. They've had places booked for months that they've given up homes, everything for. What do we do? Just throw them out and say sorry?"

Voler emitted a long sigh and extended his hands in a gesture of regret. "Oh, I admit, I admit . . . It's a harsh decision. But sometimes harshness is forced." He looked up. "I said I would be blunt. The emigrants are a mixed selection typical of the seven billion persons on this planet. Nothing exceptional or extraordinary. The space aboard that ship should be kept for individuals who *are* exceptional and extraordinary—the kind of individuals who will be needed if leadership and rebuilding on a large scale has to be undertaken."

"What kind of individuals do you think go to Kronia?" Keene couldn't help asking. Voler ignored him.

"I repeat, to let misplaced sentiments take priority at a time like this would be foolish and irresponsible. The knowledge that enabled that ship to be built originated on Earth. The wealth that went into founding the Kronian colony was created on Earth. The ship belongs to Earth."

"How are you proposing we take it, then?" someone invited. "You heard what Landen Keene said. It could melt a battleship from a hundred miles away."

Voler bunched his mouth for a moment, then replied, "We are already holding passports onto it. The Kronian delegation is still down here. We keep them here until the situation becomes clearer. Then, should it be necessary, we return them on the condition that the remaining places are filled with people of our choice. It's as simple as that."

Hayer stared hard at him. "Blackmail now? They come here as guests and you want to make them hostages. Is that it?"

Having gone so far, Voler could hardly back down. "I would have preferred a less indelicate word, but if we must use such terms, then yes. I urge us to be realistic, Mr. President. It is a time when pure pragmatism must decide."

Hayer held his gaze for a few seconds longer, then shook his head. "No, Professor. If the situation turns out not to be so bad, we would have disgraced ourselves for no purpose. If it does turn out bad, then the goodwill of Kronia might not be something we'd want to throw away lightly. This isn't a problem to be worked out by calculus. Proposition noted and considered. Overruled."

From there, the meeting went on to consider practicalities closer to home. Keene was surprised that he and Lomack were involved, but Hayer seemed to want them present. National governments and UN organizations were being alerted to prepare for collaborative action, and instructions were already quietly going out to military, police, and public services to be ready to suspend leave and vacation schedules and mobilize reserves. Obviously, just about every professional and amateur astronomer on the planet was watching Athena, and it could only be a matter of time before alarms began sounding from other quarters at home and overseas. Nothing could be done about that. Assuming the news didn't first break from elsewhere, no general announcement would be made to the media for a further twenty-four hours, by which time more information would be available from the scientific community.

The most obvious fear was of intense meteorite and dust showers from the cloud of ejection debris that had been accompanying Athena since its fission from Jupiter. The effects could be expected to be comparable to heavy, widespread air attack, with some impacts on nuclear-equivalent scale, with a small but not negligible probability of these occurring on dense population centers. Coastal inundation from ocean and offshore impacts was a virtual certainty, with hurricane-force seas likely in all areas and a distinct risk of tidal waves maybe a hundred feet high—worse if a big one hit, say, fifty miles off Miami. FEMA was cleared to activate standing evacuation plans and emergency measures at the state and city level. Military and civic command and coordination centers intended for use in national emergencies were to be readied, lists drawn up of public and private buildings with basements or parking garages, subway stations, natural caverns, and other structures capable of serving as shelters, and stocks of food, fuel, and medical supplies set aside in strategic locations. Police and auxiliary units would be briefed and equipped for dealing with looters and rioting, and the military should be prepared to take over the direction of essential services. The President's final words before leaving were, "From what we've been hearing over the past year, it seems that the place to look for more hints of the kinds of things to expect might be certain parts of your Bibles. For anyone with time left over, I'd recommend reading the rest of it too."

Keene and Lomack were asked to wait after the meeting ended. For about forty minutes they talked intermittently and drank coffee with others who were still around, and then were called into a side room where Hayer wanted to see them privately. "I kept you back because I want you two on the team," he informed them. He looked at them searchingly. "Give me your opinion on something. This argument of Voler's about needing the Kronian ship. What do you make of it?"

Keene and Lomack looked at each other. Keene took it. "I can't see that it's justified. Sure, from the guesses we've just listened to, the world is in for a bad time, all right. . . . But enough to warrant getting the leadership off the surface? Either he's overreacting, which I find hard to believe. Or he knows more than he's letting on."

Hayer nodded and looked satisfied, as if that was all he had been waiting to hear. "And I suspect that this move to send a boarding party was not unconnected. There was more to that than we were told." He paused. "The AAAS thing and everything before it are history, but the fact remains that you were right and the experts I'd relied on were either wrong, or they deceived me. Either way, how can I put any trust in what they tell me now? I need somebody whose word I can depend on to talk with those who are in a position to assess the situation, and report back to me independently of the people you just heard in there. That's you, Dr. Keene. Transportation, authorization, access to anywhere you need to go—name it and you've got it. Mr. Lomack, you've been up to the *Osiris* too and met Captain Idorf. I want you to help us defuse the situation with the Kronians before he starts sending the world messages from the ship. Do I have your cooperation, gentlemen?"

What else was there for them to do but agree? It was past 3:00 A.M., and Hayer was weary. He still hadn't adjusted fully to the responsibilities he found himself with suddenly, and there was no denying the edge of fear that Keene detected in his voice. But Keene also noticed something else. Though he might feel fear as much as any human, Hayer was able to control it. And there was a resoluteness in his face that Keene had never seen before in all the public images that had filled the telescreens and news magazines in the last six years.

Voler and Tyndam had left by the time Keene and Lomack came out from their interview with the President. So had Vincent Queal, the intelligence-agency official, and several others who had sided with them. Keene remembered Cavan saying something about the East Coast academic interests that Voler represented having ties to the defense and investment sectors, but what it might signify he wasn't sure. Neither was he in a condition to think too much about it. The time was after dawn, and Keene dragged himself away to one of the White House guest rooms to grab a few hours of sleep that could no longer be put off. It was afternoon when he awoke. After showering and shaving, he emerged to join others who had also stayed over and more arrivals who were being introduced to the situation. The President was elsewhere, reportedly at the Pentagon. Lomack had left with a group who had gone to the Engleton to repair relationships with the Kronians and prepare the way for more cooperation between Terran and Kronian scientists.

The world was still unsuspecting. While emergency and mobilization orders had begun going out as agreed the previous night, and similar measures were being initiated in other nations whose leaders had been informed, few people were as yet discerning the wider pattern and starting to talk in ways that would arouse the media. At the same time, high-level contacts in the news organizations had been notified to be ready for announcements of national importance, probably within the next twenty-four hours.

Meanwhile, reports were being logged worldwide of increasing radio disturbance and unusually bright auroras at higher latitudes due to high incoming fluxes of the particles that cause ionization in the upper atmosphere. The first whispers of Athena's approach were already reaching Earth.

26

The two primary focal points into which observational data poured from astronomers worldwide were the IAU center in Cambridge, where Voler's associate Tyndam was based and seemed to command a lot of influence, and the parallel operation at JPL in Pasadena, both of which Salio had mentioned. The dependability and possible motives of the authorities responsible for the official reporting from those centers was precisely what Hayer was uneasy about, and Keene's task, basically, was to carry out some checks by going back to the main locations where the inputs to such collecting points originated. He was given office space at the White House and assigned two secretarial staff, Barbara and Gordon, as helpers. The eventual list that they came up with in the limited time available included NASA's Laboratory of Astrophysics at the nearby Goddard Space Flight Center, where data came in for processing from the orbiting and lunar laboratories; the Palomar, McDonald, Kitt Peak, Lick, and USN observatories in the U.S., the NASA, UCLA, and Caltech observatories on

Mauna Kea in the Hawaiian Islands; the British Herschel Observatory, located in the Canary Islands; the European Astronomical Center in Geneva; and the Russian network centered on the Pastukhov Institute. Keene also called David Salio for suggestions as to possible sources in the private sector.

Salio stared somberly from the screen after giving Keene some names for him to follow up, including one at the Aerospace Sciences Institute where Salio worked. "It's Athena, isn't it?" he said finally, keeping his voice low.

Keene answered guardedly. "Why do you say that?"

Salio gave one of his humorless smiles, only this time coming closer to a grimace. "I know what kind of an object it is, and I saw how your case was being undermined from the beginning in that charade in Washington. Jean was telling me over dinner tonight about rumors she's been hearing at the hospital of emergency measures being activated on a major scale. Its orbit has shifted, hasn't it? It's going to come closer than they thought."

Keene nodded mutely. Laughter from one of Salio's children sounded somewhere in the background and was answered by a female voice calling something about it being way past time for bed. It was eleven-thirty in Washington, an hour earlier in Houston.

"How bad is it going to be?" Salio asked.

"Nobody's sure yet. That's why I need to talk to these people. I've been asked to report independently of the official channels . . . as a check." There wasn't much else Keene could say.

Salio nodded that he understood, then hesitated. "Look . . . this may sound pathetic after what happened before, but if there's any way I can help . . . Well . . ."

"It's okay," Keene said. "It wasn't just you. That was part of something much bigger. . . ." He bit his lip and hesitated. "But if they start talking about evacuation, don't wait for the panic and congestion. Get inland, away from the coast. In the meantime, if I need more help, sure, I'll give you a call. Okay?"

The Goddard Space Flight Center was located twelve miles northeast of Washington center in Greenbelt, on a sprawling site of office and experimental facilities interspersed with grassy open spaces and woodlands occupying approximately two square miles. The shapes of the buildings outlined in pools of light and patterns of orange lamps marking the roadways and parking lots expanded out of the night as the helicopter bringing Keene descended beneath an overcast of cloud. Goddard had been the planning and management center for NASA's Earth-orbiting missions and space-based observatories since its inception, and later assumed the coordinating role for all the agency's astronomical work.

A security guard was waiting to drive Keene and the pilot from the grassy landing area to Number Two Building, a long, three-story, edifice of brick walls and a white frontage with black tinted windows, where much of the work on extraterrestrial science was concentrated. They left the pilot with the supervisor in the night office and went up to a part of the top floor which, unlike the rest of the building, was brightly lit and full of people working at screens or poring over printouts and images strewn across desktops. Waiting in his office to receive Keene was Dr. Jeffrey Hixson, who headed the Interplanetary Physics branch.

Hixson was a big, fleshily built man with a flabby neck and second chin, red-eyed and unshaven. He spoke while eating a mixed plate from a batch of hamburger meals and breakfasts that someone brought in from McDonalds just as Keene arrived. There was a hollowness in his voice, and he seemed to have a haunted look. "It's going to come close—maybe even inside the Earth–Moon system. Never mind what they talked about yesterday night at the White House. Those were just guesses based on what they know about comets. This animal is in a different league from comets—I mean, totally. What we're in for is going to be *big*."

"You mean more than just meteorite storms and big dust infusions?" Keene said.

"That's a piece of Jupiter coming at us. We've never known what's really down under the gaseous envelope, but the core material that was ejected took part of what appears to be a rocky crust with it that has broken up and elongated into a stream of debris moving ahead of and trailing the main body. When that gets funneled down into Earth's gravity well, it'll be enough to obliterate whole regions."

For the first time, a measure of the panic that Hixson was struggling to control communicated itself. Perhaps the clamminess on his brow wasn't due just to his being overweight. "What kind of regions?" Keene asked.

"Let's put it this way. A month from now, countries the size of England and Japan might not be here." Hixson snatched another bite of hamburger and went on, "And it's not just the impacts that you have to worry about. Athena carried away parts of Jupiter's atmosphere, which make up a large part of the tail— heavy in hydrocarbon gases. Vaporized crude oil, Dr. Keene. If that penetrates and mixes with our oxidizing atmosphere, you've got fuel-air munitions on a continent-wide scale. They can burn at a temperature that will melt stone. With hot incoming and exploding meteorites to ignite it, a cloud like that could incinerate everything from here to the Rockies."

Keene had in fact been prepared for something like this. The Kronians and their supporters had been reconstructing this kind of scenario for years from interpretations of ancient records and geophysical evidence written all over the planet, and they had been ridiculed

or ignored. Now Keene was hearing it as if it had all
been discovered the previous night. What he needed
now was actual figures for how close the encounter
would be, magnitudes and intensities, estimates of what
they would mean on the scale of events. Hixson walked
him around the other offices and lab areas to meet the
scientists and analysts, some with computers on-line
to the tracking stations, who summarized the latest
findings and provided printouts. One of them produced
a series of telescopic images of Athena moving clear
from the disk of the Sun. The body of the planetoid
itself was obscured by the enormous tail now pointing
Earthward, twisting and contorting into fantastic plumes
and braids. It brought to mind, uncannily, ancient
depictions of the grotesque, multi-armed goddess, Kali,
advancing across the heavens to wreak destruction upon
the world. More images taken at radio wavelengths
revealed structures of magnetic fields and particle
streams extending across half the sky and already
engulfing Earth.

They went back to Hixson's office to discuss the
implications and for Keene to complete his notes.
Hixson's last words as Keene was about to leave were
to ask when a public announcement would be made.
"I don't know," Keene replied. "That's what this information is wanted for. I just report back."

"What are your own plans?" Hixson asked him. He
made it sound as if he was hoping to hear of something official that he might be included in.

"Plans?" Keene could only return a blank look.

It was only when he was in the elevator on his way
back down to the lobby that the full realization finally
sank home that this was real. It was going to happen, and he was going to be here when it did. And
for the last thirty-six hours he had been too busy and
too tired to give any thought to what he intended to
be doing about it.

❖   ❖   ❖

People had begun arriving to start the day when he emerged into the entrance lobby. The sky outside had cleared, but to Keene the morning still had a cold, bleak feel about it. His pilot was in the reception office, on the far side of a glass partition wall, leaning on the counter and talking to a woman who had taken off her coat but not yet hung it. The pilot said something as Keene came into view, and the woman looked in his direction. It seemed she had been waiting for him. Keene entered. A sign on the counter carried the name Christie Jones.

"Hi. Are you Dr. Landen Keene?" she greeted as he entered.

"I am he."

"What's going on? Anything exciting? From what I'm hearing, it sounds as if half the place has been up all night."

"It'll have to keep for now, I'm afraid. What can I do for you?"

Christie consulted a scribbled note. "I've got a strict instruction not to let you go. Somebody wants to talk to you."

"Who?"

"It doesn't say. Not someone who works here. He's waiting in Room 108. I'll show you the way."

"I'll try and keep it brief," Keene told the pilot.

"No hurry, Doctor. The coffee's pretty good here. So's the company."

Christie led Keene back out across the lobby floor, past the elevators, and along one of the ground-floor corridors. There was a display featuring models of orbiting space observatories and placards showing samples of images and other data obtained from them. "Your face looks familiar," she said as they walked. "I've seen it on TV recently, haven't I?"

"Sometimes I lecture on the College Channel," Keene said.

"Yes, that must have been it. Wow, a real celebrity."

"Hardly."

They came to Room 108 and stopped. Christie tapped a couple of times. "Come in, please," a voice called from inside. She opened the door, stood aside while Keene entered, and closed it behind him. A figure was standing by the window, wearing brown cords and a shapeless green sweater that looked as if they could have been for working in the yard. He was obviously tense, which perhaps explained why he hadn't availed himself of one of the chairs while he waited. Keene's jaw tightened. It was Herbert Voler.

The room had the basic furnishings of an office but was bare and devoid of the personal effects that denoted permanent occupancy. It looked like a room set aside for use by visitors, chosen for privacy. What was Voler, dressed this casually, doing here at such an hour, looking as if he too had been up all night? Keene waited.

"So now you know," Voler said.

"I'd phrase it the other way around," Keene replied. "It's what we've been telling you for years happened once before. Now *you* know."

Voler held up a hand as if to stay an attack. "Very well. Before we waste time getting into accusations, I admit to them. We refused to see what might threaten the things we had come to regard as the whole point of existence. Since losing them was unthinkable, we were unable to think it. Does that satisfy you? The collective psychology would doubtless make a fascinating study, but it will be a long time before this world will enjoy the luxury of being able to embark on serious psychological studies again."

"Maybe so. I don't have much time to think about it just now," Keene said.

"Of course you don't. So what are you going to do?"

"It's funny, I was just asked the same thing upstairs. I don't know."

"It should be obvious to you by now that the President has no understanding of the scale of what's going to happen," Voler said. "None of them do. Oh yes, they're counting their candles and checking the first-aid boxes like good Boy Scouts, but none of it is going to make a nickel's worth of difference one way or another. It's over, Dr. Keene—the works, the whole ball of wax. Before long, the surface of this planet may not be habitable for anything much bigger than cockroaches. Is that how you want to die—choking on smoke while you grub under rocks or fight over roots for something to eat?"

Keene answered woodenly, "I said, I haven't had time to think much about it. You do what you can do, and that's it. What's your solution—find a friend in Congress who'll cut you a better deal? That won't work this time, Herbert."

"There is one place where at least the semblance of civilized life will be able to continue," Voler said. "I tried to be realistic about it the other night, but the minds involved weren't capable of grasping what is necessitated. You're not like them, Keene. You understand reality too, even if we have seen it from different sides in the past."

Even now, Voler could consider himself among the rare few able to perceive reality—after he had been blocking it out for years? Again, Keene found himself listening to a distortion that he couldn't quite believe. The psychology at work was indeed fascinating. "Are you talking about Kronia?" he asked.

"Of course I am. Look, the only people who are going to survive this with any chance of a life worthy of the word, and perhaps raise a generation with a hope for any kind of future, will be the ones who can make it there. And the only means of getting there is the one that's in orbit over our heads right now." Keene was already staring incredulously. Voler raised a hand before he could say anything. "I admit that the suggestion of using coercive measures to gain the cooperation of the Kronians was imprudent and hasty. There's no need for anything so drastic. We can make a bargain with them that would be in their own best interests. Their ship has space available. We can offer knowledge and abilities invaluable to their colony, as well as other material resources that they'll probably never get the chance to see again. All it would need is a competent mediator whom the Kronians know and trust. Someone such as yourself, for example. . . . You see my point."

Keene did, quite clearly. Voler was unable to conceive of a situation that was beyond his ability to manipulate. He actually believed he could induce Keene to bargain a passage on the *Osiris* for himself and his friends. Keene remembered the military and intelligence people who had seemed close to Voler at the White House meeting. He was beginning to see now where the idea of sending a boarding party up to the *Osiris* had come from.

Keene looked as if he were experiencing a bad taste. "Even supposing that they offered me a place, what makes you think I'd want to take you along?" he asked.

Voler licked his lips. "Let's not allow past personal animosities to affect things at a time like this," he said. "I don't have to remind you that I possess powerful connections who would be permanently in your debt as a consequence. The future position that you could expect to enjoy in the new setting could be, shall we say, very advantageous."

New setting?

So that was it. Voler had given himself away. Already, he was talking about not merely getting to Kronia as a refugee but aspiring to running things there. Keene could guess the nature of some of the friends who would be on the list. He shook his head and smiled, managing to enjoy the moment despite the circumstances.

"No deal, Herbert. You don't seem to understand. Your kind of influence doesn't count anymore. Kronia doesn't need friends like yours. They don't have anything to offer that's wanted there. I guess you'd better go home and start boarding up the windows of that mansion of yours."

With that, he turned and left the room.

Ten minutes later, Keene was staring down at the morning commuter traffic filling the Beltway. News announcers were describing widespread radio interference and attributing it to Athena's tail fanning out wider than had been expected. There was some risk of meteorite showers, and emergency services were being ordered to take precautionary measures accordingly.

27

The first matter, as opposed to accelerated charged particles, to begin arriving was in the form of molecular clouds and microscopic dust swept ahead of Athena by the solar wind, recorded by satellite-borne instruments and measuring stations on the lunar surface. On Earth, the effect was seen in spectacular sunsets worldwide, followed, as the grain size increased, by brilliant displays of burnup trails in the upper atmosphere. From California to Calcutta, people threw barbecue parties or just ate outside to relax in the cool while watching the shooting "stars" and electrical displays. Others took the warnings of meteorite showers more seriously by putting a fire extinguisher or two in the attics and making sure to park the car in the garage.

Not all reactions were that complacent, however. Astronomers around the world were comparing results and beginning to realize that something was amiss. While some were cautious and unsure what to make of the new factors affecting orbital calculations that had been claimed at the Washington conference, others were quick to take their fears to the media. Observational data were shared over the Web as a matter of routine, and there were thousands of amateurs and enthusiasts with the software to determine that what had been predicted wasn't happening. Some were already connecting the rumors with visions of Athena being a repeat of Venus, and news stories appeared in Germany, Taiwan, and Australia asking if something was being covered up. Very soon it would be noticed that public and emergency services everywhere were shifting into higher gear, and then the stampede to get information would begin. In fact, more than a few news reporters, journalists, commentators, activists, and others who made a business of sensing things in the wind were already asking questions. President Hayer's policy, in which he had asked the other world leaders' cooperation, was still to avoid risking a premature panic by deferring an official statement until the scientific community could at least present a consensus as to the scale and extent of what should be expected.

The problem was that the stories Hayer was getting were contradictory. Hixson at Goddard, for example, was now giving figures less daunting than the ones he had supplied to Keene and had backpeddled to a position of saying that perhaps his initial fears had been exaggerated. Reports from the IAU's Cambridge center, where Tyndam was based, were confusing and seemed to vary between Hixson-like hopes for things perhaps being not be so bad, to violent disagreement, depending whom one asked. This contrasted with the input from JPL, which was consistent and bad—worse, in fact, than the predictions that Keene had heard from Hixson to begin with. And in this, the JPL line agreed with the picture Keene was getting from the other sources that he was in contact with directly.

The Russians in particular were taking the Kronian probe measurements and revisions of the electrical properties of free space in the inner Solar System very seriously, and had calculated that Earth and Athena would come close enough for their magnetospheres to intersect. This would result in titanic electrical discharges from a white-hot body that had just picked up additional charge in its grazing course around the Sun. Nobody knew what the effects on Earth's atmosphere or surface might be. The JPL scientists had reached similar conclusions. In one of Keene's conversations with Pasadena, Charlie Hu said it would be like "sitting on one of the electrodes of a carbon arc." Beyond that, the gravitational upheaval of a pass at that range would cause tides that would make the earlier estimates based on large offshore impacts seem puny. According to some European and Japanese estimates, it was not beyond the bounds of possibility that the Earth's orbital and rotational motions could be affected, in which case entire seas could slop across continents.

All a terrifying and appalling prospect. But was it true? JPL said it was, and the collective view emerging from the sources that Keene had been polling directly seemed to agree. But Hixson disagreed, and the main center that was supposed to be the official source kept vacillating. When Voler was sought for an explanation of what was going on in Cambridge, no one could find him. Hayer's predominant fear remained that of precipitating a wild overreaction needlessly. But with the media now converging on the scent and starting to bay, he only had so much time. Many of his advisors were amazed that a general panic hadn't broken out already.

"This is what we're going to do," Hayer told a progress meeting late in the evening of the day Keene returned from Goddard. He looked spent, having been up, as far as Keene knew, since the last time they'd spoken and probably taking something to stay awake. He had stated that this would be his last function today.

The First Lady, Celia Hayer, was also showing a

presence now. Tall, stately, with shoulder-length dark hair, she had always maintained a role that was strong and supportive but low-key, seeking little prominence herself in the public limelight. She had been constantly in the background throughout the day, unobtrusively filtering communications and organizing the White House staff to deal with the flood of visitors that had continued since Keene first arrived.

The President continued, "Something strange is happening with the Eastern reporting system. Some of the people we ask say one thing, others say another, and now nobody knows where Voler is. . . ." He turned to an aide as an afterthought occurred. "Did you track down his wife, George?"

"Yes, we did. She said she doesn't know where he is. I don't believe her."

Hayer appealed to the room. "You see. . . . What's going on? We don't know, and we haven't got time to make a deal of finding out. So from now on JPL in Pasadena becomes our official source. They seem to have their act together out there, and Charlie Hu has been pushing for the right side in all this from the beginning." Nods and murmurs of agreement greeted the announcement. "Lan Keene has been doing a great job getting a consistent story together out of the mess. So what I want is for Lan to go there and get this set up with Hu, and for them to go through this whole thing one more time and give us a final opinion before we make a statement to the nation. I'm going to try and hold it for another day." He looked at the harassed White House press secretary. "Can we fix it for six P.M. tomorrow, say? Have everybody here—the works."

"That means I'll need to leave tonight," Keene put in. "Sleep on the plane, which will give me all morning tomorrow with Hu—plus the three-hour time-shift bonus."

Hayer nodded and looked around. "And that brings me to the second thing. You've been hearing all day what we could be in for. Since we're going to find ourselves very short of time if it's all true, I'm setting AMANDA in motion now. What's the status of the advance team?"

"Standing by on three hours' notice," one of the staff secretaries said. "The governor of California has notified the appropriate people there."

Hayer caught the questioning look on Keene's face. "That's a standing plan for providing a second seat of government on the West Coast, headed by the Vice President, in the event of emergency," he said. Keene nodded. Hayer looked away and went on, "Then let's get them out there and begin the initial preparations tonight. Dr. Keene can go on the same plane. I'll expect to hear from you and Dr. Hu by five o'clock Eastern Time tomorrow at the latest, Dr. Keene. Is that acceptable?"

"We'll have an answer by then," Keene promised.

"Any other questions?"

"No questions."

The First Lady, who had moved to the front of the group while Hayer was speaking, came forward. "Then before anyone thinks of any, I'm going to get you out of here. It's time to give it a break, Sam. You have to save something for later."

Hayer looked around at the company. "Then, if you'll excuse me, people, your President is about to hit the hay. By this time tomorrow we should all know for sure. It's going to be a long day."

The party would travel in an Air Force jet scheduled to leave Andrews for March AFB, southeast of Los Angeles, at midnight. The AMANDA group would proceed to an undisclosed location where a West Coast headquarters had been prepared years previously as a precaution in the event of a major war—

Keene guessed it was under the mountains somewhere east of the city. Donald Beckerson, the Vice President, was expected to follow with his staff in the next day or two, after the local preparations were completed. Barbara and Gordon would accompany Keene to JPL, along with one of Sloane's scientific aides, Colby Greene, who had been working with them.

Relationships were again on an even keel with the Kronians who, it was no longer questioned, would leave Earth's governments to inform their respective peoples in their own way—in fact, it had never occurred to the Kronians to do otherwise. Accordingly, their plans for departure were moving again, the launch schedule for the emigrants due to leave from Guatemala had been reactivated, and in the meantime the communications block was lifted. They had not taken lightly the allegations made at the conference, all the same. In normal circumstances, a period of strained diplomatic exchanges would no doubt have resulted, probably commencing with a demand for a public retraction. But this was hardly a time to be making an issue of such things.

A staff car had been put at Keene's disposal, and he decided there would be time to stop by the Engleton that night on his way to Andrews Air Force Base. It would be his last chance to see the Kronians on this visit to Earth—and while nobody cared to say so openly, quite possibly his last chance ever.

The setting could have been better for what would have been one of those touching farewell scenes, had it been in a movie. While the Kronians collected together not only the belongings and material they had brought with them, but in addition all their gifts, mementos, and other acquisitions, Terran officials and administrative personnel came and went and buzzed around, including Cavan, who still had duties involved with the departure preparations. Wally Lomack had gone for the night but would be staying on in Washington to see the Kronians off. At least this time Keene's absence would have been forced.

Keene found Sariena wearing a dark jumpsuitlike garment and drew her aside for a few minutes in the suite where the reception had been given the night they first met, which now seemed so long ago—like part of another world, which in a way it was. Even now, there was no peace or solitude. Hotel staff were using the room to pack and crate an assortment of objects, and a waiter was collecting dishes from a meal brought in earlier and loading them onto a cart. Keene had said all there really was to say when he and Vicki called Sariena from Texas, and Sariena had made the appropriate responses. There was no point in repeating all that now. And besides, it would have detracted, somehow, from the understanding they had shared then—as if it needed to be reaffirmed or reinforced.

She sighed and made a gesture that could have meant many things. "How totally and unexpectedly things can change. Just when we had glimpsed what will surely be one of the most astounding discoveries in human history: the birthplace of the Earth itself; the cradle of the human race. How much more will it lead to what's still waiting to be uncovered? The work ahead will last for generations—like those cathedrals that you talked about once."

For the past few days, Keene had forgotten all about such things. For a moment, inside, he was surprised and troubled. Sariena was neither thoughtless nor insensitive; yet here she was talking about faraway futures when for all he knew his world might end in weeks. He tried to put it down to just not knowing how to react in a situation that was as unprecedented as it was painful. Maybe the cultural differences were greater than he realized, even now.

"Whatever follows, it seems it'll more likely happen out there than here," he said gruffly. "Maybe that's the way it should be . . . if that's where it all began."

Sariena looked at him and shook her head. "Oh Lan, this all feels so wrong. It's as if we're walking out somehow . . . abandoning you to this."

"There's nothing you can do," Keene said. "We had our chance long ago to be more ready. And we'll bounce back again, eventually, the same as we did before. But it won't have to be right back to the beginning again. Everything doesn't have to be lost this time. We'll be depending on you for that. It's your turn to run with the ball now, for a while. Just don't drop it."

They looked at each other silently. Sariena took a step toward him, it seemed involuntarily, and hesitated. . . . Then they extended their arms and pulled each other into a hug, both at the same time. It was the first time they had touched in any way intimately. Keene felt the fullness of Sariena's body through the suit and drew her close, oblivious to the others around them; her arms found his neck and tightened to bring the sides of their faces together. In a few timeless seconds, all the things they had left unsaid communicated themselves between them.

"I have a plane to catch," Keene murmured, finally loosening his hold. He felt her nod and draw back.

"Be sure to see Gallian before you go," Sariena whispered. "I think he wants to talk to you."

"Of course I wouldn't leave without seeing him," Keene told her. He turned one last time to the door and sent a wave back at her.

He met Gallian in the corridor, talking simultaneously to an assistant manager from the hotel on one side and a woman with a clipboard on the other, apparently on two different subjects. At the same time, Keene's driver, who had been waiting by the elevator, stepped forward. "Excuse me, Dr. Keene, but I have to remind you. We need to be leaving soon."

"Just a couple of minutes," Keene said. "Go and find Leo Cavan for me, would you? I think he's in one of the rooms that way."

Gallian excused himself from the two people he was with and steered Keene into one of the bedrooms—from the look of the clothes scattered around, quite possibly his own.

"Just to say good-bye," Keene said. "More hurried than I'd have wished, but there we are. It's been a busy couple of days."

"Things don't look good," Gallian said gravely.

"It's not your concern. Kronia did what it could."

Gallian moved closer to grip Keene's shoulder. Although the door was closed, he lowered his voice instinctively. "Landen, you don't have to go through with this, you know. Not only Kronia; *you* did all that you could too. Why not leave it now for those who wouldn't listen? With the departure schedule changed, not all of the emigrants who have places are going to make it to Tapapeque. There will be room to spare on the *Osiris*. We can take a few more in any case. Just a few days from now. . . . You can still see Saturn, Landen."

Now Keene realized why Sariena had spoken the way she had. She had been trying to put visions in his mind of what could be. It had been her way of asking him to come back with them. And while every facet of reason and rationality within him said yes, take it, nothing else made sense, something underneath it all held him back. Gallian either saw it or sensed it before Keene made any response, and released his hold.

"Sariena said she felt as if she were running out," Keene said. "Yet this isn't even her world or your world. How do you think I'd feel?" He forced a tired smile and shook his head. "Of course I appreciate the thought. But I belong here, to do what I can. Don't ask me to explain it or make sense of it."

Gallian sighed heavily, nodded, and didn't argue. "I'd kind of guessed, but I promised Sariena I would try. It's a part of your culture that I don't pretend to understand. And yet . . ." he stepped back, shaking his head, "I have to admit there is something strangely magnificent about it. Is it the same quality that makes those like Mondel—a refusal to see the obvious odds? But without it our world wouldn't exist at all. You're wrong about where you belong, though, Landen. You belong out there. But, of course, you'd have to experience it before you could know that."

Keene held his eye for a moment, then checked his watch. "Maybe one day," he said. "But not in the next couple of days. A safe voyage. And thanks for trying." A tap sounded on the door. They shook hands firmly. Gallian opened the door to reveal Keene's driver with Cavan standing behind.

"I'm sorry, Dr. Keene, but we really have to—"

"It's okay. I'm done. Let's go." As he came out of the room, he turned Cavan around to stay with him as they walked toward the elevators. "Leo, I need a word with you and there isn't time here. Ride with me to Andrews and we can talk on the way. The driver will bring you back afterward."

The elevator arrived, and they stepped in. Keene saw Sariena watching from the entrance to the suite as the doors closed in front of him. He still wasn't sure what had held him back.

The staff car moved briskly through the night streets of the capital, preceded by a police escort flashing red and blue lights. On the way out of the Engleton and for the first couple of miles in the car, Keene summarized the events of the past two days. Cavan, alongside him in the backseat, listened grimly but without interrupting.

"Something strange is going on in the reporting setup, and I'm pretty sure Voler's at the center of it," Keene concluded. "I want you to put these espionage skills that you've been developing to work, and see if you can follow up on a few things."

"My word, you are moving up in the world, Landen," Cavan said. "At this rate I'll be working for you officially before much longer. Very well, what do you need?"

"The Cambridge IAU Center, Interplanetary Physics at Goddard, and a couple of other places on the East Coast are the ones causing the confusion," Keene replied. "And they're all places that Voler has connections with. I don't think it's a coincidence. It's as if they're trying to delay a clear picture coming out of it all for a few days. Now why would they want to do something like that? Or more specifically, why would Voler?"

"I don't know. You've obviously done a lot more thinking about this than I have, Landen. So for once, why don't you tell me?"

"All right, how does this grab you? If JPL is right and it's going to be bad, Voler already knows. The moment it becomes official, all kinds of controls are going to be slapped on everyone's freedom of action. The longer he can stall that, the more time he'll have to move on whatever he's cooking up. Because that's what I think it is, Leo. A day like today, and he's not around? He's up to something."

"Hmm. It sounds likely. How much do we know?"

"When I went to see David Salio, he said something about commonalities of interests between the academic establishment and the financial-defense sector. That could give some leads as to who Voler is working with—obviously he's not on his own. I noticed at the meeting with Hayer that he seemed to be part of a group that voted together. It's no secret that Tyndam up at Cambridge and he are old cronies.

And Hixson at Goddard has to be part of it from the way he changed his tune so suddenly—I mean, what else was Voler doing there at that time? But most of all, I'd be interested to know more about this guy, Vincent Queal, that Voler seems to have a connection with. All I can tell you right now is that he's with one of the intelligence agencies, which could mean that some part of the military is involved. Let me know whatever you can find out. As far as I know I'll be with Charlie Hu at JPL, or I'll make sure that somebody there knows how to find me. They've got a direct landline, so I'll be accessible whatever happens with the communications."

They arrived at the main gate of the air base. A sentry checked them through and directed them to the terminal building, where the rest of the party due to leave for Los Angeles was assembling. As the car drew to a halt, Keene turned and extended a hand. "Let's hope it doesn't turn out as bad as some people are saying. But just in case . . ."

Cavan clasped it solemnly. "It's been an interesting few years, Landen. You know, it's a pity you didn't go to Kronia long ago. That's where you should be."

"And take care of Alicia. I never did get to meet her."

"Ah, she's crazy."

"You never told me why."

"Look at the company she keeps, for heaven's sake."

Keene paused and looked up as he climbed out of the car. There was a distinct reddish tint to the Moon. The sky everywhere was lit up continuously by brief flashes crossing an eerie background of violet, pink, orange, and green traceries.

28

Maybe because of West Coast connotations and constant mentions of the observatories in Hawaii, Keene had been half expecting somebody chubby and jovial in sandals and a beach shirt. Charlie Hu turned out to be of Oriental origins, sure enough, but lean and soberly attired in a light gray suit with necktie, even at an unearthly hour of the morning. He was in his fifties, Keene judged, with streaky graying hair and a neatly trimmed beard. He greeted Keene and his companions formally but warmly, standing as they were shown into his office and bowing slightly when they shook hands. "What in God's name are they doing in Washington?" were his first words after the introductions. "Everyone else in the world knows what they're supposed to be announcing, yet they have to send you here to ask me?"

The news media, abuzz by now that something big was about to break, were pressing the scientists, and many of the scientists were getting impatient and starting to talk. Rumors of the wealthy and famous quietly commencing arrangements to board up and vacate waterfront properties in Argentina and Brazil, the African Cape, Hong Kong, and to move themselves and their valuables to higher, inland retreats didn't help to assuage the rising anxieties of average people without such options. Religious groups of every persuasion were thumbing through their tracts and finding the fulfillment of a score of prophecies, all different. Several cities in India were seeing unrest and demonstrations demanding more positive action from the government—although precisely what action was left unspecified. Several places reported mob unrest, and a number of states were preparing to proclaim martial law.

But not everyone was overreacting. Holiday package-tour operators and cruise lines reassured customers that they would get full refunds for any schedules that had to be canceled, or a discount if they let them carry over to next year. The British Prime Minister, after returning from his Scottish estate for an emergency session in Parliament, had urged his cabinet to enjoy the fireworks display, put off for a month any plans they might have to go sailing, and returned to continue his vacation.

The mood among the workers at JPL, when Hu took the arrivals from Washington out to meet them, was very different, ranging from numbed shock through restless nervousness to open fear barely being kept under control. They hadn't had the distraction of the activity going on in Washington, and they were under no illusions as a result of contradictory accounts. After spending the night in consultation with Russian astronomers at the Pastukhov observatory, they *knew*. And although a direct collision with Athena was not indicated, some of the further consequences of the close pass that was expected exceeded even the horror stories that Keene had heard before leaving the East Coast. A white-haired astrophysicist whom Hu introduced as Margaret Ikels explained in a room where about a dozen somber-faced scientists and assistants were gathered:

"What they told you before about the electrical effects might be only part of the story. You see, the plasma tail streaming ahead of Athena generates an intense magnetic field. Earth's iron core passing through it at the distance that's predicted will become a gigantic induction generator of huge circulating electrical currents. According to our estimates, the heat generated could open up fault lines in the mantle and melt through to the crust." Ikels nodded her head to indicate a lanky, yellow-haired young man in shorts and a sweatshirt, sprawled across one of the chairs, his arm draped along the back of another, one foot resting on a third. "John has some interesting thoughts on plate tectonics that you might like to hear." Keene merely jerked his chin inquiringly. This latest revelation had left him momentarily incapable of saying anything.

"The conventional picture might be wrong by orders of magnitude," John said. "The ocean floors didn't take millions of years to spread from the rifts. That's just the answer you get when you extrapolate back the cooled-down rate of spreading that we measure today. If the Kronians are right about Venus—which is what a lot of us here have thought for a long time—it happened only thousands of years ago, maybe in days or weeks."

For several seconds, Keene stared, aghast. If the upswelling of the sea-floor ridges and sideways spreading that created the ocean floors had taken place on the kind of timescale that John was talking about, the rates of lava flow had to have been immensely greater than anything previously imagined. So, therefore, would the amount of heat necessary to produce it— which was what Margaret Ikels was saying.

"You're talking about boiling oceans, here," someone threw in from the side, as if confirming Keene's thoughts.

"So . . . in that case, what wrote the stripes?" Keene asked, finding his voice at last. He meant the parallel lines of alternately directed magnetism found across seabeds the world over. The generally accepted theory was that they had been produced by unexplained reversals of the Earth's field, occurring at intervals of thousands of years or more.

John shrugged. "The Russians think they're also tied in with all the electrical activity somehow. I guess we're about to get some interesting lessons in planetary physics. Too bad nobody will be taking notes."

A silence fell over the room. Keene saw hopelessness written on every face. Charlie Hu looked uncomfortable, as if aware on the one hand that the morale of the group was his responsibility, yet at the same time unable to insult their intelligence by trying to tell anyone that things mightn't be as bad as everyone knew they were.

"Maybe these guys should get some rest," Keene suggested, looking at Hu. In case they hadn't been informed, he added, "The President is due to make a national statement at three o'clock Pacific Time today. The main input regarding what's to be expected will come from here. Maybe we could get together at, say, around ten to compare notes and check numbers? That would give us about four hours to get a final line together."

John straightened up suddenly, his feelings now venting themselves as anger. "What's the point?" he demanded. "Do you think there's anything they can do that's going to make a difference? Look, if they want to make speeches and play survival games, that's okay by me—but don't drag me into it. I might decide I wanna spend my time getting drunk, getting high, or getting laid, but I'm not gonna pretend anything." Charlie Hu looked at his shoes. He knew that John was out of line but apparently couldn't argue.

"It's over," a girl sitting near Keene told him. "It's

taken me all night to face it, but it's real. Nobody's going to survive this, Doctor."

Keene turned away and paced across the room to a wall board covered in scrawled diagrams and calculations rendered in assorted colors. Maybe she'd had all night to get around to facing it, but he had not. There were people in Washington still of a will to do what they could and who were depending on him. He couldn't let this come apart now.

"*No!*" he said sharply, turning to confront them. "I won't accept that." His tone surprised everyone. He looked around at them. "What is this? It's easy to pretend things about yourselves when everything is going your way. It's when things are at their worst that you find out who you really are. Did any of you imagine that it was going to last forever? Life is the chance to show that you're up to doing what needs to be done, when it needs to be, the best that you can. That's still as true if the time you've got to do it in is weeks, or thirty more years, or a thousand. Everybody can be someone special tomorrow, when everything will be just right. But it's what you can be *today* that matters, when it's not." He extended an arm to point at the window, although it was still dark outside and he had no idea whether it faced eastward or not. "That's what the President and the First Lady of this country are doing. The last time I saw them they hadn't slept for two days either. They're doing what needs to be done, as best they can, because it's their job. . . . Well, I have a job too. And so do you."

He looked around. Some of the eyes met his for a moment, then shifted away. Others remained staring back at him. He was getting through to them. He went on, "I know what some of you are thinking. That might be fine when it's all for a better future. But what's the use when there isn't any future? You all heard it a moment ago: 'Nobody's going to survive this.' Well, I don't buy that either, and I'll tell you why. John said that a lot of you here believe the Kronians were right about Venus. Very well, I do too. And that means it happened before—three and a half thousand years ago. And some of those people back then *did* survive! And they didn't have what we've got today. They didn't have underground shelters, nonperishable foods and medical supplies, generators, water pumps, communications equipment, and transportation to get away from the bad spots, or our knowledge and education. And they didn't have the Kronians out there, able to preserve that knowledge and help with the rebuilding when the time came. But some of them made it. Maybe it was just a couple here and there, or the remnants of a tribe on a mountain, but some of them had what it took to rise to something more than just getting drunk and waiting to go down in the mud. It was because of them that we were here to have a second chance. And some are going to make it this time too—and because of them there will be another chance one day to get it right." He studied the faces searchingly for a second. "Who knows? Some of them could be you."

Keene moved across to a table where he had placed the papers he had been given and collected them together. "If anyone here is planning on going over the hill because there's no hope, I'd appreciate it if you leave whatever notes and figures you have available. A final, considered report *will* be sent from here to Washington this afternoon. When the President goes on camera to face the nation, I'll have done my job. Who else here will be able to say the same thing?"

There was a long silence. John's anger had subsided. He exhaled, closed his eyes, and nodded. It wasn't necessary to say anything. Finally, Charlie Hu took it. His manner was still grave, but with a new decisiveness. "Dr. Keene is right. We all need to get some rest," he said quietly. "Can I take it that we will all convene back here at ten?" There were no dissenters.

With all the rushing around in Washington, Keene hadn't learned much about the three who had traveled with him until they got a chance to talk on the plane. Barbara was built on the heavy side and moved slowly, but she was systematic and methodical in her work. Her White House job was to tide her through while she looked after an invalid mother. After that, she had planned to go abroad, maybe to take up political journalism. Gordon was the opposite: lively, impulsive, constantly on the move or on the phone with some new angle. He had intended making some kind of a career in Washington and was due to be married in August. Clearly, they were both rational, realistic people, and yet each had talked as if those plans still meant something. Keene wondered if it was because letting go of the things which at present filled those spaces in their minds would leave no way of dealing with having nothing to replace them with. Whatever the explanation, he had tried to avoid saying things that would dispel their illusions.

Colby Greene was in his thirties, slightly built with prematurely thinning hair and large, rimless spectacles that dominated his face. Originally a mathematical chemist before joining Sloane's staff via a stint in one of the regulatory agencies—which he had despised— he was knowledgeable and quick witted, with a weirdly cynical humor that pervaded everything he did. He was under no illusions about what Athena meant, but seemed almost to regard it as not especially surprising—as if some kind of disaster or other had been the inevitable destiny toward which the absurd theater of human existence had been directing itself from the beginning. "Life is a plane you never wanted to get on, which you know is going to crash," he'd explained to Keene in the bus that had

brought them from March Air Force Base to JPL. "So
what's the big deal if you get shot down a little bit
sooner?"

It all answered a question that Keene had sometimes pondered, of how people had coped and somehow managed to get through such things as genocidal
war, mass bombing, political terror, earthquake,
plague, and other situations of devastation and terror, and in particular how he himself would behave
if ever faced by the kind of inevitability they were
seeing now. The short answer seemed to be that you
pretty much carried on as normal as best you could,
for the simple reason that there wasn't a lot else that
you could do.

Since they had also grabbed some sleep on the
plane, they spent the small hours going over the
work done so far and preparing a general form for
the report to be sent that afternoon, details to be
filled in when the scientists returned later. Charlie
Hu stayed up to guide them through and offer what
other help he could. It made horrendous reading.
When dawn came, Keene found himself by the
window, watching the line of the San Gabriel Mountains slowly taking form in the first pink hint of day.
The night had been hazy, and the now constant
display of meteorite trails flashing across the sky,
which had been awesome seen from the plane on
the way from Andrews and was apparently all the
talk among jet travelers, was obscured. He stared
at the lights of the still sleeping city below, and for
a moment the picture came into his mind of foaming
walls of water brimming up behind the peaks and
bursting through the gaps between to roll over the
towns in the valley like breakers sweeping away footprints on a beach. Then he put it firmly out of his
mind and turned to Hu, who was explaining some
calculations to Colby.

"Charlie, is there a phone with a screen somewhere

that I can use?" It would be a reasonable hour of
the morning back east, even if on the early side.

"Sure." Hu showed him into one of the empty
offices and left, closing the door. A minute or so later,
Keene was talking to a sleepy-eyed Marvin Curtiss.
With all the things that had been going on, they
hadn't talked for two days.

"Lan, finally. I was going to call you priority today
if I didn't hear anything. Where are you?"

"At JPL in California."

"Good God. What do you know about the confusing stories we're hearing from everywhere? No two
sources seem to be saying the same thing."

"That's what I'm here to straighten out. It seems
there's politics involved, even at a time like this. Don't
ask me to go into it."

"I won't. But is it as bad as some people are telling
us?"

"Worse. I don't know if it's general knowledge yet,
but the President will be making a statement at six
tonight, Eastern Time."

"Yes, they announced it last night."

"It probably won't go into everything. . . . Look,
Marvin, major evacuation and emergency measures
are going to be set into motion very soon. When it
starts, the public authorities are going to be swamped.
I think Amspace should start putting a plan together
now to get its own people out to somewhere safer
and then take care of them for a while. There isn't
going to be much for them to do at Kingsville."

Curtiss compressed his mouth and nodded. "We
might really lose some of the coastal areas, then?"

"Marvin, we might be losing all of the Central
Plains. This is what I'm urging you to do. Collect all
the transportation you can muster—the firm's trucks
and buses and whatever people have got that's sturdy
and rugged, and also anything that can fly. If things
deteriorate rapidly, it may be a question of use it

before you lose it. Try to keep the people together before they start scattering, and have them sort out things they're going to need from stuff that can be left, and have it packed and ready. The rule is, travel light. Begin now on stocking food, fuel, and so on before the restrictions. Stake a claim on any piece of real estate you can get them to that's high. I'd like to include my people over at Protonix in it too."

Curtiss nodded his head and swallowed. "Yes . . . yes, of course." His eyes had a glazed look. "I'll start on it today. . . . When will you be back?"

"I don't really know yet. But here's a priority code that will get me if they start restricting the public system. I'll talk to you again tonight, after we hear what Hayer has to say."

"Very well, Lan. And thanks. . . ." Curtiss took in a long breath and shook his head. "Phew! . . . I don't know. All of a sudden you find you have to rethink everything. I'm not really sure what's the thing to say."

"Don't worry about it," Keene replied. "I've been seeing it a lot lately."

Next, he called Vicki, who had also been wondering what had become of him. He summarized his call to Curtiss and asked her to let the girls at the office know to begin their own preparations accordingly. Apparently Karen hadn't shown up the day before. Vicki thought she might have changed her plans and gone to Dallas already.

Uncharacteristically, Vicki seemed to be looking for something further to say when there really wasn't a lot more, as if she wanted to keep him there just a little longer. Keene realized with a start that, for the first time in the years he had known her, he was seeing her close to tears. "Oh . . . it's not so much me, it's Robin," she told him. "You give your whole life and do everything you can for them, and it comes to this. . . . What did he ever do?"

What was Keene supposed to say? "What do any

of the kids ever do?" he grunted. "Or most of any
of the people, come to that? There was never any
contract that said it has to be fair. This is the way
the deal came out." He wanted to be consoling, but
to his own ears it came out gruff and callous. Maybe
he was weary of the subject already; or just tired. It
seemed to help, nevertheless.

Vicki nodded and brushed her cheek quickly with
a knuckle. "Sorry, Lan. I'm being silly."

"Not a bit of it. We're all going to be getting a
lot sillier before very much longer," he told her.

29

While it was still morning in California, a train of meteorite impacts stitched its way like a gigantic bombing run over the tip of South America and across the southern Atlantic to beyond the Falkland Islands. Shortly afterward, a similar fall peppered the South Island of New Zealand, and satellites reported another shower in the North Pacific. The areas affected were thinly populated in all cases, but unconfirmed reports spoke of damage and some casualties in a couple of townships on the Chilean coast. An airliner on a scheduled flight from Wellington to Dunedin had disappeared, and a NASA observation satellite was no longer transmitting. On the Moon, seismometers were picking up steady impact activity; outside excursions were being limited to crews using earth-moving machinery to cover exposed parts of the bases with protective layers of regolith. Space transporters and personnel carriers were being readied to be brought back to Earth. It was evidently dawning on people in various places that life at the bottom of a deep gravity well could soon become distinctly hazardous.

❖   ❖   ❖

"Have you ever heard of the Carolina Bays?" John asked Keene across a paper-strewn table in the lab after they had watched the latest news update on one of the terminal screens. All of the scientists had returned on time. There had been little talk among them.

"Sounds like a foxhunt somewhere," Colby Greene murmured without looking up from what he was doing.

"No. What are they?" Keene asked.

"A lot of elliptical depressions in the ground and offshore all the way from New Jersey to Florida but mainly in the Carolinas—thousands of them; over a million by some counts if you include all the smaller ones. They're all aligned in parallel from northwest to southeast, with a raised rim at the southern end. You get similar things in other places around the world too. They have to be from bombardments by huge meteorite swarms. And they're recent—a few thousand years."

Keene tossed down his pen and looked back sourly. "Well, that's just great to know now. Where were you guys a couple of weeks ago and in the years before that when the Kronians needed some support?"

"That's not really fair, Lan," Charlie Hu said, turning from the wall board. "John was one of the people trying to get us into the Washington thing. We were cut out."

Keene nodded tiredly. "You're right. I take it back. Sorry, John. I guess we're all a bit edgier than we think."

"Forget it," John told him.

Cavan called around lunchtime to report what he had, using the landline connection from Washington and a personal encryption code for security, since regular communications channels were getting erratic. Keene talked to him in an empty office.

"This character Queal that Voler seems to know is with Air Force Intelligence, so I was able to get a couple of things from nameless friends at my former employer that I remember so fondly," Cavan said. "He's involved with high-level security at Space Command, which gives him connections. A look at message traffic over the past forty-eight hours turns up a hive of activity between Queal's office and a section of the Pentagon that handles FAST operations, headed by a Colonel Winter. And Winter turns out to be the person that Beckerson was visiting at the Pentagon the night before last, when you were at the White House meeting. In fact, it seems that Beckerson was instrumental in getting Winter the position."

"Interesting," Keene pronounced. The Facilities Security Teams were the Air Force's assault and infiltration units, trained for the penetration of air bases, launch sites, and other installations in the event of seizure by terrorists or other such situations. Not only did Keene's suspicion of something being planned that involved Voler appear to be well founded, but now it was beginning to look as if the Vice President might be part of it too.

"It gets more interesting," Cavan said. "As of this morning, your man Hixson at Goddard has gone missing too. Now that strikes me as strange, seeing as how he's supposed to be near the center of a crisis situation. So what do you make of that?"

"Something extreme, and sometime soon," Keene replied. "Any ideas?"

"Not really," Cavan confessed. "One thought I had was that they could be fixing to grab themselves a ready-equipped bolt-hole somewhere deep and safe, but it didn't add up. Voler would have no trouble getting onto the official lists anyway."

"Maybe they've glimpsed what's coming and prefer to control their own private guns," Keene suggested.

"Will it really be as bad as that, Landen?"

"Afraid so. Worse than anything you'll hear tonight. If you get a chance to get on a list for one of those deep shelters yourself, go for it."

Cavan nodded slowly and somberly. "And what about yourself?"

"I'm not sure where I go after the job's done here, Leo. Maybe back to Texas to help Marvin with whatever can be done there."

"The Kronians lift off tomorrow morning. You should have gone with them. They would have found you a place, I'm sure."

"Gallian offered me one. There were things to be done that I couldn't leave."

Cavan shook his head. "You are aware that you're crazy, I hope, Landen?"

Keene snorted. "First Alicia, now me? It must be you, Leo. You just attract crazies. That's what it is."

Something exploded in the upper atmosphere above Mali, showering debris over the western Sahara and heard from Upper Volta to customs posts on the southern Algerian border. Another breakup occurred over the Sinkiang province in Central Asia, where a hysterical surveyor on a road-building project described in a phoned interview cabins and trucks at a construction camp being set ablaze, and fleeing workers cut down in a rain of red-hot fragments. In Western Australia and parts of Indonesia, red, ferruginous dust was coming down out of the sky and turning rivers and lakes the color of blood. Herd animals from Africa's veldts to the Canadian tundra were seen moving in huge, restless, undirected surges, and swarms of birds everywhere, numbering millions, fluttered agitatedly in the trees long into the night.

Not just America but practically the entire world was watching or listening when President Hayer at last went on the air from the White House to acknowledge officially what most people by now were sensing. Grave-faced leaders of Congress flanked him on either side, along with defense chiefs and scientific advisors. Celia Hayer stood a little back and to one side with their two young children, a son and a daughter.

He did not deny any of the rumors and predictions that were circulating; neither did he go out of his way to dwell on any of them unduly in a way that would make anxieties even worse. His line was in essence a more professional and resounding version of what Keene had said to the scientists at JPL that morning. In fact, as he listened, Keene got the feeling that his own effort had perhaps been unconsciously inspired by what he had known instinctively, after meeting him, the President was going to say.

Hayer called upon everyone, individuals and organizations of every kind, to forget all the things that weren't important anymore, and perhaps never had been: paychecks and promotions, prices and profits, prestige and pretenses. All that mattered now was helping each other get through. And he was insistent on making the point that some, maybe a lot more than the world was being told from some quarters, *would* get through—and, again as Keene in his own words had anticipated—that anyone listening might be among them. It appeared that humanity had faced a comparable crisis in its earlier history and pulled through. And that had been without modern technical resources and knowledge. Surely their descendants could do at least as well. They owed that much to the descendants who would follow. He concluded by quoting a paraphrasing of Winston Churchill's words from 1940, in Britain's darkest days of World War II:

"Death and sorrow will be the companions of our journey; hardship our garment; constancy and valor our only shield. We must be united, we must be undaunted,

we must be inflexible. . . . Let us, then, brace ourselves
to our duties, and so bear ourselves that those descendants and their descendants a thousand years from now
will say of us, 'This was their finest hour.' "

It was hardly a moment for applause. But the
nation, as it listened, had never before stood so solidly
as one. But why, the question came to Keene's mind,
should it have taken something like this to do it?

Afterward, while Hayer was exchanging words with
the diplomatic representatives who had attended, a
TV reporter managed to get a moment with the First
Lady and asked her if there was any truth to a rumor
that a shuttle was being prepared specifically to
evacuate children of the privileged off the surface
when the danger reached its worst. She seemed taken
by surprise at having to make a public comment, but
recovered herself rapidly.

"Well, speaking only for my own, I can hardly do
better than follow my husband's example and give you
the British Queen Mother's response when she was
asked the same thing about moving her children out
of London to escape the German bombing. And what
she said was, 'They won't go unless I go. I won't go
unless the King goes. And the King won't go under
any circumstances whatsoever.' "

By late afternoon California time, the country was
already responding. Airlines, railroads, bus and trucking
companies placed their equipment and services at the
disposal of the evacuation authorities. Hotels, schools,
malls, and office buildings inland began working on
plans to accommodate influxes from the coasts and the
lowlands. The mayor of Denver virtually opened the
entire city as a refugee camp. Switchboards were
swamped with calls from householders offering accommodation. Late in the evening, a White House aide
called to ask Keene if he would stay on in California
to assist Beckerson's staff in briefing state administrators

on the nature and scale of what was to be expected. Keene could hardly refuse. For the time being anyway, it seemed that much of the world was finally preparing to pull together. How much good would come of it in the long run was something he wasn't prepared to brood about. The last thing anyone needed was discouragement. John was detailed to drive Keene and his companions to the hotel they had been booked into on the outskirts of Pasadena a few miles away. On reaching the parking lot, they found his car and all the others covered with a sooty ash that stuck to the windshield and needed wiping with a wet cloth to clear. The air was muggy and smarting to the eyes, and Barbara had to hold a handkerchief to her face. Colby found a dent in the roof and another in the hood. The parking lot had a grainy feeling underfoot. "Don't hold your breath waiting if you decide to claim on the insurance," he told John laconically. John said something about topping up with gas as soon as he got a chance.

Although it was late by the time they reached the city, the streets were restless with people emerging from their isolation to seek security in numbers. There was a lot of hurrying this way and that, groups standing and talking, others carrying things out of houses and loading up cars. At one corner, some people were trying to restrain a struggling man shouting obscenities at a woman with a bloody face, who was screaming hysterically. Farther on, a line of cars was backed up into the street from the pumps at a convenience store, where three big men carrying baseball bats were positioned conspicuously, watching the forecourt. John tried calling the hotel to confirm the rooms but was unable to get through.

The situation when they arrived in the lobby was chaotic, with a frantic manager trying to deal with guests unable to get credit card verification, as well as a swarm of unexpected arrivals who seemed to be under the impression that rooms should be available

to anyone on demand. Having reservations from JPL
helped, and Keene and the others obtained two
connecting rooms. For safety, they decided to have
Gordon take one of the beds in the double room allocated to Barbara, and keep the connecting door open.
When he showered before turning in, Keene found
that he had to scrub thoroughly to shift the sticky
orange dust from his skin and hair. People he'd heard
in the lobby had been talking about rivers and reservoirs from Arizona to Illinois turning red.

Despite his fatigue, he slept sporadically and
uneasily. He was awakened before dawn by Charlie
Hu hammering on the door. Keene's personal phone
was dead like everyone else's, and the hotel switchboard hadn't answered. Roy Sloane had called from
Washington and needed to talk to Keene immediately.
Leaving Colby Greene in charge at the hotel, Keene
drove back with Hu beneath a luridly flaming sky
along roads already beginning to fill with loaded-down
vehicles. He found Sloane in a highly agitated state.
The entire Kronian delegation had vanished from the
Engleton. It appeared they had been kidnapped.

30

It had been done smoothly, quietly, and without fuss; so smoothly that it was almost an hour later before anyone realized the Kronians were missing. Transportation to take them to Andrews had been expected, although without an exact time being specified since the shuttle arrangements were uncertain. Not trusting Terran arrangements, Idorf had stated that he would send down a surface lander from the *Osiris* for them; but with the increasing meteorite influx he was also taking the ship out to a more distant orbit. According to the security officer in charge at the Engleton, an Air Force major with escort had arrived and presented papers that appeared in order, the authorizing officer at the Pentagon had confirmed, and the party departed fifteen minutes later in an official bus. That was the last that had been seen of them.

Keene, using the same office that he had talked with Cavan from the day before, asked Sloane if the Pentagon contact given to confirm the order had by any chance been a Colonel Winter. Sloane had to ask

Keene to hold while he checked, and then came back astonished a couple of minutes later to announce that yes, it was. How in hell had Keene known? Keene hesitated. He didn't want to compromise Cavan's position; on the other hand, this could be the moment for getting Cavan some official help, which would probably be the biggest favor that Keene could do for him right now. In the end, he summarized the parts of the story that he was reasonably sure of, making it sound like an offshoot of his own scientific investigating and mentioning Cavan as an old friend that he'd involved to check some references. His biggest dilemma was over the Vice President, Beckerson, whose connection so far was purely circumstantial. If Beckerson was a part of whatever was going on, as Cavan suspected, then obviously it should be said; but if the suspicion was wrong, then the whole operation to set up a shadow government on the West Coast could be impaired. As a feeler, Keene slipped in a casual question as to whether Beckerson and his party were still due to follow on to California as planned. Sloane replied that they were and should be leaving late that day. So Beckerson hadn't vanished; nothing had changed. Keene decided to hold off on that issue until there was more to go on.

"It's starting to make sense now," Keene said. "Voler and his group knew early on how bad this could get. The confusion was to gain them some time before controls really start tightening up. Their aim all along has been to get themselves out, and safely to Kronia with the *Osiris*. That's what it's all been about."

Sloane stared, silently assessing the pattern for himself. "They've grabbed the Kronians as bargaining chips," he said finally.

"That was the line he tried to push at the White House meeting," Keene said. "You were there, Roy. You heard him. But Hayer shot him down. Then, when it was clear that he wasn't going to get any help

officially, he tried selling me on the idea at Goddard
the next morning, hoping I'd be willing to bargain
with the Kronians to take them. That didn't work, so
now they've taken matters into their own hands and
seized the delegation as hostages. . . ."

Sloane had followed it through and nodded slowly.
"To force their way aboard the lander that Idorf is
sending down to Andrews," he completed.

A brief silence ensued while they thought over the
various angles and options.

"Correct. And we *have* to let it land, just as Idorf
has to send it, even though we know," Keene said.
"There's no way we can afford to hold off."

"How come?" Sloane asked.

"Because we don't know how much time there is.
Put yourself in Idorf's place. Those are your people
down there, and conditions are worsening. Even if
they've got guys holding guns to their heads, you have
to bring them up because if you don't do it now you
might never get to bring them up at all. If you refuse,
who would be holding them hostage then? And the
same applies to us. That's what Voler and his people
are banking on. Idorf has to provide the lander, and
unless we can separate Voler's group from the Kronians,
we have to let it go. It's out-and-out blackmail, Roy,
I know, but we're stuck."

Sloane glowered from the screen, but there could
be no serious argument. Keene was right. "Well, at
least we know they're still in the area somewhere,"
he said tightly. "Probably they'll be gearing toward
all the action happening around the pad. If we can
locate them it might be possible to go in with a CT
team sooner, when they're not expecting it."

"Be careful. They've got Air Force FAST guys
there," Keene cautioned.

"I'm aware of that," Sloane said. "At least we have
foreknowledge now of where they'll show up and
when. One thing you can be sure of, Lan, is that from

now on they won't be able to afford one false move. We'll have our best people in on this. Andrews will be covered tighter than a presidential parade."

"Well, I'm not going to pretend to be an expert in that department," Keene said. "You've got them all there. I'll go with whatever you and they come up with." He left Sloane still frowning and looking thoughtful, glad it wasn't a decision he was going to have to make.

Further news since the previous night was that, with the failure of several more satellites and increasingly capricious atmospheric conditions, the world's communications were beginning to falter. Domestic broadcasting cut back to reserve capacity for official traffic. Although the communications difficulties made it impossible to know the exact number and doubtless caused exaggerations, more aircraft had been lost, with the result that some airlines had grounded while others were attempting to maintain a reduced level of lower-altitude services for vital needs—in some instances against the opposition of rebellious crews. On the other hand, many among the public had taken the message of the U.S. President and other leaders who had spoken in similar vein to mean that airlines were now public property and descended on the already beleaguered airports in droves. Amsterdam, a vital European hub, was closed after a panicking crowd numbering thousands, who had been arriving throughout the night, started a rampage that led to riot police being called in with water cannon and tear gas. In JPL's vicinity, police checkpoints had been set up to control access to both John Wayne and Burbank airports, while LAX reported traffic at a standstill on all approaches. Despite the appeals for dedication and nobility of spirit in the common cause, marauding and looting mobs had taken to the streets in several cities. Violent incidents were occurring already. People had been shot.

✧   ✧   ✧

When people are afraid, they stop talking about individual rights and freedoms, and draw together under authorities that promise protection. The JPL employees turned spontaneously to its administration for organization and guidance, and to Charlie Hu's admitted surprise, began showing up more or less on time, many of them bringing children that they were unwilling or unable to entrust to any other care, or simply too fearful to let out of their sight. Obviously, there was little thought of carrying on business as usual—most of which had ceased to mean very much, anyway. The Medical Department was busy treating cases of skin and eye irritation from the falling dust. A bulletin was circulated around the departments advising people to stay inside as much as possible, cover up when outside, bathe the eyes every hour in a weak alkaline solution, and avoid drinking any water tainted red. Keene was only able to catch Hu sporadically, hurrying between offices and phone calls as the Laboratory's directors tried to formulate some kind of plan and coordinate with institutions such as UCLA. A Pasadena police guard had been added to the regular security force at the main gate after a gang tried forcing its way in the previous night—nobody knew why. Police were trying to keep the populations static in places farther inland like Pasadena so that the evacuation of areas closest to the ocean could be got under way first, but not everyone was heeding. The National Guard was already deploying in the LA basin districts, where hoarding had been declared illegal and food stocks beyond a stated limit per person or family were being requisitioned for official redistribution. There were rumors that an incoming widebody, damaged in flight, had crashed on approach somewhere in Inglewood.

Hu sent a technician with two security guards to collect the other three from the hotel. They arrived with their belongings packed, including Keene's. It

seemed there was no manager, and the few staff that
had shown up were letting friends from the neighborhood help themselves to bedding, linen, and the
contents of vending machines, and selling off the
kitchen stores. With credit cards already as good as
useless, cash was becoming suspect. Preferred cur-
rencies were nonperishable foods, any kind of drink,
drugs, and gasoline. After Keene left the hotel, there
had been trouble with people siphoning gas from cars
in the parking lot, and somebody had been shot.
Gordon, still incredulous, described the scene to
Keene. "The cops were there, but then they got called
away on some higher priority. Can you believe that?
There's a guy lying dead in the parking lot, and they
have to leave! I mean, I know this is LA, but I
thought it was only like that in the movies."

Gordon was concerned for his folks and his fiancée
back in Washington. Barbara was worried about the
help who was supposed to be taking care of her
mother. Keene agreed that their work here was done
and asked Colby Greene to talk to the local command
about getting them back before things got any worse.
Colby himself offered to stay on and help Keene with
the task of briefing Beckerson's West Coast administration. "It might be safer here," he remarked, eyeing
Keene indecipherably through his huge spectacles.
"From what we've been hearing, everything the other
side of the fault might just as likely fall into the
Atlantic. I always wanted a beachfront pad."

Wally Lomack got through to Keene on the Washington line around lunchtime. He was still at the White
House but due to leave that evening on an official
plane going to Houston. His job with the Kronians was
done, and whatever happened when they reappeared
would no longer involve him. The lander from the
Osiris was on the ground at Andrews; the next move
was up to Voler's group. It was time for Lomack to get
back to Emma and his family in Texas.

"I don't know that there's much a fellow of my age can do, but what else is there?" he said from the screen. Keene couldn't help thinking that he seemed to have aged another ten years. "At least whatever happens, we'll all be together. I just wanted to say so long and all that while there's still the chance. It's been great working with a guy like you, Lan. It's a pity we won't be doing too much more of it for a while. What about you?"

"I don't know. There's more to be doing here for a while," Keene said.

"Will you be heading back afterward?"

"Right now, Wally, it's impossible to say. In case that turns out not to be practicable, I talked to Marvin about including my people there in whatever plans the firm works out—you know, Vicki and the others."

Lomack nodded. "I talked to Marvin too. Look, there's something you ought to know about. He's arranging for that minishuttle that's at Montemorelos to be fueled and kept at launch readiness. There's no hard and fast plan as to how it's to be used or when. Just a precaution. It seems like everybody in the world with access to launch capability is trying to take insurance. Everything that will move is coming back from the Moon. There's fighting going on for possession of some of the European bases. Apparently there have been some unscheduled launchings from Eastern Siberia and China."

Keene's eyebrows rose in surprise. "Already?"

Lomack nodded wearily. "Nobody's sure exactly why. But then, a lot of people aren't reacting exactly rationally, anyway."

There wasn't a lot else to say. Keene showed his hands and sighed. "Well, Wally, what can I tell you? It was good, as you say. We sure ran some rings around those guys, didn't we? I guess the Kronians have the ball for a while now. . . ."

Lomack looked away as a voice shouted something

from the background. "Yes, it's him now," he called offscreen. Then, turning back to Keene, "Roy Sloane says he wants a word. Sounds urgent."

"Okay. Try and take care, Wally."

"Good-bye, Lan."

Sloane's features replaced Lomack's on the screen. "Lan," he said without preliminaries. "They picked up Hixson. He was shacked up in a motel twenty miles outside the city with another Goddard name who must have been on the list."

"You *got* the son of a bitch!" Keene exclaimed.

"Damn right. The FBI are interrogating them now."

"Are they getting anywhere?"

"It looks like it. Hixson's cooperating and agreed to carry on normally so as not to give away that he's blown—I guess, trying to work a deal that'll get him out. Seems we're talking about an H-hour just before dawn tomorrow. We know the times, their movement plan, how they'll be coming in. With that information, our CT guys can have their units right there—plus the surprise. They say they've got all the odds."

Keene frowned as he thought about it.

"You don't look too pleased," Sloane commented.

"The intention must be for Hixson and this other guy to be collected sometime. Obviously you're going to have to let them go. They have to be there."

"That's true," Sloane agreed. "But for my money we can trust him. He's got no future with Voler now, and he's desperate. I can smell the sweat from here. With us he might have an out. That'll be enough to turn him. I know the type."

"Let's hope you're right," Keene said. He was still uneasy. Why wait that long if the lander from the *Osiris* was already down? Maybe they had a larger party to collect together than had been realized. "Are Beckerson and his party still coming as planned?" he asked curiously.

"Leaving tonight on schedule," Sloane answered. "No changes. Why?"

"Oh, just checking. I've got my own plans to think about too," Keene said vaguely. So Cavan's suspicions in that regard seemed to have been misplaced. Keene was glad that he had held back before making insinuations. He just hoped that when the showdown came at Andrews, nobody would lose their head or start overreacting in the ways that get people killed. Too many people would be there that he cared about.

An hour after Keene talked to Sloane, reports started coming in over the channels that JPL was linked into that a meteorite carpet had unrolled in a thousand-mile hail, which was falling from Minneapolis to Ottawa. Aerial shots showed parts of Detroit on fire and miles of suburbs with houses demolished, roads blocked by stricken vehicles, and in low passes, people frantically waving at the camera aircraft to send help. Footage from the ground in Chicago looked like the aftermath of an air raid: fire trucks and ambulances in smoke-filled streets littered with rubble; mangled cars; rescuers digging into piles of glass and debris fallen from shattered high-rises. A dazed woman talked incoherently about "a river of stones that came down out of the sky. They just kept falling and falling. . . ." Nobody knew the extent of the damage among the smaller townships and rural dwellings spread across such a huge area. The police commissioner in Toronto was filmed as saying, "There have to be thousands dead out there. . . . We've no way of telling. Communications are out. Everything's out. Jesus, and this is only the beginning!"

And then Charlie Hu told Keene that he was wanted at the Tracking Center in one of the other buildings, which was still managing to maintain a link to the *Osiris* by juggling with the surviving relay satellites. Idorf was asking for him, and the President

in Washington was also on the circuit. Four craft that
had failed to identify themselves were approaching
the *Osiris* and had ignored attempts to communicate.
Idorf wanted to remind whoever had dispatched them
that one of the *Osiris*'s laser bombs was armed and
ready to launch. Until the Kronian delegation was
returned safely to the ship, the hundred-mile limit
that he had declared previously still stood.

31

Keene, Colby, and Charlie Hu stood in a semicircle of tense-faced controllers and technicians, facing an array of consoles. The screens showed Idorf on the Control Deck of the *Osiris*, President Hayer with several aides and service chiefs in Washington, and various data plots. All that could be ascertained of the approaching vessels were their positions, courses, and estimates of their likely sizes from radar echoes. They still hadn't responded to signals. Nobody knew where they were from, or even if they were crewed or being remotely operated. The only observation satellite in a position to make a visual identification had been malfunctioning for several hours and couldn't be oriented in the right direction. Suspicion was that they were the launches detected earlier in eastern Asia, but attempts to contact the authorities in those regions had so far elicited either no response or denials. Colby Greene's guess was that Voler and Company—hardly surprisingly—had not been the only ones to think of escaping to Kronia by commandeering the *Osiris*. While Keene and the others had been on their way across from the other building, the *Osiris* had launched its bomb. The weapon was now sitting in a parallel orbit a little over fifty miles off, ready to fire.

"I want it witnessed that I have made every attempt to reaffirm my warning to whoever ordered this," Idorf said. "The only contacts that we have been able to make from up here all claim to know nothing. It seems that your attempts have fared no better. I am left with no choice."

"Communications everywhere are in shambles," Hayer said.

"Then it would behoove those responsible, all the more, to make their intentions plain," Idorf replied. "Consider my position. Our delegation has been kidnapped, almost certainly to be used as hostages. So we already have evidence of designs in some quarters to seize this ship. In such circumstances I have no option but to treat these vessels as hostile. As captain, I must place the safety of the *Osiris* before all else."

Hayer closed his eyes, and nodded. Several of those with him exchanged solemn looks but none spoke.

"The lead object is approaching the fire line," one of the operators handling the radar data announced from his console. Attention turned to a holo display that was copying the situation report relayed from the *Osiris*. It showed part of a translucent red sphere centered on a white, three-way cross representing the *Osiris*, with the four vessels shown as blue dots moving in from outside. Idorf had stated that he would have no part in any verbal melodramatics. The weapon would detonate automatically if the boundary was breached. Since the *Osiris* did not carry an unlimited supply of them, it was set with lasing rods registering on all four targets.

"We are transmitting at them continuously on all of your recognized international bands. . . ." Idorf reminded everyone.

Keene watched with a strangely detached fascination, having to force himself to be mindful that these slowly moving patterns of light were not part of some simulation or one of Robin's computer games, but a depiction of real events taking place some hundreds of miles above their heads at that very moment. Beside him, Colby Greene stared unblinkingly through his spectacles and licked his lips dryly.

"Lead object at the limit now," the radar tech announced.

Moments later, a different voice reported, "Detonation has been detected."

And after several more seconds: "Target echoes getting weaker, starting to break up."

On the screen showing the *Osiris's* Control Deck, Idorf turned and left without another word. And that was all there was to it. Impersonalized, soundless warfare, automated and sanitized modern style.

While the link was still open, one of the Kronian crew patched in the current views from high orbit. Fires were spreading across what looked like half the grasslands of southern Africa, with burning patches of oil lighting up the western Indian Ocean from Madagascar to Somalia. The world was turning into a ball of dirty smoke. A view away from Earth showed Athena like an immense, glowing octopus, its incandescent tentacles reaching ahead as it drew nearer.

Late in the afternoon, Keene managed to get a connection to Corpus Christi through a JPL hookup into Amspace's spacecraft tracking net and talked to Harry Halloran, the technical vice president. Curtiss had gone ahead and put together an evacuation scheme since there was still no clear direction from the city and county authorities. The intention was to move inland to Lubbock, where the state was preparing reception centers, and which put them on the way to still higher country if a further move became necessary. There had been scattered meteorite falls all over southern Texas. Les Urkin's bedroom and the family room beneath it were demolished five minutes after he went down to join his wife for breakfast. The family had packed their things and moved to Kingsville, where everyone was assembling. The downtown office was already closed. Harry couldn't say if any of the girls from Protonix had arrived, and as far as he knew there was no sign yet of Wally Lomack back from Washington. The weather over the Gulf was doing strange things, and fears were rising of hurricane and tornado conditions developing. The sea out there was like black, moving mountains. Keene told him that the JPL scientists had talked about immense amounts of heat being dumped in the upper atmosphere. Nobody was sure what the effects of the resultant instabilities might be. Harry said that cattle inland were going crazy from corrosive air and thirst. Water supplies were already the big concern.

After Barbara and Gordon left in a JPL shuttle bus to catch an overnight military flight heading east out of March AFB, Keene and Colby Greene sat in one of the labs, wearily contemplating the updates still coming in via JPL's various connections to the world. The full magnitude of what was happening was at last becoming plain, leaving them numbed to the degree that they didn't want to hear any more. There was no point.

"So what's it with you, Colby?" Keene asked. "Don't you have anyone there to rush back to as well? Never got married, eh?"

Greene pulled a face and regarded the papers lying around the desk in front of him indifferently. "Oh, I thought about it once or twice. I looked at the way it usually seems to go, and figured I'd do it the easy way—you know, without wasting all that time that most guys seem to go through."

"Oh? And what's the easy way?" Keene asked.

"Just pick a woman you don't like very much and buy her a house—then you can forget about it and get on with your life. But I never could find the right one, somehow. I always ended up liking them. . . . How about you?"

"Aw, did it once. Crashed and burned. You won't believe who she was."

"Try me."

"Her name's Fey. She's Herbert Voler's wife now."

"I don't believe it. What happened? . . . If it's any of my business."

Keene really wasn't in a mood to go into explanations. "If I just say that she found her perfect match at last, would that tell you?" he offered.

Greene nodded. "Pretty much." He rubbed his nose with a knuckle. "So will she be involved in this showdown at Andrews?"

Keene hadn't really given it much thought. "Yes, I guess she will," he said. So much for the social set and the mansion in Connecticut.

Keene's disquiet over the situation in Washington was increasing. It would be late into the evening there now, yet the latest news was that Hixson and the other man with him were still at the motel. The FBI had reported only a note delivered by messenger telling them to sit tight. If communications were a problem, it would be all the more reason to move them out sooner. Something felt wrong.

The door opened, and Charlie Hu stuck his head in. "I just wanted to let you guys know: Don't be surprised to see Guard patrols with guns in the area if you go out. There's been some trouble with looting. All kinds are coming through from the city, and we've got some pricey real estate just west of here around La Canada."

"As if that's going to matter for much longer," Keene snorted.

Hu shrugged. "I guess the same people will be

giving the orders for a while yet. But anyhow, be warned. The police chief advises that if you possess weapons it would be a good idea to carry them." Colby said nothing but opened his jacket to reveal the butt of an automatic sitting in a shoulder holster. "How about you?" Hu asked Keene.

"I went to Washington to attend a meeting with the President, remember?"

"I'll see if we can get you fixed up."

Cavan called a little over thirty minutes later. There had still been no move to collect Hixson and his companion from the motel.

"It's too quiet, Leo," Keene said. "Things should be happening by now. Either they're onto us, or there's more going on than we think."

"Exactly the sentiments I've been having," Cavan informed him. "So I thought I'd try using some of these official resources that I find I have access to now. It's really quite amazing. It occurred to me that whatever Voler is really up to, his charming wife won't be far behind. Perhaps we could get a pointer to his movements and possible plans if we knew something of hers."

"Fey? We were just talking about her here. So did you get anywhere?"

"Yes, as a matter of fact. After I'd drawn several blanks elsewhere, I tried checking the airline reservation computers. And there she was, booked to LA. The original flight has been canceled, but she got transferred to an emergency service that left Boston earlier this evening. That must have taken a fair amount of string-pulling on the part of somebody, somewhere."

"To *LA*?" Keene could only stare bemusedly.

"Intriguing, isn't it?" Cavan agreed. "And it gets more so. Who do you think is on the same flight also? Our friend Tyndam from Cambridge. I doubt very much if they're eloping together. I doubt if he'd be her type. I can only assume that they're joining the rest of the party." Cavan waited, expressionless, for Keene to figure the rest out.

Fey and Tyndam were flying to California that night. And, interestingly, Beckerson was also flying to California, practically at the same time, nominally on official duties. Perhaps Cavan's suspicion had been correct after all, and Beckerson *was* part of it! . . . But if that were so, then the whole business at Andrews had to be a diversion. Nothing was going to happen there.

"Hixson and this guy with him have been set up," Keene murmured. "They're not going to be collected at all. They're sacrificial—to keep us busy watching."

"You're getting there, Landen," Cavan said. "So the real action will be in California. The question is where. There's only one place I can think of. And with Queal and his connections through Air Force Intelligence, it all fits."

Keene stared back at the sparse frame and features watching patiently from the screen. The aim, surely, was still to get aboard and probably seize control of the *Osiris*. They already had the hostages to get them past the defenses. The only other thing needed was a vessel to get them up there. As Cavan had said, if they were on their way to southern California, there was only one answer.

"*My God!*" Keene breathed. "It's got to be Vandenberg. While everyone's waiting for something to happen at Andrews, they've been quietly getting a shuttle organized there. Queal would have the contacts to arrange it."

"Full marks," Cavan said.

"Have you talked to Hayer?"

"Yes, but he's not sure how to deal with it. If somebody like Beckerson is involved, how do we know who can be trusted? If the commander there is in on it too and we tip him off so that he warns the others away, the Kronians will never leave at all because Idorf is on limited time. The only way we'll get those people back is by letting the thing go through as if we know nothing and grabbing them when they appear. And there's only one person anywhere close who can move soon enough without drawing the wrong kind of attention. And that's you, Landen."

32

Red sulfurous dust and blinding vapors, mixed into a choking haze with the exhausts from thousands of vehicles, swirled through the headlight beams of the traffic groping its way along Interstate 5 North out of Glendale. Sheila, the technician driving the JPL shuttle bus, craned forward in her seat to keep sight, through the arc smeared by the laboring windshield wiper, of the flashing red and blue lights of the police escort leading them on the inside lane that was supposed to be reserved for official use. Outside in the murk, police, military, and volunteers in hooded capes and chemical warfare garb yelled, cursed, and waved flashlamps to direct the lines, hauled breakdowns clear, and kept interlopers out of the official lane, while fifteen million people tried to squeeze through the four main routes inland from the Los Angeles basin.

Keene, clad like the others in a military combat jacket, woollen comforter cap, and hooded smock that some JPL high-up's talking to the local National Guard commander had procured, and packing underneath it a hip-holstered .45 automatic, sat behind the Guard captain occupying the front passenger seat. Charlie, Colby Greene, and John were wedged in the other seats, along with an armed trooper, and two more troopers were at the back, inside the rear door. The bus itself looked as if it was equipped for a safari, with boxes of supplies, extra weapons, jerrycans of gasoline and water piled inside, and a layer of sandbags lashed to the roof as a protection against falling rocks. It had been decided earlier in the day to have all the Lab's trucks and buses preequipped for evacuation at short notice. Keene, Charlie, and Colby would be flying on to Vandenberg, 160 miles north on the coast, with a hastily organized Marine Corps detachment that they were to meet. John had come along to keep Sheila company and would return to JPL with the bus and its Guard escort afterward.

The plan was as simple as it was audacious—and in the time available, about as much as could have been contemplated. The first point agreed was that with no way of knowing where anyone stood, no approach could be made to the Space Command hierarchy at Vandenberg, which was headed by a two-star general called Ullman, commander of the Fourteenth Air Force, who lived on the base. However, Charlie Hu had, in connection with missions staged over several years involving both the Air Force and JPL, dealt with others there that he was willing to guess would be reliable. Admittedly, that meant relying totally on Charlie's personal experiences and gut feeling, but it was the best there was. The airbase section of the Vandenberg facility was commanded by a Colonel Lacey, who, everyone was agreed to gamble, would probably not be a part of Voler and Queal's scheme. The plan, then, was to get a small group into the Vandenberg air base, recruit Colonel Lacey's help in making contact with names in the space-launch facility that Charlie had vouched for, and figure the rest out from there. Communications problems and other pressures had defeated attempts to contact Lacey ahead of time, and they had decided they could wait no longer. Sloane in Washington was continuing to try, but failing that they would place their hope in being able to convince Lacey after they were in. That, of course, left the question of how to get an unauthorized group of people into a top-security military facility without advance clearance. Colby Greene had come up with the obvious way after they had debated several impractical alternatives: "It's an Air Force base. The sky's unloading and causing emergencies everywhere. You fly in posing as a plane in trouble that needs to get down. Then play it by ear."

One of the JPL directors had talked with the area National Guard commander, who, after being satisfied that this was coming from the President's office, had gone back through the local military chain to acquire the means. The outcome was that a Cessna Caravan with support squad was being rushed in from the Twentynine Palms Marine base and would meet them at Burbank. JPL had essentially ceased functioning as a national laboratory and was being adapted as a transit center and shelter for public-sector workers and their kin en route inland. The last Keene and the others had seen of it had been bulldozers working under floodlights in the fog to bank earth against the walls of suitable buildings, while crews sandbagged the roofs and lower floors. South of the Laboratory, the Army was taking over the Rose Bowl golf course as a transportation depot and supply dump.

Sheila muttered something and braked as the escort car in front slowed. Tail lights beyond showed vehicles ahead of it. The sound of the police cruiser's siren floated back above the traffic noise, but the lane to the left was solid. Finally, risking unlit vehicles pulled over, the cruiser swung onto the shoulder and began

overhauling the obstructions leapfrog fashion on the
inside, with the shuttle bus clinging yards behind.
Lights ahead as they pulled back into the regular lane
showed a group of military vehicles parked on the
shoulder. Two of them moved off and swung in
behind the shuttle bus as it passed, and then dropped
back to head off the encroachers. A smoky halo of
light in front of a stopped car revealed a knot of
windblown figures struggling to change a wheel on
a jacked-up camper. More lights ahead marked the
tail of a military convoy. The police escort and bus
closed up and stayed with it to the Burbank exit,
where the tailback from the exit ramp extended for
at least a quarter mile along the shoulder. The escort
led them past, and they were waved through by police
in capes and motorcycle visors directing airport traffic
at the top.

The airport approach was a confusion of cars
parked haphazardly in the roadways and others jostling for whatever space became available. Checkpoints had been set up across the road leading into
the departures drop-off area. The cruiser led the bus
to a gate bearing the sign AUTHORIZED ACCESS ONLY and
halted. A dust-covered shape, looking in the glare
from the lamps like a yeti of the desert, materialized
outside Sheila's window. He had a hood with an
enormous, fur-trimmed rim, in the shadows of which
could vaguely be discerned a transparent visor and
mask covering the lower face. Colby squeezed forward alongside Sheila, brandishing a plastic wallet
showing his White House ID and a pass from the
Pasadena regional military command.

"There's supposed to be a Marine Corps flight coming in to collect us," he shouted out the window. "It's
top priority—White House directive. What do we do?"
The yeti gave the papers a perfunctory glance, as if
acknowledging that they belonged to a world already
passing. "Wait," a voice instructed from somewhere

inside the hood, and the figure disappeared inside the gatehouse. Keene was impressed by the amount of organization that was managing to persist. Power was flowing; planes were flying. People were still at their jobs. But as he had said himself the previous day, what else was there for anyone to do?

Lights appeared in the roadway behind the bus, and a horn began blaring.

"All we needed was an asshole," Sheila sighed, resting her arms on the wheel and staring at her mirror dully. More figures came out of the shadows and went back to deal with it. The desert yeti reemerged. "I can't get ahold of anyone who knows anything. Look, there's a traffic information center set up somewhere off the Departure Hall. They've got a line through to the tower, so they'll know about as much as anybody."

"What's the name of the room it's in?" Greene yelled back out.

"You'll have to find somebody in there to tell you."

"Where do I park?" Sheila asked.

One side of the cape rose as the gesture of a shaggy forelimb. "What are they gonna do, give you a ticket?" Sheila drove around into a service yard and found space among a jumble of vehicles and baggage carts around a side entrance. The captain detailed two of the Guardsmen to stay with the bus while he and the other accompanied the rest of the party inside.

The scene inside the airport building resembled a refugee station—which in effect it was. People sat among piles of bags or huddled on blankets and sleeping bags laid out on the floor, some trying to calm cranky, overtired children, some managing to doze, others just staring blankly. There were lines at a number of the check-in desks, where hand-lettered signs identified parties being assembled and destinations. Regular schedules had been abandoned, and it seemed that which airline owned or was operating any particular

flight no longer meant very much. The public address
system endlessly paged names to call various numbers
or meet other parties at stated places. As Keene
watched, a woman with a clipboard waited while a
group whose names she had called collected their
belongings, and then led them away in the direction
of the gates. Along the far wall, several dozen young
children in wheelchairs, many of them cuddling toys,
waited while a procession of nurses brought more in
from a line of ambulances and buses drawn up under
the canopy outside the main entrance. Keene swallowed a lump in his throat and looked away.

Colby came back from the throng of people around
the Information Desk, followed by a couple of uni-
formed police. "We follow these guys," he told the
others. Sheila and John fell in on either side of him,
Keene and Charlie behind, the Guardsman and captain bringing up the rear. They passed a restaurant
area where soup, sandwiches, and beverages were
being handed out at a long table; a knot of people
were sitting on the floor playing cards; a young man
was playing a violin to a bar where there was no TV.
Many of the faces had looked bloody, but closer up
Keene realized that the streaks and blotches were red
dust lodged in creases or mixed with perspiration, and
skin sores angry from rubbing and scratching. There
was little show of belligerence. The prevailing mood
was tiredness, resignation, waiting.

The Traffic Information Center turned out to be
a large room off one of the side corridors, where a
score or so of people were working at tables covered
with papers piled among constantly ringing phones.
An improvised wall board with information entered
by hand showed traffic situations and projections, and
an Army field telephone exchange had been installed
at the rear with cables trailing out through a far door.
In one corner was a coffee pot with a tray of plates
containing remnants of bagels, muffins, and vending

snacks. A line of tables across the near end of the room formed a counter barring off the rest of the area. Clerks at the front were trying to deal with a press of people jostling for attention, while others updated the board.

"I always wondered what they'd do when all the computers went down at once," Colby remarked, surveying the scene.

One of the policeman called over a man in shirt-sleeves and a headset and beckoned Colby forward. Colby identified himself and explained the situation. The man in the headset went away to consult with one of the others, who referred to a screen that evidently was able to report something, then called somewhere on a phone. He returned to the counter.

"We have that flight logged, but it doesn't look as if it's here yet. The tower has instructions to clear it in, priority. I don't know yet where it will be directed. We'll put a call out when we know something more."

"You are aware that we're on a presidential directive here," Greene said, appearing irritated by what he seemed to take as perfunctory treatment.

"Sir, if you were here under a directive from Jesus Christ, there's nothing more I could do. When it shows up, we'll let you know. A lot of flights aren't making it."

"Ease up, Colby. They can't wave wands. We're just taking up space here," Keene murmured. Mollified, Greene let himself be ushered out to the corridor. They walked back to a part of the main ticketing concourse, where more people with children and baggage were sitting along the walls. A sad-faced black woman was dispensing coffee and hot dogs from a snack bar that seemed to have run out of all else.

"Are you people gonna need us for anything else?" one of the policemen asked.

"I'd prefer it if you stick around," Colby told them.

"We may need directions where to go when the plane shows up."

"Could you guys use some coffee?" Sheila asked them.

"Sure, why not?"

"Better make it all of us while we've got the chance," Keene said.

Sheila went to the counter and picked up a tray, John following to lend a hand. "How do we pay for this?" Sheila asked the black woman.

"You might as well just take 'em. I don't know what else to do with it."

They stood around, like everyone else—waiting. Sheila and John found a couple of vacated chairs. Colby stood to one side, talking with the Guard captain. Charlie Hu leaned back against the wall and sipped his coffee. Keene moved over to the policemen. "How bad is it getting to be out there?" he asked them in a low voice.

"It's a mess, but still pretty orderly," one of them answered. "Most people are trying to do the right thing. They're not panicking yet."

"You figure it'll get worse, eh?"

"Oh, while there's somebody to tell them what to do, and they've still got food and gas and electricity, to a lot of them it's still just an adventure. When stuff starts running out and they realize it isn't a game anymore, that's when it'll get ugly."

"We've been lucky down here so far," the other cop said. "There were some big falls north of San Francisco and farther on up the state. They've got blocked freeways up there. Lotta cars hit right out there on the road."

Two middle-aged ladies came over and drew the policemen away to ask them about something. Keene moved over to join Charlie. "You know, we only just met, and you're already beginning to amaze me. You're actually managing to look serene. What's the secret?"

Charlie smiled distantly. "Well, you know how it is. Inscrutable Orientals and that kind of thing."

Keene drank from his coffee cup. "So which particular brand of inscrutability are you from? Chinese?"

"Taiwanese, actually. But I was born in Carson City, Nevada."

"So . . ." Keene frowned, wondering how best to put it. "This business up the coast. You know things are going to get worse. Traveling might soon get really problematical. You don't have someone somewhere that you should . . . You know what I'm trying to say."

Charlie smiled again, this time cynically. "Well, yes, there is a Mrs. Hu. However, relationships are not exactly, shall we say . . . exemplary. She disappeared off to LA a week ago, I think to see the boyfriend. Anyway, I haven't heard from her since. Which is all a long way of saying, you don't have to worry about it."

"Oh, I'm sorry. Look, I—"

"No, it's okay. Thanks, I appreciate the consideration."

Sheila got up and left them—out of sensible anticipation, she said—after noticing that the line from the ladies' room was backed up into the concourse. Colby wandered away along the side of the concourse, stood looking around for a minute or two, then came back. "If LAX is anything like this, they could easily miss them," he said to Keene. Keene could only shrug.

Cavan had told them that Washington was arranging for Fey and Tyndam to be watched when they arrived at Los Angeles, but not apprehended. Beckerson's flight was routed to Edwards AFB, situated in the high desert above Palmdale—reinforcing Keene's belief that the regional command center was somewhere under the mountains in that direction. However, the plan could be to divert the flight to join up with Voler's group, wherever it was, perhaps collecting Fey and

Tyndam from Los Angeles on the way. Alternatively, another aircraft could be waiting at Edwards. Various possibilities existed as to how they might all get together. The hope was that observing how Fey and Tyndam were met and in which direction they were taken might provide further clues as to what might be expected at Vandenberg.

One of the cops left to make a circuit of the concourse. Sheila came back.

Charlie Hu returned from a newsstand with a week-old copy of *Time*, which he proceeded to thumb through sitting on the floor with his back to a wall. The front cover showed a picture of Athena rounding the Sun with the caption: WHY THE DOOMSAYERS ARE WRONG.

And then public address announced: "Colby Greene, contact Traffic Information Center. Mr. Colby Greene from Washington. We have flight information for you."

Everyone hastened back to the room with the phones and the wall board. The same clerk that Colby had talked to before told them, "It should be landing now—a Cessna Caravan, flight code MU87. Board out on the tarmac. They're bringing it right up to the door. Go to Gate 3 and wait at the top of the stairs leading down to the outside access door. Somebody will meet you there." He handed Greene a pass. "Gate-area access is being controlled. You'll need to show this."

Preceded by the two policemen, the party hurried through the departure concourse and through the check to the gates. There was a flight boarding at Gate 3 when they arrived. A girl with dusty, wind-blown hair and wearing a crumpled Delta uniform under a red-streaked raincoat led them past the slowly shuffling line and unlocked a door next to the jetway entrance. They went down two flights of steel-railed stairs to a lower space and across to a door, where the girl stopped to peer through a narrow window.

"Your plane is just taxiing up now. We'll give it a minute to make its turn."

Keene and the two leaving with him turned to face the others. There was a moment of awkward silence. Then John extended a hand and shook it with each of them. "Well . . . I guess this is it. Let's hope it works out. Maybe we'll . . ." He seemed to think better of whatever he had been about to say and left it unfinished.

Sheila followed suit, shaking hands first with Keene and Colby; then, on impulse, she threw her arms around Charlie in a hug. Suddenly, she was crying. "Oh shit. . . . I can't believe you won't be there in your office tomorrow, Charlie, with everything back the way it was. Are we even going to see you again?"

"They're here. The door's open," the Delta girl informed them.

Charlie released Sheila gently, and managed a smile. "All good things, you know. . . . It's like Lan said yesterday, you do what you have to. Take care of her for us, John."

"You guys take care too," the Guard captain said.

The Delta girl opened the door, and immediately swirls of wind-driven dust spattered through. A boxy, single-engined craft, its airscrew still turning, was waiting in the shadow of the huge widebody loading from the regular jetway above. Colby wrapped his parka tightly about himself, held onto his hood, and ducked out into the swirling orange fog. Charlie followed, then Keene. "Good luck, whatever it is," one of the cops called after them.

Acrid fumes stung Keene's nose as he followed the two hunched figures across to the plane. It had a fixed tricycle undercarriage. Military camouflage markings showed dimly in the lights from the terminal building. A shadowy figure was holding the door open below the high wing. Colby and Charlie climbed in, and Keene followed, assisted by a strong

pull from above. "Lieutenant Penalski, Marines," the
figure informed them as the door closed. There were
empty seats in the forward part of the cabin. Farther back, more figures in combat dress sat outlined
vaguely in the semidarkness. "Which of you is Dr.
Keene?" the lieutenant asked as the Cessna revved
its engine and began moving again.

"I am."

"Can we bring you up front, next to the pilot? They
didn't tell us much about the mission. You're going
to have to start filling us in right now. But there is
some good news. We can forget the plan for going
in flapping like a lame duck. It won't be necessary.
Somebody must have gotten through from Washington
finally. We got cleared for Vandenberg just before we
left."

"I warn you guys, it's still gonna be a rough ride,"
the pilot shouted above the engine noise. He flipped
his mike switch. "MU87. Burbank, we're ready for
clearance, departing Burbank to Vandenberg, IFR,
military priority."

*"MU87, Burbank. ATC clears MU87 as file, SID
departure runway one six. After takeoff, contact SoCal
Control on three-ninety-seven point nine, or if unable,
contact SoCal on one-twenty-five point four. We've
been having trouble with higher frequencies. Contact
Vandenberg approach on tower frequency one twenty-
four point nine five. If contact lost, proceed with pilot's
discretion flight procedures. Vandenberg and flight
service stations are notified via ground lines and will
be listening."*

"Roger, clearance."

*"You guys sure you want to do this? It's bad along
them hills out there."*

"Not a lot of choice here. Thanks again."

"Normally, I'd say have a good one."

The Cessna rolled forward a short distance and
stopped while a dark, humpy shape, looking like a

whale in the mists and the dark, passed across in front of them. Then the pilot got an okay from the tower to move out. Wind hit the tiny plane like a water wave as it emerged from the shadow of the terminal building, causing it to rock crazily. Keene hadn't realized how much the wind had been rising. He had the feeling of being inside a kite that was likely to be snatched away at any moment. As they turned onto the taxiway, lights outside revealed at least three wrecked aircraft pushed off to the side. Two of them looked as if they had collided while maneuvering on the ground, their wings entangled.

"There's worse moving in behind this," the pilot told him, keeping his eyes on the shapes moving in the murk ahead. "Lotta boats in trouble out there. When it hits, everything's gonna be shut down."

"How long have we got?" Keene asked him.

"Hours . . . maybe."

33

"Santa Barbara tower. Flight MU87 en route from Burbank to Vandenberg at three hundred feet south east, three miles. We're going to fly right through your airspace just off the coast." A burst of static punctuated with voice fragments filled the cabin. The pilot tried again.

"Roger MU87. We were looking for you. What the hell are you doing up in this stuff? Over."

"We just can't resist a challenge."

The cloud canopy above the Cessna was solid. Below, fingers of dark, coiling vapors blotted out and then revealed briefly the lights of the traffic on coast Highway 101 off to the right, beyond a line of breakers and beaches dimly discernible in the flickering of electrical light above the cloud. Sticky buildups on the wings, control surfaces, and windshield had made it impossible to clear the 3,000-foot hills inland, forcing the plane to head southwest along the Santa Clara Valley to Ventura, turning right to follow the coast from there. There had been several ominous *thunks* of hard objects hitting the structure, but nothing so far had penetrated the cabin.

"Okay. Watch out for three radio towers along the water's edge, two just as you pass us, one farther up. Altitudes are three fifty feet, and the position lights are out. What are you planning up ahead?"

"Follow the highway on into Vandenberg."

"I wouldn't advise it. In about twenty miles, the highway turns right and climbs through some twenty-eight hundred foot hills. Try following the railroad bed along the coast, around Point Conception to Point Arguello, where there's a navigation light. From there, you should be able to contact Vandenberg. That would put you about seven miles south, in position for approach to runway one-six. The big launch complexes should stand out. We think they still have lights there."

"Thanks, Santa Barbara. Wilco."

"Caution, traffic climbing out of Santa Barbara airport. Heavy to severe turbulence at all altitudes in this region. We're getting pilot reports of intermittent meteor strikes. Set your Vandenberg security transponder settings. Over."

"We've been dinged by a couple of those rocks too. No serious damage. But we'll be glad to get this thing on the ground."

"You must have some hot dates waiting up there."

At least, something appeared to be going right. Not only was the stricken-aircraft ruse unnecessary, but they would no longer be faced with the task of having to convince Lacey from a cold start. Of course, there still remained the possibility that Lacey could be part of the plot and was simply allowing them to fly on into the parlor, but it seemed remote.

The dark mass of one of the drilling platforms off Point Conception loomed to the left. It was showing no lights or sign of life, and was being battered by heavy seas. The pilot was having to alternate left and right turns to try and gain some forward visibility.

"I see it!" Keene said suddenly, peering through the right-hand window and gesturing as the yellow smear of Point Arguello's beacon emerged from the unfolding muddiness ahead.

"Vandenberg, MU87 is five south at three hundred feet en route Vandenberg, following railroad tracks."

Incredibly, a voice answered. *"Roger, MU87. You're expected. Barometer is twenty-nine point five-five and falling, visibility three hundred feet to occasionally zero, ceiling indefinite at around two hundred, gusting winds quartering from twenty-five to forty knots. If able, continue along tracks until you have visual. I don't think you're going to like this. Over."*

"Not many options here. What aids do we have?"

"ILS is out, and GPS is crazy. We're having trouble with the VASI lights and runway lights. You should be able to see the launch complex towers; they're still lighted. When they're to your right, fly three-forty degrees for one minute, then start a right standard-rate turn to heading one-sixty-two. When you cross the railroad tracks, the runway is a half mile farther. Report abeam the launch complex. Over."

"Roger that."

The thought came to Keene out of nowhere that the spontaneous urge to help others just because they were also humans was what Sariena had been trying to explain all along. To the Kronians it was simply a natural expression of what being human meant. Why, here, did it always seem to have wait for a war or some kind of disaster? A pool of lights curdled together oozed through the darkness on Keene's side of the plane; then another.

"Vandenberg, we're abeam the complex, turning three-forty degrees."

"Roger. We don't have you yet. Turn your landing lights on."

"Roger, lights. No joy on the runway. We should be on final."

"Keep the complex on your right and watch for the tracks."

"We just crossed the tracks. It splits, and both tracks go south on my left. Still no runway."

"MU87, the tracks should be on your right—ON YOUR RIGHT! BANK LEFT, BANK LEFT!"

The left side of the world fell away, and the haze racing through the landing light beams streamed sideways as the pilot threw the plane into a turn that seemed to bring it head-on into a succession of buffeting humps in the air; then the pattern reversed itself as they quickly rolled level again. The end of a strip marked by a few dim lights slid into view in Keene's window. "Runway to the right!" he shouted, pointing frantically. The plane banked in the opposite direction, held for a few agonizing seconds while the airscrew clawed and the overloaded control surfaces hauled it around, and then leveled out again just as the wheels thudded against solid ground. The center line was off to the left, but the Cessna had sufficient room and slowed to taxiing speed without mishap. Charlie Hu emitted an audible, shaky sigh somewhere in the shadows behind. Keene found that his palms were sweaty and he had been unconsciously rubbing them on his knees.

"Okay, we're down. Still can't see much, though. . . . Oh, wait a sec. We have headlights ahead."

"That's a follow-me truck. Follow it to parking and remain on this frequency. And welcome to Vandenberg."

The truck led them off via a connecting ramp to a taxiway. A large military transport silhouetted in the gloom began rolling forward to takeoff position. As the Cessna moved on by, two more transports became visible, waiting behind. Everything that could move, it seemed, was being got out before the wind front moved in.

❖   ❖   ❖

Colonel Lacey was a big man with wide, pale eyes set in a florid, fleshy face, lank ginger hair, and a matching toothbrush mustache. Or maybe his hair just appeared lank from his running his fingers through it countless times, as seemed to be his habit when considering a decision, through who-knew-how-many hours of the night and probably the day before. He looked haggard, with dark scores underneath the pale eyes and perspiration stains showing through the shirt of his crumpled uniform. Frequently, when a moment presented itself, he would close his eyes and draw in a long breath, as if to gain a few seconds of respite. He was also, Keene could tell—though doing a commendable job of containing it—very scared.

"Okay, I've listened, and I hear what you're telling me, and the bottom line is: I don't care," he told Keene, Colby, and Charlie Hu as they came out from a glass-walled office space where they had gone to talk privately. Lacey had received the visitors up in the tower since he couldn't spare time to be away. Lt. Penalski was with them also, having left a sergeant in charge of the other five Marines, who had been given coffee in a room on the floor below. The pilot, who they now knew to be Sergeant Erse, was with the Cessna, checking for damage and getting the aircraft fueled and cleaned. Sloane had gotten through to Lacey from Washington about two hours previously to advise that the mission would be arriving, but not trusting communications security he had not elaborated on what it was about. Around them, staff sifted reports and passed on orders, while harassed controllers tried to make sense of the fragmented information coming in and grappled with the chaotic traffic conditions. The Cessna had been one of a few landings that night. Inside the launch complex, a minimum work force was readying the few craft that could be sent up at short notice to provide additional hardware in orbit for contingencies. A large "Samson" military transport was being held back in one of the hangars to evacuate them and the tower crew after the launches were effected. Otherwise, everything was moving out.

Lacey gestured at the windows commanding views out over the field. Water was running down one of the glass panels on the far side of the floor, where a crew outside was sluicing off the encrustation of dust with a fire hose. "We have a permanent population of three and a half thousand people on this base. Ten thousand contractors' employees live in the surrounding areas, most of them with families. I've got a couple of hours to do what good I can with the planes I've got. After that, they're just junk. That's my first responsibility, Doctor. I don't care about who's going out in a shuttle. If they've got somewhere to go, good luck to them."

An adjutant with a red-streaked face, wearing a tarmac jacket, interrupted. "Excuse me, sir."

"Yes?"

"296 isn't going to fly. The valve isn't responding, and it's a strip-down to replace."

Lacey grimaced, running a hand through his hair. "Has that C-80 started loading?"

"Not yet. It's just rolling up now."

"Divert it out alongside 296. Get some stairs out there and transfer the passengers straight across. Don't bring it back to the gate."

"Sir." The adjutant turned away to another officer who was waiting.

"But we don't know what they've got planned," Keene persisted. "If they show up with a FAST team and take over the runway area, it could halt your whole operation."

"I'll take that chance when we come to it. In the meantime, my operation is best served by moving out what I can."

"Secure the approaches to the launch complexes at least. The APs aren't moving aircraft."

"What APs? Do you think we've been expecting an invasion? They're on the other side of the base, getting everyone out onto Highway One."

"Colonel." Colby Greene was visibly exasperated, managing only with difficulty to refrain from shouting in the middle of the control tower floor. "As an officer of the armed services of this country, may I remind you that you took an oath of loyalty to—"

"A week from now there isn't going to be any country," Lacey said. "You know that. I know that. And the only reason we're not getting open murder and rape on the streets right now is because most people haven't realized it yet. My first loyalty is to the people I've worked with on this base. It's a family thing now. I never took any oath that talked about protecting aliens from some other planet who didn't think our system here was good enough for them." Lacey paused to check an indicator screen above the floor showing the current departures, where the data had just been updated. "Besides, if what you're telling me is correct, I'd be doing them a favor by not interfering. That way, they'll be on their way home." From the conversation earlier, it was plain that Lacey had no particular fondness for Kronians. In a way reminiscent of the ancient practice of venting wrath upon bringers of bad news, it had almost seemed that through some devious process deep in his mind he held them responsible for Athena's having happened at all.

Keene and Colby looked at each other helplessly. Then Charlie Hu raised his hands in a placatory gesture. "Look . . ." he pleaded. "This isn't going to help. We're all under stress here. Let's recognize it. Maybe the problem doesn't need to be addressed out here at all. The important thing is what happens inside the launch complex. If we can get the right people in there alerted, they might be able to close off access to the shuttles before Voler's people get here. . . . They know what the options are in there better than any of us do. I've got some names right here of people I believe are reliable. One or two have to be in there somewhere, right on the other side of the security fence. All we have to do is call. Colonel Lacey has gotten us in this far. That's as much as we might need. Let me make some calls, and let him get on with his job."

"How can they deny access to the shuttles?" Colby demanded. "Voler and his people still have the hostages."

Charlie shook his head. "I don't know. . . . If it becomes obvious that they're not going anywhere, they might throw it in. Whoever they've got helping on the inside might turn around if they realize they're on their own. Anything that complicates the issue opens up more chances for their plan to go wrong. What else do you want in the kind of time we've got? They could land out there at any minute."

"I can deploy my men to cover the access gate from the landing area," Lieutenant Penalski offered. "In these conditions, we could have them in prepared positions right up there on the edge of the runway— even after daybreak. It's just a question of knowing where the plane will head after it lands. Maybe the tower could cooperate by directing it to us."

Keene looked at him: young, eager, as if it was going to affect his record for a promotion next year. Seven Marines against a planeload of Air Force FAST specialists. The spirit of Balaclava was not quite dead yet. It seemed to affect Lacey too. He stared at the Marine, then at Charlie Hu silently pleading for reason, Colby fighting back his anger, and finally at Keene. "I might be able to rustle together a few APs to help," he said gruffly, and strode away to a desk by the far wall to pick up a phone.

❖   ❖   ❖

They stood watching anxiously behind Charlie as he tapped in the first code at a console in a corner of the control tower observation floor. Penalski had left to collect his Marines and scout the ground while waiting for the Air Police reinforcements to show up.

It turned out that Major Sorven, who headed one of the communications sections and had been Charlie's first hope, had moved from Vandenberg several months previously. His successor was a Major Myran, but nobody knew where he was. "Can we try a guy called Crowe Thompson, then?" Charlie asked. Thompson was a civilian technician who had worked under Sorven.

The MP operating the phones sounded as if he was beginning to think that perhaps Charlie was a little crazy. "There isn't anybody in the labs. Didn't anyone tell you, it's not exactly a normal working day today?" Keene and Colby exchanged glances. Colonel Lacey, standing with them, turned away for a second to catch the dialogue of one of the controllers behind, who was getting a distress call from something coming in over the Pacific.

Charlie licked his lips. "This is important," he told the MP.

"Everything's important."

"Just hold a second, will you?" Charlie consulted his notes again hurriedly. "How about the launch complexes themselves? There are things going on in there. We can see the lights. Is there anyone answering in OLC-6 East?"

"Yeah, they're busy over in there, all right."

"The Boxcar Flight Checkout Area. Try and find an Andy Lintz. Like I said, it's important. I wasn't kidding."

"Gimme a sec. I'll check around."

Orbiter Launch Complex-6 East was a refurbished version of the old SLC-6 facility built for the primal NASA shuttle and virtually dismantled following the cutback in operations after the *Challenger* accident back in the eighties. Now it handled the newer design of one-stage "Boxcar" orbiters that were simpler, easier to assemble, and had the convenience of being prepared and loaded horizontally and under cover, to be elevated vertically only for launch. Charlie had worked for a week with Lintz on a NASA-supplied image-processing computer that had been found faulty after it was delivered to the assembly area for installation.

Across the floor, an officer who had been hunched with two operators in front of one of the consoles straightened up and turned to call to Lacey. "Sir, we've got something coming in low and fast from the east, not responding to calls. Strong radar emissions. ATC has no information."

"The lame duck's signaling that it's coming straight in," the former operator reported from another part of the floor. "They're on one engine, and it's intermittent."

"Clear the main runway," Lacey ordered. "Dispatch crash tenders and ambulance, and hold further movements till it's down." He started to turn back to the officer and the other two operators, but then looked back at the screen in front of Charlie Hu as movement caught his eye. A woman in a green coverall and yellow hard hat had appeared; but she seemed to be distracted and was looking away.

"My name is Hu. Is Andy Lintz there? It's vitally urgent that I speak to him. . . . Hello? Ma'am? . . . I said, is Andy Lintz there, anywhere?" The woman moved aside without replying, gesturing vaguely to somebody else and keeping her eyes on something distant that seemed to be happening behind the viewer. After a few seconds, a chubby, bespectacled man in a white smock showing grease stains appeared.

"Say, Charlie. . . ." He spoke in a low voice, as if not wanting to be overheard.

Hu tossed a quick, relieved grin back over his

shoulder at the others and made a thumb's-up. "Yeah, right, Andy. How's it been going? Look, I need some help, and it's really important. I'm with some people across in the Vandenberg tower right now. We think something serious is scheduled to happen in there fairly soon, and I need access to somebody reliable who can organize security."

Lintz seemed only to be half hearing, and was watching something beyond the screen in the same inexplicable way that the woman in the yellow hard hat had. The sound of voices shouting indistinctly came through in the background, and then the louder echoing of something being said over a bullhorn.

"Yeah . . . well, it might not be a good time right now, Charlie. It seems we've got what you might call a 'situation' developing here. There are guys in combat gear waving guns, and somebody just yanked the Launch Supervisor out of his office. Could be you're a little late, Charlie."

A roar from outside the tower, rising rapidly and then falling again, signaled the unknown intruder making a low pass over the base. Charlie turned in his seat to confront the stunned expressions on the faces of Keene and Colby. Lacey, his face paling, stepped forward behind them. "We're too late," Charlie repeated, his voice barely above a whisper. "All this time we've been trying to figure out how to stop them getting in. And they're in there already!"

34

Most of the others around the floor were too busy with their tasks to realize what was happening. Lacey's adjutant, however, had been following from a short distance and came across. "It was the C-130," he breathed.

Numbed, Keene merely jutted his jaw at Lacey inquiringly. "We had an old C-130 come in earlier," Lacey said. "With everything that's been going on I'd forgotten about it. It had all the proper clearances from Launch Operations. We sent it up by Security Gate Three, which leads straight through to the Boxcar launch area. That has to be how they got in."

"Queal fixed for it to be opened from the inside," Colby groaned.

"The Distress Call is on final, looking okay," the operator tracking the approaching plane from the west announced.

On the screen showing the inside of OLC-6 East, Andy Lintz looked up, sending what looked as if it was meant to be an apologetic grin to someone behind the viewing angle, and backed away with his hands raised. A moment later, the screen blanked out.

"What's that intruder doing?" Lacey shot across at the other operators.

"Going into a tight turn about five miles out, climbing slightly. Looks as if it's going to circle."

"Maybe they're not all in yet," Colby said suddenly. "The C-130 might just have been the door-opener for Queal's FAST team to make contact with the inside group." He pointed to the console where the intruder was being tracked. "*That* has to be Voler and the rest of them showing up now. They were supposed to land as soon as the move was made inside, but the runway's obstructed by that S.O.S. that's coming in."

It made sense. "Maybe . . ." Keene nodded slowly. But what could they do about it? An AP officer was trying to pull together a security contingent, but he hadn't reported back. In any case it was all too late now. All they could do was watch impotently and wait for events to unfold. To have gotten this close . . . As the realization slowly soaked in, Keene found himself feeling sick somewhere deep in his stomach.

And then the adjutant officer took a call from the tower switchboard downstairs. "Somebody in OLC-6 is asking to talk to the tower supervisor," he announced.

"Tell them to put it through here," Lacey said. Moments later, a swarthy-faced figure wearing an Air Force parka and colonel's insignia appeared on an auxiliary screen of the console that Charlie was sitting at. "This is Colonel Lacey, base commander, at present supervising tower operations. Who is this?"

"It doesn't matter who I am. All you need to know is that we have control of the OLC complex and access to it from the runway area, and we are currently holding General Ullman and his immediate staff. Just cooperate, and nobody need get hurt."

"His name's Delmaro," the adjutant murmured,

moving alongside Lacey. "One of General Ullman's staff officers."

Keene started and caught Colby's look as his eyes widened. Ullman *hadn't* been part of it! Queal's inside man was one of Ullman's subordinate commanders. They *could* have gone to the top, all along. Keene's feeling of nausea increased.

"What do you want?" Lacey asked tightly.

"Good." Delmaro nodded. "The aircraft that is about to land on the main runway now is carrying the visitors from Kronia, who are under armed supervision. Their well-being, I don't have to remind you, is a matter of considerable importance to the government of this nation. It will therefore be in your own best interests to cooperate. We require safe passage for them to Security Gate Three, where they will be received by a force from inside this complex. Is that clear and understood?"

The screen split to show a view looking out into the night, showing hooded figures with rifles moving away from the camera through a chain-link gate, perhaps taken from a vehicle parked in the vicinity. The message was that the people Delmaro represented had the gate and its approach already secured.

"Quite clear," Lacey replied.

"Then you will give the order."

Lacey hesitated, glancing at Keene. Keene could do nothing but nod. Lacey turned his head to address the controller and inhaled a long breath. "Turn the approaching aircraft around at the north end, and have a truck in position to lead it through to Security Gate Three," he instructed. "Hold all other movement."

"Very sensible, Colonel," Delmaro approved from the screen.

Now Keene was confused. If the aircraft currently landing was the one bringing the hostages and their captors—ironically, employing the same ruse that

Keene and his group had intended using—then who was in the military jet performing low, screaming turns around the base? The situation promptly got even more confusing.

"The lame duck is down," the operator reported. His voice held a puzzled note. "But it's not alone. We have a second contact following it, heading in on approach."

So now there were three out there?

"Get a view of the first from one of the crash trucks," Lacey instructed.

"Tender Two. Do you read?"

"Two here, Roger. Proceeding."

"We're with you back here. What do you see?"

"Difficult to make it out. . . . Some kind of turboprop, high-wing." A view on another screen showed landing lights approaching through curtains of smoky gloom. "No sign of engine trouble. It's running straight and true."

"Stay out there, Two. There's another one coming in behind it."

"*Another one?* What's going on?"

"We're not sure."

The lights swept by, accompanied by a passing roar of healthy engines, and the shape disappeared, heading for the remote, northwest end of the main runway, where it would turn and taxi back to pick up the guide truck. Meanwhile, the view alongside Delmaro's image showed the armed figures moving out into a dim pool of light from a lamp over the gate approach area.

All of a sudden, the other operator called out in an alarmed voice, "The intruder is descending from the southwest, lined up on Number Two runway. It looks as if it's going to land right across them!"

"*Warn it off! Warn it off!*" Lacey snapped.

"It isn't responding to anything, sir. . . . Man, it's coming down *steep!*"

"Get those crash tenders up the other end. Move 'em!"

"What in hell's going on there?" Delmaro demanded, looking suspicious.

"We don't know," Lacey answered. "Except that everyone in those planes could be about to get killed."

"The duck is at the far end, turning now," one operator sang out.

"What about that intruder?"

"It's down! I don't know how he did it. Blind radar approach. It has to be a VTOL."

"We're getting a shot of him from the crash truck now," the adjutant said. The bellow of powerful jet engines reversing thrust came from the screen showing the view from the tender racing back toward the north end of the main runway; then landing light beams appeared to the left, coming from a low, sleek shape sliding out of the night, closing until it seemed it was about to collide with the tender. The tender veered right as the driver started to evade, but then the intruder slewed around in a reckless turn that brought it ahead of the tender, going the same way.

"My God! It's heading straight at the turboprop that just landed!" Colby cried out, horrified. "They're going to hit head-on!"

And so, for an eternity of drawn-out seconds, it seemed, as the jet pulled away ahead of the tender, its tail silhouetted against the glare of the other aircraft's lights approaching from the opposite direction. But the jet was braking hard, its shape growing larger again as the tender caught up with it. The lights of the turboprop beyond grew in brilliance until everyone watching was tensed, waiting for the impact that seemed inevitable . . . and then, at the last instant, the lights slewed sideways and then canted as the turboprop was forced off the runway. The crash tender pulled up seconds later, the view from its cab showing the two aircraft stopped with just yards separating them. Figures brandishing weapons were already pouring from doors on both sides of the intruder to take up positions around the plane it had headed off.

"How far away is that other plane that was following?" Lacey called out. "Can it get down in front of that mess? How much distance does it have?"

"It's leveling out, sir. Looks like it's changed its mind."

"See, he already knows. That means they're in contact. They must be together," Charlie Hu said, trying to take it all in. Keene could only shake his head. Crazier and crazier.

"What was that other plane that just landed?" Delmaro demanded, looking worried now. "Where are the Kronians?"

"If they were in that first one, then they're stranded at the top end of the runway," Lacey said. "I can't get there, neither can you, and I'm just as much in the dark as to what's going on, whatever you think." Delmaro's composure was falling apart. He seemed about to say something, when the screen showing the scene at Gate Three suddenly brightened. He must have had a copy of the same view also, for he looked aside abruptly.

A ring of floodlights had come on, throwing the figures moving out from the gate—now revealed clearly to be FAST troopers—into sharp contrast against the darkness. There were maybe two dozen of them. Then an amplified voice boomed. *"Do not make any move! You are covered from all sides. Throw your weapons in front of you and step back three paces with your hands on your heads."* The figures came to a confused halt, some raising arms to shield their eyes against the glare, others looking at each other questioningly. *"You have three seconds before we fire,"* the voice warned.

Keene, Colby, and Charlie Hu gasped in unison

as they recognized the voice. "Jesus! . . . That's Penalski," Colby breathed. "He's doing that with just si—" Keene signed to him frantically to shut up and nodded his head at the screen showing Delmaro. Colby put a hand to his mouth and turned away.

But it was true. Confident of having full surprise on their side, the FAST squad had not deployed into what they had presumed to be deserted surroundings, but just waited before the gate for the turboprop to roll up and deliver the hostages. Penalski had just six men with him out there in the darkness. Crazy Marines!

Delmaro hadn't heard Colby, however, but was gaping on his screen, seemingly at a loss. Then the sound of a brief burst of automatic fire came from the screen showing the gate, and several of the figures ducked, presumably from bullets passing over their heads. Then, one by one, they began tossing down their guns.

Seizing the initiative, Lacey stepped forward to face the screen squarely. "You are Colonel Delmaro, I believe, right? Well, it's over. You're on your own, isolated from your hostages, and your men out here are disarmed. What are you going to do now? Shoot General Ullman? And what do you think that will achieve?"

Delmaro's eyes shifted desperately. "There are still enough of us in here to take the Boxcar up," he replied.

"Where to?" Lacey scoffed. "The *Osiris*? Do you know what happened to the last bunch that tried?" He shook his head. "Give it up, Colonel. Try and carry this through, and you're definitely finished. Quit now, and you might work out a place for yourself in whatever comes next. But none of you is going to Kronia."

Delmaro licked his lips and looked away. He seemed to be listening to others off-screen. Then he asked for a fifteen-minute hold. Lacey looked at Keene.

"Give it to them," Keene murmured. Anything that calmed things down could only help.

"Fifteen minutes," Lacey agreed.

The wind was causing sand and dust to rattle against the windows of the control tower as Keene and the others watched several vehicles carrying Air Police arrive to provide backup behind the cordon around the stranded turboprop transport. The turboprop's doors opened, and figures began emerging to surrender in the light from the headlamps of the circle of vehicles. After them, the rescuers began leading out a procession of tall forms who could only be the Kronians. They were difficult to distinguish in the heavy outer garments they were wearing, until Gallian threw back the hood of his flapping parka to reveal his white hair as he shook hands with a helmeted figure toting a submachine gun, who seemed to be in charge of the rescue troops. Keene thought he glimpsed Sariena in the background, but it was impossible to be certain. And then the figure with Gallian turned to say something to one of the soldiers, at the same time removing the sand visor he was wearing and tilting back the helmet to scratch the front of a scrawny head. Keene's knees almost buckled right there in the middle of the control tower floor. The figure who had arrived in the nick of time with his cavalry from the sky was— Leo Cavan!

Outside Gate Three, a truck filled with Air Police arrived to join the seven Marines in rounding up the incredulous FAST soldiers just as Delmaro reappeared on the screen, his face registering defeat. "Very well," he agreed. "We have released General Ullman and are turning over our weapons."

The other plane that had been following—a jet, from the sound—had been circling without making any further attempt to land. It broke off, finally, and flew away toward the south.

35

While the tower controllers got back to their business of dispatching the remaining transports, and ground crews towed the two recently landed aircraft into hangars for protection against the incoming storm, Keene, Colby, and Charlie Hu drove out with Lacey to meet the convoy from the north end at Gate Three, where others were appearing from inside the launch complex. The first feeble light of a restless, orange dawn was filtering through. Figures came tumbling out of vehicles laughing and back-slapping with relief after the tension, oblivious of the rising wind carrying needles of ocean spray mixed with the stinging dust. Colby went around shaking hands with the rescue team, who turned out to be a Special Forces unit that Cavan had "borrowed" from a friend in the Pentagon. Lacey poured congratulations on Lt. Penalski, who seemed slightly bewildered and not quite sure what he was supposed to have done that was exceptional. Keene sought out Gallian and Sariena to make sure they were all right, as well as others among his Kronian friends. And finally, he confronted Cavan.

"You've always had this habit of dropping surprises, Leo, but this time you've surpassed yourself," he shouted above the wind. "Okay. How, for God's sake?"

"Do you really want to stand out here discussing it, Landen, or shall we go inside first? I don't know about you, but I could use a cup of strong coffee. We've been flying supersonic for over two hours. I don't know how that aircraft held together. An incredible machine, Landen. Enough electronics to fly itself to China. It's a long-range bomber airframe fitted with a modified power plant for Short and Vertical Take-Off and Landing—intended for getting Rapid Deployment units to odd corners of the world fast. Called the 'Rustler.' Just what we needed."

"Where the hell did you get it?"

"Come on, Landen. I was in the Air Force for long enough as you well know. I still have friends there. Most of them have been at their wits' end for something useful to do in all this. They were only too willing to help. I've been telling you for years: I wasn't cut out for shuffling pieces of paper around."

A broad figure wearing a beret under the hood of a combat smock and wearing a pistol as well as carrying what looked like an Uzi came out of the background. His insignia showed him to be a major. "Seems it's all buttoned up," he said to Cavan. Cavan gestured toward Keene.

"This is the man in the middle of it all, Mitch. Lan, meet Major Harvey Mitchell." They shook hands.

Following Mitch was a woman wearing some kind of cap under a fur-trimmed hood, with blond hair showing on either side of her face, tucked down into her jacket. She moved over to stand close to Cavan as they came up, and smiled. Even with the outlandish garb and the spray and the wind, the first impression that Keene registered was that she was stunningly beautiful. "Hello. You are Dr. Keene. I recognize you from the television," she said. Despite everything, her voice was managing to laugh. Keene came close to falling instantly in love.

"Ah, yes. It's about time that you met Alicia too," Cavan told him.

Keene blinked. "*This* is Alicia? But how on earth did you find the time to collect her as well?"

"I could hardly leave her behind, Landen. There's no telling how, or when, or even if we'll be going back."

They moved with the others through the gate into the launch complex. Wind whistled through the fifteen-foot-high, razor-wire-topped fence. Engines opening up for takeoff roared from somewhere behind them.

The turboprop, it turned out, had been carrying just the Kronian hostages and their escorting force. Voler and the other names involved in the plot had all been in the plane following, which had flown away. Evidently, the idea had been for the inside force to seize one of the Boxcar orbiters being readied for flight and secure the launch facility, then board the hostages and their guards, with the elite arriving last, when everything was in place.

General Ullman, none the worse for his experience, met them in the Transit Lounge of the OLC-6 East complex, which was where outgoing personnel were assembled prior to launch and incomers awaited transportation. Nobody had any idea where the jet might be heading now, but with the hostages freed that had become a secondary issue. The first priority was to get the Kronians out before conditions got any worse, and the means to do it was right there, in the form of the Boxcar orbiter that Delmaro's force was supposed to have seized. The Launch Supervisor was summoned and asked to initiate preparations accordingly, while the communications section tried to get a connection through to the *Osiris* to update Idorf on what was happening.

Communications with the East Coast administration were erratic and confused. When Cavan and his Special Forces contingent left, preparations had been in hand to relocate the entire executive arm of government to the FEMA Southern Region command center in Atlanta, using one of the special aircraft originally equipped to provide a mobile headquarters in the event of nuclear war. An AWACS flying command post that was to provide communications while the Washington facilities were being moved had gone off the air suddenly, it was suspected from a meteorite hit. The Washington area had suffered heavy bombardment, with a lot of fires started. Cavan didn't know how much of the East Coast was affected, but when they took off there had been huge detonations lighting up to the north. On the flight over, they had seen large fires in the vicinity of Indianapolis.

Then it was discovered that one of the launch technicians, acting on his own initiative when Delmaro's soldiers appeared, had disabled the hydraulic systems that elevated the Boxcar orbiters to the launch position. The damage wasn't fatal, but it could take several hours to fix. And that meant that the Kronians were not going to get out before the storm.

Personnel not involved in fixing the Boxcar elevation hydraulics or trying to establish communications with the *Osiris* had been moved into the sturdier, safer structures. Grid power had gone, and the facility was running on its own gas-turbine-driven generators. Outside, the air was filled with pieces of sheeting torn from roofs, metal covers and cowls, and other windborne missiles. Fifty-foot waves had demolished the boat dock and were washing over the beaches and dunes on the north side of the base. The launch complex and runway were situated on the three-hundred-foot-high Burton Mesa dominating the area, and had escaped inundation so far, but the winds had torn loose and wrecked several launch vehicles at the exposed gantries and carried away parts of the buildings and other structures. The Boxcar orbiters were protected beneath the doors roofing their enclosed servicing bays, but there could be no question of launching them until conditions eased. In the general base area, those who had not yet left on Highway One had no choice but to sit tight. Perhaps they were better off than those who had gone.

Sitting scattered around the Transit Lounge were Keene, with Charlie Hu and Colby, most of the Kronians, including Sariena but not Gallian, a mixture of Mitch's Special Forces and Penalski's Marines, and some staff from the complex. The walls carried posters and cutaway drawings of various spacecraft, engineering charts and procedure guides, a map of the base and another showing the surrounding area, and a bulletin board covered with notices concerning things that didn't matter anymore. All the windows were sandbagged, and those not already blown in or smashed by flying objects had been taped. Cavan answered the remaining questions from a worn easy chair by one of the tables, sipping black coffee from a plastic mug. Alicia sat by him, her parka thrown over the back of an adjacent chair to reveal golden hair that fell to her shoulders in sinuous waves, and an equally sinuous body that drew glances from every male in the room.

"Landen and I had already agreed that it had to be Vandenberg. We figured the rest out from what happened at LAX. Beckerson and a small group who were with him on the flight from Washington announced a change of plan and transferred to a T-43 that was waiting for them when they got to Edwards. It took off within minutes, before anyone there knew what was going on. A half hour later, the same T-43 landed at LAX and collected your good woman, Fey, and her traveling companion, along with a couple of others that had also arrived there. Now, a T-43 is a biggish aircraft to be using for such a small number, but all the same we didn't think the Kronians were on board it. You wouldn't bring your hostages into a place like LAX. Too much risk of something going wrong. You'd keep them out of the way until the time came to produce them. But it would either lead us to them or rendezvous with them somewhere, depending on the plan."

"Now, just a minute. Let's get this straight," Colby Greene said, sitting forward. "You weren't still in Washington when this happened. You couldn't have been. I don't care how fast that Rustler is, you couldn't have got all this organized and crossed the country in the kind of time we're talking about here."

Cavan shook his head. "We were already on our way by that time—just about over Nevada?" He looked inquiringly at Mitch, who was tilting his chair back with his feet on the table on the far side of the room.

"We were close to Vegas when we got the report from LAX," the major confirmed.

Keene looked at Cavan, even more perplexed. "So what are you telling us, Leo? You'd left Washington two hours or whatever before? Without knowing where they were or when they were going to show up? You help yourself to a plane and a bunch of guys, and just decide to go joyriding west with the end of the world going on, just in case something turns up. Is that what you're telling us?"

The others around the room could do little more than shake their heads at each other, too much out of it all to really follow what was being said.

"Ah, well, it wasn't really like that, now," Cavan said.

Alicia raised her eyebrows at Keene, then looked

at Cavan. "Maybe you don't know him so well, even after all these years, Lan," she said. "You're being too modest, Leo. I'd say it was pretty much like that, yes."

"Not at all, not at all. We knew they were heading for LAX. And something had to happen pretty soon after they got there. All we needed was to be in the vicinity and equipped to react quickly." Cavan looked around the room and appealed as if to a jury. "All right, I took the law into my hands and cut a few corners. So I'll take the reprimand when it comes, right? But if I'd stopped to try it the proper way, we'd still be in Washington waiting for the right rubber stamps even now. There's an old piece of Irish philosophy that says contrition is easier than permission. The service doesn't agree, of course. But I don't think they'll be doing too much worrying for a while. As I said, I'll take the reprimand when it comes."

Keene leaned back in his seat, managing a thin smile and shaking his head. "Okay, Leo, go on. Then what?"

Cavan was about to reply, when the crashing sound of something large striking the building came from above. The lights flickered, then stabilized again. Several people started or raised their arms protectively. Others exchanged strained looks. Everyone was getting jumpy. Several seconds went by, but apart from the ongoing background of wind gusts thudding and the rattle of sand scouring the walls, nothing further happened. Cavan went on, "We got them on radar as they climbed out from LAX—another nice thing about that machine I borrowed. They headed north, and seemed to rendezvous with another plane that appeared from somewhere inland."

"Which had to be carrying the Kronians," Colby completed, nodding in a way that said he could see it all now.

"Exactly. Both of them headed out to sea for a

while, and then went into a wide turn that brought them back lined up on Vandenberg. The one carrying the hostages was in the lead, obviously intending to land first. And there was our chance. If we could get in ahead of the second plane and grab the Kronians while they were separated from the Society of Friends, there would be nothing for anybody to bargain over. And the rest you know. . . . We weren't aware at the time that an orbiter had already been seized, of course. But it worked out all right. Without the hostages to get them a safe passage aboard the *Osiris*, what could Delmaro and his force inside do with it? I must say, our young lieutenant friend from the Marines couldn't have timed things better. His move at the gate clinched it. Where is he?" Cavan looked around, but Penalski was not in the room.

"I think he's with General Ullman," one of the technicians said.

The Launch Supervisor came in through the doorway. All the heads turned, waiting. "It looks as if we might be able to get two Boxcars off if this mess ever eases up," he announced. "Forget the rest. Nothing else is getting off the ground. We've got forty-eight places in each one. There are thirteen Kronians. The Kronians have nominated six individuals for places on the *Osiris*. We have two children separated from their families, who get to go. There are eight more children with mothers only—six mothers—and they get to go. We have one expectant mother; she gets to go. That means there's room for sixty more, assuming the *Osiris* confirms that it can take them. We think it's likely that it will, since not much is going to be going up from Guatemala—but we haven't made contact yet. In the meantime, we're taking names now in the office outside of all those who want to be on the list. The places will be decided by drawing lots. Immediate family groups—that's parents with children—get one chance, but if it comes up they all go. I've got my name down. Anyone else who wants to leave the planet, step along. It's open to all. General Ullman and his family are there, just the same as the rest. Nobody's playing God over this. For once, that job's being left where it belongs."

36

Keene stood with Sariena on one side of a concrete-walled space full of motor housings, cables, huge pipes, and color coded valves in the lower levels of the complex serving the Boxcar launch bays. People were camped around and under the machinery, and children were having fun climbing about on the pipes. Those who could, kept themselves busy preparing soup, sandwiches, and hamburgers, or bringing pieces of furniture or other comforts from the offices and labs higher up; others played chess or cards, read, or tried to entertain the children. An area had been set aside for treating the growing number of casualties, from people venturing outside and being hit by flying debris to lacerations from imploding windows.

Not being as big as most of the Kronians, Sariena had managed to find some Air Force fatigues to change into from the clothes she'd been wearing since the abduction in Washington, and so looked a little fresher, if obviously tired. She had told Keene their side of the story, not that there was a lot to it. They had been collected from the Engleton by what everyone assumed to be the official bus to take them to Andrews AFB, but the escorts turned out to be captors who took them to another airfield somewhere. From there they flew several hours to a landing strip in a desert location, where the plane was covered under an awning until departing an hour or so before its arrival at Vandenberg. Their escorts were all military, following instructions, and couldn't or wouldn't disclose anything beyond what the Kronians could see for themselves. The Kronians had been held in a couple of trailers under guard. All in all they had been treated well and courteously, if firmly.

"Why not try and get some rest?" Keene said. "Even when they get the repairs finished, nobody's going anywhere until the weather lets up."

"Oh, I'll try and hold out until we get back to the ship. Then I'll sleep for a week. I'm sure all of us will." Sariena's eyes flickered over him briefly. "At least we were just sitting around most of yesterday and last night, waiting for something to happen. You should be just about ready to collapse when we get up there."

Keene grunted and shuffled restlessly, looking away. He knew that Sariena had made the remark deliberately to sound out the discontentment that she sensed in him. Keene wasn't sure himself why he felt it.

Following the example of their commanders, none of the Marine contingent or the Special Forces rescue team had put themselves on the list for the draw. Keene had been one of the six named by the Kronians for guaranteed places, but he had declined to be privileged and opted to go into the draw along with everyone else. Nevertheless, his name had come up anyway. It didn't sit well with him. The other five had been Charlie Hu, who had accepted; Cavan and Alicia, who had accepted only because Cavan had insisted on Alicia's accepting, and she had refused flatly to do so without him—but he didn't seem happy with it; the engineer who had foregone a place on the last evacuation plane in order to supervise the hydraulics repairs; and Colby Greene, who, like Keene, had opted for the draw instead but been unlucky. Gallian admitted that perhaps it had been a mistake to offer any nominated places, but it was done now and couldn't be changed.

"It's not a time to feel ignoble," Sariena told him. "Sending the women and children first might have some point on a sinking ship, where there's an intact civilization for them to go back to, but in this situation we're going to have to rebuild civilization. It's going to need people like you every bit as much as new blood. You're an engineer and a scientist, Lan. What will you do here when it's over? Charlie can see the logic of it. He's only being realistic."

Keene was reacting to an instinct that he was unable to articulate and so took the opportunity to steer the talk onto a different tack. "I used to be a scientist," he said. "But that was only until I saw what it was turning into."

"What Earth turned it into," Sariena replied. "What's at Kronia is different—the way you've always said science should be. We've talked enough about it. Don't you want to be a part of that?"

Keene leaned his elbows on a guardrail beside an access pit leading down under some machinery and sighed, giving her a tired smile. She was still selling hard—and doing a good job. "The beginnings of a whole new science," he said. "It was just starting to get interesting too, wasn't it? Did you ever think any more about the dinosaurs? When did Vicki and I call in the middle of the night? Five days ago, was it? I've lost all track."

"We had some exchanges with the Kronian scientists while we were in Washington," Sariena said. "Basically, they're intrigued by the idea. They've got a possible theory about why that estimate of yours didn't work." She meant the rough calculation that Keene had made of how much Earth's surface gravity would be reduced in a phase-locked orbit close to Saturn.

"What?" Keene asked.

"They think Earth may have gone through not one phase of gravity increase, but two. You only covered one of them."

"Two?" Keene repeated, looking puzzled.

"Somebody there came up with the thought that maybe the account of an impacting body wiping out the dinosaurs, is only half the story. If it was high in density, say, five to ten times that of the crust, and large enough, then absorbing it into the Earth's core would cause a significant increase in surface gravity. So before the impact, *two* factors were operating: the mass was smaller, *and* you had the effect of being close to the giant primary. When the gravity increased due to the extra mass being added, none of the giant life-forms that had existed previously could survive."

Keene stared at her, trying to visualize what she was saying. It did make a strange kind of sense. A planet like Earth was molten inside a sticky bag of mantle, topped by a crumbly crust—not solid all the way through in a way that would shatter. A small, dense object penetrating and being absorbed would certainly have been possible. "But we're still a satellite of Saturn," he checked.

"Right. Maybe knocked out to a looser orbit."

"So life is reduced in size, but still bigger than what we've got today."

Sariena nodded again. "And how's this for a coincidence? Taking the figures I used a moment ago, with the impacting body a fifth of Earth's initial volume, the amount you'd have to shrink a dinosaur by to get back to the same strength-weight ratio that you had under the lower-gravity conditions, works out at about forty percent. That gets you just about down to the size of the *titanoheres*—the giant mammals that lived until the end of the Pliocene."

The implication was clear. Keene scanned her face, as if looking for a hint that he wasn't jumping ahead prematurely. "So are you saying that was when Earth detached from Saturn—and gravity increased a second time to become what we've got now?" He nodded slowly to himself as he thought about it. And by that time, humans could have existed to witness it—the Joktanians and very likely others, long predating what had been thought to be the earliest civilizations. Huge, too. The giant humans had existed along with the giant mammals.

"We don't know what caused it to detach," Sariena said. "Maybe another impact event—enough to have ejected the artifacts that were found on Rhea. That's just a guess, of course, but it fits. . . . In fact, it fits with a lot of things." Keene stared at her again. And so the temporarily orphaned Earth would have begun falling toward the Sun, away from the cradle that had seen its life begin, and warmed it benignly and nurtured it. For how long would it have fallen inward?

"The ice age," he murmured.

"Yes. And when Earth found a stable orbit the ice melted, and Earth entered an age where grasslands and forests flourished where there are now nothing but deserts, temperate belts extended up into what today is the Arctic, and animals of every kind flourished in millions. The axis was more perpendicular to the orbital plane. We think those times lasted about five or six thousand years, through to three and a half thousand years ago."

"And then Venus happened," Keene said. The axis was tilted more. The climatic bands shifted and became narrower.

"Well, maybe. Some of our scientists have suggested that it could have been the Venus encounter that detached Earth from Saturn—which might explain why astronomy didn't reemerge as a science for nearly two thousand years. All kinds of things become possible once you free yourself from the insistence on gradualism that has been stifling science here for two centuries." Sariena moved forward to grip his arm. "These are the things we will be working on through the years ahead, Lan. A new science of Earth, written around a new history of humankind and its origins. Who knows what more it may turn up? The old, sterile ideas are dead. They were the products of a world that's over. A new world is being born out there. And one day Kronia will rebuild Earth, but that might be generations away. It first has to build itself. There's nothing for you to do here in the meantime. The place where you can do something that will matter is with us."

Keene looked across at the children playing among the piping. He still didn't feel at ease and wasn't sure why. "I don't know. . . . Somehow it feels like running out. A lot of people are going to need help," was the best he could manage.

Sariena stopped short of scoffing. "From doctors and priests. And maybe later, anyone who can catch a fish, grow a potato, or throw together a shack that will stand up. But it's going to be a long time before they need nuclear engineers again."

Cliff, the Rustler's young Flight Electronics Officer, who along with the pilot, Dan, made up its two-man crew, appeared at the top of a metal stairway nearby. He looked down over the machinery bays, spotted Keene and Sariena, and waved to get their attention. "You're wanted upstairs," he called to them. "They've just got a connection to the Osiris. There's no telling how long it might last."

The global satellite system had suffered appalling attrition, causing havoc with the official networks.

A connection had eventually been established via the
ground line to NORAD and Space Command's
underground city at Cheyenne Mountain near Colorado Springs, and a still-operational AWACS flight,
to Amspace's tracking facility, which was still managing to get through when the *Osiris* was above the
horizon.

Idorf was on a screen in a local control room in
the OLC complex, patched through from the main
communications center. Colby and Charlie Hu were
there with a group of comtechs and engineers, watching infrared views, taken from orbit during a temporary thinning of the haze, of the devastation farther
down the coast from Los Angeles to San Diego and
beyond. Marina Del Rey, Venice, and Long Beach no
longer existed. Whole waterfront districts had been
washed away, with street after street of wind-flattened
houses farther inland looking as if they had been
carpet bombed. LAX looked like an aircraft breaker's
yard, and JPL was a mess of collapsed buildings,
upended and scattered vehicles, and demolished
communications hardware—which explained why
there had been no success in getting a link in that
direction.

By the time Keene and Sariena arrived, Idorf had
been updated on the freeing of the hostages and had
confirmed that the *Osiris* would be able to accept the
the two Boxcar loads of additional evacuees. "But you
should begin boarding them now," he advised. The
wind you are getting is part of a general pattern that's
developing across the north-eastern Pacific, but a
calmer center is moving south toward you right now.
As soon as it gets there, you should be ready to go.
We'll transmit a beacon for you to home on."

"What's happening in other places?" Colby asked.
"We weren't prepared for the whole global system
going down at once. Since Washington went off the
air, we don't know what's been going on."

"Visibility in most places is too bad to for me to say much," Idorf replied. "There have been large bolide explosions over Eastern Europe and much of Asia. Our radar shows more to be expected in the next few days. Big waves caused by offshore impacts in the western Mediterranean have done a lot of damage along the French and Spanish coasts. Barcelona has been practically wiped out by a direct strike.

The room listened grimly. Nobody asked further questions. Keene licked his lips. "You're coming in via Amspace?" he queried.

"Yes."

"Is there anyone available on the circuit there? Can I see how they're doing while we've got the connection?"

Idorf looked away and seemed to be asking somebody something about how long they'd got. "Yes, we have someone there," he replied. "They're putting him on. But keep it brief. We're getting near the edge of our range."

The screen faded for a moment, then stabilized again to show a begrimed figure with a bandaged head, wearing a forage cap and dust-streaked shirt. It took Keene a moment to recognize him as Harry Halloran. "Harry?" he said, just to be sure.

"Lan Keene. Since we're linking the Kronians to their ship, I take it you've got them back."

"Yes, but don't ask me to tell you the story. Listen, Harry, we may not have much time. I just wanted to know how it's going there. Did Marvin get the evacuation started?"

Halloran shook his head. "Everyone's still here at Kingsville. When we began assembling them here, rumors started going around that Amspace was buying up food and gas and hoarding it, and we got invaded."

"Invaded? Who by?"

"People coming in from the coast. Some of them just seemed to go crazy—tearing the fences down and taking whatever they could grab. It's still ugly, Lan. We've had to fight to hang on to what's ours. There's been shooting. I don't know what we'd have done without our own security guys. The police are too stretched to deal with it."

"Shooting? Anybody hurt?" Keene asked.

"Sure. Some dead on both sides. The plant was like a battleground this morning. It's calmed down now, but for how long, I don't know. We're still trying to organize the move to Lubbock but a lot of people here are quitting and just going with the general flow."

Keene put a hand to his head. It had to come. But so soon? And it was going to get worse. "Harry, do you know anything about the people from my outfit—Vicki and the girls there? They were supposed to have come into Kingsville too. Have you seen them anywhere? Do you know where they are?"

Halloran shook his head. "I did see them here last night. But now? Who knows? They could be anywhere in this, if they're still around. There are people showing up and leaving all the time."

Keene stared at the screen. Sariena was watching him. Suddenly, he knew what it was that had held him back. It had been there all the time, for years, and he just hadn't let himself see it. He needed to get back there. But once he did—if he did—there would be only one way out.

"Harry, do one thing for me," he said. "Find Vicki and tell her to get to San Saucillo with whoever of the girls can make it there. And tell her to *stay* there. Whatever happens."

"Lan, we've got about—"

"*Just do it, Harry. Find her, and tell her!* This one thing. Okay?"

Halloran gulped and nodded. "I'll try."

"Not good enough, Harry."

Halloran nodded rapidly. "Okay. If she's here I'll find her and I'll tell her. What are you going to do?"

"Did Wally ever get back from Washington?" Keene asked.

"We heard he was on a plane that had to put down in St. Louis. I don't know where he is now."

"He told me that Marvin was getting the shuttle down at Montemorelos checked out. You have to know about it."

Halloran nodded. "But we never figured it into anything."

"Well, that's where we're going," Keene said.

"We?"

"Don't you want to get out of this, Harry? You've seen how bad it's getting already. You think that's the end?"

"But where is there to go in it?"

"A new world. To Saturn. Get us a pilot. I don't know about who else you want to bring. You know how many the shuttle will take. Just get to San Saucillo. I'll be there."

"But how do we know the *Osiris* will still be there?"

"Let me worry about that."

Halloran started to reply, but Idorf interrupted to warn that the *Osiris* was losing contact. Moments later, the connection was broken.

Keene turned to confront the astounded faces around him. He felt light inside, suddenly, the feeling that comes of knowing that one has finally done what some instinct that knew best wanted all along. "Well, there it is," he told them. "Scratch me off that list and let somebody else have the place. I'll see you in orbit later."

Nobody tried to argue, not even Sariena. Keene could have sworn that he saw a tear in her eyes when he looked at her, half expecting an objection. But at the same time there was a look that knew him finally, and accepted that it couldn't have been any other way.

37

When the winds eased, it was found that a fallen gantry had fouled the overhead doors of one of the Boxcar launch bays. A crew went out to haul the obstruction clear with a tow tractor. The shower of rocks and gravel had slackened, but the hazard had not gone away completely. Within fifteen minutes one of the crew was killed outright. A dozen others stepped forward to fill the place. Getting the two Boxcars away had become a point of pride for all of the launch staff and workforce.

Meanwhile, loading went ahead of the first Boxcar, which would be taking the Kronians, the balance being made up of family groups and mothers with children, the children who had become separated, the expectant mother, and after them, the names heading the draw. The second Boxcar would be launched as soon as its covering doors could be opened. After that, the facility would be shut down and the remaining personnel, including General Ullman with his wife and two daughters, flown out in the Samson transport that had been held back. They would head for Peterson Air

Force Base at Colorado Springs, where accommodation had been promised in the underground complex at Cheyenne Mountain. The only problem with that was that more people who had missed the evacuation by road for one reason or another were beginning to appear from among the shattered base-area buildings, many of them injured or in shock, and there was only so much room in the Samson. A search was being made for more ground vehicles, but many had been damaged and it was still far from clear how the situation would be resolved. Lieutenant Penalski with his six Marines and their pilot, Sergeant Erse, would wait for the launches, then endeavor to return in the Cessna to their unit at Twentynine Palms. Keene talked to Mitch, who agreed to detour via Texas and Montemorelos before attempting to rejoin the Eastern administration in Atlanta. Colby said he might as well go too. "I can't think of anywhere else that appeals to me right now," he explained. "Besides, I always wanted to see Mexico."

Sariena and Gallian stood outside the tunnel leading through the bunkerlike concrete walls to the boarding ramp in the Boxcar launch bay, while behind them the other Kronians waved farewells and disappeared into the entranceway. General Ullman, who had come to see them off with a short, official message, watched with some of his aides. Keene stood with Colby, Mitch, Penalski, the Launch Supervisor, and others from the launch crew. He shook Gallian's hand solidly, then took both of Sariena's. "Well, I guess this is it again. . . . How many times have we done this? Saying good-bye to you is getting to be a habit."

She nodded, unable to do more than whisper a low "Good-bye, Lan" in reply. Her expression and her manner conveyed as clearly as any words could have that she expected this to be the last time. Keene didn't want to dwell on it.

The technicians directing the boarding ushered through a mixed group, among them Charlie Hu, carrying a canvas bag slung over one shoulder. He stopped in front of Keene and regarded him evenly.

"Well, Lan. . . ."

"I guess it's time, Charlie."

Hu looked past Keene, and his brow knotted. Cavan and Alicia were standing watching, but with Colby and the military officers, not with the line that was moving forward to board.

"I changed my mind," Alicia said in answer to the question written across Hu's face. "I'm too much the romantic. . . . Lan going off all the way to Texas to find this woman. I have to see what happens."

Hu looked at Cavan. "I can't do anything. She's crazy," was all that Cavan had to offer. Hu frowned; then his eyes moved to Keene. Keene said nothing. Theirs, along with Keene's, meant three extra places available.

"We do have a couple with two young sons," the Launch Supervisor said, keeping his tone neutral. "They're next on the draw, but we had to put them down for the second launch."

Sariena and Gallian had gone. The remaining passengers were moving through quickly. Charlie looked from Keene to the others, and then around. The family was standing anxiously a short distance away, where they had been told to wait in case something changed. "*Shit!*" He unslung his bag, and stepped aside to join the others. Without further ado, the Supervisor waved the family forward, and a technician followed them into the access tunnel. Keene and the others began making their way up to the control room where they had talked to Idorf earlier, from where the launch would be initiated.

Thirty minutes later, the first Boxcar roared skyward trailing a plume of flame and quickly vanished into the turbulent overcast. There would be no guidance from the ground, or even knowledge that it had reached the *Osiris* unless a contact was reestablished through Amspace or via some other means. Piloting would be entirely manual and rely on the homing signal that Idorf had promised. It would take about an hour for the Boxcar to climb to the distance that Idorf had pulled the *Osiris* back to and match its orbit.

With the first launch completed, the crew that had been working to free the doors of the second launch bay was able to go back outside and resume. Until they were through, there was little for anyone else to do. Charlie Hu and Colby remained in the control room with the engineers keeping the communications vigil. Alicia, who was a trained nurse, was helping with the casualties. Keene and Cavan, the leaders of the two military squads and their aircrews, accompanied by six of Mitch's twenty-two Special Forces troopers, went out to the hangars by the runway area to check their aircraft.

Most of the buildings had sections of roof or wall torn away, and all were missing windows. The spaces and roadways between were covered with rubble and broken glass. One office block had been cleaved through the middle by a steel-frame tower which now lay twisted amid piles of desks, file cabinets, wall sections and other wreckage that had spilled from the sagging floors. A number of cars, some turned over on their sides, were buried under wreckage, two more thrown against the chain-link fence separating the runways from the launch complex. Medics wearing helmets with red crosses were tending a blood-covered figure on the ground, while APs and others struggled to extricate another. Three more forms laid out nearby were not moving.

The runways beyond were littered with fallen gravel and wind-blown debris. An earthmover with a blade would be needed to clear the way before any takeoffs could be attempted. True, the Rustler could get off vertically or from a football field if it had to, but it gulped fuel doing so. The control tower was a splintered shell open to the winds and looked out of commission, although figures were moving around inside. The other base buildings were all damaged, and a fire had started in one of them. The group from the launch complex walked on, saying little, their boots crunching on the grit and gravel. Keene stooped and picked up a piece curiously. It was still warm, not especially dense, like a bit of sinter from a furnace. A year before, it had been part of Jupiter.

People were clustered inside the open doors of the large, concrete-roofed hangar housing the Samson. As Keene and the others drew closer, they saw that a group of maybe two dozen was confronting several Air Force officers backed by a knot of APs carrying rifles unslung. The smaller hangar beyond, where the Cessna and the Rustler were parked, was still closed and seemed to have escaped attention. A big man, wearing a leather jacket, red hair hanging to his shoulders, was berating the officers loudly.

"Who was in the shuttle they launched? How many more shuttles are they getting ready in there?"

"There aren't any more. That was it," the officer at the fore told him.

"Then what about this plane you've been saving here? It's big enough for everybody. There are people hurt back there."

"It's reserved for the launch personnel and their dependants. All the space has been allocated."

"Well, nobody asked *us* about any allocating. What right does anyone have? We say the allocation needs to be gone through again, with fair chances for everybody."

"You should have availed yourselves of the road evacuation. Why weren't you there when you were supposed to be? We're trying to find more vehicles now. That's the best I can tell you."

"What good's that? There's people coming back in off the highway. They were murdered out there. . . ."

The rest was lost as Keene's party moved to the farther hangar. They let themselves in through a small door that gave access to the main area inside via offices. The floor was covered with glass from shattered windows above, and wind blowing through had left a coating of fine dust over everything. The roof had been breached at the end where the Cessna was parked, and the plane had been hit and punctured in several places. A check over the Rustler showed it to be unmarked. Sergeant Erse would have to stay on and assess the degree of damage to the Cessna. Dan, the Rustler pilot, said he'd give him a hand. Mitch assigned two of his troopers to stay behind with them.

As they came back out onto the tarmac, the radio on Keene's belt squawked. He fished it from its pouch and acknowledged. It was Charlie Hu, calling from the control room inside the launch complex, where they had found a NASA cable route to the tracking station on Hawaii, which had opened up again, giving another connection to the *Osiris*. "Hello, Lan. The Boxcar is about five hundred miles out and starting to close," Charlie said. "We thought you'd want to follow it."

"We're on our way," Keene acknowledged. "The Boxcar's going in to dock with the *Osiris* now," he told Cavan.

Cavan nodded but seemed more concerned about what was going on at the larger hangar. "Leave your other four men here as well to secure those two planes," he said to Mitch. "When we get back, draw up a roster with the others to relieve them. I want a permanent guard mounted here until we're ready to leave."

As Keene, Cavan, and the two commanders passed

the large hangar, a jeep carrying Colonel Lacey and
an AP escort drew up in front of the doors and became
the focus of attention. Leaving him to it, they continued tramping back in the direction of the gate to the
launch complex. When they were about halfway, the
gloom around them brightened, making them look up.
The light was from above, too high to be the setting
sun. Through a brief thinning of the blanket of dust
and cloud, they glimpsed Athena, looming ever more
huge, glowering redly behind the folds and twisting
pillars of its tail. Far above, a hollow boom rolled down
from something exploding high in the atmosphere. The
air had a smell of crude-oil vapors, like the areas
around the refineries on the Texas coast.

38

The bay doors had been freed when Keene and the others got back to the OLC complex. Boarding of the second Boxcar was about to commence. Mitch and Penalski disappeared to organize the guarding and resupply of the two planes, while Cliff, the Rustler's second officer, left with an airframe mechanic to help the two pilots working on the Cessna. Cavan went with Keene up to the control room.

Colby and Charlie were with a group around the console handling the Hawaii link, which was showing Idorf on one of the screens. He was looking suspicious. The atmosphere seemed confused. Idorf spoke before Keene or Cavan could ask anything.

"I was told that you were having trouble with one of the shuttles, that only one had been launched. How is it we have two craft approaching? I hope this isn't some kind of trick, I've seen enough of them already."

The Launch Supervisor, who was standing immediately in front of the screen, shook his head. "The other Boxcar *is* still here. . . . We're as baffled as you are."

"Did our delegation leave in the one that was launched?"

"Yes, of course they did."

"How do I know that? Something strange is going on here." Idorf moistened his lips. "I'm deploying an X-laser as a precaution. It can be recovered later if this is a false alarm." He proceeded to issue orders to others off screen.

"*What is it?*" Keene hissed at Charlie.

Hu indicated a display showing the projection of a hemispherical radar plot being generated by the *Osiris*'s radars. "There are two ships closing up there. One's leading the other by about a hundred miles. Nobody can figure it."

"Which one is the Boxcar?"

"We don't know."

The Supervisor turned around, saw that Keene and Cavan had joined them, and shook his head. "We don't have any ground-station or satellite data to go on anymore. What can I tell him?"

"Maybe there was something up there already that latched onto the *Osiris*'s beacon," Cavan mused.

"Maybe."

Idorf looked back. "So far we have had no identification response," he said. "Why are there two if you only launched one? How can we even be sure that either of them is the one that you launched? Once again, I have to take precautionary action." As he spoke, a blip detached itself from the *Osiris* symbol on the radar plot and began moving away toward a standoff position. Keene felt his stomach tightening. He had seen this before. Visions raced through his mind of a ghastly mistake about to unfold.

"We think one of them might just be something that picked up your beacon," the Supervisor said. "Don't do anything hasty, for God's sake."

Idorf's brow creased. "What are you implying? I can assure you that I don't relish being in this position. But need I remind you that one attempt has been made already to take this ship by armed force?"

"*What?*"

"It happened yesterday," Colby said from the back of the group. "Four of them. We're not sure where they were from."

The Supervisor glanced back, read the confirmation on Keene's and Hu's faces, and looked again at the screen. "I . . . didn't know about that," he told Idorf.

Idorf looked away, off-screen, suddenly. "Just one moment. . . ."

"What happened?" one of the techs next to Hu murmured.

"They didn't get even close," Colby answered. Idorf looked back. "Apparently we have just begun receiving an identification transmission . . . BZ650 . . ." He glanced away again. "Which is as we were given to expect."

"That's it! That's the Boxcar!" the Supervisor confirmed. Exhalations of relief came from around the room. Keene's muscles untightened. He moved forward into the viewing angle of the screen where Idorf would see him.

"Hello, Captain. It's no trick. Who the other ship is, I don't know, but I can vouch for these guys."

Idorf's expression relaxed. "Ah, Landen Keene! You, I know I can trust. Why didn't you tell me sooner that you were there?"

"I only just arrived. We've been kind of . . . busy down here."

Idorf nodded. "I can imagine. . . . A moment, Lan. . . . Yes, okay, we're getting a beam from them too, now." Again, he looked away to follow something that was going on nearby. Then, tension around the control room rose again as his face took on an ominous frown. Evidently, all was not so well after all. "They're saying they have an emergency,"

Idorf reported. "They're being pursued by an armed vessel that's attempting to use them as cover to get to the *Osiris*. They have weapons trained on them. They're asking us to fire on it."

Keene and Cavan exchanged looks. Neither had anything to offer. There could be craft up there from just about anyone with launch capability, in who-knew-what state of desperation. This wasn't exactly a time to be expecting everyone to be displaying rational behavior.

"The beam is definitely coming from the lead ship?" Charlie Hu queried.

"We can't tell. . . . And apparently it's not clear that they are receiving our signal. They're not acknowledging, just transmitting."

"Who is sending to you? Who do you have on your screen?" the Supervisor asked.

Idorf paused to check off-screen once more. "Dr. Stacey."

The Supervisor looked around, puzzled. "Stacey? Who in hell's he? . . . That's not right. Who's commanding the Boxcar?"

"Corlaster," somebody said.

"That's what I thought."

"He says he's the senior person aboard, and in control," Idorf informed them.

Somebody had produced the passenger list and was scanning it frantically, but nobody had heard of the name.

"Can you copy us here with your incoming channel?" Keene said after a few more mystifying seconds. Idorf nodded and made a signal mutely to somebody. One of the technicians seated at a console near Keene read a code and entered a command. . . . And moments later, Keene found himself looking in astonishment at the features of Herbert Voler. Colby gasped somewhere behind him. Cavan was staring in disbelief. Nobody else in the room knew Voler or recognized him. Fey was to one side of him, Queal slightly to the rear on the other with the shoulder of somebody else showing next to him.

"Well, is this your man or is it not?" Idorf snapped. "Be quick. The range is closing."

Meanwhile, Voler was imploring, "*Please*, if anyone there is receiving us, our situation is critical. This is Doctor Stacey, in command of Boxcar BZ650 from Vandenberg, calling *Osiris*. Repeat, we are being pursued by unknown craft that is armed. Suspect intention is to use us as cover to board and seize your ship. Imperative that you intervene and destroy. Your delegation is aboard with us, and their lives are in jeopardy."

Then Voler moved to reveal the view along a cabin extending behind him. Soldiers in combat jackets were in the nearer seats. And behind them, farther toward the rear were . . . the Kronians! All of them. Keene could make out Sariena's black tresses distinctly and, beside her, Gallian's white crown. Clearly, the image was being faked. As much would be evident to the others in the room as well. Besides the obvious fact that Voler's people had not been aboard the Boxcar, Sariena was wearing a green tunic, as were the others. When she went aboard the Boxcar, she had changed into freshly supplied light blue Air Force fatigues.

"This is Captain Idorf of the *Osiris*. We are receiving you, BZ650. Can you hear me?"

But either Voler couldn't or was pretending not to. "This is urgent. Boxcar BZ650 from Vandenberg calling the *Osiris*. We are closing to dock with you. . . ." Everyone in the room was looking bewildered. The Supervisor threw his hands up helplessly. "What in hell's going on?" he pleaded. "Who are those other people?"

"What do I do?" Idorf demanded.

Keene thought frantically. There was no reason for

Voler's group to think anyone might be monitoring this latest stunt, let alone anyone who knew them. They had banked on being able to get away with faking the image because they had presumed this encounter would involve only the *Osiris*. On the screen, a figure behind Voler moved aside, showing itself to be Beckerson, at the same time uncovering more of the cabin beyond. Several of the soldiers had rifles propped between their knees. The Kronians had been wearing green tunics when Mitch's force got them out of the turboprop just after it had landed early that morning—the tunics they had been wearing since they were hijacked in Washington. The picture was a superposition of Voler and the others with him, which was genuine—they were up there now, inside one of the ships—and a background taken aboard the aircraft in which the Kronians had been flown to California the day before. The two had been combined to give the impression that the transmission Idorf was receiving was coming from the Boxcar just sent up from Vandenberg. But the ship was transmitting the Boxcar's correct identification code. The Boxcar with the Kronians aboard was up there in orbit somewhere. It had to be the radar blip that was *following*.

"Charlie," Keene shot across. "Would it be feasible for the ship in front to intercept the ID code from the ship following, retransmit it, and use some kind of ECM to blot out anything else from the ship behind?" he asked.

Hu looked at him strangely for a moment, then nodded. "Sure . . . if you had somebody who knew what they were doing. Just about any ship would carry the equipment you'd need."

Keene moistened his lips. He looked back at Idorf. "That view of the Kronians is a fake," he said. "They're not there at all. The background is being manufactured."

Idorf's face hardened. "Target both objects," he instructed off-screen.

Keene felt perspiration on his forehead. Everyone else was leaving it to him now, with no idea of how his mind was working. There was no time to debate with them.

Voler and his party had left at first light in a T-43 jet transport, heading south and climbing. Keene did a quick mental calculation, then added several hours for storming a launch pad, taking up a shuttle that had been readied in hope of arriving emigrants, making orbit, and maneuvering into position. "Guatemala," he muttered aloud. "That's where they went. They seized a shuttle at Tapapeque. That's what the lead ship is." Colby looked emptily at Cavan. Cavan shook his head and shrugged. Keene followed his reasoning through, visualizing in his mind what would happen if the seized shuttle were allowed to dock with the *Osiris* by an unsuspecting crew expecting other Kronians. A FAST team, armed and waiting to go, would take the ship in minutes. And then, the full extent of what was intended unrolled itself in all its ghastliness. The Boxcar and everyone in it were sacrificial. Idorf was being urged to fire on it—with his own people aboard—to provide a diversion and maximize the surprise when the shuttle carrying Voler and his force docked.

And with extra room aboard the *Osiris* thus created, and its defenses neutralized, how many more of Voler's "elite" would be brought up afterward? With all but a skeleton crew to fly the ship eliminated, how many of their kind would go to Kronia, and with what intentions? And so it would start, all over again.

"Captain Idorf," Keene said. Despite himself, the words came out shakily. "Ignore what he's saying. There is no Doctor Stacey. Target the lead vessel only and fire. The one following is BZ650, and your people are aboard it."

If Keene's reconstruction of events was correct. . . .

The room around him had frozen into statues, all staring at him. From the screen, Idorf's eyes interrogated him silently. Both of them understood that there could be no discussion or inviting of second opinions. "You are certain of this?" was all he said.

How could Keene be? His shirt was sticking to his back, his throat dry. He closed his eyes and nodded mutely. Idorf gave the order.

And somewhere high above the Pacific, a spacecraft and several score human beings flashed briefly and turned into vapor that dispersed into the swirling gas clouds of Athena's tail.

Hawaii lost contact before Idorf was able to identify the vessel that remained.

The second Boxcar was launched a little over an hour later, into the night. By then, everyone remaining was too exhausted to contemplate evacuating before morning. There were several incidents that night involving bands from outside coming into the base, presumably looking for supplies and weapons, some involving sporadic shooting. Mitch and Penalski posted extra guards on an extended perimeter around the hangar, with the reserves sleeping under the wings of the Rustler.

PART THREE

ATHENA–
Bringer of Death

39

Next morning, two of the Special Forces troopers had disappeared. So had two girls from the base that they had been seen spending a considerable amount of time talking with. It could only be concluded that they had unilaterally deemed their military careers to be over.

The showers in the changing rooms at the rear of the hangars still worked and delivered hot water, and for fifteen minutes Keene abandoned himself to the luxury of washing away the feeling of two days and two nights spent in the same clothes, and of getting rid of the all-pervasive red dust. It got in the eyes, in the ears, and in the nostrils, and lodged in the creases of collars, hoods, and seams until it found a chink to get inside. It itched and it burned, and when rubbing and scratching broke the skin it caused sores that inflamed. "The plague of boils," Keene thought to himself as he applied a soothing cream to painful areas on the sides of his neck and the backs of his hands, then covered them with adhesive dressings. Then, wonder of wonders, he put on a clean

change of underwear, shirt, and pants from the bag
he hadn't opened since before leaving the hotel in
Pasadena.

Penalski and his Marines had not changed their
minds about rejoining their unit at Twentynine Palms.
The Cessna had taken minor damage but was up to
making the short return trip, for which its fuel was
ample. They also had enough space aboard to take
four casualties who would otherwise have had to be
moved by road. Dan and Cliff drove with a couple
of Air Force ground crew and two Marines riding
shotgun to refill a bowser at the fueling point on the
far side of the airfield for the Rustler. While volunteers from among those who were due to leave in the
Samson—now pushed up beyond 400 people—risked
intermittently falling gravel to clear debris from the
main runway, the remainder of Keene and Cavan's
groups held an impromptu conference inside the
smaller hangar.

There was some dissent among Mitch's force.
General Ullman had offered them a clearance into
the Cheyenne Mountain refuge, and Mitch's second-
in-command, a Captain Furle, felt they should take
it. Since there were no fixed orders to return East,
and it was far from certain that there was anywhere
organized for them to return to even if they made
it, their first priority should be to get the men to
safety while the opportunity was there. Although
Mitch hadn't gone into details with the men as to why
they were talking about going to Texas and Mexico,
Furle gathered it was some private business of Keene's
and didn't think it should be their affair—certainly
not something to be risking lives over. They should
put down first at Peterson Base near Colorado Springs
where the Samson was heading, Furle argued, and
anyone who wanted to do Keene a favor could carry
on from there.

"The problem with that is that we might not get

past Peterson," Mitch replied. "We didn't exactly come by this piece of equipment in a way that you'd call official. Some brass there might just take it into his head to decide that it's government property with better things it could be doing, and impound it."

"And he might have a point there, right enough, too," Furle agreed, not giving an inch. And maybe Furle had a point too, Keene had to admit as he stood listening. Normally, he would have been surprised at such discord within an elite fighting unit of this kind. But Cavan had mentioned that not all of these men had trained together in the way that creates trust and cohesion. It was a scratch force, thrown together at a moment's notice from whoever had been available.

Mitch stepped to the center of the group, his hands raised for attention. He was tall and broad, with solid, square-jawed, handsome features topped by a mane of black, wavy hair. Keene saw him as confident and capable, but with something of a flamboyant streak that put him in his element before a crowd. Good leader material and a natural as a showman, easily pictured as a performer or media personality if he had applied himself to it. But there was a lot of the adventurer there too, which perhaps went some way to explaining how he had ended up in an irregular military unit—and perhaps why he had agreed to go along with the Texas escapade.

"Guys, strictly, Terry is correct," he began. "What we did the other night was without official orders. A matter of pure initiative. But as a force, we've always taken pride in our ability to act independently when the need is there, right? That's what we've all trained for, what our reputation is built on. And there's no question that what we accomplished was fully in accord with top national priority. The President—your commander-in-chief—was personally concerned that the Kronians were returned safely to their ship, and that was what we helped him do."

He turned, appealing to all of them. "One, maybe a couple of hours longer than we'd take anyway. That's all that's being asked, guys. How long did it take us to make it here to Vandenberg from Washington? This time we're talking about four states, that's all. Half the distance we did the other night. We drop down into Texas, pick up a few people, shuttle them across the border—and then it's on up to Atlanta for dinner. Only the difference is that you'll be able to enjoy your dinners better from knowing that we finished the job."

Mitch put his fists on his hips and looked around. From the looks and the glances being exchanged, Keene could see he was carrying them. Even Furle was looking less militant. "What do you say, guys?" Mitch invited, looking at the Rustler's two crew.

"Sure—one, maybe two hours extra should do it," Dan agreed, nodding.

Cliff seconded by nodding. He was curly haired and boyish, said little but was widely liked. He seemed to have touched a mothering reflex in Alicia.

It was enough. The majority responded with nods and assenting murmurs. Furle accepted the verdict without further protest.

The bowser returned, and while the Rustler's tanks were being filled, Keene went with Cavan, Penalski, Mitch, and a squad of Mitch's troopers to the larger hangar to present compliments to General Ullman and mount rearguard while the final boarding of the Samson was completed. The Cessna, already loaded, taxied up to collect Penalski and then took off first, banking into a turn out to sea and disappearing southward at low altitude, following the coast. The huge Samson went next, rolling almost the length of the runway before lifting, fading quickly, and then vanishing into the overcast—a slightly higher ceiling than before after the previous day's winds, but still agitated and muddy. Lightning flashed distantly among the heaps of cloud, which were beginning to disgorge spots of rain. The raindrops were black and oily with soot.

Keene stood for a minute, looking at the derelict control tower and the savaged buildings around it, and across to the wrecked launch complex with its fallen gantries while the sound of the Samson's engines grew muffled and more distant. Only days before, it had all been vibrant and thrusting, a symbol of endeavor and industriousness; now . . . a preview of what was to come everywhere. Silence took over as the engine noise faded, broken only by the cawing of gulls wheeling in from over the point. A feeling of stillness and desolation overwhelmed him suddenly. He turned away to catch up with the others.

A small procession of vehicles, presumably drawn by the sounds of the planes taking off, approached from the direction of the base as a trooper driving a tow tractor pulled the Rustler out onto the tarmac. There were several cars and trucks, a Dodge van with boxes and baggage piled under netting on the roof, and a four-wheel-drive pulling a U-Haul trailer. They were way overloaded, all their occupants disheveled, many of them bandaged, most seeming dazed. Several badly injured cases were laid on makeshift beds or blankets in the trucks and the trailer. Three men got out from the front of the car leading. Three more people were crammed in the back, along with some small children. The man in front had a gray mustache and face disfigured by angry-looking, open sores. He half raised an arm feebly.

"We don't know what to do with 'em. . . . They'll never make the trip, but we can't stay here." There was nothing demanding or even expecting in his voice. Just a plea for help.

"This is a military mission," Mitch replied. "We're not going anywhere you'd want to be—probably as bad as this. Worse." An ashen-faced woman stared from the window of the car following, mechanically rocking a baby that was crying.

Alicia looked at them, then Mitch. "We can't just leave them. The plane wasn't full on our way over. We can take the worst, yes? What did you say your-self—a few hours to Atlanta? I'll look after them. That way the others will have a chance."

Keene could see the resistance in Mitch's face, the beginnings of the double standard that demands loyalty to one's own group but hostility to outsiders when survival becomes the issue. But it hadn't asserted itself strongly enough yet to prevail. Mitch turned his head toward Dan in an unvoiced question.

"How many stretcher cases?" the pilot queried.

The men looked at each other and muttered between themselves. "Eight that are bad," one said finally.

Dan did a quick mental estimate. Besides its pas-sengers, the Rustler was carrying a generous reserve of supplies, fresh water, weapons and ammunition, various types of tools and equipment. "Those, then, plus four more," he announced. "But let's be sensible about this. If somebody's obviously not going to make it, don't waste the space." Mitch looked at the man with the mustache and nodded curtly. Keene and Cavan caught each other's eye, then looked away. Although there was nothing more to be said for the moment, each had read the same in the other's look: They were going to have to learn to harden them-selves to leaving a lot of people to their fate before this was over.

The Rustler carried four folding stretchers, which were brought out. The troopers helped people from the vehicles load them aboard the plane, along with four more of the injured on improvised pallets. The worst seemed to be a woman who was moaning deliriously, both her legs crushed in a traffic accident out on the highway. After another brief conference, the men who appeared to be speaking for the group selected two couples to accompany the eight. Keene was relieved to see that all the children would remain. This was already getting complicated enough.

Keene watched the hapless group through one of the forward windows as the Rustler turned to begin taxiing out, standing expressionlessly before their vehicles. They were still there when the plane roared back along the runway and lifted off, as if not knowing where to go next.

The sea seemed amazingly calm, Keene thought as the strip of dunes and beaches came into view. Then he realized that what he was looking at was mud. The tide was out to a distance that must have been close to a mile.

At the back of the plane, the woman with the crushed legs was starting to scream.

Cliff scanned through frequency bands as the Rustler climbed. "Santa Barbara's out. LAX is out. Seems the West Coast is about out of business," he reported. Charlie Hu was behind him in the jump seat, following the procedures. "Military Sector Control is operating at San Bernardino. They're routing us over Phoenix. Come around onto zero-nine-eight degrees and make for thirty thousand to try and get over the turbulence. Two transports and a high-altitude reconnaissance flight in the area. I've got 'em on radar. Otherwise free of traffic. Still a lot of clutter. Reports of heavy rock falls in the Midwest, all flights grounded there."

"Gotcha," Dan drawled from the captain's seat.

When they leveled out, Alicia and the medic in Mitch's team, whom the others called Dash, opened up the Rustler's medical locker and went back to see what they could do for the injured who had been brought aboard. With some sedation, the woman with the hurt legs quietened down. There were two more women, both hit by falling rocks, one with a shattered arm and shoulder, the other comatose from a head wound. A man had a leg almost severed at the thigh by a piece of flying metal. Two more were head injuries, both with concussion. One had lacerations and probably fractures from being in a truck hit by a mast that was blown down. The last was a youth of about seventeen who had been blinded by flying glass. Dash confided quietly to Mitch that he didn't think the kid's sight could be saved.

Between washing and dabbing with pads, and helping to place dressings and tie bandages, the two couples—Denise and Al, Cynthia and Tom; it was funny how they had suddenly become people now that they had names—who had accompanied the injured recovered their faculties sufficiently to tell the gist of their story. They had been among somewhere around fifty or sixty friends, neighbors, and relatives from nearby Vandenberg village, many of them employees of the base, who had decided to travel inland to Arizona as a group. Less than twenty miles along the highway, they had been caught in the the gravel storm of the previous day. Seven of the party were dead, including the husband and sister of the woman with the crushed legs, who was called Joan and worked as a teller in one of the banks on the base. A group of them had brought the worst cases back into the base believing they would find help, while the rest had arranged to meet farther up the highway. There were a lot like that out there. Police, paramedics, and volunteers had set up emergency dressing stations along the way, but they were swamped.

As the Rustler with its forty-two souls aboard climbed above the denser blanket of cloud, the surroundings transformed into a shimmering panorama of surreal yellow and orange sculptures twisting and unfolding upward toward a sky woven from streamers of electric violets and pink. Beneath them, foaming curtains of vapor descended, raining amber and ochre into the cauldron that the world had become. Above it all, blurred through the watery opacity of the cloud and the plasma filaments, glowed the light of two suns.

Cavan and Mitch were up front, immediately behind the flight deck, conferring in low voices. One of the NCOs handed out breakfasts, which today consisted of reconstituted egg, sausage and hash browns, rolls with butter and jelly, apple juice and coffee. Colby sat next to Keene, staring past the seats in front and for a while lost in thoughts of his own. Then, suddenly, he said, "Those people back there. Just imagine, a week ago they were anyone you might have sat next to at a movie or met in a restaurant. Last night we mounted armed guards against them as if they were enemies. The veneer's about to come peeling off, Lan. We're all about to go back to being jungle tribes again."

Those that survive, Keene thought. He had been thinking similar things too. For what they'd just heard described had to have been typical of events that had been happening on other highways too, leading inland from San Diego and Anaheim, San Luis Obispo and San Jose, Napa and Kelso; and not just in California but every other state and all the provinces he'd never heard of in every other country too. If the rate worldwide was even a tenth as great as the sample figures he had heard, Keene estimated that the number killed would already be about equal to the total battle and civilian dead of both world wars put together.

40

The hit came with a bang like a bomb exploding in the forward part of the cabin. Keene had a fleeting impression of a flash and Charlie being hurled back from the flight deck like a rag doll; and then came a roar with an invisible, freezing fist that snapped him back in his seat. Mitch, Cavan, and a couple of others who had been near the front were swept back along the aisle in a tangle of arms and legs. Shouts of alarm came from all round, terrified screams from the back. Next to Keene, Colby had gone into an emergency crouch, head down, arms crossed and braced against the seat in front. Keene hauled himself up against the pressure and peered forward with streaming eyes. A hole the size of a door had appeared where Cliff and the electronics officer's station had been. Around the sides, torn edges of metal and a section of switch panel still attached to a finger of ribbing flapped crazily in the airstream. The plane was dipping to starboard. On the still-intact left side of the cockpit, Dan pulled a yellow oxygen mask over his face, at the same time fighting to keep control as violent judderings shook the plane from end to end. One of the smashed consoles began smoking, and moments later choking fumes poured back into the cabin.

"*Jesus! Jesus!*" one of the women at the rear was shrieking.

"What is it? What's happened?" Jed, the blinded kid, yelled from his pallet.

The pressure drop following the blast pulled air the other way, carrying bodies and loose objects toward the breach. Dan banked and throttled back, shedding speed, and the press of bodies trying to untangle themselves in the aisle fell forward and went down again. Mitch dragged himself out and braced himself half-standing between the front seats and bulkhead, where he was able to tear a fire extinguisher from its mount and smother the burning. Then he folded over and sank to his knees. Keene tried to stand up further and leaned over the seatback to find Charlie . . .

A report sounded somewhere distantly, like a bucket being struck by a hammer, and a shock jolted him. Then came two more, sharper. Keene found himself slumped over an arm of the seat; he realized muzzily after a few moments that he had passed out. He straightened up stiffly. Dan's voice shouting into his microphone came from up front over the roaring of the wind.

"Still taking multiple impacts. What's your range, what's your range? I need a vector. I have no radar and controls are jamming. Visibility nil up here." Keene looked around. Some of the others were moving groggily, others slumped unconscious in their seats or lay still on the floor. At the back, Alicia was standing, clinging to the side netting with one hand while she tried to revive Dash, the medic, with the other. Dan's voice came again, louder this time, switched into the cabin address. "Attention all. We're near an evacuation reception area, but going down.

This wagon is shot. Get everyone into seats or buckled down. Use whatever you can for padding and brace hard. This may not be the softest landing I ever made. . . . And thanks for choosing U.S. Government Air."

Keene turned and lifted Colby up in his seat. He was out cold, his face ashen, lips blue. Keene took his glasses, which were hanging from one ear, and slapped his cheeks alternately, then shook him by the shoulders.

"Uh? . . . Wha . . ."

"Colby, snap out of it. We're going down. We need you here, fella."

Colby leaned his head back and gulped in a series of long breaths. "God I'm cold. . . . The job description never said anything about this."

"You need to move. There's guys the other side of you that we have to get up off the floor."

Still wobbly, Colby moved into the aisle, and Keene followed. Mitch was up again, and several others were moving to assist, including Cavan, who seemed to be okay. They maneuvered the still-inert forms into seats or positions against the bulkheads, wedging their limbs with seat cushions, packs, and clothing. Keene went around the front seat to see to Charlie, who was crumpled across three seats and motionless. Colby helped Keene buckle him into one of the seats and pile up as much protection as they could. Then the floor tilted back, and the roar came of the engines diverting to reverse and vertical thrust. "This is it!" Dan's voice yelled. "Maybe ten seconds. Hang on!" Keene wedged a pack on his lap and hugged it to his chest, arms gripping the seatback in front.

The impact was fierce but not as bad as Keene had feared—Dan was using what power he had as a brake. They were thrown sideways, and then the starboard side of the cabin imploded amidships as the broken main spar of the wing plowed into the ground and was driven inward. The plane pivoted around the wing, grating over rocks, and slewed to a standstill with its fuselage broken into two parts lying joined at an angle. Cries of pain and fear came from all sides as the last movements and shrieks of rending metal died away. Keene raised his head gingerly. It was as dark as night, dust everywhere. Shadowy figures were moving, cursing, fumbling with flashlamps. Somebody farther back was calling for help. Keene spat blood from his mouth. He had bitten his tongue. His knee burned and his neck felt as if it had been wrung, but nothing seemed broken. Releasing his seat harness shakily, he rose to follow Colby, who was feeling his way into the aisle. A thudding concussion like an artillery shell landing came from somewhere outside.

In front, Dan was clambering back from the flight deck over a crazily leaning floor panel. *"Move, move! Get 'em out!"* Mitch's voice came through the gloom and the dust. "This whole thing could blow. Furle, are you there? You okay?"

"I . . . think so."

"Good. Go check the tail section. The rest of you who can move, give a hand with the ones that can't." One of the soldiers rose and just stood, staring dazedly. Mitch jabbed him several times in the chest and shoved a shoulder. "Behind you. Out that way. Move it!"

Ignoring the doors, the ones who were able began passing the injured and unconscious out through the break in the ruptured fuselage. Slowly, the rest came to their senses and lent help. Colby already had Charlie by the shoulders; one of the troopers took his legs. Several who had been sitting where the wing root had broken through were past any help. From the rear section, Al was helping Denise out, blood streaming down her face, while Alicia and Dash directed others lifting out the pallets and stretchers. A corporal called Legermount—strong, black-haired, always silently competent—became a human conveyor line, effortlessly carrying out one limp form after another and returning for the next.

They were on a slope of rock and sand that could have been a valley side or part of a mountain, vanishing into the dusty air. A hundred yards or so away was a ravine flanked by mounds of boulders. Mitch waved everyone toward it, then, while they were making their way across, he ducked back inside the front section of the fuselage to check that no one had been left. Keene and Dan hung back in case he should need help. Mitch reappeared briefly to go into the tail, and reappeared finally, hauling two packs of provisions and a medical chest. He threw them down and jumped after. "Let's get out of here!" he yelled. Keene grabbed one of the food packs, Dan, the other, and Mitch picked up the medical box. They got to the ravine, which was dry, and passed the items down to the others, who were spreading along the sides and finding places. And then, suddenly, the murk in the direction away from the plane lit up as if aflame, and for several seconds a ridge above them, rising to a rocky peak at one end, was silhouetted through the haze against a blaze of light from somewhere behind. Darkness closed again. Five seconds or so went by, and then the foot-jolting shock wave arrived through the ground, causing everyone standing to stagger. Cynthia and one or two others were knocked over. They all looked at each other bemusedly. And then, as if responding to the same cue, everyone not already down there threw themselves into the ravine. *"Cover!"* Mitch shouted one way, then again the other. *"Get down! Take cover!"*

Keene had landed near Tom, who was holding a blood-drenched handkerchief to Denise's head. Together they leaned over to shelter her. Keene pressed his face down into the coarse sand of the ravine bed, pulled his hood close over his cap, and covered his head with his arms. The boom came maybe twenty seconds later, like something solid hitting his head, jarring his teeth and numbing his ears. How many miles away did that put it? He couldn't think. "*Stay down!*" Mitch's voice called from a thousand miles away through the ringing in his ears. They waited, unmoving. Denise was twitching and moaning. And then earth and rocks rained down out of the sky in a torrent. Keene felt it peppering his arms and landing in drumming waves along his back. It was like being in a grave with the dirt being shoveled in. He convulsed suddenly, slapping at his leg as something hot seared through the calf of his trousers. From beyond the ravine the sound of rocks hitting the plane came like hail on a tin roof.

The rain eased gradually to become just a waning spatter of lighter particles. Keene waited, then moved to look up, feeling rivers of sand running off his neck and shoulders. The other mounds of dust around him were stirring, shaking themselves, starting to sit up. . . .

And the next impact came five seconds later.

He lost all track of how long they lay there, clawing and scraping as if trying to burrow into the earth, while detonation after detonation shook the ground and pounded at their senses. The large bolides came over with a noise that sounded like freight trains crossing the sky; others made sighing moans mixed with jet-engine-like whines. The concussions grew so frequent that it was impossible to say which blast wave was associated with which flash, and the rain of ejected debris became continuous. In a temporary lull, four of the soldiers ran to the plane to get folding entrenching spades, hard helmets, and flak jackets. One was hit on the way back and had to be dragged by the others. Keene's mind went into a numbed, suspended state, rejecting the sensory overload, ceasing to register the passage of time. Somewhere in the middle of it all, the fuel from the Rustler's punctured tanks ignited.

It was another hour, maybe two, before the infall eased and the dazed survivors finally began emerging.

Thirty-four were left. Charlie Hu had come around at last, and was miraculously okay except for head-to-toe bruising down one side of his body that would keep him wincing for weeks—assuming they lasted that long. Cavan was bearing up well, and Colby and Alicia had nothing worse than bruises and cuts. Three soldiers had died in the crash, two more in the impact storm, and six were hurt badly enough to be nonfunctional. Of the party taken on at Vandenberg, Denise had scalp cuts, not as bad as had at first been feared; the man with the severed thigh had died from blood loss, which was probably merciful; the woman in a coma had succumbed; one of the two men with head injuries had been thrown loose in the landing, breaking several bones, and was not looking good. Joan was rallying and showing astonishing strength. Most remarkable of all was Jed, the blinded youth, who seemed the most resilient of all and was trying bravely to crack jokes. Maybe it was delirium. Keene saw tears on Alicia's face as she changed his dressing.

It was mid afternoon, although the sky was too dark to give any hint. They had flown for a little under an hour after leaving Vandenberg early in the morning, which put them just short of Phoenix. The broken starboard wing and nose of the plane had burned out, but the fractured center section and tail were not completely gutted. Some usable items, including most of the food packs and water containers, were retrieved. The port wing, remarkably, while looking as if it had been shotgunned, was still in one piece. All electronics were dead, and the mobile radios unusable with the static.

Twenty-two unscathed or with minor injuries;

twelve unable to walk. There were two choices. The twenty-two could divide into two groups, one to stay with the injured while the other went to find help; alternatively, the twenty-two could simply press on together, promising only to send help if they found any. In normal circumstances, the latter would have been unthinkable. But as things were, it had an undeniable element of realism. Keene expected that Mitch, if anyone, would take the lead in stating the unmentionable but obvious: that huge numbers had already died, and more would yet, by far; that leaving the fit behind if there was no help to be found would just be condemning them along with the unfit; that any potential help they might find would be already overwhelmed and unlikely to be swayed much by the thought of a dozen more one way or the other. Alicia was waiting to hear it too; Keene could see the anticipation on her face. Maybe Mitch saw it too, and perhaps that was why he refrained. Or could it have been that even in Mitch's eyes everyone had become "ours" already?

Cavan asked Dan how much he could tell them about where they were and the reception area he had been talking to just before the crash.

"It was an Army mobile unit operating at a local airstrip where they were setting it up," Dan said. "From the fix they gave me, we must have been almost there—maybe just a few miles short. The last bearing they gave me was . . . I think, one-twenty-four degrees." He stood up and looked back, estimating the final course that the Rustler had been following and trying to reconstruct the turns he had made bringing it down. Finally, he pointed to a low pass, barely visible through the dust, a little to the left of the now-invisible ridge behind which the first impact had occurred. "I'd say it has to be that way."

Mitch nodded as if to say that was good enough for him. "I'll take a squad to check it out," he said.

"The sooner we leave, the better. Debating will only waste time." Cavan agreed but said he'd stay with Alicia, who insisted on remaining to help Dash; in any case, at his age, he said, he would only slow everyone down. Mitch didn't argue. Charlie Hu had little choice, since he would have been hard put to walk the length of a football pitch. That left Keene and Colby to go with Mitch, which seemed advisable in case their political credentials still carried weight, and Dan as the navigator. Nine fit soldiers remained, including Legermount and Furle. Mitch assigned four who were at least up to marching to stay behind under Furle's command with the injured and the civilians. The other five would accompany Mitch and his party, Legermount acting as second in command.

Keene saw suspicion in Furle's eyes as he watched the departing party sorting out supplies and equipment to take with them. "A couple of hours in Texas, then on to Atlanta," he heard Furle murmur sarcastically to one of the others as they picked up entrenching tools and went back to remove the bodies from the plane for burial along with the others.

When that task was complete, the soldiers began cutting and dragging parts of the plane to bridge a narrow section of the ravine, which they fashioned into a shelter with draped camouflage netting weighted with rocks and sand. Then they got a couple of stoves going, so at least the departing party were able to get a hot meal inside them before setting off.

41

If ever there was a preview of Hades, this had to be it. The nine—Mitch and Dan; Keene and Colby; Corporal Legermount and the four troopers—trudged in single file up the slope, their bodies stiff from hours of lying pressed against the rocks, slipping and sliding on sandy gravel that rolled from under their feet, wind-borne grit stinging their faces and eyes. Around them, a desolation of humps and boulders extended away to shadowy forms of hillsides and mesas outlined dimly in the dust-laden, sulfurous air. The knee that Keene had struck in the landing was throbbing, and after about thirty minutes he had to stop to put a dressing over the burn on his calf, which was chafing painfully. He was grateful that they had accepted the Guard-issue kit in Pasadena, including boots. His civilian shoes wouldn't have hung together for a mile in this.

At the top of the rise, Dan halted to check his compass bearing. The men stood waiting, adjusting pack straps and repositioning weapons. Then Legermount pointed; Keene looked with the others, his eyes at first

narrowing in puzzlement. . . . They were looking down
over what seemed to be an expanse of desert extending
away into the pall of dust through which something
was glowing dull red. Then, as the pattern resolved
itself, his jaw fell incredulously. The size and distance
were impossible to estimate, since in the murk there
was nothing to provide a reference of size—but a part
of the desert seemed to be burning. He felt a nudge
on his shoulder and turned. Mitch handed him a pair
of field glasses. Keene raised them to his eyes, adjusted
the focus, and peered.

The ground itself was glowing. . . . A vast, smol-
dering depression extended back into invisibility,
looking like a lake of fire behind a darker dam of
boulders and earth mixed with embers. He was looking at a crater. The "dam" was part of the wall. As
he studied it more, he made out another glow, dim-
mer and more distant, with no details discernible, that
had been invisible without the glasses. They could be
just two of thousands scattered for hundreds of miles.
Too stupefied to speak, he passed the glasses to Colby.
They resumed moving to cross the head of a valley
descending away to their left, and followed the far
side around a shoulder of mountain, all the time
angling down the slope. After about another mile they
came to a track heading in roughly their direction,
which made the going easier. Following the track, they
came across an abandoned pickup with dents in the
roof and a shattered windshield. Legermount tried
jumping a wire from the battery to the starter in the
hope of getting them a ride, but the pickup was out
of gas.

Lower down, they heard screams—not human but
shrill and whinnying, which sounded even more
blood-chilling. They found horses, dozens of them,
in a corral behind an obliterated farm. Most of those
not already dead were writhing with smashed legs,
burns, broken backs. The soldiers stopped long

enough to despatch them with bullets. A handful remained, milling around each other aimlessly, their eyes bulging in terror. Legermount looked at Mitch questioningly. Mitch scowled, then shook his head. "Hell, let 'em have what chance they've got." He waved toward the gate. One of the troopers opened it to turn the surviving animals loose.

Below the farm was a graveyard of cattle piled in heaps around a pond of red sludge. Nearby was what was left of a car that looked as if it had been hurled some distance, its wheels in the air. There were bodies inside, and two more thrown clear. What little light there had been had faded, and Mitch and Dan, leading, had to use flashlamps to find the trail. From somewhere ahead came the sound of an aircraft climbing. At least, it seemed Dan's sense of direction had been good.

The valley seemed to be opening onto flatter terrain. The ground still rose to their right, but on the other side fell away more gently and broadened. The track merged with another and became gravel now instead of just dirt, though sometimes disappearing beneath mounds of rubble and sand that looked as if they had been thrown by a giant shovel. Light began appearing below on the left, strung at intervals along a still-invisible road. Dan confirmed that it had to be Interstate 10. There didn't seem to be a lot of movement on it.

Some distance ahead, the lights became more numerous, fading into the darkness along a line veering left as if the road curved suddenly in that direction. But interstates didn't change direction that abruptly. An area beyond was still glowing. They could feel the heat on their faces, even at that distance. It seemed that something sizable had impacted square across the highway. Mitch and Dan conferred briefly. The choice was either to head directly down to the road now and follow it to what appeared to be workings in progress

to create a traffic road around the far side of the crater;
or alternatively, to stay above the road and head right
of the crater, which while more direct could mean
having to negotiate the broken rim in the darkness and
possibly being driven farther uphill again. Deciding not
to risk any further unknowns they went with the first,
taking the next track they came to pointing directly
down toward the lights. From somewhere in the direction of the highway, the muffled *whop-whop-whop* of
a helicopter rotor came distantly through the night.

In the darkness and with all the dust in the air,
the road turned out to be closer than they had
thought. They passed several houses, some stores, and
a gas station, all ruined and partly buried in rocky
debris. There were more wrecked vehicles, some
thrown topsy turvy, others pinning bodies of people
who had apparently tried to shelter under them. And
then lights and activity, accompanied by the sounds
of voices and motors, were immediately ahead.
Approaching, they found there were more vehicles
than they had realized; the lights were from just a
few with engines running that were being used to
illuminate rescue operations in progress among more
houses and commercial premises built along a service road paralleling the interstate, now discernible
beyond. Workers were shining lamps among collapsed
timbers and shoveling away rubble. One building, lit
by the headlamps of a couple of trucks in front, had
been adapted as an aid station, with casualties being
helped and carried in out of the surrounding darkness. A group of hooded and hatted figures
approached, presumably having seen the flashlamps
coming down the road off the hill. The one leading
had a bandage showing below his hat and was wearing
a sheriff's deputy's badge with a storm coat.

"Looks like we've got some fit people here. You
boys wanna enlist? We need all the help here we can
get."

Mitch answered. "We need help ourselves. Bunch of people in a plane crashed back over in the next valley, some of them hurt."

"Are you serious? They're only just starting pulling bodies out of what's left of Phoenix. Right here we've got wrecks backed up into California that nobody's gotten to yet and probably won't for days. There's about a couple of hundred thousand people in line ahead of you already." The voice was weary, not prepared to debate the obvious. Mitch sighed and nodded. It was obvious that they didn't have a case.

"Military mission. We have to try and see it through."

The deputy shrugged. "Well . . . good luck."

"Which way's the reception center?" Mitch nodded in the direction of the crater ahead. "That way, past where the big one hit?"

"Right—about two miles farther on." The deputy's face showed for a moment in the light of a turning car: young, crusted with dust, streaked on one side with congealed blood that had trickled down from the bandage. He wiped his mouth with the back of a gloved hand. "Say . . . would you guys have any spare water? We've been waiting two hours for our truck to get back. Can't take any from these people. The ones that thought to bring some are gonna need it."

Mitch passed his water bottle over. Several of the other troopers did likewise. The deputy took a modest swig, washed it around, swallowed, and nodded gratefully. "Oh boy. You've no idea . . ."

"Is that where the chopper we heard would have come from?" Mitch asked.

"Right."

"Who's operating them?"

"I couldn't tell you. The Army's in charge now, trying to get some organization together. Where are you guys heading?"

"Texas."

"*Texas?* Jeez! I'm not sure there is a Texas

anymore. It might be part of the Gulf. Everybody else is coming the other way."

"Like I said, it's an official mission."

"Well, I'm glad something's still functioning. Just follow along where they're leveling a road around the crater—there's no way you can miss it; you've got a mountain blocking the road. You can see the lights they've got set up from here. Then pick up the interstate again on the other side."

It was like a scene out of a war. There were hundreds of wrecked and damaged vehicles there in the darkness, stretching in a gigantic tailback from the crater, they realized as they came out onto the highway. Thousands. Standing amid a litter of glass and debris, roofs and hoods buckled by falling rocks, some apparently unscathed, others flung or pushed off the roadway completely. A number were burning. Twisting lines jammed nose to tail showed where drivers had weaved as far as they could before being brought to a halt. Many were helping each other check among the vehicles with flashlights and in headlamp beams, pulling out the injured and doing what they could for the ones trapped. Others just sat along the verge, in shock and bewildered, waiting for direction. Farther along, a tractor trailer had somehow balanced itself on end. A woman was wandering among the cars, frantically calling someone's name. A headless body hung from the window of a Chevrolet, dripping blood onto the asphalt. A dog whimpered at the door of a stove-in Nissan van full of tangled forms, none of them moving.

Keene walked by it all at the center of the silent column, unable to suppress a feeling of callousness, yet mindful that nothing they could have done would alter anything materially. Millions of people were dying, millions no doubt already had, and many more millions would still, and nothing was going to change it.

Crunch . . . Crunch . . . Crunch . . . Crunch . . . He
followed Legermount's tirelessly swinging heels ahead
of him and let his mind sink into numbness, shutting
out the groans, the cries, the shouts of the rescuers,
the bodies laid out in rows under blankets and tarpau-
lins. Others who were part of their own microworld
were depending on them, he told himself, and for now
nothing more mattered beyond that. *Crunch . . .*
Crunch . . . Crunch . . . Crunch . . . In such a way was
life reducing to minor achievements and small things
taking on immense significance; that kept you alive and
got you through to tomorrow. And that was good
enough. Both his legs hurt. The boots were chafing his
heels, and he could feel blisters starting to form. He
hadn't hiked like this for years. He would have to get
used to it again soon. There would be plenty of it in
store when gasoline stocks started running out.

Crunch . . . Crunch . . . Crunch . . . Crunch . . . And
so it went until the mounds of rocks and debris rose
to become a huge rampart of earth and boulders standing fifty to a hundred feet high in the light of arc lamps
running from a mobile generator. In places, crushed
and partly buried vehicles protruded from the slope.
Police, military, and emergency vehicles were clustered
along a strip that had been leveled to the left of the
crater wall, beyond which more lamps illuminated
earth-moving machines and road gangs making an
earth-and-gravel road to reconnect the severed portions
of the interstate. Mitch led the way along the foot of
the crater wall, at the top of which figures were clambering about, taking photographs of the other side and
making observations with various instruments. The
object that gouged the crater had come in from the
east, throwing most of the ejecta westward in the direction that Keene and the others had come from. As they
progressed along the edge, the wall gradually became
lower until they were walking almost on the rim itself.
The ground underfoot was hot, and the heat radiating

from inside was intense enough to keep them several yards back from the actual edge, in the shadow of the lip. Even so, every now and again one or a couple of them would venture closer for a few seconds to get a glimpse of the crater floor, glowing eerily red. Red was shining above them, too, reflected down through the dust pall by the cloud blanket. What was left of Phoenix was on fire.

A sound came of distant freight trains in the sky, followed minutes later by the rumbling of explosions somewhere to the north.

The reception center was another oasis of light and activity involving trucks and earthmovers, located a short distance from the interstate beside a small airfield littered with wrecked planes. It looked like an original cluster of buildings from a one-time military base of some kind, expanded probably within the last few days to the beginnings of a minicity by the addition of scores of portable huts and cabins, only to be flattened by the meteorite storm. The work going on currently was to clear the devastation and convert as many of the buildings as were salvageable into earth-covered dugouts and sandbagged shelters. Refugee arrivals were already being moved into one part, where food was being dispensed from a field kitchen. In another area, bodies were being carried from where they had been laid out in lines numbering dozens and loaded onto a truck, presumably for burial or disposal elsewhere.

Everything was improvised and chaotic, and Mitch's initial queries yielded mixed answers as to who was in charge. No one seemed to be, exactly, but different individuals were running different things, which they seemed to have taken charge of on their own initiative. Hopes were that it should all get more coordinated tomorrow. Eventually, they found an Army major who had set up with a small staff in a sandbagged trailer equipped with a telephone exchange operating over landlines. Apparently, he was in touch with the regional command center being established at El Paso.

Colby Greene produced his government credentials and explained that people who were involved in a vital official mission were stranded up in the hills about ten miles west where their plane had crashed, and he needed assistance. The major regarded him with much the same look as the sheriff's deputy had given them back along the interstate.

"Well, I'm not sure that kind of authority means too much anymore," he said. "And even if it did, we've got our hands kind of full right now to be worrying about a few more people ten miles up in the hills. And even if we didn't, we don't have any way of getting anyone there."

"You've got choppers," Dan said. "We heard one ourselves, coming in—when we were back the other side of the crater."

"No av-gas," the major told him. "A plane that went out of here earlier took the last we had. Two road tankers were on their way here to fill our tanks, but they didn't make it through Phoenix. We're supposed to be getting an emergency load flown in tomorrow morning, but until it gets here nothing's going out. So why don't you and your boys get something to eat, find a corner to bed down, and rest up for the night? You all look as if you could use it."

42

The tanker flight was diverted elsewhere. Back in the trailer the next morning, Keene listened with Mitch, Colby, and Dan while the major talked on the line with somebody in El Paso.

"Look, we've got half of California coming in off the interstate this morning. I need food, I need doctors, and I need medical supplies. But I can't have anything flown in, because until I've got something to refuel them with, nothing that brings any of it can get out again. . . . Base facilities? What are you talking about, base facilities? There aren't any base facilities. They got wiped out yesterday. What planet have you been on? We're having to dig ourselves holes in the ground here."

He listened a while longer, then replaced the receiver and looked at the four who were waiting. "All I can tell you is that this isn't the only area that got pounded. It's still going on in some places. Everywhere's a mess. They said they'll do what they can. We might be able to get a supply through by road from a depot I've located in California. What else do you want me to say?"

It seemed there was nothing more to be done, probably for the rest of that day. The group vacated the space they had been using in one of the previously prepared shelters, and Mitch detailed Legermount and three troopers to begin constructing one of their own. He outlined a plan for a rectangular pit five feet deep, the excavated material being used for sandbags to build up the sides, with a roof of alloy beams and corrugated steel sheet from some wreckage nearby, topped with four feet of sand. With that task under way, he left for a tour of the center, accompanied by Dan and the two other men to see what else was happening and if they could be of help. Thousands of people were beginning to appear now, jammed into their own vehicles or brought in by emergency trucks, many others walking. There simply weren't the facilities or staff to take care of the horrendous numbers of injured; trucks stacked with bodies left regularly for the mass graves that had been bulldozed behind a hill a mile or so from the center.

The entire center had become a maze of workings and diggings along one side of the airfield, made by human moles burrowing into the soil. Keene tried to put in his share of pickaxing and shoveling, but it was hard to match the pace of younger men at the peak of fitness and training, especially since his legs had stiffened since yesterday. The dust choked, even through a wetted handkerchief tied around his mouth. His lips had swollen and dried, and his tongue was painful where he had bitten it in the crash, making speaking and eating difficult. His face felt like one throbbing, open sore, and he could no longer bear the touch of trying to wipe off the perspiration.

Halfway through the morning, meteorites and gravel began falling again. There were no big detonations like the one that had gouged away part of I-10 the day before, but a steady rain continued of missiles thumping into soil or impacting on rocks

and metal with bangs like rifle bullets. People were
hit, though surprisingly infrequently. But they had
no choice but to press on. Those who weren't
actually digging or roofing stayed under cover, making whatever excursions they had to as quick dashes
from one shelter to another. In a depression a short
distance from the main area, a crew in hard hats
and Army flak jackets began erecting a derrick to
drill for water. Meanwhile, three sandbagged trucks
loaded with drums were sent to see what could be
recovered from the ruined water tower serving the
area.

By the middle of the day, Keene was realizing that
more than the years and his sedentary lifestyle were
slowing him down. He found himself alternately sweating and shivering, and once or twice almost keeled over
from dizzy fits; but he settled to a rhythm and drove
himself doggedly, resolved not to become an additional
burden to the others. When the roof was completed,
a scavenging party went away to see what they could
find to make the new abode more habitable. At this,
Mitch's men turned out to be quite accomplished, coming back with a forklift pallet and some boards for
flooring, assorted pieces of tarp, several sticks of furniture, and even a mechanic's inspection lamp with
good batteries. Finally, they were able to flop down
and rest. Keene lowered himself gratefully onto a strip
of foam rubber laid on the pallet, which had been set
aside for him and another of the men who was also
feverish, and another hit on the knee by a ricochet-
ing rock. At last, he could just lie back, let his whole
body go limp, and abandon himself to the exhaustion
that had been building for days. . . .

And then the rain started—not like a spring fresh-
ening but hammering and relentless, turning the
dugout city into a labyrinth of mud and pools through
which rivulets trickled, then poured, joined up and
grew into a network of torrenting streams within

minutes. Water seeped through the loose-packed roof and flowed down into the entrance; just as they had started to get comfortable and talked about eating, everyone had to get up, put on coats and capes, and go out again to dig drainage trenches. When they finally came back inside, Keene drifted into a series of fitful dozes that really weren't sleep or rest, coming back to semiconsciousness each time to be greeted by the drumming of the rain. At one time he was vaguely aware of Colby holding a dish of soup and urging him to eat, but Keene's mouth was too sore to accept more than a taste of water. Thoughts flitted through his mind of Cavan, Alicia, and the rest still up on the mountain; but in too much of a detached kind of way to for him to feel concern. Enough of his faculties were working to tell him he should feel concern, but the numbed remainder admitted that he didn't. Not just now, anyway. All that registered was the sweating and shivering of his fever, the single, continuous ache that his body seemed to have turned into, and the burning pain of his mouth and face. Maybe tomorrow, he would.

Rain was still falling the next morning. But the meteorites had slackened, and, wonder of wonders, Mitch announced that the road tanker from California had arrived! The major was making calls to El Paso. Keene was able to manage a breakfast of hot cereal and coffee, and afterward, finally, felt his body easing sufficiently to rest. He began drifting away, warm and comfortable at last, telling himself that he never wanted to move or have to think again. . . .

And then Colby was shaking him. Keene forced his eyes to open. Then he heard the sound of helicopter rotors getting louder, then settling to a steady roar somewhere not far away. "Lan, move. Mitch has gotten us a ride out," Colby was saying. Keene sat up groggily to find the dugout full of bustling figures collecting kit, closing and strapping packs, snatching up weapons. Colby helped Keene get his things together and pull on his parka and helmet. "They just ferried in a medical team and supplies from El Paso. They're going straight back as soon as it's topped up. Say good-bye to Phoenix. I hope you didn't want to send any postcards."

Keene pulled on his boots and took his pack as Colby thrust it at him. They stumbled out after the others into the rain. Ahead, Legermount and two others were assisting the sick trooper and the one with the hurt leg. Several times, Keene had to take Colby's arm to steady himself over the slippery rocks and gulleys. Mitch was at the edge of the airstrip, waving them in the direction of a large Sikorsky sitting with its rotor idling. Another helicopter farther back was being unloaded. Dan and one of the helicopter's crew were waiting at the door to give them a hand up and inside. Another half dozen or so passengers going back with the chopper for one reason or another were already inside. The pilot, the only other crew member, was turning and looking back from his seat, waiting for the boarding to be completed.

"That's it," the copilot called forward, closing the door while the men found places among the folding side seats and rubber cushioning on the floor. Keene was ushered forward to one of the fixed seats behind the crew stations, along with Colby, Dan, and Mitch. The copilot went up front beside the pilot, and the engine note swelled. The pilot tried a couple of times to contact someone by radio, then shook his head and flipped the set off as useless. He checked his instruments, peered through the rivers of rain running down the windshield, and prepared to lift off.

"We're looking at El Paso in about two hours, maybe a little over," he shouted above the din. "What are you guys up to in all this, as a matter of curiosity?"

"Just an official mission," Dan called back vaguely.

"You mean there are people around who still care about stuff like that?" the copilot threw in.

The Sikorsky rose and began turning. Only now was Keene able to begin collecting his swimming thoughts. . . . And suddenly his mind rebelled as the words that he had just heard replayed themselves. "El Paso in two hours . . ." *No! This was all wrong!* He turned to look at Mitch, but the soldier's face was set impassively, staring ahead at the windshield. Keene looked at Dan. Dan was looking forward between the crew seats, scanning the instruments—as if to distract himself.

Keene remembered the look on Furle's face when they had left him in charge of the group on the mountain. Furle didn't really know Mitch, and he hadn't been sure if he could trust him. Keene didn't know Mitch either, he realized. And what little he had seen cast Mitch as one who confronted brutal realities. Was this his way not only of saying that there was only one realistic option for them to take now, but presenting it as a *fait accompli*? Keene tried to moisten his cracked lips, asking himself if he could accept it. In his weakened condition, he simply wasn't up to a face-off with somebody like Mitch. He glanced at Colby, and from the concerned look on Colby's face could see that he was wrestling with the same problem. Maybe it was time, Keene told himself. Eventually, one way or another, they were all going to have to learn hardness. Was that what Mitch was telling them?

The blank wall of orange-pink outside brightened as the chopper climbed. Takeoff complete, the engine noise settled back to its cruising level.

And then Mitch said, "Oh, there's just one more thing. We have another group to pick up. They're about ten miles back the other way, where our plane came down. Twenty of 'em." At the last count there had actually been twenty-five. But the Sikorski had plenty of room to spare.

The pilot raised a hand and shook his head. "Sorry. We're on a tight schedule. I hate to say it, but twenty isn't any big deal one way or another in all this."

"This twenty happen to be important to us," Mitch told him.

"Everybody's got someone who's important. Like I said, sorry, but this isn't a taxi service. I'm under orders to return directly to El Paso. They don't say anything about going the other way."

Mitch produced his automatic and pointed it. "Now you have orders," he said.

The copilot turned around sharply, his arm reaching out reflexively, but Dan produced another pistol and eased him back. Several of the other passengers started in alarm, but none seemed prepared to risk interfering. It seemed Mitch and Dan had planned it. "Go on, pull it," the pilot challenged, showing his teeth. "Then the only way you're going to get back down is as a piece of jelly."

Mitch turned his head toward Dan. "How long did you fly choppers in the Air Force?" he asked casually.

"Oh, five or six years, probably." That was news. Keene had never heard Dan mention anything about choppers.

"You reckon you could handle this bird?"

"Sure. No problem."

Mitch looked back at the pilot. "Sometimes things work two ways," he said him. "I hate to say it, but one pilot isn't any big deal to me one way or another in all this. It's your call."

There was a long, agonized silence. Finally, the pilot sighed. "Okay, you've got it. Ten miles? Which way do I go?"

"Back along I-10 past the crater, then over a ridge to the left a couple of miles farther along. Stay in sight of the ground, and I'll direct you from there."

43

When the rain turned their shelter into a torrent, the group left on the mountain had abandoned the ravine and made a new refuge for themselves underneath the surviving parts of the Rustler. Jed was still cheerful and had been making himself useful cleaning cutlery and pots and talking to the injured. Joan was hanging on but needed surgery urgently. Two of the ones left hadn't pulled through: the man with the head injuries and fractures whose chances hadn't looked good when Keene and the others left, and a soldier with his back broken in the crash. In addition, three more were missing through a tragedy of a different kind.

After two days passed by, Captain Furle had seen himself with no other choice but to assume that no help would materialize and his group was going to have to make its own arrangements. Accordingly, he sent two of the soldiers that he had available to reconnoiter the way down to the Interstate to see if help could be summoned, and failing that to search around for a vehicle, cart, or any other means for moving the nine badly injured that they still had with them. Tom, the civilian, Cynthia's friend, had offered to go too, pointing out that two would be a perilously small number if anything happened to one of them, and he was an experienced mountain hiker. Furle had agreed, and the three departed shortly afterward. They still hadn't returned when the helicopter arrived. By the time loading was complete there was still no sign of them and attempts to contact them by radio had failed. There could be no question of tarrying longer. Mitch ordered supplies, water, and ammunition to be left for them. Furle and a couple of the troopers stacked a selection of items in the space under the Rustler's wing and prepared to clamber aboard as the Sikorsky revved up for takeoff. And then Cynthia, who was still on the ground with them, announced blank-faced that she would stay and wait for Tom. Apparently, they had lived together for eight years.

"Ma'am, you're being crazy," Furle said. "What if they don't come back? You'll die out here."

"What if they do come back . . . and I'd never see him again?"

Mitch glowered down from the helicopter door. "There isn't time for this. Grab her and put her on board," he ordered. The three soldiers closed around her, pinning her arms, and lifted her inside forcibly over her struggling and hysterical protests. Moments later, the Sikorsky lifted off once more into the violent skies.

El Paso was about as far west as it was possible to go and still be in Texas. But at least they had made it to Texas—twenty-nine of the forty-two who had left Vandenberg in the Rustler.

The scene as the helicopter came in was like the reception center at Phoenix, but with everything on a vaster scale. A quarter of the city had been obliterated

by a new crater, which had buried the former downtown area under its wall. The pilot, who seemed to have
relented after being uncooperative earlier and wouldn't
be filing any complaints, said reconnaissance flights had
shown an immense crater field extending westward
from Phoenix and to the northeast, but he didn't know
how far. The ruins of what was left of the city were
being reinforced and bombproofed, while for miles
around, earthworks, bunkers, and connecting roads
looking like extended military fortifications were
appearing across the desert slopes and among the
mountains. But it still wasn't matching the scale of the
problem. The numbers of people pouring in were even
vaster, their vehicles visible everywhere in thousands,
in some places pulled off the roadways in untidy sprawls
stretching for miles, filling the verges and any open
ground, in others tossed like the aftermath of an air
strike.

They landed at what looked like a regional airport,
amidst the kind of scene that was becoming familiar: demolished and damaged buildings, excavations
and repairs going on around the runways. One runway appeared to be serviceable. Mangled aircraft of
all types were everywhere, and the hangar buildings
that had survived reasonably intact were being shored
up and earthed over as protective bunkers for any
that were salvageable. The air, as they climbed out
of the helicopter, was hot, heavy, clammy, and
oppressive.

Leaving Furle to supervise the unloading of the
injured and find them some kind of temporary accommodation, Cavan and Dan left on what showed signs
of being an impossible task of finding them medical
attention while Alicia and Dash stayed to do what they
could. The best the helicopter pilot could suggest as
a lead to whoever was running things was the colonel in charge of flight operations, and Keene went
with Colby and Mitch to seek him out. After some

asking around they found him in the glassless but functional control tower, following the approach of an incoming aircraft on a screen connected to an Army mobile field radar located somewhere nearby. He was obviously busy, stressed, and listened to them impatiently. When Colby presented his White House papers and Presidential staff ID, the colonel seized the opportunity to have his switchboard call the office of the acting commander of the area to get rid of them. The colonel then returned his attention to the business at hand, and a guard escorted them back downstairs to wait.

Less than half an hour later, an Army sergeant driving a Ford van with netting draping its sides and a layer of sandbags on the roof arrived to collect them. Apparently, everything had happened too quickly and universally to allow martial law to be declared formally in the U.S. Military control had been instituted as an automatic reaction locally, nevertheless—as doubtless had been done in all areas retaining any organizational capability at all. In El Paso an Army general called Weyland had taken charge after just about all of the area's regular command structure and FEMA directorate were wiped out along with the fifty-plus percent of the city that was now craters and rubble.

As the sergeant talked, they negotiated their way around mounds of fallen rock and debris, wrecked vehicles, and mud traps created by the recent rain. Parts were like Boston in January, but with paths being cleared through mud and sand instead of snow. Along whole blocks, rescuers were still hauling the dead and injured from collapsed buildings. Sandbagged bunkers and shelters were being constructed wherever opportunity presented itself, and undamaged stores, homes, and offices adapted into dressing stations. But even with all the bulldozing and shoveling, the medics and nurses working frantically under tents and awnings and in hollows dug amid the debris, the mobile kitchens and relief workers handing out rations from trucks, untended cases and others too shocked or exhausted to help were everywhere: laid out along the roadsides, sitting blankly outside their vehicles, or just wandering aimlessly. The sergeant said that the services had been hard put to cope even before yesterday, which had been a massacre. Today they were overwhelmed.

The route took them west of the city along another piece of Interstate 10, with dry red mountains flanking the road on one side, and slopes leading down to the Rio Grande river marking the Mexican border on the other. They exited on a road that climbed for a short distance through a spread-out residential area that had been fairly evenly battered, and led into a valley with boulder-strewn sides and a scattering of industrial buildings and other facilities strung along the bottom. A gate through a chain-link fence, attended by sentries outside a gatehouse that had been reinforced by sandbags and corrugated steel sheeting, brought them into a parking area in front of a couple of office buildings, some sheds, and several unidentifiable structures standing below a high cliff with a mountain ridge rising beyond. Work crews in helmets, flak vests, and military fatigues were clearing rubble, filling craters, and finishing more dugout constructions. Both office buildings had every window shattered and were showing damage, especially to the upper parts.

The sergeant took Keene and the two others through a side door into one of the sheds, across a floor where stores were being sorted and vehicles unloaded, to the entrance of a tunnel leading into the mountain. He explained that Weyland had located his headquarters in a former mine working that had been converted years before into a repository for banking and financial documents as a precaution in the event of a major war. The tunnel led to a cage elevator which they took to a lower level, emerging into well-lit corridors with

white, ribbed-concrete walls. After all the destruction
and chaos of the preceding days, the order and nor-
mality of the surroundings seemed almost unnatural.

They came to an open area where military personnel at desks were working in front of a situation
board occupying most of one wall, the others covered in charts, maps, and an array of aerial photographs. A large map of the surrounding parts of Texas
and New Mexico was marked with red circles showing
what looked like craters, and various other annota-
tions. Weyland's office was at the far end, consisting
simply of a smaller space separated by a partition.
It had a desk and side table covered with papers,
more wall maps, and several upright chairs along two
of the walls. A naked bulb hung from a cord overhead, shaking slightly to the vibrations of machinery
somewhere nearby.

Weyland was tall and wirily built, on the young side
for his rank, Keene thought, forceful in manner, with
straight black hair brushed to one side and dark,
intense eyes that refused to be cowed by the situation. His face was dark with stubble, and he wore a
flak jacket over a grimy, sweat-stained shirt. The three
arrivals were shown in by the sergeant, who then left.
They introduced themselves; Weyland invited them
to take seats. He draped his elbows over the arms
of his chair and looked them over.

"I understand from the phone call that you just
got here from Phoenix, and before that you were
in a plane crash. You just about look it, too. We've
got soup, beans, and coffee going, if you could use
some."

Mitch said that sounded great but explained that
they had some injured back at the airfield who
needed medical attention urgently. Weyland stared
at them for several seconds. Then, sparing them a
lecture on the obvious, he got up, went to the gap
at the end of the partition that served as a doorway,

and called over one of his officers. He outlined the situation, and the officer went away to make some calls. Keene and Colby nodded their thanks. Keene didn't feel entirely comfortable about jumping the line. But there are times when one has to look after one's own. "And now can we get you people something to eat?" Weyland asked again. They accepted.

It turned out that the general's readiness to receive them stemmed more from a hope of being told more himself of what was going on than any recognition of a need to inform them. He had assumed from Colby's credentials that they represented, or at least could enlighten him as to the existence of, some administrative authority that had survived of a national or even international nature. He was in landline contact with the military command at Cheyenne Mountain, several regional headquarters, and also a number of FEMA centers. As far as he was aware, Washington had ceased functioning. The President, along with his family and immediate staff, had vanished three days previously with Air Force One when the administration left for the war-survival and command center located near Atlanta. The Secretary of State was supposed to have taken charge in Atlanta provisionally, but Weyland hadn't had any contact from there. A further mystery was the disappearance of the Vice President, who had left to set up a West Coast shadow government a day before the President's departure from Washington. Colby set the record straight on that score, which led to an account of the mission that had taken him and Keene to California. It was the first news Weyland had heard of what had become of the Kronians. Keene presumed that General Ullman would have reported it at Cheyenne Mountain, which seemed by default to have become the nearest that existed to a national coordinating center. Weyland noted the details, clearly with the intention of reporting them independently anyway. His

unspoken implication—that there was no guarantee
that anyone from Vandenberg had made it to Cheyenne Mountain—didn't hit Keene until a couple of
minutes afterward. Maybe he was more tired than he
realized, he told himself.

Weyland then moved to local and more immediate matters. Sitting on America's rocky spine, El Paso
was the focus of two floods of evacuees converging
eastward from southern California, Arizona, and New
Mexico, and in the opposite direction from Texas and
Oklahoma. They were arriving hungry, thirsty,
exhausted, and traumatized, the survivors of meteorite
falls, firestorms, hurricanes, and rain torrents, bringing
their sick and their injured by the tens of thousands;
by the hundreds of thousands. And there, in the dust,
the dryness, and the heat that was setting in after the
rain, they would die, as they were already starting to,
in numbers almost as large. The emergency measures
that it had proved possible to mobilize in the time
available were too few and too late. And in any case,
all the planning had been a product of the slowly
evolving thinking of years gone by. None of it had
envisaged anything like this. The worst that had been
imagined was nuclear war, in which strikes on worthwhile targets and perhaps population centers would
produce intense devastation in relatively localized
areas, but with comparatively unscathed regions
between, able to provide help and relief. But with
everywhere smitten equally, there was nowhere to turn
to. For every township and community, enclave and
locality, anything beyond the preoccupation of staying alive from one hour to the next and securing a
refuge to gain some respite vanished from the equa-
tion of reality. The result was that the whole infra-
structure by which the nation maintained itself as a
cohesive social and productive organism was coming
apart with a rapidity that in any other circumstance
would have been deemed impossible; and the same

was no doubt true for every other part of the world also.

"What you've told me confirms what we already guessed," Weyland concluded. "We're going to have to rely on our own resources to get us through this. No supraregional authority is going to emerge and start giving directions. The centers that I mentioned earlier have all got problems of their own as bad as ours here. Nobody has anything to spare. Our immediate concern is providing shelter accommodation and conserving fuel and provisions. The eventual aim is to consolidate communications between key centers along a line running through here, Denver, and up along the Rockies, that will enable mutually supportive logistics, including the restoration of a minimal power grid. With tight management I'm estimating hitting a rock-bottom situation at about three months from now, after which we should be able to start pulling things back together. In the war game scenarios, they used to figure on getting back to normal forty years after an all-out exchange. So maybe if we doubled that, we wouldn't be too far out. What do you think? I wouldn't be around to see it, but at least it would mean leading a useful life. So there's my take. Where are you people going to fit in? What kind of plans do you have next?"

Three months? Start pulling things back together? The words echoed dully in Keene's mind. It seemed that President Hayer had done too good a job in instilling hope and optimism when he addressed the nation. No concept of what the present events were leading to had yet taken root on any significant basis. Probably that was just as well.

Right now, Keene wasn't about to launch into anything that would give Weyland cause to reappraise the prospects. Nothing was going to change them, and there was probably no better way in which he could expend his energies. And besides, Keene could feel his own energy draining, even as he turned the thought over. His eyes were closing involuntarily; he felt himself sway on the chair and checked himself with a start. The surroundings seemed to float out of focus and reverberate with hollow sounds and voices that came and went. He was distantly aware of Colby and Mitch looking at him strangely, and himself murmuring that he didn't have any plans. . . .

And either he passed out then, or simply fell asleep on the spot.

44

Keene was out until the next day and awoke to a feeling of having slept solidly for the first time in a week, probably having been given sedation. His sores had been cleaned and treated. He felt stronger. And once again a shower and a shave worked their wonders. He was in a room that Weyland had assigned in the mine vaults, where Cavan, Alicia, and Charlie Hu had also been brought. Cynthia, now resigned to the loss of Tom, had come too rather than remain with the group from Vandenberg. It seemed she wanted to break from everything connected with her old life. Nobody objected. Mitch and Dan, with the uninjured remnant of the Special Forces contingent, had moved into military quarters in the upper levels.

Charlie Hu was mobile again, although stiff, and hobbled in with the others when word went around that Keene was conscious. The news was that Ullman's group in the Samson had made it to Cheyenne Mountain. Meteorite storms east of the Mississippi had been severe. Communications were poor, and nothing had been heard from the national administration supposedly being set up in Atlanta. Huge tides were developing in all coastal areas. Aircraft losses had been horrific; since the surviving equipment would have to serve for an indeterminate time, further flying, except where deemed essential by the highest authorities, was discontinued until conditions eased. In the El Paso area, rock and gravel falls were continuing steadily, with occasional showers of flaming naphtha. There had been armed confrontations over demands for supplies, access to care and shelter, and possession of ownerless goods and vehicles.

Alicia appeared just as Keene was settling down to the first food he had been able to enjoy for days. She had conceded to the inevitable and cut her hair short. Her face, while less red and inflamed than when he had last seen it, was smeared with cream and still a far cry from the cover-model complexion that had emerged from the Rustler at Vandenberg. "You're looking amazingly better already," she told Keene. "Quick recovery means there's a lot of reserve left yet. Eating well, too. Even better."

"I never thought there'd be a day when I'd say Army cooking beats anything I can name," Keene replied. "But there it is." He dug hungrily into the plate of eggs, biscuit, gravy, and sausage. "What about you? How have you been? Have some coffee."

"Apart from the outside, not too bad. My face feels as if it's been sandpapered." Alicia poured coffee into a mug for herself, adding milk from a cardboard carton.

"You've been working nonstop. How do you do it?"

"It must be my virtuous character. And then having Leo around is always an inspiration."

"There's another one who amazes me. How did you get to meet him? You know, in all the years I've known him, he's never told me."

"Oh, really?"

"No. Tell me. I'm curious."

"Oh, it was in a bar in Manhattan. I was young and new here—just took a notion to see the other side of the world. This guy was coming on strong and being a pain—you know, a jerk. Leo saw that I didn't know how to deal with it, so he moved in and gave him a lesson in charm and manners. I think I just wanted to see the look on the guy's face when I walked out to go someplace else with a man twice his age." Alicia chuckled. "Leo knew I would, because he's got the same kind of humor. Anyway, it grew from there. He thinks I'm crazy, you know."

"Does he really?"

"Don't tell me he never told you."

"If he had, I'd probably choose not to remember."

Alicia started to smile, then winced as it stretched the dried skin around her mouth. "Oh, how gallant! I love it. You see, underneath all this outside, you're just a romantic too."

"Maybe."

"You give up your place on the shuttle to go and find Vicki, and even that gorgeous Kronian woman can't make you change your mind? Of course you are! What else is there to call it?"

"Maybe I just didn't like the thought of being privileged," Keene suggested. "Equal opportunity. An old American tradition."

"Pah. I don't believe a word of it. It's just the gruff outside switching itself on again." Alicia helped herself to a spare piece of biscuit. "So tell me about her, Lan."

Keene leaned back in the chair and sighed. "Oh . . . It wasn't anything romantic. Just a kind of closeness that comes from two people who think the same way and share a lot of values and things. You know—she was the kind of person you never had to explain to about what you were thinking or how you felt, because she already knew. I don't think I even realized it myself

much until these last few weeks. . . ." Keene broke off
when he realized that Alicia was frowning at him. He
raised his eyebrows quizzically.

"Why do you say she 'was'?" Alicia asked. "You
make her sound like a thing of the past, a piece of
history already."

Keene stared at her uncertainly, then jerked his
head in agitation. "Well, I mean, it's . . ." He faltered,
unable to say the painful but obvious.

"Lan, what are you saying?"

"What else is there to say? We tried. . . . That's
not an option anymore. All we can do now is stay
here and figure out what—"

"Lan!" Alicia protested. "You can't! We're not staying anywhere. We're going on to San Saucillo like we
said. You can't change your mind now."

"But . . ." Keene shook his head. What other way
was there to put it? "Alicia, there isn't any way to
get there. All flying is over, finished. They're saving
the planes for when things get better. It'll be years
before anyone can make any again. The roads are all
choked or blocked, and whatever can move on them
is going the wrong way."

"We don't need the roads," Alicia said. "I've been
talking to some of General Weyland's staff. Stocks of
gas and supplies from south and east Texas have been
concentrated in San Antonio. A train is leaving here
tonight to bring a load back up to El Paso. There
will be plenty of room on the outward run."

"And what do we do after San Antonio, walk?"
Keene demanded. The words came out sharper and
sounding more sarcastic than he had intended. He
realized that his nerves were still on edge.

"Snap out of it, Lan. It's not like you," Alicia said.
"I don't know what we do from there. Maybe with
everyone coming the other way the roads will be
easier between there and the coast." Her eyes flamed
at him. "But you just said yourself that things are

going to get worse. How long will sitting down here
do any good? There is only one way out now, and
that's off the planet. And the means to do it is down
there in Mexico, not here."

Keene felt himself starting to object; then he
checked himself, hunched forward to rest his elbows
on the table, and stared at her. She was right. Like
a soldier who refuses to leave a foxhole under fire,
even though the position must ultimately fall, he
wanted to put longer-term considerations from his
mind and cling to the respite they had found here
after the ordeal of the last few days. The security was
an illusion that would last only so long. The more
they delayed, the worse, at the end of it all, the odds
must become. He shook his head, as if to reawaken
the sense of realism that normally resided there.

"Have the others said what they think about it yet?"
he asked her.

Alicia shook her head. "You are the first one I've
told. I assumed they'd think the same way as I did—
that there wouldn't be a problem."

Keene finished the last of his coffee and stood up.
"Then let's go and find out," he said.

The upshot was that Cavan knew Alicia well
enough not to bother arguing. Colby, in his inimitable
way, agreed as casually as if they were planning a
weekend vacation trip. Charlie Hu, more than any of
them, was under no illusions as to what was in store.
He expected there to be a lull of several days as
Athena and Earth locked gravitationally to gyrate past
each other like two passing skaters momentarily linking hands, during which time the bulk of the tail
would be directed away. The train of debris following Athena would then wrap around Earth, causing
falls more fearsome than anything that had occurred
so far. Then, after actually receding for a distance as
it swung by, Athena would be drawn back in for a

final close pass before being ejected on a trajectory away from Earth. Charlie's vote was to go for any chance of getting out if a chance was there. And Cynthia, having committed herself, had little choice but to go along with the rest of them.

The only unresolved question was whether Mitch and his men could be induced to. With conditions deteriorating and violence breaking out, to press ahead without the protection of an armed force would be folly bordering on recklessness. There was only one way to find out. First, they went to talk to Mitch.

Mitch's initial reaction was surprise that they were still even contemplating Mexico. He had assumed that they'd tried their best, the fates had come out against them, and the only thing left to consider was whether to stay in El Paso and place themselves under Weyland's command or head for Colorado. He changed his opinion somewhat when Charlie explained why the worst was far from over yet, but he still seemed uneasy at the thought of deserting his command and taking useful men away from where they might be needed. Cavan tried to set his doubts at rest.

"This is hardly a normal situation, Mitch. Your sentiments are admirable, but I have to be honest here. The figures Weyland and his staff are estimating are wildly unrealistic. They're doing their best, but they just don't have any concept of what's going on. Don't you understand? A month from now there isn't going to *be* any command worth talking about to have deserted."

Mitch pondered the point, scowling at the wall for a minute or two before turning back to face them. "You're talking about getting to a place that might no longer exist, for a shuttle that mightn't fly, and if it does, taking it up through this mess to find a spaceship that mightn't be there. And I'm supposed to believe that the odds are better than what I'd have if I stay on with this outfit. Is that what you're telling me?"

"Just the latest of Landen's crazy schemes," Cavan said, as if that explained everything. "Only this time he's got Alicia with him too."

"Sure, they're lousy odds, no question," Charlie Hu said, nodding and keeping a serious note. "But better than the alternative. I'll take them."

Mitch looked around at them. He seemed persuaded, and was running over the practicalities in his mind. "It means we have to be up-front with the men too," he said finally. "This isn't something I can order them into blindly—or would be prepared to. They have to make their own choices too."

Everyone looked at everyone else. Nobody dissented.

"So be it," Cavan said.

"The reason we've been talking about getting to Mexico is that there's another shuttle down a silo at a site just south of the border," Mitch told the soldiers a half hour later. Apart from himself and Dan there were Furle, Dash, Legermount, and six troopers: four from the group that had hijacked the chopper and two uninjured from those who had stayed with the crashed Rustler. "Now, we're not talking about huge numbers of people being there like you saw at Vandenberg. There'll be just us here, plus a handful to be picked up in Texas. That means there'll be extra room. After listening to Charlie, I'm willing to go for it. And for anyone else who's prepared to take his chances, that's the bonus at the end of the ride. But I'm not going to hang this on you as an order. It's a volunteer mission. You've all heard the arguments. Each man is free to make his choice."

Captain Furle still remembered the couple-of-hours-extra assurance that he'd heard the last time they talked about going to Mexico. "I can't say I see how it's going to change anything," he objected. "Except for making our chances worse, that is. Whatever hits here, the same thing is gonna hit there just as bad. The only difference is that here we've at least got protection and some backup that's halfway organized. There, we'd have nothing. We did what we could once, and it's over. I'm still for heading north to Cheyenne Mountain. General Ullman promised us at Vandenberg that he'd find us room there."

They showed mixed reactions. Keene could understand why. It hadn't been that long ago when he himself had been looking for excuses to stay with the apparent safety that the military bases represented. Dan decided to attempt returning to the Air Force command in Colorado too and throw his lot in with Earth, come what may. The trooper with the hurt knee and the other who had come down sick were not up to such a further mission, and two more stayed with Furle through choice. That left two—their names were Birden and Reynolds—who would go with Mitch, Legermount, Dash, and the six civilians, including Cynthia.

Keene wondered if he was the only one who understood how much smaller the Amspace minishuttle was than a regular Air Force shuttle or the Boxcars that had gone up from Vandenberg. There was no telling how many people Harry Halloran might have brought with him, assuming he made it to San Saucillo. Keene didn't relish the thought of possibly having to explain the situation to armed and angry men, should it turn out that there were no spare places after all. A likely response in that event might be an insistence at gunpoint that *everyone* submit to a draw. But first, they would have to get there. He would worry about it then, he decided. It was always possible that by that time the problem would have solved itself.

✧   ✧   ✧

Eleven in all were driven that night to the repaired siding in the railroad yards on the east side of the city, where the train to make the run to San Antonio was being assembled and fitted out. It consisted of six locomotives, three in tandem to the front and rear of a long line of boxcars and tankers with protected tops, with flatcars at intervals mounting sandbagged machine guns and posts for armed guards. Two coach cars in the center carried the command staff and guard reserves. Two flatcars pushed in front of the lead locomotive carried rails and equipment for track repairs. To reconnoiter and clear the route ahead as far as possible, a small scout train comprising a locomotive pushing several cars with engineers and a work crew, more rails and track-laying equipment, lifting gear, a couple of small earthmovers, and an Army escort had left earlier in the afternoon.

The big train rolled out shortly before midnight under the light of floodlamps and the orange glow from a sky of flame dancing among black clouds. Beyond, the diffuse incandescence from Athena showed, moving around to Earth's night side. Above the growl of the diesels and the rumbling of the wheels, distant thunder boomed continually. In the wilderness to the north and the south, patches of orange and red flickering through veils of unseen smoke glowed where the mountains and the desert were on fire.

45

The eleven shared space in one of the coaches with guards who were off duty or resting. It had open seats that could be folded down to make beds, rather than being divided into compartments, and a galley and dining space at one end next to the bathrooms. Several layers of corrugated sheeting alternating with sandbags overlaid the roof, and the windows were covered outside by steel mesh. Most of the soldiers were making the best of the chance to rest, and the lighting was kept dim.

Keene and several of the others remained awake, but there was little talk among them. They sat staring out through the windows at the Dantean sky and the intermittent glows shimmering through the dust and smoke-laden air—perhaps, like Keene, able for the first time since the nightmare began to reflect on the meaning of what they were seeing. The world they had known was being destroyed, never to be rebuilt in any of their lifetimes. Having risen to the highest peak in its history of comprehending and harnessing the physical universe, the human race had

become distracted from its quest for truth and worthwhile knowledge, and been mesmerized instead by
the pursuit of false values based on vanity and petty
ambitions. The remnant that was holding together did
so on time bought with the salvaged residues of a civilization that had already died. When the machines
became still and the bulbs flickered out, the last ruins
were ransacked for a surviving stash of cans, ammunition for a useless gun, a cake of soap, a knife, then
those left would be reduced to the condition of the
tribes that had wandered amidst the devastation in
the years following the Exodus. The only hope for
recovering in a period that would not extend over
millennia now lay with the Kronians—assuming that
Kronia itself was able to survive. The biblical accounts
had been pretty close to the truth when they said that
God periodically destroyed the world and its life, and
replaced it with a new world. Now, it seemed, He
was displeased with the latest life that had set up its
own golden calves. Keene wondered if the next form
to arise would meet with better approval as a more
faithful rendering of what life and its expression were
supposed to be. Did the Kronian model hint at a possible way? A light flaring suddenly, close enough to
be visible through the murk, then followed several
seconds later by a *whoosh* ending in a sharp report
like a thunderclap, reminded them that the bombardment had just eased for a while, not ceased.

About three hours out from El Paso, the train
halted. The lights were turned up, and the NCO
in charge ordered the guards down with their
weapons to stand to outside. A few minutes later,
an officer from the staff coach in front came through
to say that they had picked up a detail left by the
scout train ahead to warn them to slow down over
a risky stretch of patched track. Searchlights played
over the area revealed just broken cliffs, rocky
slopes, and clumps of scrub. The guard contingents

manning the flatcars were changed, and the train got under way again. Everyone began settling down except Mitch and Legermount, who sat around the dining counter at the end with the troops who had just been relieved, talking, drinking coffee, and eating. Cynthia, who had been tending Charlie's bruises and lacerations, was now huddled up with him. Tiredness overcame Keene too, finally. He stretched out, using his folded parka as a pillow, pulled his blanket close around him, and slept.

It was a little after eight the next morning when they caught up with the scout train in the rugged country between the Davis Mountains and the Tierra Vieja Mountains. They were roughly a hundred fifty miles from El Paso, having left the Rio Grande valley to cut across the large southward bend in the river, which they would rejoin two hundred miles farther on at Langtry. The scout train had halted on the approach into a shattered township, where the engineering crew were still fixing torn track and improvising repairs to an embankment. The activity had drawn out the survivors, now clustered along both sides of the tracks with the same shock-widened eyes staring from dazed, blackened faces, holding up unfed babies and injured children in the desperate appeals for help that Keene had seen a hundred times already and was sickened by because he knew there was no help, would never be help for them. But there was a lot of anger out there too. An officer came back to tell everyone other than the guards deployed outside to remain on the train.

The second in command got down from the staff coach to talk to what seemed to be the representatives—it was virtually the scene outside the hangars at Vandenberg repeating itself. The train had ample room, and the people wanted to be taken aboard. The officer tried to explain that there was nothing for them in San Antonio, where the train was going. Their hope lay in the other direction. They didn't care. After days of exposure, all that mattered was the chance of respite and to come inside anywhere that offered an escape from the terror. The problem was that the space was needed to bring supplies back. If these people were taken aboard they would never be induced to leave again, and forcing them off at San Antonio would only leave them in a worse predicament still. The officer was adamant. The best he could offer was to leave them supplies and water and pick up as many as could be fitted in on the return trip. Moreover, there was always the possibility that another train could come through before then.

With the repairs complete, the equipment was loaded and the guards climbed back aboard. Slowly, the train began moving to howls of anguish and rage from outside. Several seconds later, a window farther along the car shattered. "*Incoming!*" a voice yelled. Everyone threw themselves away from the windows and down behind the seats and the sills. But there were just a few scattered shots. It was impossible to tell where they were coming from. The guards didn't return any fire.

When the train was clear, Cavan moved over and sat down opposite as Keene regained his seat.

"It's a sad world we live in, Landen," he observed somberly. "A sad world."

Birden and Reynolds, the two Special Forces troopers who had thrown their lot in with Mitch, were both from his own unit and not part of the scratch force that Cavan had thrown together in Washington. Birden had dark wavy hair and an easy smile, and was from New York City. Raised in an orphanage, he had not done well in foster homes and joined the military as soon as he was old enough. This was the first time he could say he was

honestly glad to have no immediate family or anyone close anywhere.

Reynolds was from Texas originally—not that far
from San Antonio, as it turned out—but had moved
with his family to South Carolina as a child. He was
tall, with olive skin and straight black hair that suggested an Indian or Hispanic element, and was from
a solid Baptist upbringing. For him, serving in the
military was a way of answering a calling to serve
the nation. He tried not to think too much about
his folks back East, but his staunch belief enabled
him to accept that whatever happened was for a
reason. Keene almost envied him for that. As far
as Reynolds was concerned, they would make it to
Montemorelos and get away if the Lord needed
them for other things, otherwise not, and that was
all there was to it.

"But you're not saying we should just sit back and
wait for things to work out by themselves," Alicia said
as they talked while the miles rolled by. "I couldn't
accept a philosophy like that. I have to do what I
can."

"That was what got Charlie and the rest of us this
far," Keene agreed.

Reynolds thought about it. "No, ma'am, I wouldn't
say that," he conceded finally. "The Lord is never
ungrateful for a helping hand from those who are disposed to lend it." He added, after a moment more
of reflection, "Unlike some people."

Legermount had grown up partly in Europe, where
the family had been expanding its sporting goods
business, and come back to Pennsylvania to complete
high school and two college years. He had fled to the
military from a tyrannical father bent on molding him
into a management executive and fitting heir. "I just
don't have a head for it," he told the others. "Never
could get the hang of double entry bookkeeping. Every
way I figured it, I always ended up wanting to make

the entry on the wrong side. So I tried putting it on the opposite side from what I thought, instead. And that was always wrong too. So that was when I gave up."

"Maybe too hastily," Colby mused, cleaning his spectacles, which had still, somehow, miraculously survived. "I'm sure you'd have qualified for a high position in government accounting somewhere."

Dash had an unassuming but intense personality. He was from a small town in Ohio, had wanted to be a doctor but been deterred by the demands of med school and joined the service to acquire practical medical skills a different way. He remembered seeing Keene on TV in the weeks before the conference in Washington. "You were one of the guys trying to get scientists to take the Kronians seriously about Venus," he said. "And now everything's happening again just the way you said. I was with you. It made a lot of sense to me. I mean, the evidence was right there all the time. They're supposed to be logical people. How come you couldn't get through to them?"

"I asked that question a lot too," Keene replied. "I guess once people are indoctrinated into a system, they're unable to see things in any other way than from that worldview. What you get is experts trained to know every detail and argument of the subject, but only within the system. They can't question its premises. The notion that the whole system itself might be wrong is literally inconceivable. To do that, you almost always need somebody from outside—like you. Most of the big scientific revolutions happened in that kind of way."

Cynthia, who was doing a wonderful job of putting the past behind, looked at Charlie Hu questioningly. "Hear what he's saying about scientists, Charlie? Are you going to let him get away with that?"

"Oh, that's not us. He means those guys at Yale and Cambridge," Charlie replied.

Keene turned his head toward the window and
thought back to it all. It all seemed an eternity ago,
not just weeks—as if belonging to another world.
Outside, the clouds of dust, smoke, and ash writhed
in wind that was beginning to rise again. They passed
a creek bed choked with rotting corpses of cattle
underneath a strangely swaying black cloud that it
took Keene a moment to realize, when they swarmed
outside the window, was composed of flies. Fortunately, the window hit by the bullet had been covered with a plastic sheet. Close by, a bus had gone
down the side of a ravine, spilling bodies that still
lay where they had fallen or crawled to. There were
more clouds of flies. Cynthia gripped Charlie's arm
as she stared out tight-mouthed, her face white and
strained.

What had he been thinking? Keene asked himself. There was no "as if" about it. It *had* all been
part of another world.

Progress was slower now that they were following
behind the scout train. For long stretches the railroad
ran close to the main east-west highway—still Interstate 10, running from the Atlantic coast of Florida to
Los Angeles. The masses flocking into El Paso had been
just the beginning. For mile after mile, the train rolled
past the same scenes repeating themselves: of packed
vehicles winding their way cautiously forward through
the rock debris and wrecks; survivors from abandoned
ones huddled in makeshift shelters, others continuing
doggedly on foot; crowds pressed around emergency
service vehicles; relief camps trying desperately to cope;
and everywhere were the black clouds of flies signaling their gruesome message.

Keene found that he was registering it merely as a
record of events having happened. The sights no longer
had the ability to evoke any feelings. Twice in the
course of the day, the train had to stop for major track

repairs, each time being beseiged by supplicants who had to be turned away. On the second occasion, a group of them tried to rush the train and were stopped by the machine guns.

Nightfall found them past the halfway mark, descending from the southern Texas plateau into the valley of the Pecos. Repair crews had been pushing westward from San Antonio also, and the going actually became easier.

"You must be a man uniquely gifted with persuasiveness, Landen," Cavan said. His tone was low, not intended to carry. "Did you ever think of yourself as charismatic? It isn't a quality that I'd normally associate with my image of engineers." It was mid morning of the second day. The country to the north was dotted with fires fanned by fierce winds. Draperies of oily flame still descended from a heaving sky. Cavan was wearing Army pants and a sweater with a scarlet neckerchief knotted at the throat. The incredible thing was that he looked younger and more vibrant than Keene had seen him for years.

"What are you talking about?" Keene asked.

Cavan raised a hand vaguely. "Look at all the people you have following you to help you find this woman of yours."

Keene snorted. "Ah, come on. It's the only chance they've got to get out of this to something better, Leo. That's the reason, and you know it."

"I'm not so sure that Alicia would agree that's the only reason."

"Well, she doesn't count. She's crazy. You've told me enough times."

Cavan lowered his voice further. "But not crazy enough to think you could do it alone, without the military to help. That's why they're here, you know. She can be quite an engineer of things too, in her own way."

"Oh?" Keene knew what Cavan meant but chose to act dumb, letting his frown ask the question.

"She bewitched Mitch into it, and the others followed. He's a compulsive performer in front of any woman that happens to be around. Don't tell me you hadn't noticed, Landen."

Of course Keene had. It just wasn't the kind of thing to go making uninvited comments on. "Well . . . I suppose it's not something I really thought about," he replied. He studied Cavan's face for a moment. "Why? It's not bothering you, is it, Leo? If she did, it's as you say: to get some backup for me. Unless my judgment of people has gone to hell in the last week, there's nothing for you to worry about."

"Oh God, I've been around too many years for that. She could do worse. He's got nerve, he's dependable, and he commands loyalty. If she had any sense, she'd have found herself someone like that years ago."

Keene managed a wisp of a smile. "Well, there you are, Leo. Who's got the charisma now?"

"Charitable of you, I grant, but where would be the future? Back in the days when there was a future, I mean."

Keene looked at him reproachfully. "Don't tell me you've given up hope."

"Seriously, what do you think the chances are?"

Keene stared down at his hands. They were blistered and split from all the digging and shoveling that he wasn't used to. He looked up. "If we'd had a clear run through with the Rustler, I'd have said pretty good. But with the way things have gone instead . . . who knows? Maybe Furle was right. What else can I tell you?"

After a long wait near Uvdale for a damaged bridge to be shored up, they were held in a siding to let a loaded train from San Antonio through the other way, heading for El Paso. They reached San Antonio late that night to find the city in flames. A shrieking wind turned the buildings into torches, lighting up the overcast for miles. Spitting trails of burning naphtha left veils of smoke curling downward between the cloud blanket and the ground. The scout train had stopped a couple of hundred feet ahead. Two of its officers came back to confer with the commander on the wisdom of taking the main train any farther in until the route had been reconnoitered. The decision was to hold it back until more was known. Keene and his party transferred their kit to the lead train to go into San Antonio with it and explore what further options existed from there.

46

The railroad yard and its surroundings were an inferno of burning rolling stock and warehouses. There appeared to be no organized effort to fight or contain the conflagration. It was past being containable in any case, and from the look of things any focus of authority capable of organizing anything had ceased to exist; very likely, there wasn't enough water available, anyway.

Many people had headed for the open ground along the tracks and were trying to follow that route out of town. A crowd closed around the train as it slowed to a halt, their eyes wide against streaked, smoke-blackened faces, some wailing uncontrollably, obviously aiming to get aboard and stay there till the train departed. The soldiers accepted the injured, laying them out among the sandbags and what materiel remained on the flatcars, while the officers did their best to control the numbers trying to follow. A woman tore at Keene and Colby's jackets as they climbed down. Her face was a mass of sores and blisters in the light from the fires; her hair looked charred. *"My husband! He's trapped . . . over that way. You have to help me get to him!"* Colby disengaged himself, not wanting to be brutal but needing to keep sight of the officer in charge, who was already striding ahead along the track with two of his aides. A couple of the guards drew the woman away. Keene hastened on after the others, raising an arm to his face to ward off the sparks and cinders being driven in the wind.

An effort was under way to salvage as much as possible of the stockpiled stores. Heavily muffled figures were manhandling crates out of a burning warehouse and stacking them beside the track while others played hoses over them. A forklift following waved directions came out through the doors at the end of the building and deposited a loaded pallet. After being pointed from one place to another, the officers from the train eventually found an Army colonel and a couple of railroad managers who were trying to keep the operation moving. As Keene and the others caught up, the gist of the exchange, shouted above the roaring of the wind and the sounds of cries and screams in the background, was that it would be too risky to bring the main train in until the fires had burned down. If the track was blocked the next morning, they would move what they could out to it by road. There was no shortage of trucks, since they had been bringing loads in to San Antonio for days—although how many of them might survive the fire was another matter. Meanwhile, they could make a start by using the scout train to take back what it could carry while the connection was still there.

Mitch, Keene, and Cavan exchanged glances at the mention of the trucks. While the officers from the train were organizing their men to begin loading, Mitch identified himself to the colonel and asked which way the trucks were. The colonel, who was clad in a water-doused firefighter's smock, pointed farther ahead, beyond the blazing remains of some tank cars that had exploded. "There's a whole bunch around the loading docks that way. A lot of the drivers quit here and went out on the train that left this morning."

"Is there anywhere we can go to for gas?" Mitch asked.

"Like everything else—grab what you can." The colonel shook his head uncomprehendingly. "You don't *want* to go back to El Paso?"

Mitch shook his head. "We're going on through."

"Where to?"

"The coast, Corpus Christi."

"What in the name of Christ for? There's nothing left there."

"Special mission. . . . So there's nothing like any kind of train heading that way?"

"You're out of your mind. I just said, there's nothing left there. Mission? No kind of mission makes sense anymore. Put your men on this job instead, and you might stand a chance. Get sane."

"Sorry. We have to give it a shot."

The colonel shook his head hopelessly. There was nothing more to say. Mitch clapped him on the shoulder and moved on, waving for the others to follow. Dash and Birden stayed close behind him, Keene and Colby next, followed by Cavan and Alicia, Charlie and Cynthia. Legermount and Reynolds brought up the rear to prevent anyone from straggling. Even after everything, Keene was unable to avoid a stab of guilt as he looked back at the colonel and the others returning to their tasks.

The heat from the burning tank cars was too intense for them to pass, forcing them to detour behind a locomotive shed that seemed to have escaped major damage. A roadway flanked on one side by office and commercial buildings in various stages of burning and collapse led in the direction that the colonel had indicated. Survivors were still emerging from the side streets amid overturned autos with motionless forms inside or thrown nearby. More bodies lay scattered along the roadway. The sight no longer attracted attention.

The road ended in a large parking area outside the loading bays of warehouses serving an end of the rail yards that the scout train had been unable to get to. There must have been hundreds of trucks, lined in some semblance of order in some places, scattered haphazardly in others, many smashed or on fire. Not all had been unloaded, and in places groups of figures were braving the heat and the risk of exploding gas tanks to pass cartons and boxes down to others who were loading cars and other vehicles. Who were they? . . . Who could tell?

Mitch stopped beneath one of the high concrete lamp masts that was still standing. "The quickest way to get separated is if we all start running around without a system," he yelled through the wind. "This is the reference point we'll work from and use as base." He looked at Charlie Hu, who was clutching his side and wheezing heavily. "Charlie, you're not up to any more. Cynthia, stay with him. And Legermount, stay here too to keep an eye on them. The rest of us divide into twos: Lan, you can come with me; Leo, go with Birden; Alicia, stick with Dash; Reynolds, you take Colby. We'll take a quadrant each, and when you find something to report, you head back *here*." He pointed at the base of the mast. "In any case, check back after thirty minutes. We want a vehicle that's intact, all wheels good, preferably with the keys. If you can, check for lights, battery, and gas. Flatbed trailers would be better. If this wind gets any worse, anything higher is gonna get blown off the road. Okay?"

"Assuming we find a road, that is," Colby muttered in Keene's ear as they split up.

Keene went with Mitch toward the west side.

They passed the wreckage of several trucks and cars all entangled with another truck that looked as if it had landed on them, scraping them all into a heap. Beyond that were two more trucks almost burned out, several abandoned cars, and a truck that looked reasonably unscathed until walking around the front revealed the cab smashed in by a rock. The next two were in good shape; one had its keys in but wouldn't start. A short distance farther on Mitch tried the cab of another, then reemerged, shaking his head. As they turned away, they saw watching them two men who had been draining fuel from the tank of a tractor unit minus trailer. They looked apprehensively at Mitch and Keene's military garb and the automatic rifle that Mitch was carrying.

"It's okay, ain't it?" one of them said. "Hell, it's not as if there's any law left to be breaking."

Mitch had noticed the several cans that they had with them. "What do you guys have planned?" he asked, ignoring the question.

"Getting the hell out of here." The heftier one gestured over his shoulder with a thumb. "Our rig's shot, but we found another that'll move. No sense staying here to be roasted. Looks to me like you two guys was pretty much figuring on the same thing yourselves, anyhow."

"What have you got?" Mitch asked them. "Another tractor-only, like this, or does it have a trailer too?"

"It's a full rig," the hefty one replied. "We figured on picking up more people along the way. Chances are gonna be better for bunches of folks that stick together."

Keene and Mitch exchanged quick glances. Both nodded at the same time. "Then you've got that already," Mitch said, looking back. "There's eleven of us, including five Army. The others are over that way, not far."

"Which way you intendin' on headin'?" the smaller of the truckers asked.

"South—toward Corpus Christi."

The larger trucker shook his head emphatically. "That's crazy. Everyone's going the other way. You're on your own, soldier. They're collecting everybody around El Paso. That's where they're gonna hold out until it's over."

"We just came on a train from El Paso," Mitch told them. "You're not going to get through by road. It's blocked all the way."

"So what in hell do you think you're gonna do in Corpus Christi that's any better?" the big trucker demanded. "It's all under water. You expecting an ark?"

"Do you guys know the road down that way?" Mitch asked.

"Sure we do. Been driving it for four years."

"Okay. Then this is the deal. We pick up some people south from Alice and then head on into Mexico. Not too far past the border there's a space base that's got a shuttle down a silo, ready to go." Keene marveled at the unqualified uncertainty that allowed Mitch to say this, but he wasn't about to muddy any waters. "We launch and meet up with the Kronian ship that you've been hearing all about, and we go back with them. There it is."

The trucker looked at Mitch warily. "Man, you *are* crazy! Even if it was still up there, you think it's going to hang around for you? What makes you think they'd even have heard of you?"

Mitch fumed impotently for a second, then threw out a hand to indicate Keene. "Do you recognize this guy?" he snapped. The two truckers looked, shrugged, obviously didn't. "On TV all the time just a couple of weeks back," Mitch said. "The guy in that nuclear stunt that made the Air Force look stupid, who'd been trying to tell the world to wake up to what the Kronians had been telling it."

The smaller trucker peered more closely at Keene, squinting his eyes against the wind. "You know, it could be him too," he pronounced. "Tried to take their side in that stuff that went on in Washington."

"Landen Keene. I am," Keene confirmed.

"That's him, Buff. That's the name, all right," the smaller trucker said, nodding. Buff, the larger of the two, looked back at Mitch, uncertain now.

"You see, they know him. He's with them," Mitch said. "That's why they'll wait. Now are you with us? I'm telling you, there won't be anything for you in El Paso, even if you got there. This is gonna get a whole lot worse yet." He looked at Keene. "We could fit a couple more in, right?"

Keene just showed his hands and shook his head. "Why not? Sure." He didn't know. It wasn't a time to be calculating liftoff weights.

The two truckers looked at each other in bewilderment. "What do you think, Luke?" Buff asked, seemingly willing to be sold now.

"I dunno. . . . Goin' off somewhere all that different. Where is it? Saturn out there some place? . . ."

"There isn't going to be anything for you here," Mitch said. He looked from one to the other. "What do you have? Any folks you can get to?"

Buff looked down at the ground. "Mine were in Virginia. . . . I don't want to think about it." Luke just shook his head bleakly. Keene turned his head away, not sure how much more of this he was going to be able to take. Mitch seemed about to say something, then stopped, trying to let the obvious speak for itself.

Finally, Luke said, "Maybe, if it's like they say. . . . We should give it a try, I reckon."

Buff looked back at Mitch, tightened his mouth for a second, then nodded. "I still think you're crazy. But Luke's usually right. We'll do it."

Leaving Keene to give Buff and Luke a hand filling

the cans, Mitch went back to the rendezvous point to round up the others. "So who else you got with you in that group back there?" Luke asked Keene as they moved on to check another tank.

"One's from SICA—one of the guys who went with the Kronians on their tour. There's a scientist from the tracking labs in California. And then we have one of President Hayer's aides from the White House."

"Holy shit," Buff breathed, shaking his head.

The others appeared in a gaggle, Mitch in front, Legermount shepherding from the rear. With the soldiers taking some of the cans, Buff and Luke led the way through to the rig they had found. It was an eighteen-wheel Freightliner, aluminum sided full-box, its windows still intact and showing just a few dents in the trailer. "Are you sure this will handle in the wind?" Mitch yelled dubiously to Buff, looking up at it.

"There's only one way to find out. It'll run. That's the main thing. You wanna go looking around the whole of San Antonio for something better, go right ahead."

The two troopers helped Buff and Luke finish filling the tank, while the others loaded whatever they could find that might come in useful. Then everyone climbed aboard except Mitch, who would ride up front in the cab. Buff closed the rear doors. A minute or so later, the truck began moving.

It started rocking violently almost at once. As they went into a turn, Keene sensed it veering erratically, trying to lift. Moments later, there was a crash as they struck something, followed for a few seconds by a rending noise outside. A short distance farther on they halted again.

"Don't tell me this isn't going to work," Cavan muttered, sounding worried.

"I suppose they *are* truckers," Colby mused. "Did anyone think to check their licenses?"

"Colby, you're insane," Cynthia told him.

"That was a prerequisite for anyone wanting to work in the White House," Colby said. The truck remained at a standstill.

"Seems like they're having a conference up front," Keene observed. The troops sat stoically, waiting for what they couldn't change to reveal itself.

Cavan produced his pocket radio, usable at short range, and buzzed Mitch. "What's the problem?" he said into the mike end. There was a short pause. "He says something about a shopping trip," Cavan told the others. "Don't ask me. I don't understand it either."

At last the truck pulled away again. For what felt like a mile or two it slowed, speeded up again, turning and stopping several times. It didn't feel as if they were on a highway or making discernible progress anywhere. All the time, the trailer heaved and bucked, seeming a couple of times to be on the verge of turning over. Then they stopped again, reversed slowly, and a few seconds later the shock came of the tail hitting something, accompanied by crashing and the sound of breaking glass. The gears shifted, and the truck moved forward again and stopped. Doors slammed up front. Moments later the rear was opened to reveal Mitch and Luke.

They were at a shopping mall and had demolished the side entrance of a Montgomery Ward store. Buff was climbing in over the wreckage of the wall and doors, probing into the darkness with a flashlamp beam. "We need everybody out again," Mitch called inside. "This thing will never take the wind. We're going to have to turn it into a flatbed ourselves."

The store had been broken into already from a different entrance and was well ransacked. However, there were still axes, sledges, and other heavy tools in the hardware and garden sections, which was what they needed. For the next two hours they labored to cut and hammer the side and roof panels from the trailer, leaving the supporting ribs. From the pieces and the doors, and with the help of line and wire from the store, they fashioned a crude, ridged shelter, looking like a shallow tent, standing on the trailer's chassis between what had been left of the sides. For ballast and protection they lashed mattresses from the bedding department over the top, weighed down with bags of fertilizer and lawn food, to be supplemented by sandbags when they came across some.

Finally, Keene stood looking at the result of their handiwork. It looked oddly inappropriate. A moment of doubt assailed him. "I don't know," he said to Cavan, shaking his head. "Are we wasting our time? Is there really any point to any of this, do you think, Leo?"

"Who knows?" Cavan replied. "There's an old Irish saying: 'Now is the time for the futile gesture.' I've always thought it had a wonderful ring of magnificence about it. If anything does, it surely characterizes this obdurate species of ours. . . . Without it, I doubt if we'd even be here at all." Keene was really beginning to believe that Cavan was enjoying it.

The time by now was well into the small hours of the morning. Everyone was exhausted. They rested up until dawn, and then set out for the ring road on the south side of the city. As they negotiated their way around blocked streets and through burning suburbs, sometimes having to bulldoze wrecked or abandoned vehicles aside, a huge fireball came out of the sky and exploded to the north, sending up burning tracers dripping flames. Minutes later, another fell farther away to the west. The frequency increased as the truck made its way onto Interstate 37 South, signposted for Pleasanton.

But at least it handled manageably now.

47

Progress was slow but steady. The surroundings became emptier of people, the vehicles fewer, all going the other way. A couple of hours after leaving San Antonio, Mitch voiced the question that perhaps had been forming in many of their minds. He had come back to allow Cavan a spell of riding up front in the cab.

"Look, I know she's important to you, Lan, and it has to be a big thing in your book, but in a situation like this we have to be realistic. . . . I mean, how likely is it, really, that anyone is still going to be at this place? If this shuttle that we're betting on is down over the border, wouldn't we be doing everyone here a favor by being honest and heading straight on there direct? I hate having to say this, but . . ." He gestured at the desolation around the roadway unrolling behind them, and left it at that.

"It isn't just Vicki and Robin," Keene replied. "We need a pilot too. I told Halloran to try and find one."

Mitch looked puzzled. "But I thought you could fly it," he said.

Keene shook his head. "What gave you that idea?"

"You were on that ship that all the news was about, the one that outflew the spaceplane, right?"

"Sure, as an observer-engineer. I helped design the propulsion unit, that's all."

Mitch stared at him for a few moments of revelation while the universe took on a new perspective suddenly. "Well, shit," he pronounced resignedly. The others exchanged ominous looks but said nothing. Colby took out a handkerchief to wipe his indestructible spectacles. "Isn't it funny how life always has one more thing in store that you hadn't thought of," he remarked to nobody in particular.

Interstate 37 continued all the way into Corpus Christi. The plan, however, was to exit at Highway 281, seventy miles before, which followed a direct route south to San Saucillo, where Keene had told Vicki to wait. Since they were now entering his home territory, he changed places with Cavan to ride up front in the cab.

If anything, the bleakness of the depopulated surroundings was even more unnerving than the scenes they had witnessed from California to San Antonio. The smoke and clouds had mingled into a heaving canopy of orange and brown from which hissing streamers of flame and bursting fireballs continued to lash down over the hapless landscape of deserted townships and abandoned farms. Buff and Luke were silent, staring out in awed, uncomprehending dread. Closer to the coast now, with two circulation systems in collision, the winds alternated between violent spasms and sudden calms. With the windows closed, the cab quickly became unbearable in the heavy, humid heat that had descended. Opening them brought in fumes that produced burning nostrils and smarting eyes. The air had a greasy stickiness that matted the hair, permeated clothing, and lodged in the throat, giving everything an oily taste.

As the miles rolled by from Orange Grove to Alice, recognition of familiar places and old landmarks triggered images of the world that Keene had known. The contrast between his recollections and the things he was seeing at last brought on the dispiritedness that he had been fighting. How far, and for how long, had he been fooling himself? Whatever chance there might once have been of finding anyone had faded long ago. He'd had the chance to escape to the stars. Instead, all he was coming back to was a graveyard. He pushed the thought from his mind, wiped the sticky film from his lips, and waved away the flies.

Things went well until twenty miles or so past Alice, when Buff slowed suddenly, craning forward in his seat to peer through the windshield. "What the hell have we got here?" he growled.

"Damn!" Luke groaned on Keene's other side.

Outlined ahead was what looked like a shadowy hump extending across the highway. Closer, it proved to be part of a ridge of impact ejecta and boulders thrown from a crater somewhere to the side, with tangled branches of trees protruded in places. Buff brought the truck to a halt, and they climbed out, pulling hoods over their heads and batting away flies. The others from the rear joined them.

Reynolds climbed to the top of the ridge to reconnoiter, reporting when he came back down that the blockage extended as far ahead as he could make out. Surveys to the right and left revealed no ready way around. A number of other vehicles that had tried finding one had been left bogged down in the sandy soil. A brief conference inside the shelter yielded no alternative to turning around and finding a way through to Highway 77, which ran parallel to 281 twenty-five miles farther east, about halfway to the coast. They would follow 77 southward to below Kingsville, and then cut west to get back onto 281.

They retraced their route accordingly, and turned off Highway 281 at the first opportunity. But the patchwork of minor roads and tracks was constantly blocked or obliterated, forcing them ever farther northward until well into the afternoon, when they finally made Highway 77 just short of Robstown—almost back where they would have been had they stayed on the Interstate from San Antonio. But at last, they could resume heading south again.

For the past few miles, Keene had noticed the landscape taking on a peculiarly flattened appearance, the vegetation lying in one direction as if it had been combed, houses leaning and coming apart. And there was wreckage that seemed not to belong—house contents and belongings; parts of structures; all kinds of trash and debris—not scattered in the patterns that had become familiar but lying in endless carpets. Some of the piles included human and animal bodies, grotesquely bleached and bloated. What it meant didn't hit Keene until he saw the mounds and ribs of sand on the highway, in places holding pools of trapped water, and realized that the dark masses and clumps draped across them were seaweed. "Stop the truck!" he told Buff sharply.

From the map, they were thirty miles inland. Yet already, they had ventured below what was now the level of high tide. From the condition of the sand it appeared to have receded only recently. It would return, Charlie said, in six hours at the most. The roadway they were standing on would then be under the Gulf.

They had two choices: either turn around yet again and go back to Alice, which would mean finding a way to San Saucillo via a long detour inland; or they could make a dash south now, while the highway was above water, and hope for a way inland before it was

submerged again. Buff and Luke wanted to turn back.
Even Mitch seemed subdued, and for once Alicia
couldn't raise the spirit to dispute him. It was Cavan,
amazingly still unflagging and indefatigable, who
provided the spur.

"Six hours? We could make the Mexican border
in half that time," he told them. "There have to be
a dozen ways back across to 281 in that distance.
You've seen what kind of a mess it is once you get
into those back roads. We'd still be blundering around
there when it gets dark, and then lose another night."
Keene watched him, cutting an almost jaunty figure
in Army fatigues and a combat smock, for some
unknown reason still carrying his submachine gun
slung across a shoulder. Cavan waved an arm to
indicate the direction ahead. "Did we come this far
from California to be stopped now? The people who
are depending on us are that way, and so is our only
way out. We don't have time for any more excursions
around Texas. In any case, speaking personally, I've
seen enough of this bloody state. The more we stand
here talking, the more time we're giving the tide to
turn. So let's shut up and get on with it."

"Leo is right," Alicia told the others. "I've seen
enough of Texas too. We have to give it a try, yes?"

Buff and Luke shook their heads at each other
but said nothing. Mitch nodded his assent to the
troops. Charlie, Colby, and Cynthia turned away
without commenting and went back around to the
rear of the truck. They all climbed wearily back
aboard. Soon, Keene found himself looking out once
again at the stretch of road from Corpus Christi to
Kingsville that he had driven so many times. But
he had never seen it like this. The road was thick
with flotsam and trash as well as fallen rubble,
making progress slow. There were upturned cars,
downed trees—even wrecked boats carried from the
coast. Through the outskirts of Kingsville, the

remnants of houses demolished by impacts had been broken up by the water and dispersed. The whole area looked like a shantytown in the wake of a hurricane, extending for miles.

They were ten miles or so past Kingsville, anxiously watching east for the first signs of the wave front, when Keene saw the figures ahead, standing across the roadway. They were holding automatic weapons trained on the cab of the truck. Two standing ahead were waving it down. Farther back in the haze was what looked like a barricade on the road. Keene took the radio from the shelf below the dash panel and buzzed Mitch in the trailer three times. At the same time, he felt for the automatic in the holster at his belt. "Forget all the stuff you've seen in movies," he muttered to Buff. "They could cut this tin box to ribbons in seconds with those things. You'd better pull over."

48

Keene counted eight of them, muffled in a variety of coats with hoods or hats, a couple wearing poncho-like capes. Their faces were all dark, although whether this was their complexion or due to the effects of smoke, dust, and dirt was impossible to tell. They looked exhausted and desperate.

"Okay, stop it right there," one of the two who had come forward ordered. He had a thick beard and was wearing a torn gray jacket with a hood that revealed tangled hair protruding around the edge. With six rifles trained from fifty feet farther back, there was no question of accelerating through the line. Buff halted the truck and looked down from the window. The leader had a lean, high-cheeked face with narrow, yellow eyes. He motioned with his rifle for them to get out of the cab. "Let's see what we got here. You're going the wrong way, doncha know? Now we've got us a ride going the right way. Come on, everybody out!"

"*Not so fast!*" Mitch's voice barked from the trailer behind. The leader's head jerked sharply to look back

462

past the cab. Keene moved his head to view the nearside mirror and saw three barrels protruding from gaps in the forward end of the shelter. "This is an Army Special Forces fire team. We are in here, behind cover. You are out there, in our sights. Your call."

The leader glanced uncertainly at the other, wearing a purple scarf across his face, who was standing just behind. The others farther back shuffled awkwardly or stood in bewilderment. One of them started to back away cautiously. *"Hold it right there!"* Mitch's voice ordered. The man froze.

Then the leader waved at them to lower their guns, and his face split into a grin of broken teeth with gaps. "Well, sa-ay. It's okay, we don't want no trouble, man. We were, like, just bein' careful, you know. Doesn't do to take chances, the way things are. You never know who you might run into. But you're still goin' the wrong way, man. We've been where you're headin', and there ain't nothin' to go there for. It'd make more sense to just turn around and get us all out o' here."

"That's fine. So you can lay the guns down," Mitch answered. The leader hesitated. In the cab, Keene raised his automatic above the window level where it was visible, leaving no doubt who would be the first to go. The leader nodded to his men and put his own gun on the ground. One by one they hesitantly followed suit. He turned back toward the truck and spread his arms wide, again switching on a broad grin to show he was the most reasonable fellow in the world.

Mitch appeared from the back, accompanied by Cavan, cradling his submachine gun in the crook of an arm. Legermount and Birden got out too, but remained in covering positions by the rear corners of the trailer. Keene climbed down to join them, still holding the automatic. Other rifles were still being aimed from inside the shelter. "Okay, now we've established a talking relationship, what's it all about?" Mitch asked. "Did you people just decide to go out for a walk or something? Look around. Don't you know this is going to be seabed in a matter of hours?"

"Yeah, we know all about that, all right." The leader looked back along the highway. "But whatever your plans are, you people ain't gonna get no farther in any case. There's a bridge down just back there. Nothin' the other way for us to turn around for— 'cept wait for the tide to come in like you said." He waved toward the side of the highway. "Then we saw that boat there and figured we'd come across to check it out—think maybe it'd see us through till we found somethin' better, like maybe another truck. Then you showed up."

Keene looked the way the leader was pointing and noticed for the first time the hulk lying on its side against a gravel bank about a hundred feet off the highway. He turned with Mitch and Cavan to peer past the men still cordoning the road. The wind was gusting, but not to the levels that it had reached earlier. Flies attacked in vicious, swirling flurries. Ahead, he could make out, now, the canted surface and bared pilings of what he had taken to be a barricade across the roadway. More figures were standing on the near side of the break.

"Where are you making for?" Mitch asked.

"Corpus Christi, then thirty-two to San Antonio. What other way is there?" The leader shrugged as if it were a pointless question. "Where the hell did you think *you* are going?"

"It's a long story." Mitch squinted into the distance. "So how bad is this bridge?"

"Not even good for walkin', man. Washed out. We just about got ourselves over, an' that's it. Like I said, you ain't takin' that truck nowhere that way."

"Let's have a look." Mitch waved to Buff, who

slipped the truck into gear and eased it forward. The leader directed a torrent of Spanish at the others back on the road. They parted sullenly. The leader and his second led Mitch and Cavan through them, the truck following ten yards behind.

There were four more in front of the bridge, three women and a boy, maybe in his mid teens. The leader said something in Spanish as he approached, sounding as if it was meant to be jocular but evoking only a suspicious look from the youth as he saw the strangers carrying guns and his own people without any. Moving to the edge of the break, Keene saw that the bridge spanned a shallow ravine containing a creek. The structure had collapsed on one side, shedding most of the pavement except for the right-hand shoulder, which hung as a succession of tilted slabs and flakes to afford a precarious crossing from the far side. The ravine was littered with trash and debris washed up by the tide and carried down by the creek from farther inland. The wreck of a small coastal freighter lay half buried in mud a short distance below the bridge on the seaward side. Keene guessed that the boat being slammed against the bridge had caused the initial damage, and the flood waters had taken things from there. On the far side of the bridge was an ancient green truck of the kind used for local deliveries, with a miscellany of boxes, bicycles, plastic-wrapped bundles, and suitcases tied to the top. Mitch and Cavan came up to stand alongside him and silently took in the scene. It told its own story.

"You see what happened," the leader said, waving. "We get that far, and that's it. We don't wanna go back anywhere we've seen, man, I'm tellin' you. Then Augusto sees the boat over this side here, and we come over to check it out. Figure maybe we're gonna need it when the water comes in again, you know? So now, what you say? That big truck can easy take all of us. You ain't goin' anywhere this way, in any case. We don't give you guys no trouble. I mean, what else you gonna do, just leave us here? Come on, man. We all gotta stick together in this, you know?"

Mitch swatted flies away from his face and looked at Cavan for guidance. "Looks like there might not be any other way," Keene heard him say above the wind.

"What about my guys back there?" the leader asked. "Is it okay for them to come back now? We're all friends together, right?"

"Over there, where we can see them," Mitch said, waving at the shoulder on one side of the roadway. "Have one of them pick up the guns and leave them by the truck." The leader yelled back to relay the directions in Spanish. Buff and Luke had come down from the cab and were staring at the bridge and the strip of highway disappearing into the swirling vapors beyond. Luke turned and said something; Buff shook his head stolidly. The others were appearing from the back and coming around to inspect the situation. "You guys bring some women too," the leader commented, tugging his beard and grinning approvingly.

"What else are we going to do?" Mitch said. "Shoot them? We don't have any choice but go back toward Corpus Christi. We can't just drive away and leave them here to drown?"

"I suppose we have to take them that far," Cavan agreed. "Then it would depend on what we decided. Are we still talking about finding a long way around, or do we give it up and head back for San Antonio?"

Mitch pulled a face and looked toward the sky. The booms and rolling of distant thunder had intensified in the last few hours. "I don't like the way this is going. It feels like it's building up toward the Big One that Charlie talked about. I don't want to be anywhere near any ocean when it hits." Cavan looked at Keene to invite comment, but in a way that said Mitch was speaking for both of them.

"What's happening?" Charlie asked as he joined them.

Cavan gestured. "See for yourself. The only way now is back. What we do when we get to I-37 is the question."

Alicia was turning her head from side to side, as if searching for a way around. "But . . . San Saucillo?" she said. "What about the shuttle?"

"What do you want us to do, fly the truck over?" Mitch asked her.

"What's the deal? Are we trying for the long way, then?" Colby asked, moving into the circle.

"That's what we're debating," Cavan told him.

"Athena's closing in," Charlie said dubiously. "Every tide is going to be higher than the last."

"How far inland could the next one go?" Cavan asked, looking alarmed.

Charlie showed his hands in what could be the only honest answer. "How can I tell you? Maybe to Saucillo." In which case, he didn't have to add, there would be no point in spending maybe all day tomorrow looking for a long way around. It would achieve only the guarantee of their getting trapped also. Cynthia moved closer to Keene and squeezed his arm as if in a gesture of sympathy for how he must be feeling.

"You people talk much longer, and we're gonna need that boat up there anyway," the leader called over at them.

Mitch looked away, indicating that as far as he was concerned there was nothing more to be said. Cavan stood waiting for Keene to acknowledge the inevitable. Alicia shook her head protestingly but could add no words that would change anything. Even Colby was reduced to an awkward silence. Keene stared across past the bridge; unrealistic, romanticized images poured into his mind of Vicki, Robin, others, waiting somewhere. Everything in him rebelled at the obscenity that was being forced upon him. His gaze came back to the battered green truck, weighed down by its almost comical burden of accoutrements. And finally, the obvious dawned on him.

He stabbed a finger, pointing. *"There's your answer!"* he threw at the rest of them. Their eyes followed, then came back to him disbelievingly.

"What are you talking about?" Mitch asked uncertainly. Keene was past debating; in any case, there was nothing in the way of reason or logic left for him to debate with. He turned and began shouldering his way back between the others.

"What are you asking us to do?" Alicia pleaded as he passed her.

"I'm not asking anyone to do anything. I just know what *I'm* doing." Keene walked to the end of the truck, climbed up into the shelter, and began collecting a share of rations, water, and other oddments to fill his pack. They had brought spare rifles and magazines. He selected a standard Army pattern and a pouch filled with clips. Alicia and Colby arrived as he clambered back down off the tailboard, Cavan not far behind. Alicia gaped at him for a moment, then grabbed his jacket with both hands, pulled him close, and kissed his cheek.

"Have you gone completely mad, Landen?" Cavan called ahead.

"Why me? Wasn't it you who was mad a short while ago?" Keene gestured the way ahead. "You said it yourself. There's people depending on us. You change your mind if you want, Leo. I'm going on."

"But . . . you heard Charlie."

"All the more reason to get moving, then."

Alicia started saying something to Cavan. Keene came back to the leader, who was watching, confused. "How far did you come in that?" Keene asked him.

The leader waved vaguely. "Was a long way from south, a place you never heard of."

"It runs? It's got gas?"

The leader made a face, shrugging. "Well, is like you expect, you know. We take some from a car we find here, a truck there. But is good for a few miles yet, sure."

"Okay. Then I need the keys." The leader seemed to hesitate reflexively. "Hell, come on! It's not going to be any more use to you." Keene said.

The leader stared at Keene for a moment longer as if confirming that he was dealing with someone crazy, then shrugged and looked away. "*Augusto. Come here,*" he called, and followed it with something in Spanish. One of the men came forward and produced a set of keys. He removed a couple carefully and presented them to Keene. God alone knew what he thought he'd need the rest for.

Keene looked quickly around the rest of his party, the troops, Buff and Luke still standing together. More than anything, he was conscious of time relentlessly passing. "I would have wanted a better way to do this, but it's what we've got," he told them. "You're all great people. It's been a privilege. Let's consider the rest all said, eh?" Some of them managed a response; others just stood mutely, as if unable to believe it was happening. Keene glanced back at the leader and indicated the green truck with a wave. "And if you want any of that stuff off there you'd better get your people moving, because I'm dumping it." Slinging the rifle around behind him to leave both hands free, he moved onto the bridge. Behind him, the leader's voice launched into a tirade at the others.

Picking his way over the chunks of broken concrete was trickier than it had looked. The sloping surfaces were slippery, making it necessary to find footholds in the breaks and where possible hold onto the jagged edges higher up. In places he had to move on exposed steel reinforcement, greasy and treacherous, causing his body to tense involuntarily as when sensing insecurity walking on ice. All the time, the wind gusted and raged around him in its attempts to pluck him off. He was perhaps a quarter of the way across when Alicia's voice floated through from behind. "*Lan!*" Holding tightly to the stance he was on, Keene raised his head to look back. She was coming around the truck, lugging a pack in one hand and what looked like a medical kit in the other. Cavan was behind her with another pack and his submachine gun. "*We're coming with you.*" Such was Keene's concentration at that moment, that the message only partly sank in. He kept his head turned for a few seconds, letting the gesture say what his position prevented him from articulating, and then looked back to his task.

Near the midpoint, he came to a section where the group crossing the other way had tied ropes as improvised handrails—the worst part, with all the pavement gone and the creek visible below, from where the smell of decay reached his nostrils. Clutching the ropes and the girders, he had no defense against the flies. The sky to the west lit up with an incoming fireball landing closer than most. Keene braced himself for the boom and the shock wave, waited until they had passed, and carried on.

Then he was once again among flakes of shattered concrete, and by comparison the going seemed easy now. The last few yards, and he was standing on unbroken roadway again, in front of the green truck. At close range it looked even more antique than before. He walked up to it. All the glass was gone from the passenger side of the cab, and what looked like the rear window from a different vehicle had been lashed in place of the truck's absent windshield. The sides were dented everywhere and missing a few panels. Keene picked out a scattering of what looked suspiciously like bullet holes. Grunting to himself, he turned back to look for Alicia and Cavan. They were close together on the bridge, Cavan helping Alicia at the awkward center section.

But that wasn't all. There was another figure some yards behind them . . . and another two farther back still, just moving onto the first stretch. Keene peered, and after a few seconds made them out to be Colby, followed by Charlie and Cynthia. A tall figure that had to be Mitch was walking from the truck, at the same time slinging a large pack over a shoulder; as Keene watched, two more jumped down from the rear of the trailer and followed. *They were all coming!* Keene wiped the grime and perspiration from his face. It felt sticky and stubbly, but all of a sudden none of the discomfort mattered. Something warm and uplifting, brushing a depth of the spirit that in his life had seldom stirred, flooded through him. He rubbed an eye with a knuckle. More than just the fumes, he realized, was causing his vision to blur. He turned away and climbed up into the cab.

He first tried the engine. After a couple of backfires and two unsuccessful attempts at starting with different setting of the choke, which was manual, it finally coughed into life with a celebration of blue smoke from the tailpipe, indicating burning oil. Looking out through the improvised windshield, Keene saw the figure of the leader on the far side, beaming and giving him an enthusiastic thumb's-up as if to say, *See, I wouldn't fool you.* For what it was worth, the gas gauge claimed almost half a tank. Check with a dipstick before setting off, Keene told himself.

By the time the others began arriving off the bridge, he was already tossing out filthy blankets, piles of clothes, and pots of partly eaten food from the back. The inside stank of tobacco and pot, too many unwashed bodies crowded together for too long, and fear. While he was still clearing space, he heard the sounds of the rest of the baggage being cut free from the roof. Legermount and Dash appeared at the doors and began heaving in packs and equipment. Keene climbed out and found Cavan and Mitch poring over a map that they'd brought from the other truck. "Come on, we need you, Lan," Cavan said. "This is your country we're in now."

"Buff and Luke aren't coming?"

"It appears not," Cavan said. "Perhaps they decided that trucks, not spacecraft, were more their line." Keene realized that for some reason he had half expected it.

"Here," Mitch said, handing Keene his radio. "You want to wish them luck?" There was still a set programmed to the same frequency in the cab. Keene took the unit and pressed the call button. Across the bridge, one of the figures near the truck turned around and walked back to the driver's door.

"Yeah?" a voice answered in the radio that Keene was holding. It sounded like Buff.

"Lan Keene here. So you guys aren't coming along after all?"

"Well, you know how it is. . . . I could never really see me up in one o' them spaceships, anyway. And these people aren't so bad. Someone's going to have to get them to San An or wherever they want to go. And then Luke and me figured that if it works out that it's possible, we might try heading back east when the worst is over, and try to find our folks—just the way you're doin'. I reckon like maybe you gave us some inspiration. Anyways, we're set on giving it a try."

Keene swallowed. There wasn't a lot left that he could say—or the time to say it in. "Well, you've been a big help to us. Good luck."

"We'll take whatever comes. Hope it all works out for you."

Keene clicked off the radio. The others were already aboard, Legermount waiting on the driver's side of the bench seat. Keene and Mitch squeezed in with him, while Cavan went around to the rear. Nobody else from across the bridge was coming back to collect any belongings. Evidently, the things they had found in the larger truck would suffice. Legermount fought the shift into reverse with a frightful grinding of gears, backed around onto the shoulder, then engaged forward and turned onto the highway. A series of blasts from the other truck's horn sounded behind.

As they lurched their way among the washed-up debris, broken paving, and fallen rock rubble, Mitch nudged Keene's arm and pointed ominously in the seaward direction to their left. Through the patches of brown haze twisting in convolutions with clearer air drawn in off the sea, a line of fuzzy whiteness had become visible, extending as far as they could see to the south ahead of them and northward behind, paralleling the coast.

49

They had to get back across to Highway 281 running parallel with them farther inland, and then south along it to the San Saucillo site. The road they were on ran a little above the flat expanse of land to their left, stretching away twenty-five miles to the coast. Watching the approaching line of foam as it appeared and disappeared in the murk, Keene put it at two miles away at most. If Charlie was right about progressive tides getting higher, and they took 281 as a likely guess for the next high-water mark, the water's average rate of advancement from the former coast would be between six and seven miles per hour. That meant it would reach Highway 77, the one they were on, in around twenty minutes. Timing the truck's odometer with his watch told Keene that they were averaging close to twenty-five miles per hour, and with the state of the road and the obstacles, Legermount wasn't going to push any more. The turnoff that Keene normally took when driving to San Saucillo was fifteen miles farther south, which at this rate would take them thirty-six minutes. They weren't going to make it. It was as simple as that.

He looked up at Mitch after timing another mile and shook his head. "Scratch the plan for taking the exit that I said. It isn't going to work."

"Great. So what do we do?"

"A few miles ahead, the road goes down into a dip where it crosses a valley with a creek—kind of wide and shallow. You come up the other side onto a ridge that extends west. Our only chance is to try and pick up a farm track or something going that way. We'd be running ahead of the tide and should gain on it. Saucillo's on high ground too, so if we can make 281 with time to spare we should be okay."

Mitch turned to Legermount, relaying the proposition unvoiced. Legermount nodded and said nothing as he wound the wheel around and then back, keeping his eyes on the road.

They passed a succession of overturned vehicles, carried off the roadway and containing disheveled, water-sodden corpses, that looked as if they had been caught in a previous tide. As the truck began descending into the dip that Keene had mentioned, a bus filled with people, its roof loaded up the way the truck's had been, appeared going the other way. "We can't stop," Mitch said sharply. Legermount didn't have to be told. He slowed down enough to gesture back with a thumb and wave his hand negatively. After the bus had passed, he took his eyes off the road intermittently to glance at the mirror, finally shaking his head. "They're not turning." Keene sighed, but there was nothing to be done. God knew what those people were doing here in the first place.

Looking to the left as the ground began to slope, Keene could see the approaching front plainly now, still maybe a half mile off but with a tongue surging ahead into the valley that the road descended into. It was not a placid, beachlike rising of the tide accompanied by rolling breakers, but an angry, boiling wall of foam, flailing the land ahead with wreckage, debris, and pieces of uprooted trees as it advanced, while behind, the ocean rose and heaved in impatiently jostling hills of water and wind. Keene felt a coldness at the base of his spine and a sweaty slipperiness in his palms. The tension of the other two in the cab communicated itself palpably. A wheel hit a rock, and the truck bounced sickeningly. Legermount swore under his breath.

As the road leveled, the first fingers of water were streaming across the lowermost point ahead. They were below the level of the oncoming crest, now a churning cliff of water bearing down on them. A building of some kind on the creek bank came apart as they watched and was swept away in pieces. Parts of the roof reappeared again, bobbing and cartwheeling in a surge of whiteness that engulfed the roadway just yards ahead. Then, momentarily, the surge retreated, but the truck slowed as it hit the resistance of water, throwing the occupants forward.

"Don't slack off now! Go for it!" Mitch shouted.

Legermount straightened his leg as if he were trying to push the gas pedal through the floor. Keene felt them sway as a swell caught them on the side, and for a moment he thought they were afloat without traction. Just at that moment, he could have done without being an engineer with the picture in his mind of the probable state of what was under the hood, and what water would do to it. But it was time they were due a small miracle, and somehow the motor shuddered and roared defiantly through to claim a tiny victory of abused technology. The road began rising, and while the land to the left and ahead of them was still being swallowed up, they had gained some margin, however temporary. Keene leaned out and looked back. The water was already far into the valley, cutting off the opposite side like a strait separating an island. He knew that the road dropped again not much farther on. Very possibly, the water would have covered it already. They had to get off the highway before then.

Beyond the ditch, the road was now bounded by a wire fence strung between wooden posts with a plantation of young firs on the far side, mostly flattened or uprooted and thrown together in tangles. The fence was down in places and sagging in others under debris that had been thrown against it, but there could be no crossing the silt-laden ditch between it and the road. Keene scanned the margin ahead anxiously. Just as it seemed that they were going to have to start descending again, he spotted a shoulder ahead where the ditch disappeared into a pipe under a gravel ramp crossing to what looked like a gate. "Slow down," he yelled across the cab. Legermount eased off the gas. Below, to their left, a sheet of ocean extended away where there had been nothing but land an hour before.

There was a gate, but it was intact between concrete posts and appeared locked. Behind it, a fire break led away between the trees, offering just a watery, sandy surface littered with branches and downed trunks. "That's gotta be a way into a trap if I ever saw one," Mitch said.

"That's something we'll have to risk," Keene replied. "It'll be worse farther on."

"How do we get past the gate?" Legermount asked.

Keene took in the situation rapidly. "Forget the gate. We can take out the section of fence next to it."

Legermount steered the truck onto the ramp and brought it nose-up to the section of adjacent fence. Before it had stopped, Keene was out of the door and on his way back, hammering on the side with a fist as he ran. Birden opened the rear door from the inside. "Tool bag!" Keene shouted. "We need cutters . . . maybe claw hammer, pry bar." Colby threw the bag out, then tumbled out himself, along with Birden and Cavan. Keene tore the bag open, took out a large set of cutters, and ran back to begin attacking the fence, snipping the mesh squares vertically down a line by one of the posts. Mitch found a pair of heavy pliers with cutter edges and went to work at the bottom, while the others held the strands back as they parted. Keene looked back across the highway behind the truck. Fountains of white spray were already exploding upward from below the end of the ridge. *"That'll do it!"* he yelled at the others. "Let's get moving." While Birden and Cavan held the cut section of fence aside, Legermount eased the truck through the gap.

"We might need help if anything needs clearing," Mitch told Birden. "You ride shotgun outside Legermount's door."

Keene stepped up into the cab as it passed. Mitch followed him but remained standing, holding the door open. Birden did the same on the other side. The others threw themselves in the rear while Alicia held the door from the inside. Legermount eased the clutch up. For a moment the rear wheels spun and skidded sideways, and then they gripped. They began snaking a way through the fallen trees and heaps of washed-up brush. But the way turned out to be not so bad as they had feared, the fallen branches giving traction in the sandy soil. The soldiers riding the cab only had to get down twice to haul obstructions aside before they came to a dirt service track, following the remnants of a power line, that led in the right direction and it looked as if it might keep to the ridge. They stopped long enough for Birden to return to the back of the truck. Mitch hauled himself in beside Keene, closed the door, and leaned his head back, letting his helmet rest against the cab wall to release in a long, slow gasp the tension he had been accumulating. Legermount reached forward and slapped the dash panel of the truck affectionately.

"Well, I'll be darned," he breathed. "The old gal done did it."

"We still have Mexico to make," Keene reminded him.

Legermount settled down more comfortably behind the wheel. "The way she feels right now, I reckon we could make Argentina," he replied.

The service track brought them to a wider farm road, which they followed south for a mile or so before curving around to follow the contours in a more-or-less westerly direction once again. They emerged onto Highway 281 at a point Keene recognized as being only a couple of miles north of the turnoff to Amspace's San Saucillo launch site. As they turned left onto 281, they could see water northward, away to the right. That would be the valley of the river that bounded the north side of the landing field, Keene informed the others. Past the landing field, the river curved south, marking the perimeter of the two-mile safety zone around the launch pads. Depending on how far upriver the tide had penetrated, and if the water had reached 281 farther south, the San Saucillo facility could have become an island on three sides by now.

50

It was like coming back to a place of fond remembrances and finding everything bulldozed away for a new highway intersection or a shopping mall—except the recollections weren't from some idealization of distant growing-up years but a matter of mere weeks ago. The last time Keene saw the grounds bordering the approach road had been from the helicopter taking him and Vicki back to Kingsville after flying from Montemorelos, when cleanup crews had been collecting the trash left after the launch demonstration. There had been stone falls and cratering, and the area to the south was charred and blackened. Disabled vehicles stood along the roadside, all of them dented and holed, several burnt out, most with wheels missing and hoods and trunk lids open, stripped of movable essentials.

Loud concussions sounded from the north. The sky was the eeriest they had seen, causing even Mitch to gaze up wordlessly with an awed expression that probably came as close as he was capable of to dread. With the clearer masses of air coming

in from the ocean, the canopy that had remained
solid for days with dust and smoke from the con-
flagrations inland was now a turmoil of fiery clouds
rolling down to blot out the landscape at one
moment, then a minute later opening into vast vaults
of emptiness extending upward like inverted canyons
between walls of incandescent colors. All the time,
the rumbling of distant thunder and the booms of
bodies passing above or exploding in surrounding
regions merged in a background of noise punctuated by occasional nearer detonations that were
becoming practically continuous.

There was something ironic about the way the
familiar sign by the main gate had survived unscathed,
still proclaiming it the entrance to AMSPACE INC.
ORBITAL LAUNCH & FLIGHT TEST FACILITY. The gatehouse
was demolished, and there were gaps torn in the outer
security fence. The parking areas beyond had been
pulverized, and Legermount had difficulty finding a
path through the wrecked vehicles. A mound of
recently bulldozed earth near the ruin of what had
been the Sports and Social Club perhaps explained
the absence of bodies.

Immediately ahead, one end of the main administration building had collapsed, while the remainder presented the familiar scene of a windowless
facade with shattered upper levels open to the
winds. The second floor was now a reinforced roof,
and below, the ground floor had been turned into
shelters behind earth banks and walls of sandbags.
A number of wrecked military trucks suggested that
the site had been used as a relief or evacuation
center, probably on account of its large landing field.
Behind the front offices, the flight preparation and
assembly complex was for the most part a burned
ruin, above which the larger vehicle assembly building had split down the middle into two parts that
now hung outward in a deformed V against the sky.

Legermount brought the truck to a halt. They sat surveying the scene.

"So this is what it all came to, eh?" Mitch said after a silence. "The end of the dream."

Keene was too overcome by images of how he remembered it all to respond. Legermount murmured, "Maybe Reynolds is right. It all needed a new start over again—but with different people."

"Don't tell me he's got you as a convert," Mitch said.

Legermount shrugged. "I dunno. But looking at the way it all happened . . . It makes you think."

They felt the jolt of the rear door being opened. Moments later, Cavan, still toting his submachine gun, appeared by the passenger-side door. Mitch picked up his rifle and got out to join him. They stood, letting their eyes roam over the desolation. "Well, is there any hope here, Landen?" Cavan asked finally.

"There's always hope," Keene replied, sliding across the seat to get out.

"So where should we begin? Isn't there a pad area too, somewhere?"

"It's two miles away at the other end of the airfield." Keene shook his head. "Anybody who was waiting wouldn't hide back there. The only way out of it is up."

"Look, I hate to sound pessimistic, but shouldn't we agree on a time limit on this before we start?" Mitch said.

Just as Keene eased himself down off the end of the seat and straightened up, an amplified male voice rang from the administration building ahead of them.

"DO NOT MAKE ANY SUDDEN MOVES. YOU ARE BEING COVERED. EITHER LEAVE NOW, OR ONE PERSON ONLY COME FORWARD UNARMED AND STATE YOUR BUSINESS."

Keene looked along the bottom level of barricaded windows and sandbagged openings but could see nobody. Cavan moved a few yards from the truck, presumably to show no hostile intent.

"What's happening?" someone said from behind. Keene glanced back and saw Colby peering around the rear corner of the truck from inside.

"Near the center, just right of the main doors," Mitch said, keeping his gaze ahead.

"Interesting, but at the moment, academic," Cavan observed. "I'd say we have little initiative in this particular matter, Mitch."

"I guess you're right."

Keene moved out from the truck, keeping his hands high to show he wasn't carrying a weapon. "I'll go," he muttered to the other two. "This was supposed to be my party, anyway."

He began moving forward, picking his way through the rubble and glass fallen from the building. As he approached, he caught a movement from the place Mitch had indicated: a sandbagged opening into one of the ground-floor rooms where there had formerly been a door and adjacent window. Closer, and he saw that it was a figure in a woollen cap and combat jacket, covering him with an automatic rifle. "That's far enough," the figure called in his own voice when Keene was about five yards away. Keene halted. The figure straightened up from behind the sandbags to see him more clearly. Keene caught a glimpse of another farther back, also holding a leveled gun. "Okay, who are you, and what do you want here?" the one in front asked. Keene drew a breath to launch into the simplified explanation that he had been composing in his head. . . . And then, instead, his posture relaxed, and his face creased into a grin. "What's so funny?" the figure demanded.

Keene waited a second or two. "Have I really aged that much? Although, I suppose it wouldn't surprise me. Or is it the fancy dress like yours?"

"Look, I'm not in a mood for games."

Keene gave it a moment longer. Then, "Oh, stop it, Joe, you stupid shit. It's Lan Keene, for Christ's sake. I'm sorry we took our time getting here, but the traffic was a bitch. . . ." He broke off and could do no more than shake his head as the flippancy drained from him. It was Joe Elms, who had piloted the NIFTV the day they took on the Air Force spaceplane. He had the same reddened, blistered face as everyone else, with the beginnings of a beard, and looked more like a guerrilla fighter than a spaceship pilot. But it was Joe.

Even now, Elms came out warily, the other behind him still covering. He moved closer and peered disbelievingly. "It *is* you. . . . You look like you've been in a volcano. Jesus, have we all changed that much?" Elms turned to the other and waved for him to lower the gun. "It's okay, Sid. *It's them*. They made it!" Elms looked back at Keene, his expression dazed. The message seemed only now to be sinking in. "We . . ." He gave up and shook his head.

Keene looked past him at the younger man stepping out over the parapet of sandbags. "Sid? I know you. . . . Sid Vance, right? You came with us to the *Osiris*." It was the Sid who had won the place on the shuttle, the kid from Navigation Systems Group, just out of college, who had been with Amspace a month.

"I never gave up on you," he told Keene. "I kept telling them. You just never seemed the type."

It hadn't fully sunk in yet with Keene either. Only now was he beginning to realize how much, inside, he had been steeling himself for the worst. There was only one more question. He interrogated Joe with a look for a second as if hoping to divine the answer before he dared ask it. "And Vicki?" he managed finally.

Joe nodded. "She's here. Robin's hurt his arm, but he should be okay. Too bad we didn't have a doctor. We had some trouble here a couple of days ago, and he took a bullet. I did what I could . . ."

Keene didn't hear the rest, partly because the relief that swept over him, and the strange, sudden weakness that came with it, almost causing him to collapse. The other reason was that he could see into the room behind the sandbagged opening; another person had appeared framed in the doorway at the far end. Keene was unable to make out the face or expression in the shadows; but without really trying, in some unconscious reading from years of learning her postures and her body language, he knew it was her.

Keene moved away from Joe and Sid and stepped over the low wall of sandbags into the room. It had once been an office but had been turned into a watch post, with an improvised bed, a collection of coats, capes, hats, and weapons hanging along the opposite wall, and the desk serving as a general table. Vicki didn't make any immediate move but stood staring from the doorway as if paralyzed. Keene was distantly aware of Joe's voice outside saying something over the bullhorn. He crossed the room slowly and looked at her. She was wearing jeans with a stained shirt and sweatband around her forehead; her hair was matted, and her face, he could see even in the dim light, was cracked, swollen, and streaked where perspiration had carried away the grime. He didn't think he had ever seen anyone look more wonderful. Her eyes looked him up and down silently. Keene waited for the offbeat remark, the dry understatement. He could see her mind running over the combinations, rejecting one after another as not fitting the moment. And then, instead, she just came a step nearer, hugged him with both her arms, and buried her face against his shoulder. Keene pulled her tight, rubbing his face onto her hair. He felt her gripping tighter, then starting to shake as everything she had been storing up found release. In that strange way things had always been with them, it was the things they didn't say that said the most. Finally, he drew back enough to speak.

"About Robin. Joe said . . ."

"His arm's broken, but it seems clean. We tried to set it."

"I've got a couple of medics with me. He'll be okay." A hundred questions were tumbling over one another to get out. Keene shook his head, not knowing where to begin. "What about the others?" he asked. "Karen, Judith?"

"Karen left for Dallas with her boyfriend before the evacuation started. Celia came here with me but left with the military. I never heard from Judith. . . ."

Keene could see the tears starting, her fighting to hold them back. "I guess we won't be going back to the Bandana this time," she whispered.

"I never liked the music there, anyway."

Now the stupid talk. It had to come. They were never going to change. And then Vicki abandoned the attempt and hugged him close again, and he kept holding on because he felt his face wet too and didn't want her to see. And all the time he wondered to himself why this was the first time they had ever let each other know their feelings like this.

The noise of the truck pulling up outside and the voices of the others finally parted them. Another figure appeared from the corridor behind the door that Vicki had come through, thirtyish maybe, with sandy hair and stubble, dressed in baggy pants and a red T-shirt. Vicki said his name was Jason, an Amspace prelaunch technician that Joe had brought with him after Vicki relayed Keene's message. Jason had actually worked on some of the equipment installation at Montemorelos and knew the layout there. And that was it: just the four of them, and Robin.

Keene was perplexed. "No others? Harry Halloran? Wally? Ricardo?"

Vicki shook her head tiredly. "Sorry. Harry got here but he didn't make it through. I don't know about any others. It's a long story."

Cavan came in with Joe, who from the shouts and laughs Keene could hear outside had already passed out the news that Vicki was here. "We've been on the move since first thing this morning," Cavan was saying. "Everyone could use a meal. How are you stocked here?"

"Not too badly. Our dining room is across the corridor. The menu's a bit restricted, but there's plenty of room. We've got the whole place to ourselves."

"We'll need to be ready to move out as soon as the water recedes."

"And travel overnight?" Joe sounded skeptical.

"There's no choice," Cavan said. "The next tide will cover this whole place." Joe whistled. It seemed he hadn't realized things were that close.

Alicia and Dash came in with a medical pack. "Where's Robin?" Alicia asked.

"This way," Jason said, turning to lead back the way he had come. Keene followed them to a room across the corridor that was evidently being used for living quarters. Robin had been napping on a couch, from an office suite or reception area somewhere, that had been made into a bed. He had his share of blotches and facial sores like everyone else, but he was clean and looked rested. From his expression as he rubbed his eyes and looked the arrivals up and down, he evidently couldn't say the same about them.

"I never knew you dressed like that," he told Keene. "It's like out of some movie. You look like you should be in a war somewhere."

"Me?" Keene objected. "You're the one who got shot in the arm." Robin conceded the point with a rueful nod. "How does it feel?" Keene asked.

"Oh . . . it could have been worse, I guess."

"We've got a couple of people here who are going to take care of it. Professionals. You'll be okay."

"Mom told me about Earth being a satellite of Saturn, and the gravity being less then, and that's how the dinosaurs existed. Is that the way you think it really was?"

Keene shook his head incredulously. At a time like this, *that* could still bubble to the surface of his mind? "That's only part of it," he answered. "Half of science is going to have to be reconstructed. You're going to be a busy guy when you get older."

Alicia, who had been waiting near the door with Vicki and Dash, moved forward. "We'd better take a look at that arm," she said.

"I get squeamish about these things. I'll leave you to it," Keene said, moving toward the doorway.

"Do you really think I could get to be involved in work like that, Lan?" Robin called after him.

Keene winked back at him. "You'd better believe it."

Robin's upper arm had been hit by a ricochet, but the break was a simple one. Alicia and Dash reset it and announced that it should heal without complications. Over bowls of a spicy beef and vegetable stew that Joe had concocted, accompanied by hunks of crusty buttered bread and, incongruously, a selection of not-bad wines purloined from a cabinet in the Executive Suite, the arrivals told their story and listened to a condensed account of events at San Saucillo.

The trouble at Kingsville, which Harry Halloran had described when Keene called him from Vandenberg, had resulted in different groups deciding to go their own way instead of the concerted early evacuation that Keene and Marvin Curtiss had hoped for. When Vicki began recruiting for a group to go with her to San Saucillo and wait for Keene, others had conceived the idea of organizing a launch from San Saucillo themselves and trying to join the *Osiris*. By that time the military was using the San Saucillo airfield as an adjunct to the vulnerable coastal bases around Corpus Christi to fly essential cargos inland. One shuttle was launched but exploded in the boost phase—it was thought from a meteorite hit. After that, the pad area rapidly became unserviceable and further attempts were abandoned. Most of the others gave up then, and left with the military when they pulled out three days previously. "We might have done too," Vicki concluded. "But some kind of local gang came in— because of the stuff the military had left behind. But that wasn't enough; they wanted what we had too. There was fighting. That was when we lost Harry, along with a couple of others who'd stayed. They got away with the truck that we'd kept, so we were stuck here. So you can see why Joe was jumpy when you showed up in that circus truck. I mean . . . what kind of breaker's yard did you find it in?"

"Don't jest. It's still your only ticket out," Keene reminded her.

There was little more to be done when they had finished eating. Joe had made sure to have everything they needed to take sorted and packed in case a quick getaway was called for. They had also collected a supply of gasoline, which the troops transferred to the truck's tank, with a reserve in the rear in cans. They took an extra half hour to sandbag the truck's roof and fix spotlamps on the cab door pillars for the night drive. Mitch used an ax to cut a hole through the wall at the back of the cab to allow communication with the rear compartment.

As distasteful as it was for Keene to have to admit it to himself, having the numbers reduced did simplify things. The normal load for a minishuttle of the type at Montemorelos was twelve persons—which had been the size of the party that visited the *Osiris*. As things were, they had fifteen adults plus Robin. By throwing out inessential equipment and eliminating fuel for reentry, Joe felt they could accommodate the extra. But he wouldn't have wanted to push things any further than that.

While the others were loading the last items, Keene went out the back of the admin building to stare one last time over the landing field and toward the pad area, where so much of the latter years of his life had been invested. Although night was coming on, the flaming sky was creating enough of a lurid light to see. The scene looked like the aftermath of a battle with the litter of abandoned military equipment, vehicles, and a number of wrecked aircraft, including a cargo plane that had been picked up by the wind and cartwheeled into one of the heavy transporters on the tracks bordering the landing field. As he watched, something burst like a falling bomb somewhere near the far end of the main runway, toward the ruins of the pads. Boots crunched on the concrete behind him. It was Mitch.

"We're ready to go, Lan." He stopped beside Keene and followed his gaze. "End of the dream, eh?"

"Maybe the beginning of another," Keene said.

"You mean out at Kronia?"

"That's where the ball will be for a while now."

Mitch looked at him. "Is the *Osiris* still going to be up there, really?"

Keene sighed. That was something he hadn't wanted to think about. It wasn't on the list of things he could change. "Let's just play things the way that's got us this far, Mitch," he answered. "One crisis at a time."

They walked back through the building to the waiting truck. Keene decided to let Vicki spend some time introducing herself to the others and rode up front again with Legermount and Mitch.

For once, fortune seemed to have worked in their favor, and on regaining Highway 281 they found that the tide had cleared it rather than introducing new obstacles. Although the meteorite bombardment continued to increase, they made the sixty-odd miles to the border in close to two hours and, setting the last of their immediate worries to rest, the bridge across the Rio Grande at Reynosa was still passable. And more, the coastline now to the east of them bulged seaward, taking it farther away, which would give them an additional margin of distance when the tide returned to its next high point.

51

They were a few miles into Mexico, when the entire western sky lit up for ten or twenty seconds in a sheet of yellow that illuminated the surroundings like an eerie, off-color dawn coming from the wrong direction. It could only be what the scientists had feared early on: A huge area of hydrocarbon-vapor-saturated atmosphere had ignited. Legermount halted to stare incredulously. Mitch was equally stupefied. Keene felt as if his insides were turning cold. "Get out of here!" he shouted at them. "We can't stay exposed out here. Get under a bridge or something."

Mitch shook himself back to reality. "How long have we got?"

"If that thing is a hundred miles away . . . maybe ten, twelve minutes."

They pressed on, but nothing like a bridge or flyover materialized. When they had left it as long as they dared, Keene directed Legermount to steer off the highway at the bottom of a cutting they were in, and to park as close as he could get against the rock face forming its side. Keene ran around to the

back and threw open the door. *"Everybody get out
and get down! Cover your heads and your ears!
There's a shock coming in, and it's going to be a big
one!"*

Bodies tumbled out and scattered to find niches
among the rocks and sand gulleys along the verge.
Keene waited to help Vicki and Robin down, and then
guided them to a muddy fissure near the base of the
cutting face, which Colby and Reynolds were hastily scraping deeper with entrenching tools. They threw
themselves in, hands and whatever padding they could
find clamped over their ears, Keene using his body
to shield Vicki protectively. Even so, the pressure wave
when it arrived was excruciating, and he heard
Cynthia scream with the pain. In its wake came a
howling wind that tore dust off the ground in sheets,
blowing branches and whole trees past the end of the
cutting and pinning the truck on two wheels against
the rock. Out in the open, they wouldn't have stood
a chance. As things were, it was two hours before the
tempest fell sufficiently for them to risk moving again.

When they emerged from the cutting, the sky to
the west had dulled to a red maelstrom boiling along
the horizon, shimmering with lightning that was all
but continuous. With the wind, they would not be
able to maintain the rate they had managed from San
Saucillo to the border. It was ninety to a hundred
miles to Montemorelos, the last stretch being uphill
into the highland beyond Cruillas. They had something like eight hours in which to get away, racing
against not only the water on one side now, but a wall
of fire advancing from the other.

They did well for the next sixty miles. While the din
of bolides passing through the atmosphere, and of air-
borne and impact detonations, grew to terrifying
dimensions, the rising tidal incursions had emptied the
coastal region of population, and the road remained

free of traffic. And grotesque though the images were that they fashioned from the landscape, the fire to the west and the incendiary skies illuminated the way ahead and gave early warning of obstructions.

But past the San Fernando River, things changed. Emergency evacuation plans had evidently been less advanced south of the border, or less vigorously implemented, and the truck began running into the stragglers still heading for the high ground. Although relatively few in number, they were the slowest and most heavily laden, creating agonizing moving bottlenecks, seemingly at every narrowing of the road or uphill stretch. And crossing over the road to try and pass was invariably frustrated by another driver swinging out ahead and moving only slightly faster than the obstruction, and who once in possession of the passing space, stayed there.

"This isn't looking good," Keene announced over the noise as he checked his watch. "We made pretty good time for a while. Now we're losing it all again."

"What do you want us to do, shoot 'em?" Mitch yelled back.

Stalled vehicles were also an impediment. At one point, a car right in front of the truck lurched to a halt suddenly, hit by a falling rock, and Legermount was only just able to avoid hitting it as figures tumbled from the doors. A mile farther on, a group of people by a stranded van were waving frantically, several of them running out into the traffic lane and trying to grab the doors of anything that slowed close to walking speed.

"How is it back there?" Keene shouted back over his shoulder through the hole Mitch had cut in the cab wall.

"Bumpy, but we're surviving," Cavan's voice answered. "We've felt a couple of hits on the roof. Let's just hope we don't collect a big one. What's it looking like outside?"

"Grim."

A big explosion occurred a mile or more to the left. The shock came, followed by a volley of debris. There was sharp *crack* from somewhere near Legermount's head, and the side window shattered. A truck a hundred yards or so ahead slewed off into the ditch. Legermount gripped the wheel tighter and kept going.

The new site at Montemorelos was up on the plateau away from any major route, and Keene had hoped that they would lose the other traffic when they left the highway. But it didn't work out that way. Word of the likely size of the impending tide must have gotten around, for everyone was turning off to follow any road leading in an upland direction. Congestion built up, and it seemed that everything would come to a standstill. But though it brought greater immediate hazard, the increasing intensity of the bombardment proved to be the saving factor. Few of the other vehicles had protected roofs, and as the hail of stones from above grew heavier, more of them pulled off the road for the occupants to scramble out and seek shelter underneath, enabling the truck to pass through.

The makeshift windshield exploded inward, covering Keene and the others with rivers of shards; Mitch knocked out what was left with the butt of his rifle and yelled at Legermount to keep going. A tracer of flaming naphtha hissed down and draped across the road ahead of them, but they carried on over it, bucking and bouncing to the smell of burning rubber from the scorched tires. To the right a hillside was on fire, showing the forms of trees as blazing silhouettes.

The village of Montemorelos lay among scrubby hills at the top of a long rise from the coastal plain, a few miles before the launch site itself. There was no route farther inland, and by the time the truck arrived, lines of vehicles were jammed around the outlying area. Maybe their intention had been to sit out the high tide here, and then descend again to the highway and get to the main Sierra Madre range during the next period of low tide. Very likely, many of the refugees hadn't thought beyond simply getting to the nearest high ground. But now, with nothing but a wall of flame to the west, they were choked along the lanes and pulled off into the surrounding fields under the increasing downfall, with nowhere to go. Some were trying to improvise shelters out of the vehicles or farm buildings, while others seemed to have lost their heads and were running around aimlessly or just sat immobile as if seized by a stupor. The spotlight that Keene was directing from the cab window picked out people struggling to get others out of a crumpled car, more falling out in the open. Ahead, one side of the village was in flames; even as Keene watched, something landed among the houses, throwing up a shower of debris in the glow.

The main thoroughfare through the center was jammed with vehicles, wreckage, and milling people, and several times Legermount had to stop and back up to find a way around the alleys between the houses. People pressed around constantly, either trying to stop the truck to get help or to gain access to it after losing their own transport. It would have been suicidal to stop. There was no way of telling if any of the cries, angry shouts, and thuds of fists and other objects beating the sides were due to the truck's hitting any of them; there was nothing to be gained from thinking about it.

Keene had worried that some might have taken it into their heads to look for shelter among the launch site constructions, even though there was nothing else beyond the village in that direction and no route inland. However, past the village center the way

became clearer, and as they came to the outskirts it
began to look as if they might have a clear run for
the last few miles. Then, as it rounded a bend in the
road, the truck came upon several cars and a van
pulled over to the side with a cluster of figures
apparently trying to repair something.

At the truck's approach, several of them stepped
out in front of it, waving it down with flashlamps,
giving Legermount little choice but to brake or run
right over them. There was just time for Keene's
spotlamp to pick out the stove-in side of the van
and the mixture of capes, parkas, and uniforms—
whether police or some kind of military, it was
impossible to tell—when a harsh voice barked something on the driver's side. A figure outside grabbed
for the door, but Legermount had already locked it.
An arm came in through the broken window to seek
the inside handle; Mitch lunged at it with his rifle
butt. At the same time, another figure twisted the
lamp from Keene's grasp and opened the passenger door. Whoever they were, they were desperate
and panicking. Their van was out of commission, and
they wanted the truck. There was more shouting,
and Keene felt himself gripped by the jacket and
pulled from his seat. He managed to produce his
automatic, but a gloved hand swiped it aside. For
an instant he was looking at a swarthy, mustached
face framed by a parka hood pulled up over a
peaked cap, eyes wide, teeth bared; he saw a pistol coming up toward him and knew that moment
of slow-motion awareness, like the split-second
before a car crash when what's about to happen is
clear but a dreamlike paralysis makes it impossible
to intervene. . . . And then Legermount fired three
times in quick succession across the cab with a
handgun, and the figure cried out and recoiled
backward.

Shouts were coming from inside the rear of the

truck. Looking back through the cutout in the cab wall, Keene saw light flooding in as the doors were torn open and more figures appeared, waving rifles. Somebody fired a shot from inside but without effect. The ones outside began raising their weapons to aim into the truck.

Mitch yelled *"Down!"* and fired a burst back through the length of the truck from the cutout. Keene slammed the passenger door. A form loomed toward him; he aimed the automatic, and the shape ducked away as Legermount hit the gas pedal.

But as the truck pulled away, a bright lamp from outside illuminated the interior to show Cavan trying to untangle his gun from a pack, Dash reeling off-balance and tumbling from the sudden jolt, with the others frozen in confusion. It would be a slaughter in there. The truck would never pull away fast enough, and Mitch, blinded by the light shining in from outside, couldn't see to protect them.

Legermount hit the brakes, and even while Keene and Mitch were slamming into the dash panel, crashed the shift into reverse and gunned the truck backward. A series of sickening thuds accompanied by screams came from the rear end. The light disappeared abruptly, and Keene felt a wheel lurch over something. Legermount braked and reengaged forward gear. Again, the gruesome lurch, and they picked up speed. Shots followed, a few hitting the bodywork, but the truck was away by now. Keene put his face close to the cutout. "Anybody hurt back there?" he called through.

Cavan appeared outlined against the frame of the still-open door a few seconds later. "No . . . I think we're all okay. Would you believe it, Landen? The first chance I get to actually use this bloody thing, and it gets caught up in the straps. Maybe the desks were more my line after all."

❖   ❖   ❖

The last stretch of road up to the launch site was clear and deserted. From the final bend at the top of the slope, the view to the side looked down over the direction they had come, visibility being better now as a result of the conflagration to the west, drawing in clearer air from the Gulf. Several new craters glowed below on the plain, while beyond, shining pink in the ghastly light, the line of the inrushing tide was already visible as an immense wall dwarfing the scale of the previous one.

52

Finally, they came within sight of the launch facility. Apart from the ubiquitous rock debris and some superficial damage in places, the structures stood intact. The gates were still locked. Jason and Joe ran forward and severed the padlock hasps with bolt cutters. Legermount took the truck through, waited for them to reboard, and Keene pointed the way to the access building serving the silo that had been made operational. Again, Jason and Joe came around with tools to force open the doors. As the last lock gave, they waved the others out from the cover of the truck. Legermount gave it a friendly parting slap before grabbing his kit and hastening away.

While Jason and Joe disappeared inside with Legermount, Keene and Mitch stood by the doorway ushering the others through while Cavan saw them down from the truck: Cynthia and Charlie; Colby with Vicki, helping Robin; Alicia, followed by Dash; Birden and Reynolds. . . .

"There's one more," Keene called. Cavan looked momentarily uncertain. "Where's Sid?" Cavan turned back toward the truck. Keene went over as Cavan shone his flashlamp inside. Sid Vance was still sitting at the far end, his back to the wall, his face blank. Keene threw Cavan an ominous look and climbed in. "Sid?" He nudged Vance's shoulder cautiously. Vance keeled sideways silently, then doubled over. Keene lifted him back up while Cavan played the flashlamp from the door. Sid's head lolled limply to one side. There was a single bullet hole in the front of his jacket, hardly any blood. Keene checked his face and raised an eyelid with a thumb, then turned away, shaking his head.

"I never really found out who he was," Cavan said as Keene got back down.

"Just a kid who always hit lucky—until this time," Keene said. He looked past Cavan and stiffened suddenly. Cavan turned and looked back. Three sets of headlights were coming up the road from the village.

"It seems that our friends back there don't intend letting the score go unsettled, Leo," Keene said. "You might get a chance to use that gun yet."

They went in, found Mitch, and set him about organizing some defense while Keene, Jason, and Joe went on down to the service bays adjoining the silo to check the situation. Only dim emergency lights were on, running off a battery system in the generator room that had also been left driving the refrigeration plant for the liquid oxidizer portion of the hybrid fuel mix. That was the most crucial part. It meant that the oxidizer storage tank was ready to deliver to the shuttle now—the operation had to be done at the immediate prelaunch phase. Had the refrigeration been turned off, liquefying the oxidizer would have taken hours. With a supply ready to flow, transfer could be accomplished in about fifteen minutes. Keene breathed a silent prayer of thanks to whoever the engineer had been who allowed for this kind of situation.

Jason threw switches along a panel and started the standby diesel generator. They had power. Keene heard him go into the control booth, and moments later lights started coming on in the concrete-walled rooms and equipment bays, through the stairwells and corridors, and among the ramps and service platforms around the silo above. Keene went through to the pump room and ran quickly over the valve settings. As he started up the oxidizer transfer process, Jason's voice came from the general address system serving the area. *"Okay, Joe, you should have power. The access hatch should be at green, bridge extended."*

"Right. That's what we've got," Joe's voice shouted down from the access bridge to the shuttle, higher overhead.

"The onboard system's showing live. I'm disconnecting power umbilicals and switching everything to internal. Okay, start getting everyone inside."

The lower gantry through to the silo was down. While Jason went through the blast door into the silo to release locking pins and safety latches, Keene went up to the monitor panel at the access level to begin retracting the service gantries and power up the silo's covering doors. Charlie Hu was at the bridge crossing the gap to the white body of the shuttle. Joe had already gone through to commence flight-deck procedures.

"We're still missing some," Charlie said. "Where are Cavan and the troops?"

"Securing the outside. It looks like trouble followed us up from the village."

"What about Sid?"

"Sid didn't make it." Keene saw Charlie's hesitation, wanting to contribute something more. "Go on inside and make sure the others get strapped down, Charlie. There's nothing you or they can do. We can't have everyone out there." Charlie nodded, turned, and disappeared into the hatch.

Jason appeared, having finished his chores below. "Just the oxidizer to complete," he announced.

"I can take care of that," Keene said. "Where can we get a connection to the flight deck?"

"This way." Jason led him back to a control room outside the blast wall of the silo and activated a screen on one of the panels. It showed the face of Joe, working systematically inside the shuttle.

"Roger," he acknowledged.

"Can we get some remotes from the security cameras outside?" Keene threw as an aside to Jason. "And see if you can pick up Mitch or Cavan on the band they were using." He turned to the screen showing Joe. "All in order here. How are you doing inside?"

"Well, if you never heard of seat-of-the-pants spaceship flying before, this is gonna be it," Joe replied. "I've got a reading on the outside wind. We could never launch in this with a regular sequence. I'm programming the side thrusters to fire as we come up out of the hole and create a horizontal counter thrust. Just hope I've got these numbers right."

Keene had never heard the like of it. "I don't have a lot of confidence in first-time guesses," he answered dryly.

"That's why you need a pilot, not an engineer."

A shudder ran through the structure as something large impacted not far away.

"Lan, look at this," Jason called from another console.

"Keep the line open, Joe," Keene said to the screen, and moved across. Jason had operated one of the external cameras to view the main gate into the compound. The three cars had arrived outside, but somebody had driven the truck back and parked it there, blocking the entrance. As Keene watched, a helmeted figure jumped from the tailboard, ran a few paces, then turned and threw something back inside. Seconds later, the truck flamed into a torch.

Keene remembered the spare cans of gasoline they had loaded at San Saucillo. *"Who is that crazy bastard?"* he yelled.

"I think I've got Mitch here," Jason said, passing Keene a mike.

"Mitch, can you hear me?"

"Just," a voice acknowledged distantly through a blur of static.

"This is Lan Keene. That's not you at the gate?"

"I'm on my way up to the roof with Legermount and Dash. Birden and Reynolds are covering the entrances."

That accounted for five. Then it could only be Cavan. "Oh Jesus," Keene groaned. "Head for the front, Mitch," he shouted into the mike. "Leo's gone out there to delay them. He's going to need cover."

"Got it."

On the screen, two cars were bumping their way along the outside of the fence toward a place where something had torn a gap. The third car was still outside the gate and had disgorged a figure who began firing at Cavan through the fence. Cavan turned and dropped to one knee, and for a heart-stopping instant Keene thought he had been hit. But it was just to aim, and Cavan dropped his target with a quick but accurate burst. However, more were appearing from the car. With one gun against several, and being out in the open, Cavan would have no chance. He rose and began zigzagging back across the compound. But with the distance still to go, there was no way he was going to make it.

"Perimeter lights!" Keene snapped at Jason. Jason reached for a panel beside the console and began flipping switches. White light enveloped the gate area, throwing the burning truck into relief and highlighting the figures clustered against the fence. One of the soldiers from the building—either Birden or Reynolds from what Mitch had said—ran forward into view and began firing at them. They retreated in confusion into the darkness farther back, and Cavan sprinted for the building, followed by whoever had covered him. Meanwhile, Jason had managed to direct a second camera at the two cars making for the gap, which was now also clearly visible in the fence lights. One of the cars stopped suddenly, figures tumbling out and throwing themselves for cover, evidently from fire coming from somewhere, probably the roof. The other veered off into the shadows and doused its lights.

"Is it you doing that, Mitch?" Keene asked into the mike.

"Right. We're on the roof at the front. Good move with the lights. How's Leo?"

"Looking good."

One of the lights over the gate was shot out. Seconds later, the two nearest the gap through the fence went the same way.

"I'm just about done here," Joe's voice called from the screen showing the flight deck in the shuttle. "We need everyone on board."

The third car was coming out of the darkness, heading for the building. Behind it, several dark forms came through the gap and began spreading out. One of them fell. Muzzle flashes were coming from the others and from the car.

Then Keene realized that there was something odd about the background in the scene. Unless his sense of direction was confused, the view from the roof in that direction should have shown the plain below, lighted up by the fires and the glowing meteorite craters. Instead, it was black and featureless except for flecks and patches of white. He stared, puzzled for several seconds; and then, suddenly, a chilling feeling ran through him as he realized it had turned into ocean. And then, even as he watched, the fires of the village they had just passed through, maybe one or two hundred feet below them in his estimation, dissolved under what he could now make out to be an oncoming front of churning foam.

"*Mitch! It's time to pull out!*" he shouted into the mike. "*Look down the hill!*"

"*Christ!*" Mitch's voice exclaimed.

Keene turned to Jason, "I'm going down to wrap up the lox. We need to open the silo doors."

"I can do it locally from the ramp." Jason crossed the room at a run and disappeared out the doorway.

Keene flew down the stairs to the lower level, checked the gauges, and shut off the pumps. As he retracted the umbilical, the sound of firing came from inside the building. He climbed a steel stairway to a platform above the pump area and entered a passage as Birden appeared at the far end, stopping to send a burst of fire back from the cover of the corner, then ducking back around as it was returned. In the other direction was a steel door that led through to the access stairs. "*Birden!*" Keene yelled out. "*This way.*"

Birden looked back and saw him. "Dash is coming through. Hold that door."

Keene ran to the door and pulled it open. Behind was a work area with a tool bench. Birden stepped out and fired again as Dash appeared around the corner and ran past him. Keene held the door while Dash went through. At the far end of the passage Birden fired again and turned to follow. Keene waited, holding the door. But before Dash could cover effectively one of the pursuers appeared and cut the running figure of Birden down with a stream of bullets. Keene found that he was still staring, horrified, when Dash slammed the door.

"*He's gone! Move!*"

They dragged the bench behind the door and tipped it over to form a block, then started away again; but Keene, on a second thought, turned back and took down a heavy sledge from a wall rack while the bench rocked from the pounding against the far side of the door. Turning again, he found that Dash had waited to cover him in case the door gave. They raced for the stairs that would take them up to the access bridge.

They arrived to find Mitch bundling Cavan across the bridge into the shuttle, and Legermount and Reynolds holding off more pursuers at the far end of the boarding antechamber, where one body was already lying on the floor among splashes of blood. Dash followed Cavan and Mitch across the bridge and disappeared inside. Keene stopped just past the blast door to wait for Legermount and Reynolds. Looking up, he saw the silo doors open, revealing a circle of orange-streaked sky. Jason must have already gone through. Legermount detached and ran through with Reynolds covering and took the door. "Where's Birden?" he asked Keene.

"Out of it."

Reynolds backed through, firing from the hip, and went through to the shuttle. Legermount waved for Keene to go after him. Keene shook his head, motioning with the sledge in both hands. Reading his intention, Legermount swung the door shut and stood back while Keene delivered a series of heavy blows to jam the hinge and latch mechanisms. By the time Keene tossed the sledge down and turned away, Legermount was across the bridge and in the shuttle, waiting at the hatch.

Inside, Dash and Reynolds were fastening themselves into harnesses; the others were all secured. While Legermount closed the hatch and settled down, Keene paused to find a grin for Robin, who was hunched between Vicki and Alicia, looking pale. "Bearing up okay?" Keene said to him. "That's the worst over. We're on our way." Robin nodded, managing to keep a brave face. Keene squeezed Vicki's shoulder in a way that said everything would work out okay—it wasn't as if he would ever have to answer for himself if it didn't.

"Okay, I've seen Mexico," Colby said from his seat. "Can we move on?"

Keene went forward to join Joe in the crew section and buckled himself into the flight engineer's seat. He would have to handle the electronics too, since they had no Ccoms operator this time, but that didn't make a lot of difference to anything, since there was nowhere to communicate with. The first thing he made sure of, however, was that the computers still contained the navigation beacon and homing codes that had been used for the rendezvous with the *Osiris*. A quick run through the checks showed engines, fuel, power, hydraulics, environment, and cooling all looking good. He keyed in the command to retract the access bridge, and an auxiliary screen with a vertical view down between the silo wall and the body of the shuttle showed it sliding back cleanly into its recess.

"Tank and pump pressures good, temperatures good, auxiliaries functioning," he told Joe. "Do we want the whole list?"

"With guys out there wanting to shoot this thing full of holes? Hell, no. Let's get outta here!"

"Then you're all set. We have delivery. . . . What's this? *Oh, my God!*" Keene stared at the screen, horrified, as it showed the blast door at the bottom of the silo being opened from the other side. A group of figures in helmets and combat gear ran out, brandishing guns, onto a concrete ledge flanking the duct that directed the exhaust out to a water-cooled pit on the far side of the structure—Keene and Jason hadn't bothered to flood it; what would have been the point?

Joe's finger was already straightening against the button.

The figures came to a confused halt and stood

gaping up at the tail and booster nozzles of the spacecraft towering above them. Then, realizing their mistake, they began a frantic scramble to get back through the door.

"Ignition."

53

Keene counted seventeen gut-wrenching hits or lightning strikes on the structure as the ship climbed through the winds, the flaming clouds, and the meteorite storm. But it stayed together, and as it emerged from the atmosphere the occupants got their first view of Athena since the last transmissions before the satellites were knocked out, and the shots that had been relayed from the *Osiris*. The nucleus was clearly visible now, appearing six times the size of the Moon, which meant that it was well inside the lunar orbit. It hung as a malevolent, white-hot presence, its tail of dust and incandescent gas engulfing and extending far beyond the Earth, with twisted and braided secondary streamers discharging immense sparks through the plasma envelope to the main body and between each other.

The regular flight-planning programs were unable to compute a stable orbit through the changing gravity now permeating the region. Charlie Hu, Joe, and Keene calculated a burn that would send them coasting out on a long ellipse away from the two bodies as they closed. Although it meant expending an alarming portion of the remaining fuel, their estimates indicated that it would be better in the long run than constantly having to fire to correct a closer-in orbit. And with the ship's vantage point lengthening, its occupants watched the devastation of an entire planet as the encounter between Earth and Athena entered its final, cataclysmic phase.

The seas of fire that they could see engulfing parts of the southwestern and central U.S. were repeated across huge tracts of every other continent also. From the size and sharpness of the spiral chasms carved in the smoke-laden atmosphere, they were generating winds more ferocious than anything seen previously. Watching in horrified yet compulsive fascination, they were able to glimpse through the slowly shifting patterns fragments of what was happening on the surface.

The tides filled the valleys of the Amazon, Mississippi, Congo, Ganges, and Yellow Rivers, rising over the southeastern states all the way to the Appalachians in the U.S., covering the plains of southern India and Argentina, and creating temporary seas that immersed London and Paris, Baghdad, Beijing, and Montreal. When the water receded, a mud bank running from Florida to Venezuela turned the Caribbean into a six-hour lake; Britain reemerged amid a plain of lakes extending from Norway to Spain; Asia became reconnected to Australia except for a narrow channel twisting its way between Borneo and Celebes.

As the magnetospheres of Earth and Athena intersected, colossal electrical bolts began flashing incessantly not just between parts of Athena but directly down upon Earth itself. After two days, Charlie, who had been trying to make measurements from the ship's imaging displays, announced that the tidal extremes were getting less even though Athena was still closing. It confirmed the fears that Keene had

heard voiced back at JPL: The motion through
Athena's field was making Earth an immense Fara-
day generator, heating the beds of the oceans and
actually inducing boiling in places, causing sea levels to fall by hundreds of feet. The recondensing
vapor turned into a pall of cloud miles thick, which
the winds stirred with the browns of the hydrocarbon gases and the smoke from the continent-wide
fires to draw a curtain over the death throes as Earth
and Athena commenced the slow mutual gyration that
would mark their closest pass. But the broad story
told by the shuttle's infrared scans left no need for
every ghastly detail.

Under the close gravitational influence, the crust
seemed to slip in its rotation. Softened and melted
toward the surface by the induced heating, it buckled and tore into huge north-south running paroxysms
of earthquake and upheaval. The great African Rift
opened up into a two-thousand-mile-long lake of lava
that could be seen widening hour by hour, soon to
become a new ocean, while to the east the tip of
India extended into a ridge of upthrusting, colliding
slabs of seabed snaking its way southward across the
equator. The trench system running from Japan via
the Phillippines to Indonesia was opening too, and
starting to cleave Australia—very possibly, Charlie
guessed, presaging a continental uplift somewhere in
the western Pacific. They were literally watching the
next world being born, even as the old one died.

The shifting of the spin axis caused oceans to slop
across continents. Swathes of blue and green cold
advancing hour by hour across the previously yellow
and orange hot areas on the false-color infrared images
told of miles-high cliffs of water bursting over the
Appalachian barrier to descend upon Cincinnati and
Pittsburgh, surging up into the funnel formed by
Siberia and Alaska to spill over into the Arctic basin,
and turning the southern Himalayas into an

archipelago. With the surface charted simply by its temperature variations, the images quickly lost all resemblance to maps that were recognizable. In any case, it was already clear that those maps would hence be of interest only to future historians, geologists, and archaeologists. "Could *anything* survive that?" Vicki whispered amid the horrified silence that had enveloped the cabin for hours.

"Nothing could survive that," Joe murmured. His voice was numbed.

"It happened before, not all that long ago," Keene reminded them. "And some survived then. It may have been just a handful, scattered across a mountaintop here and there or a few places that the floods didn't reach. But it was enough."

"Go forth and multiply, and repopulate the Earth," Reynolds recited softly.

"But could it really have been this bad?" Vicki persisted.

"They didn't have the technology either," Charlie said. "Some of those down there might pull through, even with all that." Keene didn't know. All he could do was look with the rest of them at the dark ball that Earth had become and know that in the cities disappearing under towering walls of foam in the darkness beneath, the forests and grasslands that had become carpets of ash, the exposed seabeds being consumed under spreading lava plains, the splitting mountains and sinking islands, humans and life of every kind were dying in billions. The things he had seen in the past week had hardened and wearied him to the degree of showing little external sign, even to this. Vivid though the pictures were that he created in his mind, nothing in his experience enabled him to relate to the the calamity he was witnessing. But inside, in his soul, he wept for the tragedies taking place everywhere, a million every minute, on the scale he was capable of grasping. He wept for all the

Marvin Curtisses with stepdaughters who would never play their cellos to a public audience now; for the David Salios with pretty wives and young children who would never see Europe; the Wally Lomacks and their grandchildren; the Washington cab drivers and their wives who weren't going to retire to Colorado; the Lieutenant Penalskis, Colonel Laceys, and General Ullmans who had stayed to carry through their duty; the Buffs and Lukes who had gone back to find their kinfolk.

And he mourned the passing of the culture that had emerged from squabbling European tribes to produce the cathedrals of Cologne and Rheims, the paintings of Michelangelo and the music of Bach, the calculus, the steam engine, the Boeing 747, the IBM PC, and yes, even Wall Street. Would visitors from another age return one day to take pictures of New York's steel skeletons standing stark against a sandy desert, or to excavate the ruins of Tokyo and its seaport among some range of inland hills as others had the pyramids or the ziggurats of Nineveh?

The momentum of the two bodies' turning embrace parted them, and Athena at last began withdrawing to find whatever future was destined for it among the other objects of the Solar System. As a macabre finale to its act, it recrossed the lunar orbit close enough to draw the Moon toward itself until the Moon started to break up. It receded with what had been Luna slowly transforming into a trail of debris, curling around to circle Athena like a triumphal garland. The bulk of the material could be seen plunging down in a torrent to be consumed into Athena's incandescent surface. The residue would accompany Athena as a ring system, a trophy from its victory, which it would carry across the heavens as a taunting reminder for thousands of years to come.

54

The ellipse carried them out past what had been the Moon's orbit, into regions of space that were cleaner. However, being intended for short missions, the shuttle was not equipped with solar panels or a long-life power source, and use of the sampling instruments and external imagers had to be limited. The craft had evidently sustained some damage during the lift up from the surface, for nothing could be picked up on radar. Neither could a signal be received from any surviving ship or other source that might be out there. This naturally raised the question of how they could be sure that *any* of the communications equipment was functioning properly—in particular, the beacon that was supposed to provide a signal for the *Osiris*. As time continued to drag by, the more sinister but obvious question raised itself of whether the *Osiris*'s failure to materialize might be due not to any malfunction of the shuttle's equipment, but the fact that the *Osiris* was no longer out there at all.

As nerves grew frayed, and fears worked on by the mind acquired the substance of virtual certainties,

Keene was the one who had to bear the brunt. It
wasn't simply that something that the others, now
relieved from the pressures of just staying alive, were
beginning to see as a Mad Hatter scheme from the
beginning, had been his conception. With the change
in circumstances and environment, roles had altered,
and he had become the leader that all of them recognized now. Keene had acknowledged Charlie's
seniority within JPL. Mitch had accepted Cavan in
Washington as the natural commander of the force
mobilized to go to Vandenberg, and then assumed the
dominant part himself when the situation changed
from political intervention to virtual combat. Now they
had returned to the world of technology and space
engineering; and the natural person to take charge
in it was Keene.

He did his best to reassure them, telling them to
put themselves in the position of the Kronians aboard
the *Osiris*: the only representatives of their culture
to be within hundreds of millions of miles of what
had happened. "Imagine you're all scientists, like
Charlie," he appealed to the others. "You're in a
unique position to record close-up and take back
records of events that nobody alive will ever see again.
Priceless data and information. What are you going
to do—just head off home and ignore it? Of course
you're not. But you wouldn't exactly want a ringside
seat, either. You'd pull back to a safer distance.
They're out there somewhere. We're on a long, eccentric orbit. It'll take some time, sure. But they're
there."

"But even supposing they are, what's to make *them*
think that *we're* still here?" Legermount persisted.
Legermount had been restless and brooding now that
the action was over. Cool, competent, and given to
few words when there were demanding things to be
done—the ideal second to someone like Mitch—he
was affected the most by the passivity of being shut

up, waiting for something that was beyond their control to happen.

Which brought them back to the original point: How did they know the beacon was working?

"It's still a good point," Cavan agreed.

Keene wasn't sure if any of them had the expertise to do very much if it wasn't, and he doubted if the ship carried the full range of parts that might be needed anyway; but it quickly became clear that not even knowing if they had a chance would drive everyone slowly crazy. He and Jason talked about rigging up a simple transmitter-receiver that they could launch on a tether and communicate with by wire to test the ship's receivers and see if a beacon signal was being emitted. But Robin, looking livelier now, his arm strapped comfortably and doing well, reverted to his habit of spotting the obvious that had been missed. "Couldn't somebody be let out and just do it in a suit?"

Of course, that was the way to do it. And with Joe resigning himself to the position of driver and galley steward in this operation, the natural choice of who should go fell upon Keene.

Joe helped Keene put on one of the three EVA suits that the shuttle carried as a normal complement, and Keene squeezed into the narrow entry space inside the main hatch, which was fitted with an inner door to serve the double function of acting as a lock. Joe pressured the chamber down and opened the hatch from the flight deck. Keene rechecked the tether attached to his harness, its mounting, and the straps holding the test set that he would use in addition to the suit radio. Then he shoved himself through, orienting to align the gas thruster on his backpack. Moments later he was coasting away, turning to watch the distance steadily increasing between him and the vessel, apparently

motionless in space. It looked a lot more scarred
and battle-weary than he had imagined.

"Hello, Joe? This is Lan, testing. Anybody
there? . . . Lan Keene to ship. Hello, Joe, are you
reading? . . ." Nothing. He flipped on the portable
unit that he had brought and tried the first frequency
they had set. "Jason, are you reading? . . . Come
in, ship. This is Lan, out on the line." Silence. He
tried the other frequencies, ship standby, and emergency bands. Still the same. Worried now, Keene
raised the forearm carrying the suit controls and
switched to the wire circuit. "Joe, can you hear
me?"

"Nice and loud, Lan. How are we doing?"

"Not good. I've been trying you and Jason on all
the channels. You didn't get anything?"

"Negative. . . ." There was a pause. *"Jason says he
was tuned all the while. Not a thing."*

"I don't like this, Joe."

"Me neither. Have you tried the beacon yet?"

"I'm just about to now." Keene looked down and
switched the portable unit to receive mode. He
realized then that his chest was pounding. His breathing was shaky in his helmet, the clothes next to his
body clammy with perspiration; his mouth and throat
had gone dry. In the next few seconds he might find
out that they were all destined to die out here. He
selected one of the Kronians' homing settings and
plugged an audio decode connection into one of the
suit circuit's external jacks. . . . And a moment later,
he was shouting out aloud in a relief that was almost
crushing.

"YEAH! . . . OH, YOU BEAUTIFUL, BEAUTI-
FUL SHIP! I COULD MARRY YOU, YOU BAT-
TERED PIECE OF BEAT-UP JUNK!"

The tone was coming through clear and strong in
his helmet. It was the sweetest music he had ever
listened to.

"Lan? . . . We're okay?" Joe's voice inquired, sounding a little unsure.

Keene nodded to himself, feeling drops of perspiration run off his head. "We're okay, Joe. The receivers might be out, but the beacon's singing. We're getting out of here, Joe. They're going to be coming for us."

"Yeah, well, that's great." Joe didn't seem fully to have absorbed it yet. *"Lan, don't do that to me again."*

They reeled him back in, still ecstatic and intoxicated by the sight of the stars, and for a few minutes with the weight of what had befallen Earth actually gone from his mind. It was only when he was almost at the hatch and about to guide himself in that his thoughts went back to the radar display he had watched at Vandenberg of the blip closing in toward the *Osiris*. The connection had been lost before they'd had a chance to be sure that the unharmed craft really *was* the Boxcar as Keene had assumed. If he was wrong, then none of the Kronians would ever have arrived at the *Osiris* to tell their story of Keene's last-moment change of plan; and whether the shuttle was transmitting a signal or not wouldn't make very much difference, since with Idorf and his ship long ago seized, nobody would be looking for it.

The grim set that the thought imparted to Keene's face must still have been in evidence when he emerged through the inner door into the cabin, and Jason helped him off with his helmet.

"What's the matter, Lan?" Vicki asked. "Joe said everything was all right. You look as if there's bad news."

Keene looked around at their apprehensive faces, the silent pleas to be reassured. He couldn't dump this latest doubt on them now, he decided. But neither could he lie to them. There had to be some bad news.

"I didn't realize how much you all stank," he told them instead.

They turned off all the unessential electronics, wound the environmental control and air recirculation down to minimum, and made do with just the dim emergency light in the cabin. Keene surreptitiously increased a little the carbon dioxide level that the monitors would set to. It would relieve the load on the system and make people drowsy, passing the time more easily, lowering their oxygen consumption, and making them less likely to vent their anxiety in querulousness. All the same, Legermount tossed and fidgeted until it seemed he would start dismantling the ship with his hands, just to find something to occupy himself. Reynolds was just the opposite, calm and accepting in his belief that all was in the hands of a higher, wiser power.

Mitch and Cavan talked idly about military affairs and the old days, not realizing how much it sometimes affected the others, and wondered what the future might be for their line of business on Kronia. Dash revealed a literary bent and began composing a detailed account of all he could recall, at first using any scrap of paper that came to hand, later getting Keene's okay to transfer to an on-board laptop whose drain wouldn't make a lot of difference to anything. When Dash wasn't writing, Jason and Joe would take the laptop forward to the flight-deck seats and play chess. Colby went off into long excursions of thought that resulted in few revelations, returning periodically to use the laptop for notes of his own that he was compiling, or to quiz Keene about workings of the ship that aroused his curiosity. He also attempted to entertain Robin with a variety of coin, card, and pocket-item tricks, none of which would work. Colby's explanation was that he'd never realized how much they depended on gravity.

Vicki and Alicia talked about science, history, life in America and in Poland, and personal reminiscences involving Keene and Cavan. Charlie and Cynthia continued getting to know one another, making an effort to forget the lives that were gone and swapping stories about Kronia as if deliberately rejecting any possibility that they might not be on the threshold of new lives about to begin. Charlie was also intrigued by Robin's novel thoughts on such things as planetary evolution and biological origins, and they talked about the Venus encounter, the Joktanian discoveries of humans who had lived beneath a sky dominated by Saturn, and the science that would have to be rewritten.

"I was just starting to get to know a planetary scientist in Houston when . . . you know, it happened," Robin said. "His name was Salio. He said the whole time scale that all the books teach was much too long—that it had been invented that way to justify theories that don't hold up anyway. Everything happens much more quickly. It's all going to have to be rethought. Is that what you think?"

"Well, I never thought about it much at all until the last few days," Charlie answered. "But you saw how it happened: new oceans starting to open up, mountain chains lifting while we watched! And it must have gotten even worse after Athena closed in and we lost track. But the information that we've got will be keeping scientists busy for years. You saw how those lava sheets were pouring up out of the rifts in those last images?"

"Yes." Robin shuddered at having to remember.

"I've been thinking about them ever since. There were huge electrical discharges going on between Athena and Earth all the time the sheets were spreading. I figure *that's* what could have caused the magnetic stripe patterns on the old sea beds. The conventional line is that they were written over millions of years by unexplained reversals in the Earth's field. Well, maybe it didn't take millions of years at all. Maybe it was just days!"

Vicki was listening, looking skeptical. "Could it have cooled quickly enough in that short a time?" she asked dubiously.

"We don't know what was going on down there under all that cloud," Charlie pointed out. "Hundreds of feet of ocean had been boiled into the atmosphere. Suppose that under the smoke cover it precipitated out again as ice. Maybe that could cool a surface skin sufficiently to retain magnetism. I don't know. I haven't analyzed the numbers yet."

Keene clipped to an anchor line on the wall and stretched out to rest, tired of following it all. Or was it the carbon dioxide level? He looked around the cabin and yawned. Most of the others were settling down except Dash, who was busy with his narrative, and Cavan and Alicia up front, talking in low voices. . . . And an irritating clanging that he'd just noticed.

It stopped for a few seconds, then started again.

"Is that you, Legermount?" Keene grumbled irritably. "Stop rattling the cage. We're trying to settle down."

"It's not him this time. He's out of it," Reynolds's voice mumbled.

"Then what?" Keene straightened away from the wall, alert suddenly.

Colby turned and showed his empty palms. "It's not me." Joe looked up from something he had been fiddling with close to one of the lights and shook his head.

It came again: *Clang, clang, clang. . . . Clang, clang, clang. . . .*

Keene's head jerked around sharply. There was nobody in the direction that it was coming from. . . . Just the entry hatch. His and Joe's eyes met for a second.

"Oh my God!" Joe whispered. He tore free from his anchor line and hurled himself forward to the flight deck section with Keene following.

"Hallelujah!" Reynolds murmured.

Cavan and Alicia were already moving out of the crew positions to make room. Joe's trembling fingers raced over the touchpad to activate the imagers; Keene powered up the controls for the external cameras. A screen came to life showing a drifting starfield as the shuttle turned. Keene rotated the camera outward to get the view abeam of the ship. And, slowly, the most beautiful sight he had ever seen moved into the frame: one of the *Osiris's* surface landers riding parallel perhaps half a mile off.

"It's them! They're here! That's them banging on the door!" he heard himself shouting. Joe brought up the lights. Within seconds, everyone in the cabin was shouting and hugging, laughing and crying. Keene grabbed one of the rifles, which for some reason they had brought aboard, and hauled himself into the entry space behind the hatch. *Thunk, thunk, thunk.*

Joe had a camera trained along the outside of the shuttle's hull. Two figures in bulky, Kronian-style suits were outside the hatch, one poised to beat the surface again with a metal hand tool, the other holding the end of some kind of tube pressed to the hull. Keene beat against the ribbed inner surface of the door again. *Thunk, thunk, thunk.* On the screen, the figure with the tube started making excited gestures and pointing at the ship. The other leaned forward.

Clang, clang, clang sounded from outside the hatch.

Keene responded deliriously. *Thunk, thunk, thunk . . . thunk, thunk, thunk . . . thunk, thunk, thunk . . .*

The lander moved in to make a docking connection, and the fourteen exhausted survivors from the shuttle were transferred over. The two Kronians who had come across were Sariena and Thorel, the engineer from the *Osiris*'s crew. Sariena had wanted to be one of the first to greet them if they were found.

Kronia was sending all the help that could be mobilized. In the meantime, the *Osiris* had been searching the vicinity for days. A number of other ships from Earth had also managed to get away, and the *Osiris* had collected a full complement to take back. The shuttle that Keene had been hoping to organize when last heard of was the last it could afford to wait for. Idorf had been ready to give up, but Gallian wouldn't hear of it.

Events after the launch of the Boxcar from Vandenberg had been as Keene deduced. A second, mysterious ship had inserted itself ahead of the Boxcar as it closed, transmitting fake signals claiming to be the Boxcar pursued by a would-be attacker attempting to use it as a shield. Keene's on-the-spot guess of which one to fire on had been correct. On a sadder note, after all the heroic effort that had been put in, the second Boxcar sent up from Vandenberg later had never been seen. Just one more tragedy among the billions.

Thirty minutes later, the Kronian vessel detached and drew away under a mild nudge from an auxiliary thruster. On a screen inside, Keene looked at the empty, silent hulk turning slowly in the sunlight, presenting on its side the last, scarred rendering he would probably ever see of the Amspace Corporation logo.

The lander's main engine fired, and the craft pulled away into a curve that would take it to the waiting *Osiris*.

FURTHER READING

The scientific ideas in this book are based largely on the work of Immanuel Velikovsky (1895–1979). Many readers of the hardback have asked where they might learn more on this background, or catastrophist views in general. The following sources would provide some good starting material.

(1) Immanuel Velikovsky's three major works:

Worlds in Collision, 1950
The book that started the whole controversy, identifying the comet of the Exodus as Venus, originating from Jupiter.

Ages in Chaos, 1952
Reexamining ancient history in the light of catastrophic events.

Earth in Upheaval, 1955
The evidence written into the Earth's geological and biological records.

All available from Buccaneer Books, POB 168, Cutchogue, NY 11935

(2) Carl Sagan and Immanuel Velikovsky, by Charles Ginenthal, 1995

Over 400 pages presenting findings from space missions and other sources that are consistent with Velikovsky's claims, while contradicting the experts who vilified him. Available from:

New Falcon Publications
1739 East Broadway
Tempe, AZ 85282
Tel: 602-708-1409

(3) Velikovsky and Establishment Science

A comprehensive rejoinder to the publication *Scientists Confront Velikovsky*, which followed the 1974 AAAS conference. What really went on, earning Velikovsky a standing ovation that the media didn't mention. 144pp. Available from:

Lewis Greenberg
226 Richmond C
Deerfield Beach, FL 33442

(4) The Velikovkian

A journal dedicated to studies of the evidence for global catastrophes in human times, along with such related issues as the ancient historic record, evolution and extinction, the dynamics of the Solar System, methods of chronology and dating. Normally 4 issues per year of typically 100-120 pp. each, with occasional special-topic issues. Editor-in-Chief: Charles Ginenthal.

Some titles from recent issues include:

"Comparing Magnetic Fields: Neptune and Uranus,"
   by Charles Ginenthal
"Velikovsky's 'The Dark Age of Greece,'" by Clark
   Whelton
"Puzzles of Prehistory," by Roger W. Wescott
"Revisiting Venus's Heat," by George R. Talbott
"The Emerging Revision of Ancient History: Recent
   Research," by Martin Sieff
"The Origin of Craters on the Moon and Large Lunar
   Boulders," by Charles Ginenthal
"Thales: The First Astronomer," by William Mullen
"Ocean Sediments, Circimpolar Muck, Erratics,
   Buried Forests, and Loess as Evidence of Global
   Floods," by Charles Ginenthal
"Phobos and Deimos," by Lynn R. Rose
"Shattering the Myths of Darwinism," by Richard
   Milton
"The Relevance of the Velikovsky Scenario to the
   Homeric Question," by Hugo Meynell

Send inquiries to:
Charles Ginenthal
Ivy Press
65-35 108th St.
Forest Hill, NY 11375
Tel: 718-897-2403

(5) *Aeon*
A journal of myth, science, and ancient history,
frequently exploring theories of different early Solar
System configurations.

Information at: http://www.ames.net/AEON/

or from:

Ev Cochrane
601 Hayward
Ames, IA 50014
e-mail ev.cochrane@ames.net

(6) Society For Interdisciplinary Studies
Biannual catastrophist journal providing articles and papers on a wide range of related topics, books sources and reviews, and digest of Internet coverage.

Send inquiries to:
The Membership Secretary
Society for Interdisciplinary Studies
10 Witley Green
Darley Heights
Stopsle, Beds LU2 8TR
U.K.

Web: http://www.knowledge.co.uk/xxx/cat/sis
E-mail: SIS@knowledge.co.uk

ABOUT THE AUTHOR

James P. Hogan is a science fiction writer in the grand tradition, combining informed and accurate speculation from the cutting edge of science and technology with suspenseful storytelling and living, breathing characters.

Born in London in 1941, he worked as an aeronautical engineer specializing in electronics and digital systems, and for several major computer firms including DEC, before turning to writing full-time in 1979. His first novel was greeted by Isaac Asimov with the rave, "Pure science fiction . . . Arthur Clarke, move over!" and his subsequent work quickly consolidated his reputation as a major SF author.

He has written over a dozen novels, including *Paths to Otherwhere* and *Bug Park* (both Baen), the *New York Times* bestsellers *The Proteus Operation* and *Endgame Enigma* (both available from Baen), the "Giants" series (Del Rey), and the Prometheus Award Winner *The Multiplex Man* (now in a new Baen edition). Hogan currently splits his time between residences in Ireland and Florida.

DAVID WEBER

The Honor Harrington series: *(cont.)*

Flag in Exile
Hounded into retirement and disgrace by political enemies, Honor Harrington has retreated to planet Grayson, where powerful men plot to reverse the changes she has brought to their world. And for their plans to succeed, Honor Harrington must die!

Honor Among Enemies
Offered a chance to end her exile and again command a ship, Honor Harrington must use a crew drawn from the dregs of the service to stop pirates who are plundering commerce. Her enemies have chosen the mission carefully, thinking that either she will stop the raiders or they will kill her . . . and either way, her enemies will win. . . .

In Enemy Hands
After being ambushed, Honor finds herself aboard an enemy cruiser, bound for her scheduled execution. But one lesson Honor has never learned is how to give up!

Echoes of Honor
"Brilliant! Brilliant! Brilliant!"—*Anne McCaffrey*

Ashes of Victory
Honor has escaped from the prison planet called Hell and returned to the Manticoran Alliance, to the heart of a furnace of new weapons, new strategies, new tactics, spies, diplomacy, and assassination.

continued ☞